USA TODAY BESTSELLING AUTHOR
# Dale Mayer

## SIMON SAYS...
# HIDE

A KATE MORGAN NOVEL

SIMON SAYS... HIDE (KATE MORGAN, BOOK 1)
Dale Mayer
Valley Publishing

ISBN-13: 978-1-773364-74-2
Print Edition

# Books in This Series:

The Kate Morgan Series
https://smarturl.it/DMSimonSaysUniversal

Simon Says… Hide, Book 1
Simon Says… Jump, Book 2
Simon Says… Ride, Book 3
Simon Says… Scream, Book 4

# About This Book

Introducing a new thriller series that keeps you guessing and on your toes through every twist and unexpected turn....

*USA Today Best-Selling* Author Dale Mayer does it again in this mind-blowing thriller series.

The unlikely team of Detective Kate Morgan and Simon St. Laurant, an unwilling psychic, marries all the unpredictable and passionate elements of Mayer's work that readers have come to love and crave.

Newly promoted detective Kate Morgan stands up for the victims in the world, never backing down or giving up. From a family of victims, Kate will not tolerate those who take advantage of others. The worst ones prey on the hopes of desperate people to line their own pockets.

And when Kate finds a connection between more than a half-dozen cold cases to a recent case—where a child's life is in jeopardy—she'll make a deal with the devil himself to protect the child.

Having the gift of Sight, Simon St. Laurant knows that once he uses it, he can never walk away. But when nightmares of his own past are triggered, Simon can't stand back. Determined to help, Simon vows to save these children—even if it means dealing with the cranky and critical Detective Kate Morgan.

**Sign up to be notified of all Dale's releases here!**
https://smarturl.it/DaleNews

# A Behind-the-Scenes Glimpse into Dale Mayer's Simon Says Series

With this new Simon Says series, it seems some background information from me, the author, might be in order. For one, Vancouver is a city where I have many happy memories of my decade-plus years growing up there. As an army brat, I spent most of my childhood years in Vancouver, as I ventured into adulthood. For all the good memories I do have, several are not so good. That's partly what brought this series to light.

The city of Vancouver, like all big cities, has the wonderful surface layer that hides a dark underbelly. The contrast between dark and light has always interested me. I write on both sides of this coin constantly. The good against the bad, the light of day against the dark of night. The positive versus the negative. The funny compared to the dark. Laughter paired with suspense. It keeps me happy and the words flowing.

I was at a conference with several friends years ago, and I mentioned I wanted to do a new thriller series. The ideas easily flowed forth—which they do naturally with me anyway. But this time, my two main characters, Kate and Simon, fully popped into my mind, both the physical appearance of both as well as their personalities. I didn't touch the concept for another full year, until I sat down and wrote the first book, Simon Says … *Hide*. Then self-doubt hit, and I pushed it aside, ignoring it for another year. But Kate hammered away at me inside my head, wanting more page time, so I sat down to write the next four books of this Simon Says series.

Writing fiction, particularly crime fiction, presents its own challenges, especially when you marry that with the fiction license—joining reality with imagination. Meaning, I did my best to line up truth and facts and yet kept my license to create needed bits of information to ensure that the story worked. Remember. These are stories. They are not real cases, not real people, nor real events. In fact, given urban density, at the time you read this story and the others in this Simon Says series, the Vancouver street names, traffic patterns, and even beaches and community neighborhoods could well have changed.

I do thank the Vancouver Police Department for their patience in answering my multitude of questions throughout the writing of this series. They were very helpful in sorting out the divisions between the various community and law enforcement groups that work together to protect and to serve and to keep safe Vancouver and all the neighboring cities.

Remember. All these people, places, events are fictional, creations of my mind. I wrote these stories for entertainment purposes only.

Enjoy!
Dale Mayer, Author of the Simon Says Series

# CHAPTER 1

*Vancouver, First Monday in June ...*

NEWLY MINTED HOMICIDE detective Kate Morgan sat on one of the many benches positioned in this child-friendly park, watching the kids play on the swings in downtown Vancouver. She'd passed her first three months in her new position amid the craziness of too many murder cases to count. Vancouver, BC, was like any big city around the world and had its share of criminal activity. The city had its issues—just being on the coast and blending many different nationalities—yet somehow it all worked. Plus it was home for her. Always had been.

Because of those life-and-death issues, Vancouver had three homicide units, usually with six or seven detectives in each unit. She chuckled. At one time, the two other units called themselves Team Canuck or Team Flames, showing how hockey crazy Canada got. She didn't know what her unit used to call themselves, as she was the odd-one-out still. New enough to know her place and not so new to misunder-stand the team needed time to meld.

Her ever-assessing gaze watched two men on a bench on the far side of the park. One got up, tossed a bright yellow ball at the other and then, with a raised hand, turned and walked away.

Her focus flitted to the storm approaching in the distance, assessed its threat, and dismissed it. Rain was part of the reality when living on the coast. The more pressing threats in her world were the two-legged predators. She'd known the dangers ever since her younger brother had disappeared, even now, twenty-five years later with still no trace of him. She kept a copy of his file on her desk, as a reminder of the work she'd dedicated herself to. Timmy was always close to her heart. She could only hope to get closure, as she worked to give closure to others.

Sudden movement on her left had her watching a lean man of average height, walking into the park and staring at the kids on the swing. Something about his gaze set her nerves on edge. He was slightly turned away from her, only letting her see his jeans and well-worn jacket with the upturned collar. He perched on a nearby bench seat, seemingly fascinated by the boys' antics.

The single male on the far side stood suddenly and strode her way, tossing the yellow ball and catching it smoothly with every step. He gazed at the street beside her, unconcerned for the kids or other adults. His focus was internal. From the power suit he wore, business deals most likely.

As she turned back to the other man, he'd disappeared. Her gaze zipped to the boys at the swings. They were still there. Relaxing slightly, she studied the park exits. Both men had left at the same time. From opposite sides of the park.

It shouldn't have meant anything.

But it felt like it did.

Her phone rang just then. Rodney, one of her team. "We found another one. Prepare yourself. It's a little boy."

## *Tuesday*

SIMON ST. LAURANT had had a bad week. He twisted in bed, kicking off the blanket. His body shimmered with sweat. He drifted in and out of sleep. He'd been up until two in the morning in one of his friendlier gambling games and had crashed soon afterward. Now it was five in the morning, and the last thing he wanted was to be awake. He rolled over, pulled the sheet over his sweating body, and closed his eyes.

As he tried to fall asleep again, he drifted down the same godforsaken dark street, just a halo of light coming from the streetlamps across on the other side. A small man, holding the hand of a very young boy at his side, walked quietly down the street. The little boy asked, "When will we be there?"

"We'll be there soon," the older man promised.

Something was just so damn wrong about that picture that Simon kept telling the little boy to run, wanting to reach out and drag him to safety. But, even as Simon reached out a hand, he saw that it wasn't real, that he wasn't there, that he couldn't grab that little boy and escape. As the older man walked under the streetlamp, Simon caught the hungry look on the man's face. A predator's look. Yet not clear enough to identify him.

Simon woke immediately, sat up, and groaned in frustration. "Why that same goddamn freaking nightmare?" he cried out, before flopping to his back yet again.

He was exhausted, his mind overwhelmed, as he drifted once again into the deepness of sleep. This time he landed in a small room, with lots of toys on the bed and on the floor. A bed that broke his heart because it had a plastic sheet for the little kids who might wet themselves. A blanket was atop the bed but was otherwise empty. Simon's mind knew that a light was on the side of the room and that Simon would see the child soon, but he didn't want to go there. He kicked himself out of the dream, sitting up again, shuddering in the dark. "Damn it," he muttered, rubbing his eyes. "What fresh hell is this?"

Almost as if by asking that question, his body stiffened. He fell backward again, and this time he was in a different room, and the bed was bigger. It had little pink roses around the base and unicorns across the headboard. A little girl sobbed her eyes out, curled up into a tiny ball, hugging a teddy bear. The problem was that fancy little bed was completely out of place, surrounded by bare concrete walls and old cracked floors. The lack of carpet or any other niceties suggested this would not be a nice little home for her.

Instead Simon saw the bloodstains on the mattress around her, the pain and the terror in her heart, and the loneliness in her soul. He wanted to hold her and to tell her that it would be okay. But the same words rippled through his mind: *Hide. He's coming.*

Then everything went dark …

When he woke again, he lay in his bed, staring at the ceiling, dry-eyed, but felt as if he'd bawled his entire life away. Every part of his body hurt, especially his soul. He sat up, felt like he was thirty years older than his thirty-seven years on this planet. Thirty-seven years of pain and fighting to get the upper hand, trying to make sure that he wouldn't be a victim in this world again.

Years ago he'd sworn to be a victor instead. He played the game, but he didn't let others play him. That wasn't part of his new reality. Not anymore—not for a long time. He looked down at his bed, the bottom sheet literally pulled off the mattress and twisted beneath him, while the top sheet was crumpled on the floor beside him.

"Looks like I had a party—and not the fun kind," he muttered, as he slowly straightened. He stretched, turned to get the kinks out of his neck and his back. A bad night had the effect of turning his spine into a pretzel that he could spend hours trying to untwist. He needed a hot shower to complete the job. Yet every time he went under the water, he kept seeing images of the boy that he'd seen in the first nightmare this morning.

It made no sense, when he'd seen many other children throughout his lifetime of nightmares, but, for some reason, he identified with that one. That night terror always upset him because he didn't know that child. It wasn't Simon as a child, and he didn't understand the dialogue, didn't remember it from his own life. What he did know was that these nightmares had to stop.

If he had a friend who was a doctor, he might have talked to him or her, but unfortunately he didn't even have that. In truth, speaking out loud of this weakness, ... in the wrong hands, that knowledge could crush Simon. As he walked naked to the shower, he knew something had to change; he couldn't keep going on this way. The nightmares had restarted suddenly, for no current reason, and they were getting stronger, clearer, and more traumatic to view.

He should get away for a few days. Book a gambling cruise to take his mind off this mess. Maybe see Yale there. Simon's gaze caught sight of the yellow child's ball that Yale had tossed to Simon, the two men out of the blue both at the park yesterday.

Simon often walked that corridor and had come upon his old friend, looking sad and depressed. It had been nice to see Yale unexpectedly. Normally they'd be in on the same poker games or cruises, but he hadn't seen his old college friend in over six months.

Much happier after their visit, Yale had laughed, as he'd tossed him the ball, and said, "For old times' sake."

With a shrug, Simon stepped under the rain showerhead and let the hot water slosh over his head and down his back to the tiles below.

As soon as he was dry and dressed in lightweight pants with a linen shirt, perfect for summers in Vancouver, he picked up his blazer, flipped it over his shoulder, and headed out. He needed coffee in a big way, but he also had to escape the solitude of his own thoughts, preferably out in public, where he could disappear into the crowds. He walked off the elevator, crossed the lobby, and headed toward the front door, held open by the doorman.

Once outside, he stopped for a long moment, lifted his head, and sniffed the early morning Vancouver air. The nearby harbor, with that scent of salt, plus the noise and the bustle of city life, all of it melded together beautifully. With a smile he turned and headed toward his favorite coffee shop.

# CHAPTER 2

K ATE WALKED TOWARD the open room, the bullpen full of desks, singled out her own, and threw herself into her chair, her fingers hitting the keyboard with the same ferocity.

"Wow, bad night?" Owen asked from behind her.

She shrugged, as she logged in to check her email. "Aren't they all?"

She was the newest member to the division, supposedly worked within an active base team of six—with access to an analyst and two assistants—plus Sergeant Colby Stevens, the head of their team. One of the assistants was out on leave, so the temporary replacement was sinking deeper under the workload each day.

"Thought you went out with your new guy last night?" Owen teased her.

"In your dreams," she snapped back.

He was the one happily married member of the team, with one boy and one girl, the perfect little family. That alone was enough to get a rise out of her. How the hell did he manage that with this job? She really wanted to know. She barely had time to braid her thick hair each day, keeping it out of her way. Plus he never missed a shift, but yet somehow he was there for all his kids' special events and birthdays. When he was on the job, he was fully here. Yet it seemed that he gave his all to his family. They were lucky.

Now she had more reason to hate his teasing. She knew he had a huge grin on his face, particularly if he thought he'd gotten a rise out of her. Her love life was a constant joke. Because there wasn't one. She tried to keep the team out of it, but it was damn near impossible. This is what happened when you worked closely with guys. Two women were in the group, her and Lilliana. And, if ever two women were opposites, it was them.

Kate liked to consider herself a fighting machine, but, in truth, she had to work harder, faster, than anybody else, just to prove herself to the others. She was tall, lean, didn't give a damn about makeup or looking good. It's not what she was here for. She was all about the job. Lilliana was one of those pretty women; blonde, coiffed, makeup perfectly applied, always looked good—even though she was a detective. Yet she was as smart as Kate was. Although there was just something about Lilliana that made the guys like her a whole lot more.

Kate could read fast and could digest information quickly, but her real talent lay in solving puzzles. It had taken years of dedication to become a detective. It was a coveted position, and, anytime an opportunity came up, it meant somebody else had retired, quit, or unfortunately died on the job. And that's what had happened to the detective she replaced. He'd been killed during the investigation of a major crime. It had taken the department six weeks to hire somebody to replace him, and, even now, she felt the disapproval of those around her.

Not so much disapproval because it was her as much as she was someone else.

She would never fill Chet's seat. It just wasn't possible.

He'd been six-five, a 280-pounder, with a ready laugh. A guy everybody had loved. He'd done his job well and had been on the force twenty-five years. According to the others, he'd wanted to die on the job; he just didn't want to die ten years early.

"Chet always came in with a smile on his face," Rodney said from her side.

She winced at that. "And for the one-hundredth time," she said, without turning around, "I'm not Chet."

"Is that not the truth?" Lilliana said on a laugh as she walked in. Somehow she always looked put together. Her jeans were high-end, her shirts designer.

It was all Kate could do to arrive clean, as few holes as possible in her jeans and her T-shirt, and no way would she ever show up in heels. She shook her head. Not that they had to wear the same uniform, as if still street cops, but Lilliana had these clothes that somehow made her look like a professional, whereas Kate always felt like she was barely getting the hang of things.

When the phone rang beside her, she just glared at it.

"See? That's one of the things here," Rodney said helpfully from beside her. "When the phone on your desk rings, it means somebody is trying to call you."

She shot him a look, picked it up, and said, "Detective Morgan, what can I do for you?"

It was Audrey, the new clerk out front. "Somebody here to see you."

"Who is that somebody?" Kate drawled. "Santa Claus?" As Audrey went off on a gale of laughter, Kate pinched the bridge of her nose.

"Oh, I do love your sense of humor," Audrey said, "but, no, he just came in off the street. He wants to talk to a detective."

"If he came in off the street," Kate said carefully, "he's not looking to talk to me."

"The sergeant said that anybody new coming off the street was supposed to talk to you first."

Kate took a long slow breath. *Of course he did.* "Fine," she said. "I'll be there in a minute." She put the phone down very quietly. Even then, the members of her team all around her were smirking. No way they weren't, and honestly—if she weren't the low man on the job—Kate would be too. Still, she would put in her time and do the job. A job she was damn glad to have finally gotten.

After making whoever it was out there wait for ten minutes, she stood, grabbed a pad of paper and a pen, and stepped out of the room. She heard the bullpen conversation as she left.

"She's in a great mood, isn't she?"

"Clearly she didn't get laid last night," Lilliana said in a delighted whisper that made all the guys perk up and smile.

As Kate walked past the Colby's office, he called out to her, "Kate, what's up?"

She looked at him and said, "Just going to talk to somebody out front, a walk-in with info."

"Good," he said. "I'm glad you're settling in."

She nodded and kept walking. She was patient. That the team hadn't clicked yet just meant it would take a little longer. Chet had been well loved—the wound only scabbed over, not fully healed. She had put her time in on the streets and had worked damn hard to make detective. Now she was here; she was one of them. She should be happy that she was doing the drudgery because it wouldn't last. Besides, even being new was better than still trying to make the grade.

As she stepped toward the receptionist area, she saw one man sitting on a bench. Could already tell he was tall and fit, his dark hair immaculately groomed. He was dressed in a silvery-gray suit, and he wore it like it had been tailored directly on him. *Rich guy.*

Instinctively she didn't like him. Something was slightly familiar about him, but she couldn't place it. Something about money, something about the posh style, it grated on her. But then she was from the wrong side of the tracks. Born there, she had never found a way across to the other side. This guy looked like he was born with a silver spoon in his mouth. As she approached, he stood and reached out a hand.

"Thank you for seeing me."

She noted the faint French accent. *Probably a Quebec transplant.* Not a Vancouver native, like Kate was. She shook his hand, wearing the same professional air that had gotten her where she was, and said, "Let's step into this room, where we can talk." She then led him into an empty interview room nearby.

As he sat down on the far side of the table, she closed the door, dropped into her seat, pen in hand, facing her notepad, and asked, "What can I do for you?"

He just sat here, without saying a word.

She looked up at him, folded her hands in front of her, resting them on the pad of paper, and waited. She found that waiting often made even the guiltiest of suspects nervous. But not only wasn't he nervous, it was almost like the waiting helped him to settle. She frowned.

"You are the one who came here," she said gently, struggling for patience, when what she really wanted to do was get up and walk out. Files were stacked up on her desk; the backlog of work was never-ending, and she always had her private work that she kept secret, though she knew it really wasn't. Only she was so damned busy that she hadn't had a chance to look into that particular cold case. Keeping Timmy's file on her desk was a constant reminder to not forget her brother. As if that would ever happen.

The man across from her finally spoke. "I'm probably just wasting your time."

"Good to know," she said. "In that case, we are done here because, sadly, I have no time to waste." With the pad and pen in hand, she stood, opened the door, and motioned for him to leave. But he hadn't moved. She looked at him and asked, "So which is it? Are you wasting my time or not?"

He leaned forward and said, "I guess I need to tell you, so you can figure it out."

She cocked her head to the side, disappointed that she couldn't return to her desk; still, he intrigued her. He wasn't here because he wanted to be here, and she didn't think much could force this man to do anything. Shutting the door with a little more force than necessary, she walked back over and sat down.

Now she waited again.

He grinned at her, a lightning-fast sexy smile that immediately had her back up. "Are you always this difficult to talk to?"

Her left eyebrow shot up. "How do you know I'm difficult to talk to?"

"Because you're sitting there, trying really hard to not boot my ass off this chair and out of the station," he said. "And I really appreciate that you've given me some time to work through this in my mind."

She felt like a heel, but, from the look in his eyes, she

knew he'd done it deliberately. She tossed down her pen, slouched in her chair, crossed her arms over her chest, and said, "Anytime."

"I'm having nightmares."

"We're not shrinks. You know that, right?" she said in a droll voice.

"Great," he said. "I'm trying to pour out my soul here, and you're not helping any."

"That's because I'm not a shrink."

"Ha, ha, ha," he said. "I know perfectly well where I am. I'm at the police station, and I need to get something off my chest."

Kate grabbed her pen, leaned forward, her gaze intent, as she studied him. "What did you do?"

"I didn't do anything."

She studied him for a moment, slid the pen back down again, and slouched, resumed her arms-across-her-chest position. This time she crossed her legs too. "So why are we here?"

He gave a startled laugh. "You know what? You'd make a great doctor."

She stared at him in confusion.

"Your bedside manner is perfect."

She just upped the voltage of her glare.

"Look. I don't want to be here either," he said in frustration. "I've come to this police station three times and walked away each time, before I ever made it inside."

"Congratulations, you made it inside," she said. "Are we done now?"

He stared at her and then laughed. "Of all the things I ever thought I would come up against, not even having a chance to talk wasn't one of them."

"You've had lots of chances to talk," she said, "but you're not talking."

"Same nightmares over and over again over the years, but now really concentrated in the last week," he snapped. He clasped his hands together in front of him, a small yellow ball squeezed in between.

She studied the child's toy, wondering why it was firing in her memory. There were thousands all around the city just like it. Forcing her gaze back to stranger, she studied his stiff back and rigid jaw. "Not helpful," she said, and she managed to keep her tone completely flat.

He shook his head. "Same little boy every night."

Her gaze narrowed. "Do you like little boys?"

He fisted his hands on the table, leaned forward, and said, "The same little boy being walked down Hastings Street under the shadow of the lights, a little boy not more than five, maybe six, years old, holding the hand of some old guy, who scares the crap out of me."

"Interesting," she murmured. She studied him closely for any signs of deception, but nothing was really there, as far as she could tell. He was telling the truth, as he believed it to be, but, so far, he hadn't said anything definitive yet. "Can you identify the little boy?"

"Only that he's got some lollipop in his free hand, and he's wearing a little Burberry coat," he said. "I can't tell what color it is."

"Why is that? You said there were lampposts."

"He is walking under the lampposts, yes, but everything is in shades of grays."

"Your nightmares are in gray?"

"This one is, yes."

"So then what happens?" she asked, intrigued in spite of

herself. She didn't know what it had to do with the police, but she could imagine that a dream, *nightmare*, as he'd said, that would happen over and over again would really piss off a guy like this. That fascinated her as much as anything.

"I just hear this voice that calls out, 'Timothy.'"

"*Timothy?*" she said, questioning, her body stiffening at the name.

He nodded.

"*Timothy?*" she snapped, her feet flat on the floor. "Is this some sick joke?"

He looked at her in surprise. "No," he said. "What are you talking about?"

She stared at him and then gave a hard headshake. No, he couldn't know. Besides, her Timmy had gone missing during the day, not the evening, and had happened a long time ago. "Look. I don't know what your nightmare is all about," she said, "or why you think you need to tell me about it. I'm a homicide detective, in case you didn't know." She stopped, took a deep breath. "But if you don't have anything else, then this interview is over."

"This is an interview?" he asked curiously.

"Look, sir," she snapped. "Do you have anything else you feel like you need to tell me?"

"Yes," he said, "I just know that—because of the styles of clothing, the shades of gray—this happened a long time ago."

"*Know?*"

He stared at her.

Yet he seemed more confused than mad. "And?"

Her fist clenched on her lap, she stared at the half-moons that her fingernails had embedded into the palm of her hand in order to stop the scream from reaching up her throat. She wanted nothing more than to grab this guy by the throat and to shake the truth from him.

"The trouble is, it goes from that image to another image within a little room," he said, "with toys and a toddler's bed, but no child is there, just a blanket. But it's got some plastic wrapping around it that's a different color, not so dark. Unfortunately then it goes to an absolutely beautiful little girl in a fancy little bed." His tone was heavy. "The little girl in the bed is crying her eyes out. She's in a basement. It looks like a basement or maybe a cellar. I don't know," he said. "She's got just a blanket, and blood's on the bed. She is crying, as if her heart is breaking." And then he fell silent.

She sat back and looked at him. "And it's the same nightmare over and over again?"

"The same one for a week now," he said bitterly. "Until last night."

"What about last night?" she asked, but inside she knew. Dear God, inside she knew.

"Last night, another child was added to the sequence," he said. "A little boy, a little bit older, like six, maybe seven. I don't know children's ages. Skinny, curled up in the bed, but he wasn't even breathing. In the nightmare I zoomed down, and he was just lying there, and I couldn't see him moving or breathing. There was like a weird outline to him."

"Did you see anything that can identify these children? Or where they are located?" she asked lightly. But she was gripping the pen in her hand so hard that it was in danger of breaking.

"I would have said no," he said. "I would have said it could be any child, anywhere in the world. That's one of the reasons I never came in to the cops before. Although I've had these particular nightmares for the last few weeks, I've had them off and on in various forms for years. I've always just ignored them, but now I can't ignore them anymore."

"Why is that?"

"Because this newest little boy has a name on the bed above his head. It read 'Jason.' No last name, just the first name."

"And you can't give me any physical description of him?"

"Emaciated to the point of being starved," he said bluntly. His tone still easily portrayed the horror of what he had experienced in his nightmares. "He's drawn, skinny, like you could see inside him. His skin was almost translucent."

"And, if the child were dead, how long has he been dead?"

He shook his head. "I got the impression it was recent. But I don't think he was—" And then he stopped, shook his head, and looked away. "I don't put any credence into this," he said. "So you probably shouldn't either."

"Well, I don't have anything to put credence into yet," she said drily. "So why don't we just go down this mythical pathway and see if anything is there?"

"Have you had anything to do with psychics before?"

"Hell no," she said forcibly. "I only believe in what I can see and hear and feel."

He stared at her. "Of course I would be talking to you."

"Do you consider yourself a psychic?"

"Hell no," he said. "But I can't help but wonder if these nightmares don't have some kind of fact-based realism."

"Fact-based realism?" She had never heard that phrase before. "If you had given me anything to identify any of these children with," she said, "I could look them up in the files."

"It's the first time I saw a name on the bed," he said, "but I definitely got the impression the child had been there for a while."

"Starved to death?"

"I'm afraid that was probably the least of his problems," he said softly.

She studied his face, seeing the pain, the tired lines in the corner of his eyes, the faint anger masked around his lips, as he clenched them tight. "It makes you angry, doesn't it?"

He glared at her, not liking the sound of that. "I didn't do anything to these children," he said, "but whoever did hasn't stopped."

She sat back. "Why do you say that?"

"I think, when I saw the first nightmare," he said, "since it seemed to have been such a long time ago, I ignored it. But then I had another one and then another, and each time they came back around, another child had been in the group."

"If that's true," she said, "then whoever this person is has taken four."

Then he shook his head. "No," he said, "because it's quite possible he's taken a lot more, and I just haven't connected."

"*Connected?*" she pounced. "So you are thinking along psychic terms?"

"No," he said quietly. "I'm not thinking on any terms. I just know these damn nightmares won't leave me alone, and last night I saw the name Jason. And the child maybe was six, and I can't give you any more than that."

"Well, it's not much," she said, "but I'll need your contact details."

SIMON SAYS... HIDE

He just stared at her.

"If it does turn out to be something, I obviously have to contact you again," she said. "Not to mention the fact that every visit here is recorded."

He swore softly.

"Is that a problem?" she asked. And again she studied him intently. Everybody gave away so much in their body language that they weren't aware of. But, in his case, no, he kept his cool, even as the small tic in the corner of his jaw pulsed away. She watched it, fascinated, because she never understood if it was a muscular thing or a nervous sign. But, in his case, it was neither.

He was thinking hard. He turned to look at her, nodded, and said, "My name is Simon St. Laurant," and he went on to add his phone number and address.

"That's a pretty high-end area for you to live," she said, staring at the False Creek North address she'd written down.

"For *me* to live?"

"For anybody," she said smoothly. "In other words, it takes money to live there."

"If you say so," he said curiously. "Money comes. Money goes," he added. "I try not to worry about it too much."

Her pen stopped in the act of writing down his address. "Isn't it nice that you can say that," she said. "Most of the world can't."

"I'm not most of the world," he said, once again settling back into that arrogance she'd seen in him when he'd first arrived.

She nodded, stood, and said, "I'll see you out."

"Will you check?" he asked abruptly, as they reached the entrance door, where he would walk back out onto the street.

She nodded. "I'll check."

He flashed her a brilliant smile that had her stopping still in amazement. "That's all I can ask," he said, and he turned and walked out.

Behind her, the Audrey, from the front desk said, "Wow." In a lowered voice Audrey added, "He's gorgeous. Did you see the way he moved? Like a panther, so smooth." She giggled. "And you got to talk to him too."

Kate said in exasperation, "Well, I had to, obviously."

"You're just lucky I'm here to run interference for you," Audrey said, with a cheeky grin. "In his case, I'm more than happy to. I wonder if he's married?"

"Don't know. Don't care," Kate said and headed back to her desk. Anything to do with psychics made her back away. *Charlatans*, the whole lot of them.

But the one thing burning in the back of her mind now—well, other than the mention of her brother, Timmy—was how the hell this Simon guy had heard about Jason, a six-year-old boy who'd been missing for six months and whose emaciated body had just been found.

# CHAPTER 3

*Friday Morning*

T HREE DAYS AFTER St. Laurant's statement, Kate still had
no answers. But, from the little bit nonpsychic Simon
had given her, she did confirm he was talking about Jason
Holloworth, who'd gone missing while walking home from
school one day. He was supposed to go outside to wait for
his mother, who had been late to pick him up, so he decided
to start on his own because he was only a few blocks from
home.

But he never made it.

According to his mother, he was always on the skinny
side and had issues gaining weight. He was six and a half at
the time of the abduction but looked closer to five. His
seventh birthday came and went, with no sign of the child.
Everyone was still hoping he would be found alive and well,
until four nights ago, when his body was found floating in a
harbor, not very far away from this Simon's address.

She thought about that and looked over maps of exactly
where the body had been found versus where this guy's
apartment was. They were less than half a mile apart. Still, in
that area, half a mile was a long distance, as that area had a
high-density population. She wasn't even sure what to do
with this information from Simon. She was pretty damn sure
her sergeant didn't want to know anything about it. It's not

like Simon had offered anything helpful, but still, she felt duty-bound to report it. Even if not credible. Besides, she knew all about charlatans. He might not look like the normal ones they saw at the station, but that didn't change anything.

She also didn't know what to do about the little boy Simon had called Timothy. *Timmy.* Just the mention of her brother's name caused a lifetime of hurt.

It was just about lunchtime, so she would stop to talk to her boss on her way out. She grabbed her wallet, pulled out a few bills to stuff into her pocket, tossed her wallet back into her desk drawer, and walked down the hallway, heading for the front door. She would grab a bowl of soup around the corner at her favorite Jewish deli. She absolutely loved their food, and it didn't matter what the special was, she'd have it and consider herself lucky. As she walked toward Colby's office, her footsteps slowed. When she got there, she saw through the glass window that he was alone.

He called out, "Come on in, Kate." She opened the door and hesitated. "Come in." She came in, took a seat when he motioned to it, and asked, "What's up?"

"Three days ago we had a guy walk into the station," she said. "He had these nightmares."

His eyebrows shot up. "So we're talking to people about nightmares now?"

"I heard him out," she said. "It was about him seeing a series of children in his nightmares, from a little boy that he said the vision seemed to be from years ago to another little boy, who he said was more recent. Several others popped in and out in a continuous stream of ugly situations. The recent boy appeared dead in his dream, and the name on the bed above his body read 'Jason.'"

Colby leaned forward. "Jason?"

"Yes," she said. "When I heard that, I went and double-checked the records to see if his statement followed the description of Jason Holloworth," she said. "Apparently he was already very, very skinny and had a great deal of trouble gaining weight. The stranger who walked in"—she looked down at her fingers as she tried to remember his name— "Steven St. Laurant, I believe. No, Simon St. Laurant," she corrected. "He had put his age at six and very emaciated."

"This guy sees himself as some kind of psychic?"

The corners of her mouth quirked up. "I did ask him that," she said. "He was almost offended."

"Why?" her boss asked. "Unless he was involved? Knew the victim? Knew the family? Saw the boy alive? Dead?"

"I don't know," she said. "I just wanted to let you know what he said."

"Have you done anything with his info?"

"I logged it, but that's it," she said. "We got a little busy with a couple other cases, so I haven't followed up."

"It is crazy right now. Check the details that he gave you on the other children, when you get a moment," he said. "Maybe something else will line up too."

"And if it does?"

"There's the question, isn't it? At that point we'll get the team on it. First make sure he isn't the person behind it all," he snapped, as he stared out the doorway. "We've seen that happen a time or two."

"I don't understand the psychology behind letting the police know about these cases if you are the one actually perpetrating the crimes."

"The psychology of the criminal mind is something we could spend lifetimes trying to understand, and we still never really will. Talk to our psychologist on staff about the subject someday. You'll never get her to shut up." he said. "So we don't believe this guy, check it out, and make sure that we have some understanding of where and what he's doing," he said. "Then we'll haul him back in and have a more detailed conversation with him."

"Will do, when I get back," she said. "I'm heading down to Marco's for the special today."

"Oh, what's on special?" he asked, looking up with interest.

"Doesn't matter," she said. "I always love it anyway."

He laughed and waved her off.

She took the stairs, needing the exercise and the stress relief. Since she'd joined the division, it seemed like she worked harder, longer, and more intensely than she ever had. She'd spent twelve years on the force, trying to make detective. Now that she was here, for some reason she thought some of her stress would reduce. Instead, she was in this constant battle to prove that the department had made the right decision in hiring her. Too bad no one else seemed to agree with that decision, but they would eventually.

HE WALKED ALONG the shoreline, loving the fresh roll of the waves, the smell of the sea, that salty tang to the air. It made him feel refreshed, renewed. His life was one long sad history, but he was making the best of it, finding little areas to make himself smile. Somebody should have taken him out a long time ago; he'd even gone looking for help at one point. But nobody seemed to care; nobody seemed to have the budget; nobody seemed to want to help, so he just turned to his nature and embraced it instead. A part of him hoped one day he'd get caught, but another part knew that, at this point, he'd do anything and everything he could to stay free to continue playing his games.

He was well past being fixed or rehabilitated or whatever society thought they could do with him. And he wasn't ready to give up his pastime just yet. As he wandered along, he smiled to see the groups of families with children. It wasn't quite warm enough to be in the water, but people had sand buckets, digging and making sandcastles and just generally having fun. He watched one father sit beside his two young sons, and he murmured, "Good job, Daddy."

On any given day, he'd easily find half-a-dozen children unaccompanied or whose parents were otherwise distracted, either fighting or on their phones. On any given day he could walk into a park or a beach somewhere and see another potential guest at his place. Somebody to put a stab at happiness into his dark world.

It's not his fault that he needed to snuff out the life in them within a few days to weeks. He tried to keep them longer. Especially Jason. Something was supremely sweet about that little boy. But he was obviously sick right from the beginning. He'd been skinny and had gotten skinnier over time. It was really too bad because his parents should have taken him to the doctor a long time ago.

As it was, he'd given Jason the nicest few months that he could. But still, Jason had died, and he'd hadn't even had to do the job himself. Poor Jason; he'd deserved so much better. He shook his head. Life was a bitch.

He turned to watch a toddler heading toward the water. He looked around for a parent and didn't see anyone. He watched, open-mouthed, as the little one went crashing into the water and fell headfirst. Then he laughed because his mom had been in the water, and she had scooped up the little one, who was laughing and crying at the same time. He smiled at that. "Don't see that too often," he said. But the toddler was screaming from the cold water and yet laughing with happiness.

With a smile, touched at the obvious love between the two of them, he turned and walked down the path a little farther, feeling lonelier than ever.

The beach here wasn't groomed on a regular basis, which was nice, so he could always find driftwood and shells, little bits and pieces that floated in on the tide. He was out here more for himself, rather than looking for anybody to join him again. Jason's death had hit him hard. He'd been a good little boy, a happy little boy. He hadn't liked his new owner very much, but that was to be expected.

Something about Jason's soul made him feel like he could reach out and touch that happiness. He often wondered, if he could maybe just capture the light in these children, their innocence, if it would help redeem him. As if what he was doing was somehow helpful. Positive. But then he just shook his head and laughed at his foolishness. He'd realized quickly enough that anytime he snuffed out one of those little lights, nothing else happened. Death was death, and, once they were gone, they were just garbage to be taken out and disposed of.

He didn't even know how many he'd disposed of over the years, but there'd been dozens. Twenty-five, maybe even thirty. He kept a book, but he didn't like to keep count. That was too egotistical. He didn't like to compete against others either because he didn't really see himself that way. And he didn't want anybody to remember him by his numbers. Nobody would remember him kindly. Too many dead children now. He'd been doing this for so long; why should he stop now?

If his mother knew, she'd be horrified. His sister knew, but, well, she would understand because she had a twisted bent herself. They'd inherited it from their father. But somehow their sweet little dense mother had never really understood. She wasn't quite all there now either. Last time he'd spoken to her, the Alzheimer's had kicked in pretty heavily, and she kept asking him if he would bring home cat food. They never had any pets.

He couldn't remember even bringing home a stray. Well, a turtle one time. Maybe when he had been what, fourteen? He didn't know what age she was stuck at in her own mind, but it was obviously decades ago. He'd ignored her for years after that, just like she had ignored him when he was younger. His sister had called him a week ago to say Mom's health was failing. He hadn't been sure what she wanted from him on that. Finally she burst out and asked, "Will you even be sorry when she's gone?"

"She was a pretty minor aspect of my life," he said. "She'll be even more minor in her death."

His sister had found that hilarious. He smiled because she was just like him.

"Dad's dead, you know?" she said.

"You've told me that dozens of times," he said patiently. Again he didn't know why she kept bringing it up. But he figured it was just to get a rise out of him.

"You never could prove yourself to him."

"Good, then I don't have to bother trying, do I?"

"But I wish you'd stop trying to be like him," she said in frustration. "You're better than that."

He smiled a secret smile, knowing she couldn't see it.

"Of course I am," he said. "I'm the devil's spawn."

"What does that make me then?" she retorted. "The devil's spawnee?" She giggled.

He didn't even crack a grin over that one. "No, we're both the devil's spawn," he said, "two peas in the same pod."

"We are twins for sure," she said, "but I don't think we're all that much alike." Her tone had been very doubtful.

"Oh, I think we are," he argued. "We are very much alike."

"No," she said. "You have that weird twisted side to you. I'm nothing like that."

"Give it time," he said. "You just won't indulge in your hobby yet. With some time and a bit of freedom, you will."

"No, it's nasty," she said, "and it's not my hobby. It's yours."

"Yes, but you like to hear all about it, don't you?"

He caught her there because, although she didn't dare do what he was doing, preferring instead to be outraged and disgusted at his "hobby," she always wanted to hear the details. And maybe that's all she could do. Maybe she couldn't be honest with herself or with him; maybe that's just how it worked. He was okay with that too. He knew how deep their connection went, even if she wouldn't acknowledge it.

"Jason died," he said abruptly. "A few days ago."

"I'm sorry," she whispered. "I know how special he was for you."

"Very special," he said, his voice softening. "I'll really miss him."

"He was ill already, you said."

"Yes," he said. "I knew he wasn't long for this world. I just wanted to make his last few months the best they could be."

"And the best that they could be for you too," she said in a dry tone.

He shrugged. "Doesn't mean I don't miss him."

"No, I'm sure you do."

"I'll replace him," he said suddenly, knowing that question was coming up. It always did.

"Don't you think," she said, "maybe it's time to walk away from your hobby?"

"No," he said. "I just don't want a long-term guest again. It really hurts to lose them."

"Well, if it hurts you, think about what it's doing to all the families."

He'd no civil answer for that one.

Even now he smiled, as he walked along the beach. It was nice to talk to her about it; it was nice she understood. She was the only one who would. It made him feel not so alone. And he kept telling himself that he really didn't want to have another guest for a while. He still felt the effects of Jason's death. And it really did hurt.

It wasn't fair; Jason had been so young and so innocent and had only wanted to have a decent life. But, of course, with his parents, that was a whole different story. They hadn't looked after him; they didn't deserve him. They should have taken him to specialists and made sure he got the help he needed. But they hadn't cared enough. How sad was that?

At least he'd cared, so, in the end, Jason hadn't died alone.

### Saturday Morning

SIMON WOKE UP Saturday morning and stretched slowly in bed. The sheets slid gently across his smooth naked skin, making him feel luxuriously awake, as he slowly registered the fact that he'd actually slept last night. It was his third—no, fourth—peaceful night after visiting the police station. Maybe that's all it took. Maybe he only needed to talk to the cops to have it all off his shoulders. Smiling, he sat up, wondering what he wanted to do for the day. When he'd gone to bed last night, he'd deliberately not made any plans, wondering if he would have a decent night or not.

Then he looked over and found he wasn't alone.

He glared down at the woman, wearing just panties, sprawled across his bed. He shook her shoulder. "Annalise, what are you doing here?"

She raised her head with a jerk, blinked, and let her head crash back down again. "Oh man," she said and then yawned.

"What are you doing here?" he repeated.

"You said I could stay."

He shook his head. "No, I didn't. Hell, I was alone when I went to bed."

"Well, you would have," she said, rolling over and pulling the sheet over her shoulders. "You just didn't let me work on you hard enough."

"How did you even get in here?" He searched the cobwebs of his mind but didn't remember seeing her. He ripped the sheet off her and said, "Get up, get dressed, and get out."

She sat up and glared at him. "Why are you such a grouch in the morning?"

"Maybe because you weren't invited last night."

She got up and stormed into the bathroom.

He didn't even care. He just wanted her gone. He cast his mind back to last night, but he was damn sure that she hadn't even been in his awareness. He frowned, as he wandered his small apartment. Her clothing was laid out across the nearby chair and on top was a key, *his* key. What the hell?

When she came out of the bathroom, still in just her panties, she walked over, pulled her dress up and over her head, and slipped into her heels.

He held up the key. "Where the hell did you get this?"

She gave him a casual look and said, "I found it."

"You let yourself into my apartment last night?" That didn't make him feel any better. Better to have no sleep than to sleep through someone sneaking into his place, while he snoozed on.

"Sure, why not?" she said. "I already knew you were up for an easy lay. Of course you weren't exactly all action last night," she said, with a disgusting snort. "Matter of fact, you wasted my night."

"What the hell?" he said in outrage. "If I'd wanted you over, I would have invited you. You don't just walk into my place because you somehow got a hold of my key."

As he held the key, he tried to *see* just where she had gotten it from. And he thought of Caitlin. "Caitlin gave it to you?" he said in disgust. "How many of these damn keys does she have?"

"She made a bunch," Annalise said, with a trilling laugh, as she headed to the front door. "I'll tell her that I struck out, but at least I got a good night's sleep."

"Yeah, well, you can tell Caitlin that she can fuck off too," he said. "We broke up six months ago. Why the hell is she sending women my way?"

"Because she figures that, once you understand nobody's as good as her, you'd have her back."

"Not in this lifetime," he roared.

She closed the door with a *snap* behind her, but her laughter stayed in the room. He walked over, locked the door, and called the locksmith. Within minutes, he had the order in for early the next day to come change the locks on his door. He set the key down. It had been months since his ex-fiancée had tried something like that. He couldn't believe she'd done it again.

When his phone rang, he looked at it and then tossed it on the bed in disgust. Somehow Caitlin wasn't getting the message. Simon shook his head. What a mistake he had made with her. He wouldn't do that again. What had he been thinking when he got engaged? *That he wanted normal. That he wanted a partner. That his solo life had served its purpose for all those years. That he wanted … more.* However, today just reminded him—yet again—that normal wasn't for him. That a partner he could trust was not in the cards. That living his solo life protected him. That he shouldn't want … *more.*

He walked into the bathroom to shower, only to find that his uninvited house guest had left a mess here too. He stepped into the shower, hating the smell of her perfume and old hair spray. He doused himself well with soap and shampoo to clean up the stench. When he stepped out, he felt better, but just the sight of the mess in his bathroom pissed him off all over again. After such a great night's sleep, when he saw his bed, with her indentation and some of her long hairs and even her hairpins on the bed itself, he immediately stripped it down and threw it into the laundry.

He couldn't believe Annalise had done that. And he couldn't believe he'd slept through it. How the hell had that happened? He hadn't slept well in a long time, but sleep deprivation was no excuse. Then he remembered the half bottle of scotch, now sitting empty beside him on the bar. ... Well, that explained him not waking to her arrival and would be the last time he'd do that for a while.

Moodily, he started a cup of coffee and then sat in front of the huge picture window to enjoy the view. He had a two-seater couch arranged in front of the circular windows that showed him the city of Vancouver from his penthouse apartment. He sat here, sipping his coffee, trying to quell the rage inside.

He picked up the phone, turned it on, and called his ex. "You do that again," he said, "and I'll take apart your house of cards and make sure nothing's left for you to pick up the pieces from." Just when she wanted to protest, he turned off the phone and tossed it on the couch beside him.

The last thing he wanted to listen to was any more excuses from her. They'd had months of ups and downs on a daily basis. The sex had been hot, and the rest had been awful. When he couldn't stand any more of the chaos and the constant drama, he broke it off. Only she'd refused to listen. And she'd taken her revenge in a constant irritating string of emails, texts, phone calls. Then resorted to some mad retaliation by sending her girlfriends to his doorstep. This was the first time one had entered unannounced. She'd also be the last.

He was so done with it. He was done with so many things. Hopefully his police visits were done too. He sipped his coffee and stared out at the city, wondering why everybody in his world lived such a shadowed life. He could crush business opponents; he could clean up at any card game. But, when it came to relationships, well, he hated to say it, but apparently he sucked. It was time to change his game, only he wasn't sure exactly how. He didn't want any of those damn recurring nightmares either.

Control was everything to him, and no one and nothing would take that away from him.

# CHAPTER 4

### *Saturday and Sunday*

K ATE SPENT THE next two days, her whole weekend, trying to fit in searches on the missing children, according to St. Laurant's minimal descriptions. Only her time was at a premium. Vancouver had had two murders the previous night; one looked to be an open-and-shut case, but the other one was still dodging them. The detectives on her team had hours of interviews left to do, walking the streets and talking to passersby. They'd managed to snag a couple patrolmen to give them a hand going door-to-door, but nothing shortened the legwork that needed to be done.

### *Second Monday in June*

WALKING INTO THE office early on the third day, she was tired and cranky. She hadn't slept. They'd been out working a case until well past two in the morning.

When she dropped her phone on the center of her desk with a louder-than-normal *snap*, Owen looked up and snickered. "You know that getting laid is a great stress relief."

"If that's the only reason to get laid, I'll skip it, thanks," she said. She walked to the counter and picked up coffee, bringing her cheap mug back to her desk, where she set it down carefully. She might drop a lot of things, but she treated her coffee as gold. The guys had tried to replace her cheap mug several times, but she wasn't having it. It was her favorite cup; it was thick, held the heat, and it was bigger than all the others. And that meant that she got at least one and a half cups of coffee per mug, compared to what the rest of them were getting.

Besides, they were in cahoots to empty the pot before she got hers. It drove her crazy at the beginning, and they were in sync over it all. And, if that were the case, then she was better off just letting them do their thing and ignoring them. She was still all about the case and the victims. Right now she had more of both than she was happy with. When the temperatures outside spiked—which, yeah, in Vancouver wasn't much of a real heatwave—violence spiked. Tempers flared, dispositions shortened, patience disappeared, and all kinds of things that wouldn't normally happen, happened.

The one possible open-and-shut case was a fight between husband and wife. They'd been out on the beach all day. Both of them were hot and suntanned—badly sunburned actually, she added mentally with a snort. They'd been drinking beer and smoking marijuana for most of the afternoon. Somehow they got into an argument at home over munchies, in which she stole his bag of chips. He grabbed the knife and pinned her to the wall with it, jamming it deep along her breastbone.

When Kate took her first sip of the hot fresh brew, she sat back, closed her eyes, and just let it slip down her throat to her stomach. She could almost imagine the caffeine being injected into her bloodstream. Surely it wouldn't be more than ten years before caffeine was actually something you could shoot. Hell, they injected everything else. Why not coffee too?

As she sat here, her eyes closed, she let some of the case information roll through her head. No other people were in that one house, just the husband and wife, and they'd been seen arguing on the beach earlier. His fingerprints were all over the knife, and he was blubbering like a baby when they found them. Kate wasn't sure who had called it in though, and that bothered her. She sat here, her fingers slightly drumming her desktop. Because somebody *had* called it in. That was the only sticking point for her.

Meaning that person knew something, but, if they had witnessed the event, where were they, and what was their role? The husband was incoherent and swore he hadn't called it in; then he had also said that he hadn't killed his wife. Said he'd passed out. And, when he woke up, his wife had been dead. But Kate had checked both their phones anyway, and neither had made the call to the police. And it certainly wasn't random that the cops had showed up.

So something was going on; she just didn't know what. The others on her team didn't seem to be particularly bothered about it, but she was. Something was very strange about having a crime scene like that, where it seemed clearly open-and-shut, yet still no way to know who made the 9-1-1 call.

"A Good Samaritan caller," she said, but she hated that. It was too perfect an answer. How had someone seen? Looked in a window? If so, why? Or had they been there at the time—and, if so, had that person killed the wife?

As much as she liked every case cut-and-dry, every *T* crossed, every *I* dotted, every question mark exactly where it needed to be, this case didn't feel that way. She sipped her coffee. She worked through everything else she knew about the case, but absolutely nothing was unusual, *except* for that call. She thought about it and leaned forward, then picked up her phone and called Dispatch. After identifying herself, she said, "A 9-1-1 call came in at 2218 last night. Do you have a recording of the call?"

"Of course," the dispatcher said, "but I'll need to pass you to my manager, so you can get a copy of it." Kate waited. The manager came on the line. "Yes, we have that," he said. "Give me a moment, and I'll send a copy over."

"And can you tell me if there's any ID for the caller?"

"No," the dispatcher said. "Nobody ID'd."

"So somebody made the call but didn't answer your questions?"

"That's the way it happens sometimes," he said. "I've sent it to you. You can listen for yourself."

After hanging up, she brought it up on her email and went over the very short recording. It looked like a thirty-seven-second call.

"This is 9-1-1. Do you have an emergency? Please tell me your name and your address."

"He stabbed her," said the hushed voice. "He stabbed her dead."

"Name and address," the dispatcher's voice said again. "Please, sir, I need your name and address."

But the only address he gave was the address of the murdered woman. Kate found that interesting. So he knew where it was and knew enough about the scenario to call it in. But, when it came to identifying himself, he didn't. He had immediately said, "You need to send somebody there, before he can hide his tracks," he snapped. "Now."

And he hung up. It wasn't even thirty-seven seconds. The first part was just the dispatcher, picking it up and answering, going through the standard spiel.

"Interesting," she murmured. "So what the devil is this all about?"

*Something about that voice.* Something she wasn't so sure about. She thought about the psychic case days earlier and shook her head. No, it wasn't that. It was obviously *not* Simon's voice, at least not speaking in a normal voice. But it would be odd to have two weird scenarios like this in just a handful of days.

But then again, a full moon was coming, and she swore to God it brought out the crazies. She'd heard several people at the hospitals talk the same way. Somehow a full moon made people do things they wouldn't normally do. Had a third person been in that house? And had he somehow led the husband on to kill the wife? Or had some third person just been a bystander? Maybe he'd been a pizza delivery guy and watched through the window. She understood why he wished to stay out of it, but it would certainly make her feel better to know who had placed that call.

"Good morning," Colby said, as he walked into the bullpen.

She opened her eyes and stared at him.

He looked at her directly. "Long night, huh?"

"You could say that," she muttered. She picked up her coffee again and finished it. As she stood to refill it, he said, "You might as well sit down. Because, one, the coffee is gone. And, two, we've got a meeting in three minutes."

"Three minutes is enough to get more coffee," she protested and stared longingly at the corner she had to get around to get to the coffee.

"But not to make a new pot," he said. "So, in this case, no, it's not."

"Why is the coffee always gone?" she groaned.

"I think it's a standard police problem," Colby said. "The coffee is *always* gone."

"It shouldn't be," she said, "damn it." But she sat back down and watched as everybody else walked in with full cups of coffee. She glared at them and asked, "Did you all finish the coffee?"

Just then Audrey poked her head around the corner and said, "I put on a fresh pot. Two minutes to fresh coffee."

At that, Kate gave her the first bright smile of her morning and said, "Good, thanks. I want to make sure I get a cup."

Audrey looked at her funny and said, "Didn't you already get several cups? The guys said you did." Immediately Audrey broke up, the others laughing too.

Kate shook her head and returned her attention to Colby.

"First order of the day," he said. "We need to wrap up the file from last night. It's nice to see an open-and-shut case. It helps our numbers. Send it through, and let's get that one done with. As for the second one, I understand we still have canvassing to do, so you can pull in two more plainclothes men—or a couple off the beat, if you need to," he said, "but I want all the information by the end of the day."

He looked over at Kate. "What about the guy who came in a few days ago? Did you check out all his descriptions?"

She shook her head. "I was only halfway through the list when we caught two live ones, so everything else went to the back burner."

He looked at the stack of files on her desk and frowned, but she just let him look. She didn't say anything after a moment, and neither did he. Her sergeant looked around at the other desks, and she knew they were all mostly empty. That's the way they all rolled. Most of them stuck to the cases that were on their desk because usually enough of them were here to keep them all busy. The often worked the same case but, if not necessary, they worked independently.

She was the eager beaver, poking into things in the past, but then that's what she did.

"Kate's looking for a promotion already," Lilliana said from the background, eliciting a rumble of muted laughter from the rest.

"She might get it too," Colby said simply. "At least she looks like she's been busy."

The others just glared at him, and he smiled. "If anybody's got any problems, I'm in my office until ten," he said. "Then I've got press meetings after that."

And, from his tone, everybody knew that was his least favorite way to spend the afternoon. It made her feel better to think that he wouldn't be enjoying his day any more than she was. She immediately brought up her keyboard and started hacking away at the emails that had come in overnight. A lot of the officers had gone out last night, taking statements and interviewing witnesses.

Well, she had too, but there were just too many to canvass on her own. The interviews were coming in via email. She absolutely loved that system. It gave her a copy of the statement, a name, and a time and date stamp. And, of course, she compounded the issue by printing off all the statements because she was a very visual person. She pulled everything together from the printer.

As she walked back, Audrey poked her head around and asked, "Did you get coffee?"

She stared at her for a moment and pulled out the cases

that matched her printed interviews, then shook her head. "Don't tell me that it's gone."

"Not if you get there fast," Audrey said in her chirpy voice.

Kate snagged her cup, walked around the corner, just to see Owen replacing the empty pot.

He looked at her and laughed. "Jesus, you're really off your mark today, aren't you?" he said, as he walked away to give her room.

She made a pot herself. She stood here, guarding it, until it was done dripping. While she was doing that, she went through the pages she'd printed off. Nothing here was different. Nobody had seen anyone else. It was just the two people in the house on a long-term basis, as far as anybody knew.

No visitors, no guests staying over, no boarders, no deliveries, or anybody else in the vicinity. They fought a lot, did drugs a lot, and drank a lot. Nobody was surprised at this end. Knowing that, Kate had no reason to stop this from moving forward. She shut down her mind on this issue but noted a question for herself on the page.

"You ready to let that one go?" Rodney asked. "You know it's open-and-shut."

"It's open-and-shut *except* for whoever called 9-1-1," she said.

He stared at her and frowned.

She nodded. "I've listened to the 9-1-1 call. He doesn't identify himself, but he does give the correct murder address and says that our suspect stabbed the victim and that somebody needed to get there before he had a chance to cover up what he'd done."

"So," he said, "the caller was probably the husband."

"It's not his voice, and he was nowhere near that collected when we were there. If it were him, he used a different phone, as that call wasn't made from his cell."

"Remember? The world is a stage, and everybody is in the drama club," he said. "They let us see what they want us to see and try to tell us whatever story they can tell us."

"Maybe so," she said, "but it sucks."

"Life hasn't changed at all in the last three months," he said. "You were a hell of a good cop for years. Now you're a hell of a good detective. But just because you moved up doesn't mean the quality of the humans we deal with did."

She winced.

"What about Jason? Anything on him?"

"No," she said. "I haven't found anything on that one. I'm still waiting on the autopsy report, and the coroner is still waiting on the drug test to come back."

"In other words, we're nowhere," he said. I'm sure the Integrated Child Exploitation Unit will want to be kept in the loop, even if we find out something else was going on with the boy's disappearance. Although it might be a bit early to contact ICE yet."

"Personally," she said, "that seems to be where we were right from the beginning, when Jason first went missing."

"Not necessarily," he said. "We have one open-and-shut murder case. Now lock it down."

She nodded, not having any other reason—except for the 9-1-1 call—and took care of the rest of the paperwork and sent it off. Just as she stood and turned around to get coffee, somebody grabbed the pot ahead of her. She frowned, following the hand to find Colby. She watched as he filled his cup. Then he looked at her and said, "Where's your cup?"

She pointed; he filled it up. "Now at least you're getting one."

"Why don't we just get one of those massive coffeemakers," she said, "and then we won't run out so fast."

"Or," he said, "we should just get one of those little pod systems, where you can make a cup every time."

"Then we just fill the dump with more waste," she said.

"Didn't realize you were such a conservationist."

"We're killing the planet," she said, "and I try not to go too crazy but, jeez, one coffee filter, one pack of coffee, it should do more than four cups of coffee."

"It does," he said. "You forget eight of us are here and our analyst, Reese. Of course she helps the other teams, as well as do our assistants."

"That just supports the argument that we need a big commercial unit." Glancing at his face, she added, "I wish we'd hear from the coroner on Jason's case."

"What about the family?"

"They've been informed," she said quietly. Those jobs were the worst. "And they, of course, have no idea what's happened, nor if that location where he was found was important."

"Nothing? Not an inkling on that location?"

"False Creek is an area they know of," she said. "Definitely a wealthy community but they're at the lower end of that margin," she said. "As expected, they're devastated, but they didn't have anything new to offer."

"Of course not," he said, "they never do. He's been missing what, six months?"

"Six months, two days, and three hours," she said, her tone even lower.

His sharp glance landed on her face and bounced off

again. "He is a priority," he said. "I don't need to remind you of that." He turned and walked into his office.

No, he didn't need to remind her. Any child's case, particularly this one—a missing boy, who shows up dead and in the condition he was in, six months after he's been kidnapped—definitely wouldn't be a secondary case. But, so far, they didn't have anything. She kept hoping the Forensics Division might find something, anything. At this point all they had was the passerby who saw the little body floating in the water. She'd interviewed that witness herself.

The only good news was, the child hadn't been in the water very long. They cased all the cameras in the vicinity, but they hadn't captured any sign of how the child arrived. Of course, about a one-quarter-mile-long section wasn't covered by any cameras. Had the killer known no cameras were there? Maybe her team should be looking at somebody who worked the area or for the city workers who had access to the cameras.

Thinking about that, she walked back to her desk, carrying her coffee, and sat down at her computer, doing searches for the traffic cams. Logging into the site that she finally had permission to get into, she checked the city cameras heading into that area an hour before the boy was found. There was some seriously heavy traffic, which made no sense, being a weekday.

If it had been a Friday night, yes, but Thursday night? It seemed like there was even more. She ran the date through another Google page to see if something had been going on in Vancouver. And, of course, there was. It was one of the seasonal games. That would explain some of it but not necessarily all the traffic.

Still, she went through the traffic that headed in that

direction, but, because the boy was small, he could have been in a back seat; he could have been in a trunk; he could have been in a truck with a topper, and he could have been in a van. Jason was small enough that he could have been in a duffel bag. She searched every vehicle, noting she had just so many options. Too many to narrow it down. The last deceased male child to be found was in Richmond, a hell of a long way from his home.

Were they related? She brought up that case—a little boy named Tam Wong. He'd been missing for six weeks, before his body was found, showing signs of malnutrition and abuse. Jason had been found nude but wrapped in an overlarge jacket. Oddly enough Tam had been found in a similar scenario; he had been nude except for somebody else's too-big pants. A zap strap on the feet and a belt around the top held him inside. That alone made these two cases connected.

Looking at that and jotting down notes, she searched through other cases of dead children, looking for mis-matched or oversize clothing for the victim or no clothing at all. She came up with a couple others who were possible. One was from six years ago, and another was from four years ago. She frowned because that would be every two years, although the timeline between the last two would have shortened that up. And the oddity in that was a little girl had gone missing four years ago. She'd been four, four and a half, at the time that she'd disappeared, but her body had never been found. So why the hell had it come up on her search? She noted that a pile of clothing had been recovered. It had been her clothing, plus an additional dress that had been too large for her.

"Weird," she murmured.

She printed off that page and the other ones that she had, gathering the case numbers so she could pull the physical files. She much preferred a hard copy, even though everything was digital these days. She could have asked Reese, their analyst, to pull the material, but she didn't want to at this point. It could end up being nothing, and everyone was swamped already. It was faster to search in digital but easier on her eyes to review the information in printed copy. She had compiled quite a case file list. She wanted a place to put them all up, but this room didn't have adequate wall space for it. She frowned, as she connected four more cases similar to Jason's—one from fifteen years ago and one from eight years ago—and now she had eight.

She got up with the list of case numbers and walked to Colby's office. He looked up and said, "I hope you've got a really big problem that will save me from going to these meetings this afternoon. Maybe a terrorist cell just blew up? Or a serial killer? Have we got a hijacking? Something?"

He looked so hopeful that she had to chuckle. "Most people in our business don't hope for murder and mayhem."

"And, of course, I don't either," he said, throwing down his pen. "But I really don't play the political game well."

"That's a lie, sir," she said cheerfully. "You play it very well."

He looked at her and said, "What are you after? You're never nice."

"Ouch," she said, staring at him. "You don't have to be so harsh."

"The truth is the truth," he said. "What's in your hand?"

"Eight cases," she said, wondering if he were serious. Was she such a bitch? Realizing he was waiting, she added, "So far."

"Eight cases of what?" he asked, his tone hard and cold.

"Eight cases similar to Jason's."

His shocked gaze widened; then he shook his head. "No way in hell," he said. "We would have noticed."

"Only one thing connects them all," she said. "The clothing that they were found in didn't fit."

He stared at her and crossed his arms over his chest, as he tilted his chair back and kicked his legs up onto the top of the desk. "That's pretty slim."

"Maybe," she said, "but it's in all of them. Except this one's a little different." And she held up the info sheet on Christina.

"What's different about her?" he asked, reaching for the sheet. She handed it over, and he quickly read it. "I remember this. She went missing, never to be seen of again."

"Except her clothing was found," she said.

"That's not all that unusual," he said.

"And along with it was another dress that was too big."

He looked up at her from the piece of paper in his hand. "And your point is?"

"It has the earmarks of the other cases," she said, "but no body."

SIMON SHOULDN'T HAVE made that 9-1-1 call. He knew he shouldn't have, and it was really, really pissing him off. But, every once in a while, these visions were so damn strong that he knew he would have to do something about it. And, when he read about it later in the news, he'd been right. But that didn't mean he should have done it. Anything that could confirm it was his voice would just get him into deep water.

He already knew the cops would use every angle, every bit of evidence against Simon, and there would be absolutely no way to back out of the mess.

Life sucked, and then you die.

That was the motto he'd heard. But his was the opposite. *Life sucked; you made it better, so it sucked less.*

Still there'd just been something about this murder, and Simon knew that somehow that guy would walk if Simon didn't turn him in.

It didn't make any sense because what he had done was so clear-cut, but Simon couldn't take the chance. He hated the fact that now, all of a sudden, he was this Good Samaritan. He knew shit happened, but he didn't want to be the one who was around when it did. He could take care of his own, and he had many times, but no way in hell did he want to start taking care of everyone else. He'd pulled himself out of the gutter and planned to never go back. Nothing ugly was allowed to touch his world. And it didn't, at least on the physical side. But, for whatever reason, somehow something had gotten in under his skin and into his psyche.

And he was unnerved enough to worry about it.

When his phone rang a few minutes later, he answered it. "What?"

First came silence, and then a female said, "This is Detective Morgan. You came in to speak with me a few days ago."

"Oh," he said, and immediately images of the tall, lean, physically fit detective flooded through his mind. *Chestnut-colored hair, huge chocolate-colored eyes, wide mobile mouth.* He was always hungry—in one way or another—when he thought of her. "What can I do for you, Detective?"

"Do you have any other details?" she asked. "On the

boy, Jason."

"You mean, you believe me?" He snorted. "Guess that makes you more the fool than me. And, no, I don't have any more details for you. Thanks for calling." He hung up. And once again he tossed his phone. It was becoming a habit. If he could toss it away, then he could also toss away his connection to the world, as if that act would cleanse his soul.

Needing to get away, he walked to the bakery, ordered a bagel from behind the counter, and then walked to the butcher, where he picked up some fresh cheese and ham. By the time he was on his way home, he was hungry and stressed. He slowly rotated his neck and his shoulders, choosing to walk up the flights of stairs in his building and maybe wear himself out a little bit more. By the time he made it to his apartment, instead he was even more irritable.

He walked to his door and unlocked it, then pushed it open. His phone rang. He let it. When it finally stopped, he said, "Good riddance."

He put down his purchases, then checked the ID of his caller. The detective. He frowned. If he didn't answer her, she would probably hound him.

Then he noted four other missed calls. "I was gone thirty minutes," he snapped to the empty room.

He put the phone carefully on the counter, as he brought out the bagel, sliced it, then buttered the halves.

He knew the cop couldn't stand him already. He didn't know where the restrained animosity came from, but it was there. And, considering her job, he probably didn't have to look very far to find reasons why.

His Quebec-born grandmother had had the sight—after all, that was what led her to finding Simon at the age of six, and he would go as far as to say that maybe he had inherited a little bit of her ability. But he didn't want more than that. He had only had four years with her, but her gift was not something that had made his grandmother's life any easier. On the contrary, it just made it harder and more impossible. She'd been both revered and hated. Who the hell needed that? His grandmother had warned him once that, the moment he went down this pathway, there was no turning back. *Pas de retour en arrière.* He'd laughed at her. *Ne pas y aller.* Not going there.

She'd given him that narrow glare that she'd been so damn good at and said he didn't have a choice; he was already on it.

He stared at his phone and wished to hell that whatever that first misstep was, he hadn't taken it. Grandma had been proven right, and he knew that this one-way path would only get worse.

# CHAPTER 5

*Third Monday of June*

THE DAYS JUST slammed hard from one day into the next. Somehow it was the third Monday of June already. Kate worked her ass off all day, every day, and crashed blindly every night. Nothing like the pain of trying to figure out what had happened to a missing or a murdered child. It brought up all kinds of memories that Kate tried to dampen down. And it wasn't working. The longer she worked on Jason's case, the more she thought about Timmy, her kid brother. She'd pulled up everything there was on his case and had nothing, absolutely nothing to show for it.

Her brother had gone missing two and a half decades ago. Kate had been responsible for looking after him, but one moment he was there, and the next he was gone. Her mother had blamed her ever since, never relenting from that position, placing her in foster care immediately. Even after her mother had been in rehab several times, her phone calls were nothing but a sickening tirade over and over again about how Kate had ruined her mother's life by letting Timmy die. Now in a long-term-care facility, her mother was nothing if not consistent in the verbal and mental abuse that she rained on Kate.

Fact of the matter was, Timmy had been five. But Kate herself had only been seven. And she'd been put in charge of her younger brother. When she'd come out of her classroom to find him on the playground, she'd forgotten her homework, so ran back inside to grab her books, and, when she returned, he was gone. But she was to blame.

Somehow a seven-year-old had paid a price that should never have been put on a child. And she'd never stopped looking for her brother. Anytime a John Doe showed up, anytime a child was found, even after decades, Kate's heart leaped. And anytime they found a tiny corpse, decomposed beyond recognition, she knew instinctively that it was him—only to be proven over and over that it wasn't.

Nobody here knew how bad her childhood had been. No one here knew about her secret guilt or why she held up prickly barriers against the world. A couple knew about her brother but only that he'd gone missing. Not the details of how her life had derailed at that point. And how could she explain that the people who should have been there for her weren't and the people who she should have been there for were gone?

She trusted herself, but she didn't trust anybody else. That made for a pretty tough working relationship. But she'd do whatever the hell she had to do to keep this job because this was what she'd wanted, ever since her brother had gone missing. Come hell or high water, this was her role in life. And she was bound and determined that she would find her little brother. Somehow ...

"Penny? You know? ... For your thoughts?"

She frowned and looked up to see a smooth, way-too-expensively-dressed, and overly coiffed Andy—their fifth team member. "Not worth it. Isn't there some broad you're supposed to be picking up for dinner?"

"That's tonight," he said. "You really need to get your

timing straight."

"And my jokes apparently," she said. She studied him. "You're looking pretty dolled up. Did you even go home last night?"

"Of course I didn't go home," he said. "I never do. That's the way I like it. You do know if you'd loosen up a little bit yourself, you might like it too."

"I, at least, like to know the name of the person I sleep with," she drawled.

He flushed.

And she stared. "Oh. My. God. You can't remember who the hell it was last night, can you? So they all roll into this jumbled mess of images? Is that it? What do they call that? A collage, that's it," she said triumphantly. "A collage of faces. The bodies have the prerequisite parts but, other than that, not a bit of difference between them."

He stared at her, shocked.

She shrugged. "What the hell?" she said. "Too crude for your refined sensibilities? Am I not allowed?"

"No," he said. "You're supposed to be sweet and feminine."

"Then I'm in the wrong job," she said bluntly. "Don't get me wrong. Sex is good for everybody," she said. "But, when you have so much, with so many different partners, that you can't even remember who the hell you're with"— she checked her watch—"like four hours ago, you've got to ask yourself, *Who or what are you running from?*"

With that, she grabbed her coffee cup and headed out of the room. An odd silence filled the bullpen behind her. She shouldn't antagonize everybody, but, since she'd joined the detective division, replacing Chet, incurring the obvious animosity of the rest of the team, she had instinctively come out swinging, before anybody could get under her skin.

She sipped her coffee and stared out the window, trying to relax. This Jason case was getting to her. She needed to find something, anything to give to the parents, to give to her sergeant, to give to the rest of the team. If she could find a crack, they all would be there to pry it wide open. However without that crack … Damn it. Her sergeant had been beyond upset at her eight cases, and he'd asked her to go deeper, to make sure that there was absolutely no mistake.

The connection was slim, but it was there. The thought that a child pedophile, a serial killer, had been operating for that long here in the city was bad news. The fact that she had been the one to find the connection would also not go down well with her team. Or that she'd kept her finding from them. She knew of and had worked with the Missing Persons Division irregularly, depending on whether their cases overlapped. But, when it came to children, everybody was affected, no matter what department.

When someone behind her called out, she turned and looked at Lilliana. "What's up?"

"I would ask you that," she said. Lilliana, ever-perfect, sauntered closer, holding her delicate china mug full of coffee. "You're even more abrasive than usual."

"It's the case. Is that an issue?"

"No," she said. "We were pretty rough on you, when you first got here, but we thought, by now, things would have calmed down."

"And they probably will," she said, "but they haven't yet."

"I'm sorry," Lilliana said. "I was one of the forerunners, who chewed into you pretty good when you first arrived."

"It's never easy replacing somebody," Kate said. "And, in

this case, there's no replacing Chet, but his seat needed to be filled, and I got the job."

"And we know that," she said, "and, of course, he was a good friend of ours. Seeing that chair and not seeing the big guy there every day is still really hard for everyone."

Kate thought it was an apology, but she wasn't too sure. She listened as Lilliana explained a little more.

"It's not that you personally weren't wanted," Lilliana said gently. "*Nobody* was wanted. We even went to the department head and asked if we could operate as is, save the budget, you know, not hiring someone else," she said, "but they wouldn't allow us to do that."

"Ah," Kate said. "Knowing you'd all rather have no one than me doesn't help."

"Sorry about that."

"Whatever," Kate said. "You wanted a four-man team. Duly noted." Inside though, it was nice to get a little bit of give in the relationship between the two of them. She sipped her coffee, and Lilliana continued.

"Technically," Lilliana added, "we were a seven-man team."

Kate snorted. "Where have you been hiding the other two? We could use the help."

Lilliana nodded. "I guess we're really at six. The five of us and Colby makes six. I can't count Nix. He's switched to Darren's team. Trudy replaced him, who almost instantly got pregnant and keeps extending her maternity leave. We may never see her again either. Von replaced her and got injured on the job. With each surgery, he's got two months to recover. Once back, he'll be on desk duty for a while." She sighed loudly. "So maybe you ought to cut Andy some slack."

"Why is that?" Kate asked.

"We need him, and he's still in the hump-and-dump-them stage."

She stared at her in surprise. "I'm sorry?"

Lilliana shrugged impatiently. "You must have heard about it. You know? After you have a breakup, you have a lot of affairs, just so you feel like you still have it."

"Glad I missed that stage," she said in a neutral tone.

"Well, I didn't," she said, "and Andy is in it."

"Okay," Kate said. "So what then? When he makes digs at me, I'm not allowed to bite back?"

"Actually it's a good thing you do," Lilliana said. "We'll respect you a little more."

At that, Kate stared at her. "If you say so." She shrugged and turned to walk away.

"And you're right about Andy."

Kate halted, then turned to look back at Lilliana. "What part?"

"He is running away," she said. "His wife of twelve years left the marriage with his best man from their wedding. Andy is hurting, and he is running. But it's his way of handling it, so maybe lay off a bit."

"It was broken already." He stared down at the phone in his hand. "Honest," he said. "I don't know how the hell it happened, but it's broken already."

"Already?" his sister cried out in alarm, her thin high-pitched voice rose as it came through the phone.

"I think something was wrong with this one," he said hurriedly.

"No, no, no," she said, "you can't take the sick ones."

"I didn't think it was," he said, bewildered. "It's broken."

"How broken?"

*Silence.*

"Oh, God, did you kill him?"

"Her," he said absentmindedly. "Her."

"Jesus Christ," his sister said. "Bro, we've talked about this. You need to let up. Before you get caught."

"I can't," he said. "I was lonely." His voice cracked, as he stared out the window. "There's what? Two-and-a-half-million people in and around this city?" he asked. "And nobody even knows I'm alive."

"A lot of people know you're alive," she said earnestly. Then she added, "And, if you don't watch it, a lot more people will know, and that's not what you want."

"Why not?" he asked. "I mean, *lonely* or *notorious*. Is there a difference?"

"Well, they are two sides of the same coin maybe," she said, puzzled. "But the more people know about you," she said, "the more people will know what you're doing, and you could wind up in jail again."

"Well, I'm not spending the rest of my life in prison," he said in that matter-of-fact tone of voice he used all the time. "You know that."

"And I don't want to lose my brother," she said. "So please be careful."

"I was so careful," he said, hating that he'd changed to that childish singsong voice again, as he stared down at the little girl on the couch. He'd only had her a few hours. But she was dead, … broken. "But it's broken."

"Damn," she said. "Can you just wait a bit before you

dispose of her?"

"Well, I can't dispose of her the same way as the others anyway," he said. "You know that."

He could almost hear his sister swearing in the background. She didn't really understand what he was doing and why he was doing it, but she was always here to help him deal with it.

"Look," she said. "It's too many, too fast."

"Well, I didn't mean it to be," he said, "but it's broken."

"What are you doing about it?" she said after a moment. Her tone was calm, and she was trying to be reasonable.

He didn't like the reasonableness either. "I'm not sure," he said, "but it's broken. What do you do with things that are broken?"

"Don't throw it in the trash," she warned.

"Of course not," he said. "What do you think I am?"

"You're my brother, and I love you," she said softly. "But you've got to stop doing this. You've been caught once. You can't a second time. It's different now."

"That's the first time you've ever said that to me. You've always partaken, like a voyeur," he said. "I'd give you all the details, and you'd always be right there with me. Why are you separating from me now?" He hated that. It made his world feel even smaller.

"I'm not," she rushed to say, but he'd already heard that soothing tone in her voice. Her attempt to *handle* him.

"Yes," he said, "you are. You're unhappy with me, and I don't like it."

"I'm not happy that she's dead," his sister snapped. "You only moved Jason's body out what, ten, eleven, twelve days ago?"

"I was lonely."

"Take up dancing lessons then," she cried out. "Go to a pub, get laid, do something to meet people."

He snorted at that. "Well, as you know, I can't dance," he said, "because I've got two left feet, and I'm completely tone-deaf," he said. "Besides, it was a while back but I was at the park, sitting and talking to all these nice people," he said, "and that's when I saw her."

"The child?"

"Yes," he said in a dreamy voice. "She was running across the park with a balloon. She was so happy, so innocent. I just really wanted to touch that. She was so full of love and laughter, and her mother obviously cared. I mean, they were hugging each other all the time. I mentioned her to one of my cronies. He grabbed her. I was pissed initially, but then I realized he'd done me a solid, as I managed to buy her off him. It took a bit, but eventually I got her for myself."

"So why did you break that?" his sister asked curiously.

Just hearing that note in her voice again made him feel better. She was always trying to figure him out. Always trying to make some sense of it. "I don't know," he said, "but I wanted to be a part of it somehow. I wanted to see, if she was with me long enough, if she would treat me like she treated her mother. If she would look at me like she looked at her mother."

"But you never could be her mother."

"I know that," he said, "but it doesn't change anything, not really. I still needed to try."

"And how did she react when you took her away?"

"She was screaming," he said sadly. "She kept crying for her mother, and, when I told her that I could be her mother, she told me to go away. She said that I was a mean old man.

Just like the other one."

"Ouch," his sister said. "And I suppose that made you angry?"

"Well, I didn't think so," he said. "I mean, these little kids, they don't know what they're saying. She'd just never been in an experience like this before, so I couldn't really listen to the words she was saying."

"No, of course not." But his sister spoke with a heavy tone.

"It really was fast," he said. "I didn't have any fun at all. I just wanted to be a part of what they had."

"I'm not sure," she said, "that you are completely there."

"Of course I'm completely here," he said, adding a note of warning. "Just the two of us are involved in this. You're the only one who knows, and we'll keep it that way."

"I'd never tell," she said, the weariness in her voice making him worried. "But sometimes I wonder if it's too much for me to hear."

"You love the details," he cried out. "That's how we bonded way back when. It's never changed."

"Maybe I'm just getting old," she snapped.

"We're both getting old then," he said. "We're twins."

"Duh," she said. "But sometimes I hear these details, and they're not fun for me."

"That's because you're not with me," he said. "I've told you that we can get two. I mean, lots of children are out there. It might take a little more planning, but we could get one each. I've never gotten the ones I really wanted."

"Is that true?" she asked again, that curiosity back in her voice.

He smiled, pleased with the angle he had picked up. She always had questions, and, when she had questions, she was engaged. When she was engaged, he knew she was his. "There might have been a couple I wanted, but then I decided that they weren't a good bet," he tried to explain. "You know? Some kids are watched better than other kids. Or sometimes you see them walking, and you realize that something's wrong with their leg, or the mother comes over with medication, so you know they're sick or things like that," he said. "Obviously I want as healthy as I can get."

"And yet you took Jason."

"I know," he said. "He had that ethereal look to him, as if he already had one foot in the grave, one foot in the angel's realm. Seriously something was so angelic about him."

"And he lived for quite a while," she said, marveling.

"Well, I treated him really well," he said. "I had to, you know? Because I really, really loved him."

"I know you did," she said, her voice softening. "He was special for you."

"He was." And the tears choked his throat again. "And I thought maybe she'd be special too. But it's broken."

"Why do you keep saying *it*?" she asked.

"Because *it* is an *it*," he said. "Not a *she* anymore. Not a *he* anymore. It's dead. It's just an *it*. It's now a piece of garbage that I have to get rid of. A broken toy," he said sadly. "And what do I do with broken toys?"

"You have to get rid of them," she said, with that old weariness in her voice again. "And then you replace it."

"Exactly," he cried out. "See? You're the only one who understands me."

"Sometimes I wonder if I understand anything," she said sadly.

"You do," he assured her. "You know you can ask me anything. I'm happy to tell you."

"I know," she said, "except for that one question I keep asking that you refuse to answer."

"Well, stop asking that one then," he said crossly.

"No, you said you'd tell me anything. So, tell me why you're doing this."

"And I keep telling you," he said, "it's because I'm lonely."

"That's a reason. It's not a motive," she said.

He frowned. "They are the same thing," he said, getting angry at her for splitting hairs over a simple word.

"No, that is a reason that you give to others, but it's not the motivation inside you that's telling you to do this," she said, her voice getting hard and angry too.

Every time they talked about it, they ended up back at the same point.

"You can listen to what you want to listen to," he said, "and I'll listen to what I want to listen to. The bottom line is that this is the way it is. I'm not changing."

"Yes," she said, "that we can agree on."

And, with that, she hung up.

# CHAPTER 6

*Tuesday Morning*

THE NEXT MORNING Kate was sipping her coffee and running through the files. It was 10:15 a.m. already. She set the computers for multiple searches, and then she went case by case by case, looking for any elements that linked to the theory she was working on. On one of the images, she caught an ever-so-tiny nick on the inside of the left wrist. She stared at it, magnifying it many times over. She went back to her other seven cases, all eight similar to Jason's, and found something at the same place but too grainy to clearly see it.

*Was it possible?* Excitement gripped her. She flicked through Jason's digital folder but didn't have a good picture of Jason's left wrist. She picked up the phone and called the coroner's office.

"Jason's wrist," she said, "left hand, above the wrist bone," she said. "Is a tiny mark there?"

"I can check," Dr. Smidge said. "The photos are in the file. Can't you see the mark on the images?"

"Something's there, more of a shadow on the photo," she said.

"You seem to be pretty excited about it," he said in a dry tone.

"Anything that we can find is a help," she said. "No, I

don't know in what way, but, if a mark is there, this might connect a bunch of other cases."

"Then I don't want a mark to be there," he said forcefully. "The last thing we need is a child serial killer."

"You mean, another one?"

"I know," he said. "Already too many in this world. But we don't need one here in Vancouver."

She heard the morgue drawer being opened and a tray being pulled out.

"Left wrist?" the coroner asked.

"Left wrist, above the bone," she said. "On the inside corner."

He looked at it. "*Hmm.*"

"What does that mean?"

"Well, something's there," he said, "but it's pretty indistinct."

"Can you take a couple good photographs of it?"

"Or you can come down here and take a look at it yourself," he said. "I'll take a couple photos too."

"Done," she said. "I'll be there in thirty." She hopped to her feet, grabbed her jacket, stuffed her phone into her pocket, and bolted out the door. As she got to the elevator, she heard Lilliana call out.

"What did you find?"

"Maybe nothing," she said. "I'll let you know if I can confirm it." She would have taken the stairs, but the elevator was right here and empty. She dropped to the ground floor, then raced to the coroner's office in the hospital, what was usually a twenty-minute drive away.

He looked up with a nod and said, "That was fast."

"It's important," she said quietly.

He studied her face for a moment. "Well, you seem to

be excited about it, but I sure as hell hope you're wrong."

"I do too," she said. She followed him to the back room, thinking about all this short, rotund man with the wispy white hair had seen in his career thus far. Dr. Kerry Smidge had a little more than ten years to go in this industry before he retired, but he'd already seen it all. He had the demeanor of a leprechaun but the attitude of a junkyard dog, and somehow she appreciated both. At least that's what she kept telling herself.

He walked over to the wall of drawers. He pulled out the one with Jason's body on it. Already autopsied. He pulled the sheet back to show her the left wrist. Bringing out a camera, he took several more photographs.

She pulled a magnifying glass from her pocket and took a look. And whistled. "Goddammit," she said, "it's the same."

"What are you thinking it is?"

"Originally I wondered if it was a wave pattern," she said, "but do you see that little bit underneath, that half circle?"

"Yeah, what about it?" he asked. "And honestly it's so faint here, I can't imagine that it was done recently."

"No, I suspect it wasn't recent at all," she said. "I think it's supposed to resemble a set of lips. Like a kiss."

## Wednesday Morning

SIMON WOKE UP to the bright Wednesday morning, out of sorts and hemmed in. Craving fresh air, he dressed, grabbed his lightweight raincoat, and walked out. He waved at the doorman and headed down the front steps at a brisk pace.

He took several deep breaths of the moist refreshing air. Applauding his decision, he picked up a coffee and took the next right. The constant misty atmosphere continued, but dark clouds threatened more. First stop was the nearest building he was rehabbing.

He strolled up to the front, stopped, and stared.

"Doesn't look much better, does it?" said the general contractor, when he saw Simon.

"Didn't really expect it to, did you? It's one hundred years old and needs the work."

"Other buildings would take less money," he said.

"Other buildings don't interest me," he said. He hadn't explained why he'd chosen this building, and he wouldn't. Not now. Plus Gary hadn't worked for him for long. It was nobody else's damned business but Simon's. That's the way he liked to keep it. He looked at the work in progress, nodded, and said, "Keep going."

He strolled away. He knew that his contractor was watching him as he left, but he didn't give a damn. Simon was long used to people wondering who he was and where he and his money came from. As long as they questioned in their own minds and not out loud to him, he didn't give a shit.

He'd built his life to what it was today. He avoided close relationships, which really made him question that major detour he took with Caitlin. It was easier to *not* deal with people, since he didn't generally like them. He had four other buildings projects that he was working currently. It would be a long afternoon.

He kept looking up at the sky, wondering if he would be lucky enough to miss the deluge. As it was, he was inside one of his other buildings, when it started to pour. He delayed his exit until the rain eased, and then he made a quick run to the next building. He could have taken a cab or even driven, but neither appealed to him today. Fresh air, even if it was damp and spongy, was still better than vehicle exhaust and the pain of parking.

By the time he had finally finished doing what he needed to do, he stood and stared at the weather for a long moment. The rain had eased off; the evening sky had darkened with clouds, and the city lights shone on the water. Vancouver was almost completely surrounded by water and enjoyed a spectacular view of the Pacific Ocean and the mountains behind.

It was truly a wondrous geographical location. But, like every big city, there was an underbelly. Anybody could come and make a living here, but not everybody could come and make a killing financially. Although plenty were doing well, a lot more were closing down businesses because they couldn't handle it. Opening a business was not a get-rich-quick scheme, although a lot of people opened with that attitude. He wished them luck, but he also knew that it wouldn't likely work.

Vancouver was a hard city, a tough city, even harder for newcomers. A lot of people came for the glitz and glamour but forgot entirely about the fact that every city had problems and that every big city had those who thrived on those in trouble. It sucked, but it was the way of the world. Predators were everywhere.

He turned and headed home. He was a good twenty blocks away, and it would take him a good hour to walk. That's when he remembered where he was, and—if he scuttled down two blocks and over two blocks—he would come out to Mama's place, one of the few restaurants that thrived in Vancouver. It was said that one restaurant closed and another one opened every day of the year in the city.

Mama's place had defied all logic and had managed to stay alive for seventeen years. Mama, the Italian woman who he appreciated far more than most, had married a Mexican man, and together they had blended their flavors, along with their personalities, to become a successful small mom-and-pop restaurant. Simon supported as many mom-and-pop shops as he could, just because they struggled so badly.

He enjoyed a nice high-class restaurant sometimes too. The glitz and the glamour were definitely not a part of his regular world, and at times he was happy to be in the trenches. As he walked into the restaurant, Mama saw who it was and cried out, coming over to give him a big hug. He wrapped his long arms around her ample curves and hugged her gently.

"You're all wet," she scolded him. "You could get sick."

"I hope not," he said, with a smile. "Really can't afford it."

"Of course not, of course not," she muttered, busy brushing water off his jacket. "You're staying for dinner?"

"No," he said. "I'm not."

She stopped, looked at him, with such an expression of horror on her face.

He chuckled. "But I was hoping you could do me up a take-out order."

"It's not good for you," she said. "You need more than just taking food home. Best is to stay and to relax, with good food, good friends, and a good glass of wine."

"At least this way I get good food," he said gently. "Otherwise I'll just end up going home and not eating at all—or ordering pizza." The genuine look of shock on her face had him laughing gently. "Go make me something," he said. "I don't mind what. Whatever it is that you think I should have."

She frowned and said, "We have a new special."

"Perfect," he replied. "Just make sure it's lots."

She chuckled. "Have I ever sent you with less?" That was the one thing she always did—made sure he was well-fed. He paced the small room, looking out the window, as the rain pounded down once again. When she returned with a large bag and two small take-out containers, he just shook his head. "I don't need that much."

"This way, you will have lunch tomorrow," she said comfortably. "And, in this weather, we won't get many customers," she said, "so we will have lots of leftovers."

He quickly paid for the order, gave her a smile, and said, "You are too good to me."

"No, it's you who is good to us."

With that, he walked back out into the rain. He made a mad dash for a couple blocks, until the rain eased, and then he slipped across into one of the lesser-known areas, taking a shortcut across the city. Most people didn't walk through this area because it was well-known for drug deals and back-alley attacks, but a lesson he'd learned a long time ago, from another life, was to stiffen your spine and to walk like you mean it.

"Nobody will attack you if you look like you're ready for trouble. They have to be twice as strong, twice as fast, and twice as mean to make sure they can handle what they are dealing with," he murmured out loud, imitating his grandmother's voice.

Another trick his grandmother had taught him was to draw in his energy tight and to turn it ever-so-slightly red, giving it more of an angry tone. Anger lent extra energy to anybody, which meant they had more fuel for a fight than most people wanted to take on. And, of course, nobody disturbed him.

When he came out on the other side, he was only one block back from the high-end part of town. It always amazed him that a strip of blocks separated low from high, the wrong side from the right side. He was comfortable in both but definitely preferred the high side. Poverty sucked.

As he walked up the steps to the front door, the doorman raced to open it for him. Harry took one look and said, "You always refuse to take an umbrella."

"I always forget," Simon said, giving his head a slight shake, sending water droplets everywhere. "At least I remembered food." The doorman walked ahead and pushed the button for his elevator. As he stepped inside, Simon said, "Have a good evening, Harry."

"You too, sir. Make sure you dry off, before you catch a chill."

As the elevator opened up at the penthouse, Simon wondered why everybody was so concerned about his health. He hadn't been sick in decades. He wasn't exactly sure why, but again he had learned a lot of tricks a long time ago, and nobody would understand. So it was a trade-off.

Life itself was a mystery, but certain corners of it he definitely knew how to manipulate. Inside, he put down the take-out food, quickly stripped off his jacket, and loosened his tie. He grabbed a towel, gave his head a light scrub, tossed the towel back on the hook, and he walked to the fridge, where he pulled out an already opened bottle of wine. Popping the cork, he poured himself a hefty glass and then tossed the cork. He'd finish the rest of the bottle tonight.

With his wineglass, he walked over to the table. As he sat down, Mama had given him something like tortillas and nachos or something; he wasn't exactly sure. Foil packs of something. Tortillas had been in one, and, when he opened up the others, he found raw veggie strips and then meat. He quickly made himself a wrap and tried it.

It was delicious, he was still figuring out the myriad tastes. By the time he hit the middle, he was loving it, and, when he finished with the first one, he was already reaching to make a second one. After he'd had three, he put the rest in the fridge. Then he picked up his phone, walked over to the couch in front of the full-length windows overlooking the city of Vancouver, and sat down with his second glass of wine.

He was tired and still not sleeping well, but at least he hadn't woken up with any strange woman in his bed—or anybody else for that matter. Just then his phone rang. He glanced at it, winced. His ex-fiancée. He ignored it, and it stopped, but it immediately rang again. This time he reached for it, picked it up, and said, "What do you want?"

"Good evening, Simon. This is Detective Morgan calling."

He stared down at the phone in confusion. He'd been so damn sure it had been his ex. "Did you just call me a few minutes ago?"

"No," she said, "calling you once is enough for me, thanks."

His lips twitched. Just something about her abrasive tone always made him feel better. Which made no sense. "What can I do for you, Detective?" he asked, as he settled into the corner of his couch, with his glass of wine.

"I need details," she said briskly. "More details."

"Why? You didn't believe me in the first place," he said, stiffening slightly at her words. He felt himself immediately building up walls to push her away, to push it all back. He'd worked hard these last couple nights to not have any more of those damn nightmares and to try and forget her.

"I may have found a connection," she said, "and I need more details."

"Connection?"

"A connection between the different kids you're seeing."

He sucked in his breath. "What connection?" he asked harshly. "Are you serious?"

"I'm not calling out of joy," she said sarcastically. "I'm sure you have a pretty damn good idea why I am calling," she said, "and it's sure as hell not some social call."

"That's too damn bad," he said lightly, "because I'm pretty sure we'd be really good together."

"I don't give a shit," she said, "because that's not happening."

Instantly a vision ripped through him—the two of them hot and sweaty in the sheets. Lust drove right through his groin.

"Cut the bullshit! Can we get back to the question at hand?"

His eyebrows rose, and he felt the smile tugging away at his lips again. "I don't have any details. Remember? I told you these were just bad dreams."

"Bad dreams that have disturbingly eerie details," she snapped. "In your dreams, did you ever see a mark on the wrist of one of the children?"

He frowned and sat up. "What kind of a mark?"

"That's what I'm asking you."

"I don't give a shit if you believe what I'm saying or not,

Detective, but I don't play games."

"This is a game to you?" she asked. "Something about a child's life is just one big game to you? I don't know what the hell makes you tick, and I don't care—except for these cases. If anything leads you to believe these cases are anything other than a dream, you need to concentrate and get me more details," she urged.

"I thought you didn't believe in psychics?"

"I don't," she said in a tight voice. "You're all con artists after people's money."

"So you're giving me money for the information I give you, right?"

"Of course not," she said, just as smoothly. "But rest assured, I've met plenty of cons, just like you."

"Yet you called me tonight," he said. "So isn't that a bit of a contradiction there?"

"Depends on what kind of information you give me."

"Nothing," he said, and, pissed in spite of himself, he ended the conversation. He tossed the phone on the couch and glared down at his body, reacting to her voice, to his vision. "Like hell," he said. "You can think about something else next time. Because she is out of the question."

When his phone rang again, he ignored it. It finally stopped ringing, and ten minutes later it started again.

He glared.

He picked it up to see his ex-fiancée's name. No way he was answering that. When his doorman called from downstairs, he didn't want to answer that either. "Hey, Harry. What's up?"

"A lady is here who wants to talk to you."

Simon reached out to touch the bridge of his nose, sure that it was the damn detective again. "If she's got a badge, you pretty well have to show her up," he said. "But I'm not happy about it."

"Badge?" Harry said in surprise. "She hasn't flashed any badge."

"Then it's a hell no. I don't want to see anybody," he snapped.

Harry hesitated.

"Who is it, Harry?"

"It's your ex," he said.

"I *definitely* don't want to see *her*." And, with that, he hung up. As he walked away from the intercom system at the door, it rang again, and he started to get furious. "Harry, I said no."

"Please," his ex-fiancée cried out in the background. "Dear God, please."

Something about her tone made him stop and freeze. "What the hell?"

"I know. I know," she cried out. "Please, just listen to me."

"Are you kidding? After all the shit you've pulled?" he said. "Why would I listen to anything you say?"

"Because I'm desperate," she said.

"You're always desperate," he snapped. "Nothing new or different."

"It's not me," she said. "It's my nephew, Leonard."

"What about him?" he asked.

"He didn't come home from school today. It's Wednesday, and he had nothing scheduled for after school today."

Instantly he froze. "And?"

"You know," she said urgently. "You know."

"I don't know anything about your nephew," he roared. "Why the hell would you dare to even suggest such a thing?"

She burst into tears, and he heard the sobs in her voice. Through the phone, Harry spoke again, "I'm really sorry, sir. I'll make sure she doesn't come back again."

"You damn fucking well better not," he said, and he slammed down the phone. He tossed back the rest of his wine and walked over to the bottle and refilled his glass. That killed the bottle, but it sure as hell wasn't doing much for his mood. He sat back down on the couch, staring at the wine, as it swirled in his glass. When the phone rang again, it was his ex.

A text came through next. **He is missing. You can help.** Simon didn't answer. Just stared at the message. **You know you can. Please.**

He got up and, carrying his wine with him, walked into the bedroom, put the glass down, and stripped down, heading for a hot shower. As he stood under the hot steaming spray, he let it slosh over his body and directly onto his face. The hot beating water pounding his skin. But the pounding in his psyche wouldn't stop.

Absolutely nothing would stop this, would it?

He desperately wanted all these people to go away. To have some control, hoping he could get it to slide back into oblivion. But it was too late. Something inside had broken free and had opened up, and there was no going back.

He didn't like people. Didn't trust anyone. Especially himself and whatever this weird ability of his was. It had been wrong before. At a time when he'd needed it. No way he could depend on it now.

Especially not if children's lives were at stake ...

# CHAPTER 7

## *Wednesday Evening, Late*

K ATE STARED AT the phone, wondering if she should try calling Simon St. Laurant again. He was avoiding her, and that pissed her off. She hoped he went to bed tonight and woke up covered in sweat from the nightmares. Mean of her maybe, but she needed answers, and she didn't know whether he was responsible in some way or not. However, if he had anything more to offer, she wanted it.

Working with a charlatan went against everything she believed in, but, to get justice for these kids, she'd deal with him. Since she didn't believe in psychics, the only other answer in her mind was that he was part of this. And, if he was, she would make damn sure he paid for it.

She covered one wall of her apartment with big sheets of butcher paper and then posted pictures of the children, the victims, along with her notes and timelines. It just made no sense. Huge gaps were in between, like several years even, and she didn't know whether that meant that she was missing more victims or the victims had been kept longer back then or something else had interfered with the perv's murderous activities. Was it random, or was there a pattern to this? The unknowns were really driving her crazy, but then they were what drove her to find the answers. It's what made her a good detective, while driving everybody around her nuts.

Her personal methodology was more like that of a lone ranger than a team operative. When she'd had her detective interview, they had asked her about that. She told them that she could work with a team, but she was more effective on her own. It had been made clear to her that she needed to include everybody on the team. All she could say was, she was working on it.

She stood back and studied the nine cases on the wall, Jason's and the other eight that were similar. She knew in her heart of hearts that there were more. Possibly a lot more. The only thing she had to go on was that weird mark on the wrist, and it was really faded on some—to the point of nothing visible at all—yet always a piece of clothing that didn't belong to the victim was with the bodies.

It made no sense, but then serial killers didn't ever make sense. Not to her. That didn't mean it wasn't still important to figure out why these people did what they did. If anything, it was even more important because somebody had to stop them. To do that, she needed to understand these killers.

It was late. She didn't want to go to bed, yet she was tired, but these kids—her gaze flitted to the wall and away—they were eating into her psyche. She was starting to dream about them. Nightmares really. That brought St. Laurant back to mind. She shoved her hands into her pockets. If Simon were involved, she hoped his actions choked him to death.

But, in the meantime, she would do everything she could to stick close to him. Tomorrow was her day off, and she planned to see what he was up to. And that meant she had to get to bed. As she checked her watch, she groaned. It

was already two in the morning. How had it gotten to be
that late?

### Thursday Morning

WHEN HER ALARM rang at seven the next morning, she
groaned, rolled herself out of bed, and stumbled into the
shower. She made herself a pot of strong *bite her in the ass*
coffee, poured it into a thermos, and headed out the door.
She was in front of Simon's False Creek North penthouse
apartment building by 7:30 a.m. According to the doorman,
he usually went for a walk in the mornings. Some days he
was gone all day; some days he left again in the afternoon.
She didn't know what the hell he was up to, but something
was going on because she'd done a full rundown on him and
hadn't come up with much. He owned a company, Novel
Investment, which said nothing. He was just too damn clean
for her liking.

Not even a parking ticket was on his record. Neither was
a marriage or a child. She also hadn't run down any family.
Foster care, yes, but no sealed juvie records either. It was
damn suspicious. Nobody was perfect, especially not a guy as
smooth and as silky as this one. She walked past the entrance
to his apartment and over to the pretzel seller across the
street. She bought one hot off the cart.

Then she sat down on a nearby bench and ate while she
waited, enjoying the beautiful scenery of the harbor. At ten
to eight St. Laurant came out, dressed in a suit, looking just a
little too dapper for her. She'd only gotten five hours of
sleep, and who knows what the hell he had had. By the looks
of him, it was way more than her, and, for that, she hated

him already. She got up, tossed her pretzel wrapper into the garbage, and followed him, staying a block behind.

When she crossed the street to the next block, a man behind her asked, "Detective, what are you doing here so early? Are you looking for me?"

She knew she was made. She glanced at him, took a sip of her coffee. "What the hell?" she said sarcastically. "Everything isn't about you, by the way." She'd always learned it was much better to be offensive than defensive. It seemed to work this time too. He frowned and looked around. "We do have crime in the city," she said.

"Maybe," he said. "So what brings you out so early?"

"I have to meet someone," she said. "What are you doing out here this morning? Why aren't you lying on your silk sheets?"

"They're actually linen," he said. "Much nicer on the skin."

She gave an irritable shrug. "Whatever."

"I'm guessing you sleep on cheap polyester," he said, with a sneer. "And don't even know the difference between linen, polyester, silk, or cotton."

She shrugged and said, "I just sleep."

"Not last night, you didn't," he said, his gaze intent.

She deliberately turned away from him. "See you later," she said and headed to one of the big public buildings up ahead. Except he wasn't deterred.

"I'm going this way too."

"Sure you are," she said in a tone of disbelief.

"What? Now you think I'm following you?"

"Yes," she said. "I'm looking into these kids." She locked her glare on him. "Remember? The ones you dangled information on, then pulled back."

"I didn't dangle any information," he said in frustration.

She slid a sideways glance at him. He definitely did look like he was frustrated. Why? What was his game? If he wasn't involved, he knew who was. As far as she was concerned, at this moment, that was the same thing, but she needed whatever information he had. "Whatever information, whoever you think is doing this, whatever you know," she said, deliberately avoiding the fact that she thought he was involved, "you need to tell me."

He stopped, looked at her. "Are we back to that again?"

"Back to what?" She opened her eyes wider.

"It wasn't me."

"Of course not," she said, rolling her eyes. "It's never you."

He took a slow deep breath. "You really think I'm involved though, don't you?"

"I don't know jack shit," she said. "I know that I have a boy in the morgue and cold case files involving several dead children," she said, "and that is never good."

"Apparently another one went missing last night," he said, thinking about his ex-fiancée.

She stopped, turned, and looked at him. "What?"

"Somebody I know."

"What I want," she said, "is the name of whoever is involved in this. If you know," she said, pointing her finger at him before poking him in the chest, "I want to know too."

"I don't know anything about these kids," he said. "But my ex called me to say her nephew was missing."

Her eyebrows shot up. "What? Did she report it?"

"I didn't even think to tell her to call the cops," he said in confusion. "I should have though, shouldn't I?"

"Well, let's hope somebody did," she cried out. "Why'd

she call you? What the hell would you do about it anyway?"

He didn't have an answer for it; he just stared at her.

Yet something was in his gaze, something that made her stop and frown. "What were you planning on doing?"

"I wasn't *planning*," he said, his voice hard and clipped, "on doing anything." He ran a hand through his hair. "You carry on," he said. "I've had a change of plans." And, with that, he turned and walked away.

Only she wasn't through. She raced up behind him, grabbed his arm, and turned him around. "What do you know about this missing boy?"

The look in his eyes was haunted. "I don't know any-thing," he snapped. "For all I know, the boy and other cases are unrelated."

"I hope so," she said. "Otherwise we have a problem in the city."

He took a slow deep breath. "Some of those cases are very old."

"Yes," she said in a soft voice. "Isn't it time to help us put a stop to it?"

She didn't know if she was getting to him or not. She knew that, if she told her boss about this, he'd have her bring Simon in, and they would sit there and interview him for hours until he broke. And maybe that's what they needed to do. She just wanted to see if he had a child with him. If they took him in, and he had somebody hidden somewhere who would slowly die, that would be even worse. She didn't want to do anything that would endanger another child.

She watched as Simon disappeared on her. She pulled out her phone and called Missing Persons. After identifying herself, she asked for Jennifer, someone there she knew. When Jennifer came on the line, Kate asked, "Do you have a missing boy? As in a last-night kind of thing?"

"Yes. It was called in around dinnertime. The Amber alert went out a few moments later. Didn't you, hear?" she asked curiously. "The little boy is seven, normally walks home with friends. Yesterday the friend was sick, so he walked home alone, but he didn't make it."

"No updates?"

"No." Jennifer's voice turned heavy. "He just disappeared off the face of the earth."

Kate winced at that because, of course, they never did. It just seemed that way. They could search high and low, but it was damn near impossible without something—someone— to point them in the right direction. Over two-and-a-half-million people were in the city and its surrounding areas; any one of them could be holding that child. And unfortunately the child could already be dead. "Let me know if you get any updates," she said.

"Wait, wait, how did you hear about it?"

She quickly explained about Simon.

"I want to talk to him," Jennifer said.

"You do that," Kate replied. "He's not very helpful though."

"Do you think this guy is involved with your case?"

"Somehow, yes," she said. "I just don't know in what way."

Jennifer hesitated.

"You talk to him," Kate said, giving her Simon's name and number. "If we could just save one child, maybe I'd get more clues for the next."

"Do you think he's got one?"

"I'm not sure what he's got or what he knows, but he knows more than he's telling me. I'm sure of that."

And she hung up.

"THAT DIDN'T TURN out the way I expected," Simon
snapped to himself. Something was so very irritating and so
very magnificent about her. He wanted to hate her but knew
they were well past that point. What she didn't understand
was that she and Simon were on a trajectory that would take
them someplace personal. Hell, he could read the signs, even
if she was in denial. A trajectory he would do anything to
avoid. The last thing he wanted was a cop in his world. He
hated them, always had. And, from the looks of it, she hated
everybody like him too.

It was Thursday, and a weekend cruise left almost every
Friday afternoon. He checked his watch, got on his phone,
to confirm the next few weekends were available, leaving his
options open. Even if the gambling lost him money, he
needed to get the hell out of town for a bit. He didn't want
to be anywhere close by, if something went down with
Leonard. God, he hoped not. No child should endure that.
But a solid alibi might change Kate's opinion of him.

As soon as he hung up the phone, it rang again. This
time it was the Missing Persons Division. His heart chilled
that the detective had passed his name on to somebody
handling Leonard's case. "I don't know anything about it,"
he snapped. "Talk to my ex-fiancée. She was the one who
called me."

"I have," the officer said. "And she said that you know
more than you're telling."

He stopped and stared out across the ocean. "I don't
know anything," he said heavily, feeling the pressure weigh

in on him. "I can give you a full rundown of where I was all of yesterday and today," he said. "And you'll see I was nowhere close."

"Why don't you tell me about that first?" she said. He quickly went through the list of addresses where he went to check on his jobsites.

"These are all yours?"

"Yes," he snapped. "They are all mine. They are building projects."

"That's a lot of potential locations to hide a child."

Everything inside him went still. Just the thought was so abhorring, he wanted to upchuck on the spot. Either that or pound the next person he saw into the ground. The closest one available appeared to be an old lady, somewhere in her mid-seventies, pushing a square shopping cart in front of her. That was probably not a good idea. He finally said, "Listen. Either arrest me or leave me alone." Then he hung up his phone.

Standing here for a long moment, he looked down at his hands, not surprised to see a tremor sliding through them. Of all the criminals in the world that he could possibly be, a pedophile was not one of them. Not after his own nightmares at the hands of one. Of course the cops would look at that and might actually see motive. Supposedly victims of sexual abuse grew up to be sexual abusers themselves. Simon shook his head at that disgusting thought. The cops seemed to see the abuse as grooming or training.

So far, he'd avoided having anybody looking into his background too much. Most people saw him on the front page of the newspaper, a philanthropist, as he worked on this charity or that. But, at the very best times, he was out of the public eye, away from everybody. He didn't want anyone in his life, and he didn't want anyone close to him. Case in point, Caitlin. Simon had screwed up there.

Such anger was inside him that he wanted to call the detective and to swear at her for having passed on his name. Even as he was dialing, he looked away—all she was doing was trying to find a child.

So, he could hate what she'd done, but he could never hate her reason for doing it.

Making a strangled sound, he shoved his phone into his pocket and stormed back the way he'd come. He had a full day ahead of him. But he'd already wasted an hour, and, at the moment, it looked like his day would just get worse. Using the anger to fuel his efforts, he made it through half a day, before storming back to his penthouse. By the time he got in his front door, his phone was ringing again. It was his ex. "Now what?"

"Did the cops call you?"

"Of course, since you set them on me."

"I didn't know what else to do," she cried out. "He's missing. Don't you understand that?"

"I can't help. Don't you understand that?" he roared back. "For six months, all you've done is make my life a living hell, and now, because your nephew is missing, you think I'll turn around and do something for you? What do you expect me to do?"

"I was hoping you would," she said, her voice very small. "I was hoping you wouldn't hold anything I've done against an innocent child, who you could help."

"What are you talking about?" he said. "I don't know anything. I can't tell you who picked him up or where he is."

"No," she said and hesitated a moment, then went on. "But I know what you're like in the night."

Everything inside him stilled. He took a slow long deep breath. "What do you mean by that?"

"You have nightmares," she said. "You are always crying out about kids. I used to wake up and sit on the bed and watch. Sometimes I even taped you."

He sank on the couch in shock. "You what?" The acute betrayal was so loud and so shocking, he didn't even know what to say.

"I got rid of them," she cried out. "I didn't know what to do with them anyway. I wanted to ask you about them. Then I realized how angry you were."

"*Angry,*" he said, in a very silky voice, "doesn't begin to express how I feel right now."

She took several deep breaths. "I got rid of everything. I promise."

"I doubt it," he said. "You are exactly the kind of person who would use it for blackmail."

"No," she said, "I won't."

"As long as?"

"As long as you help find my nephew," she whispered.

"So, in other words, you didn't get rid of them, and now you *are* blackmailing me," he said. "Nice. Very nice."

"I'm sorry," she said brokenly. "I have to help my nephew."

"And, of course, you went to the cops right away, right?"

"Well, I didn't go right away," she said crossly. "But I called as soon as I could."

"Your nephew," he said, "were you responsible for picking him up and bringing him home yesterday?"

*Silence.*

He nodded. "Now I get the picture," he said. "You're feeling guilty because he was your responsibility, and you didn't look after him properly." He gave a harsh laugh. "Doesn't that figure?"

"I need your help," she said. "He's just a little boy."

"If I help, it will be for the boy. It won't be for you. Or your stupid recordings."

And he hung up the phone. But inside, a fury like he hadn't felt in a long time rattled through his soul. He sat down at his desk and made plans.

———— ⚡ ————

"A CHILD IS missing?" He stared at the TV. "Well, I haven't got him," he said. "Too damn bad. I wouldn't be sitting here all alone if I did." Of course he wasn't completely alone. He still had the little China Doll girl, propped up on the couch beside him. But he couldn't keep her for long. Not that it was a *her* anymore and was just an *it*. But, with everybody out looking for this newly missing little boy named Leonard, he would have to watch carefully for a chance to get rid of *it*. He sighed. "What am I to do with you?"

But his gaze kept going back to the TV. When a child went missing, everybody got up in arms. He knew; he'd been responsible for over thirty or so going missing himself. He looked at the ledger he kept off to the side. Beautiful memories. His sister wanted that ledger badly. But he'd never let her know where it was. He'd also never let her come over to his place, and honestly she never wanted to because she didn't want to deal with the truth of the children. He figured that, somewhere in the back of her mind, she was still hoping he was making it all up.

Before he had started this hobby of his, he'd fantasized about it nonstop. And, as he had gone down his pathway, she had gone down another. She was a doctor, fascinated by what he did. He sometimes wondered if they would have a relationship if he was anyone other than who he was. *A specimen to study.*

He stared over at the broken China Doll beside him and said, "Tonight, tonight, we'll put you to rest." Just then an announcer on the television talked about the Amber Alert again.

"Aren't we done yet? My God, you'd think there weren't enough children in this world," he snapped. "It's just a boy. Just one, honestly, when probably a dozen went missing tonight, but you only care about the one on the news." An image of the boy flashed on the TV. He looked at it in wonder. "Oh, he's beautiful," he said in delight. He leaned forward to see the name flash on the bottom of the screen. *Leonard Hanover.*

"Well, Leonard, you know something? If you are found," he said, "you might just have to go missing again. Or do you have a brother?"

He quickly brought up the internet on his laptop, searching for Leonard Hanover. It came up with all the same news articles that he was currently watching. A little rundown on the family but not much. A little more research showed that he was the only child of a single mom.

"Yes, yes, yes," he said. "You're perfect. Now we might just rescue you from someone else in order to take you for ourselves." He smiled. "Wouldn't that be great?" he said. "If I find out who took you and then take you back," he said, "they'd get blamed, and nobody would know about me." He really loved that. And then he stared out the window, wondering. He knew a couple guys, twisted and odd when it came to kids. Guys like him. They belonged to a secret group.

He glanced back at the China Doll. "Two birds with one stone. What were they up to? I'll get rid of you and pick him up, if I can find him," he said, and he rubbed his hands together, absolutely loving the challenge facing him.

"This is a great twist," he said. "So much more than I'd hoped for." He glanced back at the TV. "It's okay, Leonard. Hold on. I'm coming."

# CHAPTER 8

*Thursday Afternoon*

J ENNIFER CALLED KATE back almost two hours later. "I checked Simon's whereabouts and verified where he said he'd been. He wasn't seen anywhere close to the school either, so, at the moment, I don't believe he had anything to do with Leonard's disappearance."

"Interesting," Kate murmured, wondering at the relief coursing through her, "and what about the aunt who was supposed to be looking after Leonard?"

"She still says that Simon knows something about it."

"Does she say what?"

"That's the problem. She's gets cagey at that point, so I'm not sure how much of her story I can believe."

"Maybe none of it," Kate said tiredly. "I think he professes to be some psychic."

Jennifer snorted. "Oh, great, just what I need," she said. "Who the hell needs that shit in their case?"

"Right? Yet the minute we have a missing child, all the crazies come out of the woodwork," Kate said.

"But this guy came out ahead of time, didn't he?"

"Well, you could say that," she replied. "The trouble is, I don't think I believe him."

"But you can't find a way to disprove him, is that it?"

"You could say that," she said, "and it really sucks."

"I get it," she said, "but nothing much you can do about it."

"I'm keeping an eye on him anyway," Kate said.

"Just make sure you keep your focus on the cases and not get sidetracked by your suspect."

"Wasn't planning on it," she said, "but something's going on here. There's something, I know it. I just don't know what he's involved in."

"And, of course, that doesn't mean that it's anything relating to this case," Jennifer said in warning.

"I know," she snapped. "But I can't get him out of my mind."

"I'll send you the file," Jennifer said. "See if anything pops."

"Good enough," she said. "I'll go over it, see if I can come up with anything."

"It's already almost twenty-four hours," Jennifer said, her voice heavy. "You know what that means."

"I know," Kate said, "but we have to keep up hope."

"Yes, I'm in the wrong business for that."

Kate heard the hard *click* of the phone, as the call disconnected. She sat back in her chair, rubbing her eyes. She had attempted to follow St. Laurant this morning, and now it was midafternoon of the same day. A frustratingly useless day. Just then Colby called out for her. She looked up to see him motioning at her to follow him. She got up, grabbed her coffee, walked in his office, behind him.

"What do you have for me?" he asked.

"I can tell you about the markings on the wrist," she said, "but we don't have decent enough photos or any mention of the marks in the old cases."

He leaned forward. "What markings?"

She brought up photos on her phone and said, "The coroner found it on Jason, after I mentioned it."

Colby stared at it, shook his head. "What is that?"

"As near as I can tell," she said, "it's like a faint wavy line, making a cartoonish set of lips."

He looked at her in disgust. She shrugged and showed him a slight image. "Seriously?"

"I can't tell you any more than that," she said. "I don't know what it means."

"Well, I don't like what it implies," he snapped.

"None of us do," she said mildly.

"I know. I know," he said, "but I was hoping you could find a connection. Or rather I was hoping you wouldn't find any connections."

"I found a couple."

"And?"

"That's the problem," she said. "There isn't enough yet to bother mentioning. I'm still looking."

"Any progress on who's behind all this?"

She shook her head.

"What about the psychic?"

"He knows more than he's telling," she said. "I just don't know what."

"That's it then," he said. "Bring him in for questioning. And it's time for you to tell the team." She hesitated. He looked up at her and asked, "Problems?"

She stood, shoved her hands in her pockets, and said, "Maybe it'd be better if you told the team."

He dropped his pencil, sat back, and looked at her. "Problems with the team?"

She shook her head. "Nothing I can't handle."

"Call a meeting," he said. "I want to be there."

She nodded and walked out. As she returned to the bull-pen, where everybody was working, she said, "Colby asked me to call a meeting now for everyone. We're going into boardroom two." She walked into the boardroom ahead of everybody, wishing she had her files from home with her.

When Colby walked in a few minutes later, he said, "We may have a problem. As this is supposed to be a team effort, I'll tell you right now that I had Kate do this on her own, and, now that she's found a few things, I want the team to look at what she's found and to tear it apart," he said. "If you can't find holes in this and if you see the connection that she sees, we've got a problem on our hands. A very big problem."

She watched the team as their expressions went from curiosity to anger at him for assigning her a private job, then back to curiosity.

Colby said, "Detective Morgan, explain, please."

She nodded. "Sixteen days ago, we had a man walk into the station," she said. "We all made fun of it at the time. He had information about children's cases from his nightmares," she said, "but he didn't know when, where, how, why, what, who, or anything else," she said, as she raised her hands in frustration. "As you can guess, by the end of my interview, he was deemed somewhere along the line between fanatic and psychic. I didn't know where on the crazy list to put him. I just knew that he was on there somewhere."

The others groaned. Andy said, "These psychics don't know much. And what they know is never helpful."

"True, and that's how I felt about it too, when Colby tasked me with the job of proving that the info was full of shit."

"Like we've got time for that," muttered Owen. Except Colby looked at him; he winced and said, "Sir."

"Oh, I get it," Colby said. "But, every once in a while, we also have to consider the fact that sometimes, just sometimes, we are wrong, and people actually do have information."

"So what did this guy have to say?" Lilliana said from the back of the room.

Kate replied, summarizing Simon's visions and as much of the work that she had sorted out in her head. "I don't have my files here," she said. "I was working on this at home, so everything is currently up on my board there."

"Tomorrow morning—or the next morning if shit hits the fan—but as soon as possible," Colby said, "I want it all recreated here. On this wall. Whatever cases you found, whatever bits and pieces you've got, I want to know," he said. "Tell them about the mark."

Everybody leaned forward.

"What the hell is going on here?" Owen said. "We used to be a team."

"*You* used to be," Kate said. "I arrived as the rejected newest member."

He had the grace to look a little ashamed. Then he shrugged and said, "Hey, we're all dealing with something."

*Silence.*

She continued. "The mark is on Jason," she said, "the dead little boy we found over a week ago. It's faint, as in barely discernible faint, but, when we enlarged the images, we saw it. I've only got it on my phone right now." She brought it out and showed the same one she'd shown to Colby. She passed her phone around, so they could all look at it.

One by one they shrugged and wrote it off as nothing.

"That same mark is on eight other cases, going back as

far as fifteen years ago," she said flatly.

*Silence.*

"What?" Lilliana cried out. "You're serious?"

"I'm dead serious," she said. "Unfortunately seven of those eight are dead too. One little girl remains missing. I highly suspect this pedophile has been operating a lot longer than that, and I don't have any idea how many related cases there may be. I'll get Reese on it now."

A general skeptical grumbling went through the group.

"Also there's another similarity."

They just stared at her.

"What's that?" Rodney asked suspiciously.

"Each of the dead children was found with a piece of clothing that wasn't theirs," she said gently. "Close, but not quite the same."

"And DNA?"

"No DNA in the other files. The clothing found on Jason wasn't his and is currently with Forensics."

"Well, if the clothing was washed, it's no longer viable to collect any evidence from," Lilliana said.

"Quite probably," Kate said. "I think this guy has a closetful of odd clothing, all in children's sizes ..."

"Jesus Christ." Rodney sat back, as he tossed his pencil on the table. "So, what is this? A lone ranger club now?"

"Well, let's see," she said. "What cases have you been working on for the last three months?"

He slammed his chair forward and said, "I've been working on the god-damn Waxner projects." He just glared at her, looked at the others. "We were doing fine until you came."

"Good. I got it," she said. "Chet was great. Chet was your buddy, and he was a hell of a good guy, cut down too early in life. And, damn it, it's not fair. But it happened. I'm sorry for that. I really am," she said, her voice hard. "And I get that it's been a shock, something none of you want to adapt to," she said. "But Chet is gone, yet I'm here. Now this is what I found, and I'll continue to work the case. So either join in or fuck off. I don't much care," she said calmly. "Actually I'd prefer to work alone, but that's not my call." With that, she sat back in her chair. Looking over at Colby, she said, "Back to you, Sergeant."

He stared at her, then looked at the rest of the team and asked, "Seriously? Even three months in?" He looked over at Rodney. "Are you working on cases you haven't told her about?"

Rodney flustered, tried to bluster his way out of it, but Lilliana stepped up. "Yes, we do have a couple."

"What the hell?" Colby roared. "I didn't bring her in here to work on her own cases. She brings a different perspective that you need to be open to. This stops now. Do you hear me? Every one of you will stay late until you go over the cases that you are working on, until you're *all* brought up to speed. Do you hear me?"

They all stared at him, and not one of them argued. Eventually there was four nods. He turned to look at Kate. "This goes for you too. Do you understand me?"

She gave a clipped nod. "Yes."

"From this moment on, if I find anybody is lone rangering a case, they will be up for reprimand," he said. "And I'm okay to kick your ass off the team, if I have to," he said. "I get that we had a great team with Chet. But he is gone, like Kate said. She can't step into his shoes. She has no intentions of doing so, and she shouldn't have to. He was a good man and a great detective. She's made detective grade, and you have to give her a chance to prove herself. Honestly, after all this, I think she already has. She's found all kinds of things here that none of us even noticed. That's not acceptable. Somehow this unit has fractured. Fix it or I will." At that, he turned and walked out.

There was a moment of silence, and Kate stared at the rest of them. She didn't say a word because whatever they did now would make or break the next few months.

Lilliana stepped up and said, "Okay. Now that we have it all out in the open," she said, "let's go over the cases. Let's do it all together, so we've all got the latest on everything." It took a moment, but the others nodded; the atmosphere was stiff but workable.

And they spent the next hour sharing with Kate their progress on the various cases, much of which she already knew, because, as much as they thought they were keeping it quiet, they weren't. She worked in the same area with the same analyst and assistants and even the other two detective teams, which thankfully were on the other end of the hallway. But since they hadn't bothered to share, she had done her research on her own. Still, she had three cases that she was working on with two of them, but it bothered her that they were working on two other cases and hadn't updated her. Still, she listened, grabbed materials that they had, photocopied it, and stacked up the files.

"What are you doing with that?" Rodney asked, nodding at the stack she had in front of her. "We like digital."

"Good for you," she said. "I'm taking this home, so I can catch up on it tonight," she said. She grabbed her jacket and her keys, snagged the stack, and walked out.

It was all she could do to hold down the sense of betrayal she felt inside. Making detective had been everything she had cared about for so long. She had her reasons, and she sure as hell wouldn't share any of that with them. But the fact was, she *had* made the grade.

And every one of those assholes out there who were after kids? Well, they had just better start shaking in their boots because she was coming after them, one by one.

# CHAPTER 9

*Thursday Afternoon, Late*

KATE HEADED HOME, but, before she'd gone even halfway, she got a text from Missing Persons. It was her friend Jennifer. **Is this your buddy?** And she sent through an image.

Kate clicked to see the image. And then she sent a text back. **Yes, that's him. Why?**

**He's been flagged as a person of interest.**

**Have we got a tail on him?**

Jennifer called her back. "Sometimes texting is just too damn frustrating," she said.

"I get it," Kate replied. "Did you put a tail on him?" It was hard to contain the excitement in her voice.

"You like that idea, don't you?" she said. "Let's just say that, after the mother, aunt, and other people mentioned him, he came up as suspicious."

"Suspicious as in *charlatan* or suspicious as in *pedophile*?"

"As somebody who might know something," she said, "and I'm not above using whatever assistance there is."

"Got it," she said.

"Down on Main Street, as in an hour ago."

"Interesting location," Kate said. "Any idea where he is?"

"Why?"

"He lives in the False Creek North area."

A whistle came through. "So he has money?"

"Yes, remember the charlatan part?"

Jennifer chuckled. "You don't like anybody in that field."

"I don't," she said. "I don't like anything about it or him."

"But, then again, that doesn't make him a conman."

"Maybe not," Kate replied, "but I don't trust him."

"Or you don't trust yourself?"

She gave a bitter laugh. "Hardly the issue at the moment."

"Maybe. Are you following him now too?"

Kate crossed the street to flag a cab and to head to the same area. "I wasn't, but, because of the way he is acting, we should keep a close eye on him. I'm tempted to go down there myself."

"What would that tell you?" Jennifer asked.

"I don't know," Kate said. At the moment, not exactly an easy question to answer.

"If you want to watch …"

"*As long as I don't get in the way*, I know," Kate said. "I'm likely to head down too."

Off the phone, she looked around. Instead of finding a cab, she saw an approaching bus, which would take her downtown. She hopped on and got off when she hit Granville Street. It was a Thursday evening, and lots of people mingled around the downtown area, with its several movie theaters, lovely little restaurants, late-night pubs and bars. It was a great time to be in Vancouver.

Unless you were a little boy.

And unless you were a pedophile, she hoped, because a lot of people were out looking for these perverts. She sent

Jennifer a text and gave her the location. **Where is the tail?**
**Heading south, down to the Pacific Centre.**
**On it**, Kate typed. She adjusted her route toward the
direction she'd been given. When she passed the Pacific
Centre, with no sign of Simon or anyone else, she quickly
checked in again.

**He's gone into the mall**, Jennifer replied.

**Interesting.** She frowned. She looked around, wondering at the sense of eeriness, as if she too were being watched.
That was often the case with the cat-and-mouse game that
occurred whenever she was tailing somebody. It often
seemed like she was being tailed too. With someone like
Simon, she wouldn't at all doubt it. Something was, although she hated to say it, almost otherworldly about him.
Something weird in those silvery-gray eyes.

A guy shouldn't have eyes like that, nor should he have
those long lashes. Most women she knew would love to have
those lashes naturally, instead of opting for the bother and
the expense of extensions. His complexion was also smooth
too; he woke up beautiful with no effort at all. She hated
him for that.

How come men could get up and just be perfect, with
no makeup, no curlers or irons or whatever the hell? And she
bet he never had to endure a five-product facial regime. She
was always so stressed by the demands of her job that at least
one zit was coming up somewhere on her face. She didn't
give a shit where it was though, just that it hurt. She did the
standard scrub and wash before bed and, in the morning,
just got up, brushed her hair after a shower, braided it, and
she was out the door.

She didn't have time for the forty-minute rigmarole that
so many women did. Her friend Zoe had told Kate that it

only took ten minutes, but, when Zoe showed Kate how that ten minutes went, it ended up being twenty-five. Her friend smiled and said, "With time it gets faster."

"Screw that," she muttered. The last thing she had time for was makeup. Even now, she pinched the bridge of her nose to keep her eyes a little more awake. A child was at stake here, and she jogged down the steps to the end of the mall, her eyes quickly adjusting to the fake lighting. Her phone buzzed.

**He is heading toward the Robson Street exit.**

She swore, raced back up to the main road instead of walking through the mall. She quickly jogged a couple blocks, heading toward the same exit. She got there just as Simon came up the steps. She stopped for a moment, but he didn't even seem to care; he walked calmly forward, following some North Star, as if he had some internal guidance. He walked with a purpose, and she had no idea what that purpose was.

At the far side of the street, a homeless man playing a guitar on a corner smiled hopefully at her. She studied him for a moment, then turned her back on him. But still she had that weird chill about being watched. She spun around a couple times unable to shake that feeling. Finally she got tagged. The call was from Missing Persons.

"What the hell is your problem?" Jennifer asked. "Our tail is following him and wondering why you keep looking around."

"Because, damn it," she muttered, "it feels like I'm being watched."

"Well, my tail has about had enough of seeing you," she said in frustration.

"That's fine," she said, "but somebody else is out here in

this game."

"Like who?"

"I don't know yet," Kate said. "I'm going off the grid. Your tail knows I'm out here," she said. "I'm not disappearing. I'm just going a different route." And, with that, she hung up.

She walked around, took a corner, and cut through the alleyway, then headed up on the far side, so she was ahead of Simon. Mostly because she knew the angle he was walking, and he was heading toward the park entrance. He wasn't likely to go all the way around the bridge, up to the top and across. That was miles yet. But a lot was going on down here, and she wouldn't doubt that he had a specific purpose in mind. But that didn't mean that the missing child Leonard had anything to do with it. She just hoped this wasn't a wild goose chase. Not when a child was at stake.

Sure enough, she caught sight of him again.

His phone rang, and she watched as he answered it. But he didn't gaze left or right, he just kept going straight forward. Something that really bothered her was that, every time he walked up to a crosswalk, the opposing traffic was stopped with a red light, so he could walk across without changing his stride. She watched him a couple times and thought it was a coincidence, but now she realized it was anything but. She wondered if he had some mechanical device in hand that altered the traffic lights. She frowned and then quickly sent her contact a message. **The damn lights keep doing him favors.**

**So? He's lucky.**

**Or has a device to control it.** She got a question mark back. With a heavy sigh she frowned; of course they would think she was crazy. But something was eerie about him to always cross on a perfectly timed green light without breaking his stride. As she came up to the intersection that he'd sailed right through, the light changed. She frowned, but, since there was no traffic, she darted across. She could almost see him laughing at her from up ahead.

Then he called back and said, "You might as well come walk with me."

"Hell." She headed out and joined him. She also knew that whoever was following him from Missing Persons would be pissed.

"Why are you out here after me?" he asked smoothly.

"I'm not," she said, "but I sure as hell would like to know how you end up crossing in perfect sync with the lights all the time."

"Just lucky," he said.

She shook her head. "Lucky is fifty percent of the time. Maybe even sixty," she said. "With a hundred percent of the time, no luck is involved."

"So what now? You're accusing me of interfering with the traffic lights?" he asked.

"Maybe," she said, "if I could ever figure out what the hell you're doing."

He chuckled. "You're such an untrusting soul."

"I don't trust anyone out here," she said. "Even you."

"Good," he said calmly. "I don't trust myself either." She stared. He shrugged and said, "When you live your life, you learn whether you can trust anyone out there or only trust yourself."

"I know I can trust myself."

"Good for you," he said, but his tone deepened. "What I do know is I can trust everyone out there to do whatever it is they want, knowing it'll be in their personal best interests. If you don't expect anything more than that, you never get taken. Now trusting yourself? That's a whole different story."

She stopped in her tracks, thinking everything he said was completely backward. When she turned and looked up again, he'd disappeared from sight. She walked forward to find him leaning against a wall inside a doorway. She just stood and glared at him.

"Have a good evening, Detective." And the door opened for him, and he stepped in.

She studied the building. It was a private club. She'd heard he was a bit of a gambler but didn't know to what extent. Her phone rang, and she knew who it was. "He's gone into a club."

"And you completely broke the tail," Jennifer said in outrage. "I'm catching complete hell here thanks to you."

"Well, he saw me, and he asked me to walk with him. I didn't have a whole lot of choice at that point."

"What the hell?" she said. "You know this isn't a game. We have a child missing."

"I know," she said. She frowned, thinking. "I'm back-tracking."

"Why?"

She stopped and turned. "Because a panhandler was back there, and Simon tossed some money into his tray."

"And?" Receiving no answer from Kate, Jennifer continued. "Good thing you're not on my team," she snapped. "I would have fired your ass for that stunt."

"Maybe so," she said, "but I'm not done. The evening is young." With that, she turned and pocketed her phone.

She didn't know what was bothering her, but something was. She headed back toward the area where she'd seen Simon drop some coins in the panhandler's tray because, at that time, something had changed. As she came back, the panhandler moved quickly down the street. She raced behind him.

"Wait," she said. But instead of waiting, he pulled his jacket tighter and moved faster. "Stop," she said. "Police!"

He broke into a blind sprint. What had appeared to be an old man suddenly looked to be someone in prime shape, as he raced down the street ahead of her. She'd already been running, but he quickly dodged into one of the back alleys, and, by the time she got there, he'd already disappeared. Standing here, swearing, she was pissed beyond belief.

Not only had she not caught him but he'd completely fooled her the first time around.

She didn't have any photos of him either. As she walked down the alleyway, gathering her breath, the coins had spilled from his tray. She bent and took a look. One was an oddity, like a casino coin. Instinctively she knew whose it was. She pulled a tissue from her pocket and quickly wrapped it up and tucked it back into her pocket. Why had he dropped that here? Just then her phone rang. She pulled it out.

"We got a sighting of a lost little boy two blocks away," Jennifer said. "Where are you?"

Kate quickly gave her location. "Who called it in?"

"We don't know," Jennifer said in frustration. "But he said the little boy needed to be picked up because somebody else was after him."

Kate raced back out onto the street and started searching. "Where? North, south, east, west?" She was frantic as she ran toward the coordinates. Just as she hit the corner across the street, she saw a little figure up against a doorway. She bolted in that direction, just as another man came closer to him. "Get away from him," she roared.

He turned and looked at her, startled. Then he hurriedly stepped back. She only caught the briefest glimpse of him, as he bolted down the opposite side of the street away from her. She bent down to see it was, indeed, a little boy. "I've got him," she said into her phone a moment later. "Another man was literally ready to snatch him up again."

"A good man?"

"No," she said, her voice deadly soft. "No, I wouldn't say so. But I don't know. Maybe I'm being too harsh."

"Is he alive?"

She reached out, checking the little boy, and he whimpered and cried. "He's alive," she said, "but I don't think this is the one you are looking for."

"Why the hell not?" Jennifer asked.

"Because this one is only two, maybe two and a half," she said. "Easy, little one. Just take it easy." The little child started to sob. He held out his arms; she sat down on the steps beside him and tucked him into her lap. "This guy is little," she said. "And he needs help."

"Is he okay?"

"I don't know," she said. "He is exhausted and cold." She could tell from his body temperature through the clothing. "And he's crying, in case you can't hear that."

"Got it," she said. "I have an ambulance heading toward you. Hold him close. We are still looking for the other boy—Leonard. Damn it. What the fuck is going on? Did you get a good look at the other man?"

"No." On instinct, she said, "Send somebody after him. He headed down Thurlow. See if you can run him to ground."

"Okay," she said. "I have two others in the neighborhood. Description?"

"Midcalf overcoat, dark brown scarf, looking a little odd. Something weird about his eyes. Black gloves."

"Got it," she said. "You stay with that child."

"He's not going anywhere," she said. In fact, he was curled up against her chest, her big coat wrapped around him. And, although he still sobbed, he was calming down. She heard the sirens in the distance. "It's okay, little one," she said. "The police are coming and so is an ambulance." He just tucked in closer and hung on.

And she knew she wouldn't hand him over easily. As soon as the ambulance arrived, she pulled out her badge, showed the EMTs. They nodded and came over to talk to the little boy. When she opened her jacket, and one of the men reached for him, the little boy started screaming. She winced and tried to soothe him, but there was nothing for it. She had to hand him over, so he'd get checked out. Very little light was back here in this alleyway, but the medics had flashlights, and, once the little boy was on the gurney, she didn't even need lights to see that his pants were bloody. She looked up at the officers. "Please tell me that it's not—"

They wore grim faces and said, "We'll get him into the ambulance first and get him to the hospital. Did you find any ID on him?"

She shook her head. "None that I saw in this light. It seemed more important to hold him close at the time," she said, but her heart was being wrenched from her chest as she listened to the little boy's cries and anguish. "Dear God," she said, "get him some help."

"We will," he said.

She quickly took a picture of the license plate on the ambulance to make sure that nothing else happened with this little boy. She didn't even know why she was doing that, except that everything in life right now seemed upside down and backward, and she wouldn't let this little guy go without a damn good reason. The fact that he was exhausted was one of them though.

As soon as the ambulance left, two police officers came and asked her for the details. She quickly gave them an outline. "One man was looking to snatch the child."

They looked up from their notes at her. "Are you thinking he knew who the child was?"

"I don't know," she said, "but something really weird is going on here."

"We're also still missing that seven-year-old," he said.

"I know." Just then she got a phone call from her unit.

"Kate, this is Owen," he said. "We've got another body."

She closed her eyes, stared up at the sky, and said, "I'm on it. Where am I going?"

"You're almost there," he said. "Take two blocks, turn right, head up one."

"You already know I'm here? How?"

"Heard you found a child." After a heavy pause, he added, "Good job on that, by the way."

"But?"

"The *but* is, we're standing over a little girl. This child is dead."

WELL, THAT DIDN'T *work out quite the way I thought it would.*

Simon had ditched Kate at the first club, but, not liking the odd sensation inside him, he'd only stayed for fifteen minutes, then had headed out again. He'd walked toward a private game that he'd considered hitting later but figured early would work too. Except, as he'd started walking, his instincts had kicked in, sending him in the opposite direction. He wasn't even sure where the directive was coming from, but he felt compelled to follow until it. He hit the alleyway shadows and saw something gleaming in the darkness.

Sorrow and anger had kicked in with equal force. He stood silent for a moment, then made the phone call.

And had left right after speaking with the first officer on the scene. He'd left his information and had promised to return later to speak to whoever notified him.

And had promptly joined the private game, now around the time he'd originally planned to step in, and had several stiff drinks. Anything to blank out that image of the dead girl from his mind.

Simon folded back his cuff and pushed up his sleeve, as he waited for the next round of cards to start. He had a stack of chips in front of him, but it wasn't too high. This was a game he'd been planning for, for several months. A game of revenge. On a cheater. It was one thing to wreck somebody else because you're good at cards or because you had inside knowledge.

It was another thing to have a cheater drain somebody else who didn't have the money to lose. Simon planned to take the cheater to the cleaners tonight. The one man the cheater had cheated wasn't here and wouldn't likely be back ever. He'd lost way too much on another night and would spend months, if not years, paying it back.

That's the problem when you got into these games. You got in heavy, and things got ugly.

Simon had a beer beside him, and the smell of smoke was heavy. He wished to hell they'd all stop smoking. It clogged his nose and filled his lungs. It would be days before he'd get it out of his clothing. As he waited for the cards to come his way, he checked out what his opponents all had. Making a decision, he bounced one chip in and said, "I'm good."

"Seriously?" said one man, with an honest laugh. "You are holding at that?"

Simon placed his cards facedown, nodded. "I am." And he just stared back at the man. Some of these guys he knew; some knew him. Some knew of him.

One of them tossed his cards into the center and said, "I'm out."

"You can always get another set of cards," his neighbor protested.

"Not if he is holding his," he said. "It's just much easier on my bank account this way."

The guy snorted. "I don't believe it," he said. "I'm in."

Simon wanted two cards, and he tossed in a coin and raised him one, so round and round the game went. He didn't take any more cards, but he kept playing to the pot. Finally the other guy settled down, and he laid out four in a row. Simon nodded, then laid out four aces. A chorus of groans came all around the table, as he pulled in his pot.

"Jesus Christ," his opponent said. "You're one lucky bastard."

Simon shrugged and said, "Hey, I've been here lots and left without winning anything." Because he had deliberately set that up, they all knew it to be true. Yet this was Simon's night, and he would make sure it was a good one.

"Hope you're not walking home with that money," the

losing cheater said. "You're likely to get mugged."

The evening proceeded much the same. Simon would win a little, lose a little, but he kept his stack, and, over time, it built and it built. Finally his neighbor tossed in his cards and said, "I'm done for the night."

Simon looked over at him and nodded. "Good call," he said. "I think it's time to leave too."

"You can at least give us a chance to win some of that back," the cheater said.

"What do you want to do?" Simon asked. Then he shoved everything into the pot. "I'll take you on," he said. "Push your little pile in against my big pot."

The man's eyebrows shot up; he looked at the two stacks, and he nodded. "This is all I've got for weeks," he said, "but hell yes. Absolutely." All the others were out, so Simon and the cheater did a quick twenty-one hand, and, within seconds, Simon flipped over his cards. Then he scooped up his opponent's money and added it to his already big pot. He looked to the owner of the club and asked, "Can I get a bag, please?"

"Jesus," he said. He got up, came around with the club bag, and handed it to him. "I don't think we've ever seen anybody walk away with that kind of money."

"And yet I've probably put that kind of money into this place over the last couple months," Simon joked. But he was aware of an ugliness emanating from across the table. He looked over at the cheater. "What's the matter?"

"You must have cheated," he said.

Simon froze, and a sudden stillness fell around the room. "Did you just call me a cheater?"

The man stuck his nose up pugnaciously and nodded. "Hell yes," he said. "No way you got that hand."

"I didn't deal it," he said. "I didn't have anything in my hands except the two cards I was given. Why the hell would you think I was cheating?"

The guy looked at the dealer. "Because you will probably split it with him at the end of the evening."

An outcry came from the others.

"Watch your mouth," said one of the men. "It's one thing that you're sitting here, pissed off that you lost after all the times you've won in here," he said, "but you don't get to call anybody a cheater just because you're pissed."

"Oh, yeah, I know he's cheating. I've seen that con before."

Simon sat back down, the bag of money in his hands. "What con?" he asked.

But the man looked frustrated. "No way you did that honestly."

"And why is that?" Simon asked, staring at him with a note of humor. "Are you a cheater yourself? Is that what you think this is? That you've been out-cheated?"

The other guys laughed.

The cheater got up and said, "I'm definitely done for the night." As he walked to the front door, he turned around and said, "You better watch how you walk out."

"Wow, that's a hell of a threat," Simon said. He looked at the rest of the table. "You all okay if I walk out of here?"

"Not too impressed with your timing," one said. "But, yeah, absolutely. Cheating is not your deal. But, like he said, make sure you are careful."

"Got it," Simon said. "Thanks for the warning." He tucked the bag under his arm, pocketed his cell phone, and said, "Gentlemen, it's been a pleasure." And he walked out. Just silence was behind him. But ahead of him, he knew would be a trap. No way the cheater would let Simon walk out of here. What Simon didn't know for sure was if one of the men behind him wouldn't let him walk out either.

He wrapped up the ball of money as tight as he could, tucking it into his outside pocket, so he had both hands free, and then he stepped out to the street. When the whistle of air came, he had already ducked and was moving. But unlike most people, he didn't move away. He turned and headed directly for the target. The cheater stood there, waiting for him. A gun in hand, the cheater wasn't expecting Simon's right fist that clocked him on the jaw or Simon's left leg that came up and took out his gun hand. When the cheater went down, his head smacked hard onto the concrete.

Simon stood over him and said, "Seriously? You wait out here to shoot an unarmed man?"

"I need my goddamn money," he said painfully.

"Well, you're not getting it," he said. "Did you really think you could get away with all that cheating?"

With eyes opened wide, the man sputtered, "How did you know?"

"Because I can recognize a cheater," he said. "You've been stealing from these men for months."

"Have not," he said.

"Not only that, you completely bankrupted the last guy."

"He shouldn't have been here. I was teaching him a lesson," he said.

"Well, guess what? That lesson is now yours," he said. "Get out of the game before you end up playing a game that you can't win." And, with that, Simon turned, and he walked away. He'd kicked the gun away, but that didn't mean the guy wouldn't go for it again.

When Simon turned around and saw him reaching for it, he hid in the alleyway and waited. No way to know just how stupid the cheater would be. When he heard raised voices, he realized the other players from their game had come out. Simon stepped around the corner, even though the guy had a gun. "Now you tell them," Simon said, "how you've been cheating them for the last couple months."

But the cheater shook his head. "You're the one who's been cheating them. The proof is under your hand right there."

"I've been playing here for years," Simon said. "I've never cheated. You've been fleecing them one by one," he said. "You think that gun will help you?"

But the shooter raised it and pointed at Simon. "I should have killed you when you stepped out."

"You actually tried, as I recall," he said.

And, just like that, the cheater pulled the trigger. But an empty barrel clicked. He stared at it, shook his head, and said, "No way. I loaded this thing."

"Well, try it again," Simon said, and again the man fired at him. Trying over and over, but it was empty. He threw it away in disgust. "How the fuck did you do that?"

"No idea what you're talking about," Simon said cheerfully, noting the other guys closing in on the cheater. "Have a good night."

As Simon walked away, he considered what to do with the money. And had a perfect answer. As he kept going, up ahead was one of the more hidden women's shelters in town. They had to be obscure so their abusive husbands and boyfriends could not find them. He walked up, rang the doorbell. There was no answer at the door but someone over an intercom asked him what he wanted.

"Is Lisa here?"

"The manager?"

"Yes," he said. "Tell her Simon is here to make a deposit." While he waited, he opened the bag and frowned, grabbed out a large handful of bills, rolled it back up again. When the door opened, and a woman stepped out, her gaze was fearful as she looked around. He said, "Hold out your hands."

She looked at him in surprise, until she saw the money. She immediately held out both hands.

"Spend it all on the women's shelter," he urged.

"Simon, your previous donation helped to fund two more years. We appreciate you, but you don't have to keep doing this."

"Like hell," he said. "You take care of yourself."

And just like that, he turned and walked away.

---

THAT'S NOT HOW he had intended the child swap to go. When he'd questioned his group, he'd heard about the child from another one. This wasn't the child everybody was looking for but another one, a little boy. He desperately wanted him. But apparently, when this asshole realized the cops were trailing all pedophiles from the most recent Amber Alert, he had dropped the boy somewhere in a public place.

He'd talked to the asshole only an hour earlier, tried to get the youngster for himself, but the perv had refused, said he was going downtown to drop him there. It had taken a bit to get the directions, but, as soon as he had, he'd seen the boy up ahead. Almost in reach. And he'd been so close, so damn close. Then he saw the woman racing toward him, shouting, and knew he would be too late.

Had she seen him? He really hoped not because he didn't want to deal with that right now. He'd kill her if he needed to. He'd killed others for less. It was all about secrecy ... and staying away from the cops. He didn't even stick around long enough to see what she'd done with the child, but he knew instinctively that she would care for him and would make sure he was okay.

He'd have done the same. He'd have looked after him, and the child would have been grateful too. That was all he wanted anyway—somebody who would love him. At least some of the time that's what he wanted. Other times he didn't even know what the hell he wanted.

So be it.

He quickly dialed his sister's number. "What do you want at this hour?" she groaned. He stared at the phone. "I didn't even think about that," he said. "What time is it?"

"It's got to be close to midnight," she said. As she fumbled around on her side of the call, she said, "Damn it, bro. It's two in the morning."

"I need to talk," he said. She sighed, and he could imagine her sinking down again into her pillows, lying there, with her eyes closed.

"About what?"

"I almost got a little boy tonight."

"Almost?" *Silence.* "Normally you don't tell me about your failures."

"Well, in a way it's a success," he said, "so I'm trying to find the good part."

"You're very confusing tonight," she said.

"I heard that another pedophile had this little boy but was running scared with the Amber Alert. You know registered pedos in the kidnapping area are rousted first," he said. "I'm fairly well-known for shaking them down, so, when I put out the word that I was looking for the little boy, I was hoping that he would just give him to me."

"And he didn't?"

"No, he didn't," he said. "He let him go in some damn dark corner of downtown. A tiny little boy just left in the doorway like that," he said. "Who the hell would do that? He just deserted him on the street corner. Anybody could have picked him up."

A half snort came from the other side of the phone.

"What the hell?" he said. "Are you laughing at me?"

"I'm laughing at the pedophile who stuck a child on the street corner, and you're worried about *just anybody* getting him."

He thought about it and then said, "Good one. Yeah, very funny. You're right. But I would have looked after him."

"Of course you would have," she said in a soothing voice.

He needed that. She let him rant and yell until he'd finally wound down. "See? That's why I called you," he said. "I needed this talk."

"I'm glad to help," she said, "but could you possibly avoid calling so late? This was a lot, even for you."

"Well, I keep trying," he said, "but tonight was different." By the time he finished talking, his sister wasn't answering anymore. "Sis, are you still there?" He heard a murmur come over the phone, and he glared at it. "The least you can do is listen to me."

"I tried," she said, "but now I'm asleep, so goodbye."

And instead of the *click* of the phone, he heard the

phone drop and knew his sister was off to dreamland, as he should be.

But it had been a busy night. He'd gotten rid of the broken China Doll, but he'd missed his chance at getting a little boy who would have looked up to him and would have been beyond happy to have been taken care of by him. Now he was all alone in his damn apartment, and he hated it. Something was so depressing about being here. At least while the China Doll was here, he hadn't felt quite so lonely. Of course it was broken, but, even broken, it was something. Now he had nothing again.

He frowned at that; he hadn't heard whether the seven-year-old Leonard had been found or not, and that worried him. It worried him because still other pedophiles were out there. Hell, he knew many of them. He should get his pick of the kids. He hadn't shaken down a couple other pervs yet; maybe he needed to. Maybe somebody else had Leonard that he didn't know anything about.

As he thought about it, he wondered if Leonard's family wasn't doing this for some other reason. He hated it when families used kids to fill their pockets. Talk about abuse. He loved his kids. When families did something like that, it made life impossible and miserable for their kids. Nobody ever charged the parents. Nobody ever gave a shit about the poor kids then. No, it was all about what *he* did wrong. It was ridiculous.

That little China Doll would have been great, if she hadn't died. He didn't even know how she died. He stared down at his hands and shook his head. He'd given her a bath in alcohol to make sure there were no signs of what he'd done. She'd been so sweet and so perfect and obviously very sick before he ever got her.

The same with Jason. That little boy had been in terrible shape. He'd loved him and had done everything he could to keep him alive, but eventually Jason had died on him. It was just so damn sad. Already he felt the tears collecting in his eyes, but he didn't want to cry again. He didn't want to cry over Jason; it was just too hard. He absolutely loved that kid.

He brought up the news article that he'd seen online and saved the picture of the little boy Leonard to his desktop. He felt his heart tighten as he saw that face. He really wanted him. But where the hell was he? It didn't make sense. Unfortunately it actually did because lots of guys just like him were out there. Guys who were lonely, guys who were looking for their special companion to make life not quite so rough. Hopefully he could find Leonard and could bring him home. He also thought about who else he could take that child from because that was the key to everything. It was one thing to know somebody else had him, but no way he would let that stand.

He would take Leonard for himself.

# CHAPTER 10

*Friday, Very Early Morning*

IT WAS A damn long night. Kate worked straight through Thursday into the wee morning hours of Friday. The success of protecting the little boy was followed by an absolutely aching defeat, as Kate stood next to Owen, over what appeared to be a six-year-old girl, her skin perfectly china white. Her beauty—that simple innocence—shone through in the darkness. Kate stepped back and asked Owen, "Who found her?"

He pointed to the side of the road and said, "That man over there. Simon St. Laurant. I spoke to him when I arrived, and he said he'd come back later and talk to you. But I see he's there now."

She glanced across, Simon staring at her. He lifted a hand, as her breath sucked into the back of her chest. She looked down at the little girl, then back at Owen. "Any other witnesses?"

Owen nodded at the cops. They shook their heads. "Just him."

She nodded. "I'll go talk to him. Why isn't the coroner here yet?"

"He's on the way," Owen said. "Everybody is busy to-night though. A couple bad accidents and some gang-related shooting downtown. Then this one."

"By morning there will be half a dozen more too," she said sadly. "Unfortunately that's the world we live in."

"It is, but it would sure be nice if it weren't."

She crossed the street, turning her hands in her pockets, while she studied Simon. As she approached, she said, "What the fuck?"

Simon shrugged. "What was I supposed to do? *Not* call it in?"

She reached up and rubbed her face. "It would be nice maybe if you just weren't involved every time I turn around," she muttered. "Particularly with these cases."

"You have to pick which side you think I'm on, Detective," he said, "because this sitting on the fence could get a little rough."

"I know which side you're on," she said. "And it's not my side."

"Are you so sure?" he asked.

She glared at him. "When did you find her?"

"About twenty minutes before the cops arrived," he said. "I was at the club, having a couple friendly card games, and, when I was done, I walked out and came this direction and found her."

"But this isn't False Creek," she said, looking at him.

"What does False Creek have to do with it?"

"I don't know," she said and then groaned. "Did you see anyone? Was anyone around her? Did you remove anything from her?"

"I didn't see anyone. I didn't see anything. I didn't see any vehicle. I didn't touch the body, and I didn't remove anything from her."

She nodded. "Were any lights on in the nearby apartments, anybody hanging around? Were there any shadows, any footsteps, any noises that didn't fit?"

"No," he said, shaking his head. "Nothing like that."

She nodded. "Fine. So how did your game go tonight?"

He held out the bag with what was left of the money. "It went great."

She shook her head at the size of the bag. "Jesus Christ, at least ten thousand must be in there."

"Twice that, at least," he said calmly.

"High stakes," she snapped. But she turned and stared at Owen and the local beat cops, still looking at the body. She couldn't give a shit about the money in his pocket. All she cared about was the life that had left that little body.

"How long were you looking for her?"

She shared a glance at him. "I never got any report that she was missing," she said sadly. "So that's giving me a whole new investigation."

"Well, I didn't have anything to do with it."

"Just a magnet for trouble though, huh?"

His tone turned grim. "Only lately."

She stopped, turned, and looked at him. "What changed?"

He stared right at her, his gaze completely unfathomable.

"For something like that to happen in your world," she said, "usually something changes."

He gave her a shrug and a blank smile.

Frustrated, she said, "Well, that's your problem, but make sure you stay the hell away from my cases."

"And if I don't?" he asked, his tone turning silky.

"I'll make sure that I drag you into each and every one of them," she said. "You're either a charlatan or somebody who gets his kicks out of seeing the police running around, chasing after this killer," she said. "Or you are the killer himself. I'm okay to lay any one of those labels on you, though I'd much prefer that last one."

"You need proof for that," he said.

"And what?" she said. "Are you too smart for that?"

"Oh, I don't know about that," he said, "but it's definitely an issue."

"I don't think so," she said, "but now we have a problem."

"What's that?"

"Now you are in too many of my cases. I've got a missing seven-year-old boy, and we've got a dead little girl," and she frowned, as she recognized the ages. "And we've got all those kids from those crazy nightmares of yours." With that, she turned and headed back to the crime scene. Only to realize she hadn't asked him about the toddler she'd found alive earlier.

SIMON WATCHED THE detective leave. Something was elusive and yet addictive about her. They were playing cat and mouse, only he didn't know what the end game was. He detested the police, detested authority of any kind. Particularly people who took a paycheck and didn't give a shit about anything beyond that.

Jobs weren't people; they weren't hearts and souls. They weren't dreams and hopes and wishes. When it came to a lot of cops, they didn't give a shit about any of that. They were just about black-and-white statistics, needing to make an arrest to keep their paychecks flowing. He didn't think she was the same kind of paycheck-collecting cop because something was different there, something damn weird about her. No. Not weird. *Unique.* Yeah, he'd go with unique.

Yet she was right about one thing—something had changed. He just didn't know what had triggered it.

He patted the money bag in one pocket, then pulled out the small yellow ball he still kept in the other. Not sure why, except it was a reminder of Yale, who'd tossed it to him as he was leaving the park that one day. With that, he turned and headed for home. As he walked, he passed several others out, cruising around and enjoying life. But something in the back of his head said that he was up against some other elements.

He kept walking forward, searching the alleyways as he crossed them. Once again, he heard a weird sound that had him flattening against the wall, turning to face the threat. And, sure enough, there was his cheating opponent from the game earlier this evening. Only now his face was puffed up and red, his nose bleeding. Simon stared at the man in surprise. "Whoever did that to you, well, I'm surprised they even let you walk away."

"They didn't," he spat on the ground. "I woke up on a bench a few blocks away. But don't worry. I know who is really responsible for this."

"Not me," Simon said mildly. He looked at him and said, "You've still got the gun, I see."

"No," he said. "It's a second gun."

"You went home and got your spare?" He thought about it and said, "That takes a certain amount of tenacity, especially if the rest of you looks anything like your face. I'm sure premeditation won't be hard to prove."

"You fucking cheated," he roared.

"You've been cheating for months," Simon said. "What makes you think you could get away with that forever?"

He stared at him. "I can't go home," he said. "You don't understand. I can't go home like this. My wife will kill me.'"

It amazed Simon that these guys could face down all kinds of danger, even get their faces punched in, but the thought of going home and confessing to their wives what they'd been doing terrified them. Big strong men, shaking in their boots. "Yes, you can." He turned and walked away.

"Wait," the cheater called out.

Simon turned, looked at him, at the gun, and said, "If you shoot me, then you best make sure you kill me. If you're after the money, most of it is gone already."

The cheater stared in shock. Simon pulled out the bag to show him. At the sight of the much smaller pile, he looked like he would walk away. Simon shrugged and turned his back on him again.

A shot fired behind him.

Simon stood for a long moment, eyes closed in resignation, then turned to look. "Shit."

# CHAPTER 11

*Friday Morning, Later*

B Y THE TIME she crashed in bed, Kate was so past exhausted, she didn't have time for a shower. Waking up four hours later, she knew that was all the sleep she would get. She dragged herself from bed to stand under the hot water, as it sloshed over her shoulders. Her apartment still had boxes from when she'd moved in two years ago. It was the story of her life. She ate on the run, slept on the run, and everything else just came to a grinding halt.

She'd had a couple quick relationships over the last few years, but that was it. Now she didn't even bother with those. Nobody understood her work; nobody understood her drive, and that was okay. She was who she was, and she'd be damned if she would give that up for anybody else anymore. She'd done that with her prior relationships, but she wouldn't ever again.

She opened the fridge and found nothing to eat. She groaned. "I've got to get to a grocery store someday," she murmured. Neither was there any more coffee. She rubbed her eyes, put on her holster and her jacket. Next, she put on her boots, which were looking more scuffed and well-worn than they should be, and headed out the door. She stopped at the first vendor and grabbed a pretzel, wondering how she was supposed to live on carbs alone. As she headed to the office and walked in, straight to the coffeepot, she noted she was the first one in.

She filled her big mug and sat back down and munched through the rest of the pretzel. The others all came in after her. They looked at her and groaned.

"Are you always so fucking early?" Owen asked.

"I couldn't sleep," she said. "What do you want me to do?"

"I don't know. Roll over and try again?"

She shrugged. "It is what it is."

"We don't have anything to go on yet."

"Maybe, but we do have to get somewhere on it."

"Have you actually started working?"

"No," she said, "too tired."

"Great, you're still human."

She stared at him in surprise. "I'm pretty-damn sure that's not what you were gonna say."

"Yeah, it is," he said. "You're always first in, and you're always last out. You're always so damn perfect that you're making the rest of us look like shit."

She gave a startled laugh. "No," she said, "I'm just doing my job so I get to keep it."

He stopped at that, looked at her, and nodded. "That makes sense, and, by the way, I still could shoot you if you didn't leave me any coffee."

She was just so damn busy with all these cases now that she was eating, drinking, and sleeping them. She didn't dare give herself a break because those kids hadn't gotten one either. The last thing she wanted to be was a cop who was asleep at her job when yet another child was taken. She also knew she wasn't to blame if it did happen, but the idea was pretty hard to live with.

By the time everybody was in, Colby stepped out into the bullpen area. "Report."

"We could let her do that," Owen said.

She stared at him. "You were the one who told me where to go."

"To go where?" Colby asked. "What were you doing downtown anyway?"

"I was stalking Simon," she said, a round of snide laughter came behind her. "The psychic," she snapped. "With the info on the kids' cases."

Colby looked at her in surprise. She shrugged. "I followed him downtown, after talking to Jennifer in Missing Persons. They put a tail on him, so I went to join in on the fun. St. Laurant ended up in a private poker game and a couple oddities. We didn't find Leonard, the missing seven-year-old boy, but I did find the toddler," she said. She checked her watch. "And I checked the hospital this morning. I'm supposed to call at eight for an update."

"But he was alive?" Lilliana asked from behind her.

Kate nodded. "Alive, bloodstained pants, but I don't know if that was his blood or someone else's. It broke my heart to hand him over though," she said, staring at Colby. "I had just passed him over to the ambulance crew," she said, "and was standing there, trying to regroup, when Owen called me to tell me they had found the little girl."

"And how did that get called in?"

Owen looked at her; she looked back. "Simon St. Laurant."

Colby's eyebrows rose to the surface. "Him again?"

"Yeah, I warned him that he was a little too involved in my cases," she said, "and either I would haul him in and see how he was involved, or he better get the hell out of my world."

"Haul him in," Colby said. "That is an order. We don't want anybody with that kind of information walking around town."

"I get it," she said. "I talked to him last night. Well, way after midnight this morning."

"And?"

"I'm not exactly sure," she said. "I don't think he had anything to do with it. He said that he just came upon her."

"What, another psychic tip?"

"I suspect he'd say *intuition* more than anything." Her phone rang just then. She looked down and frowned. "Jesus. It's Simon."

Colby said, "Answer and put it on Speaker."

She groaned, hit Speaker, and said, "What do you want?" She knew the other detectives were startled at her response.

"I want to talk," he said.

"That's good, since my sergeant just ordered you brought in for questioning."

"Oh, that's nice," he said. "Where do you want to meet?"

She looked over at Colby, and he pointed at his feet. "I'm not kidding," she said. "Colby wants you in here for questioning."

"Well, you tell Colby he can go fuck himself," he said. "I just came from the hospital, and you've got another body here."

"Did you kill this one?"

He gave a startled laugh. "No, I didn't. He actually shot himself."

"And why would he do that?" she said, slowly rising.

"Because he was at the game last night and lost everything."

"And?" she asked. "There's obviously more to that story."

"Probably," he said, and she heard the fatigue in his voice. "He accosted me on the street and accused me of cheating—which is projection, by the way. He was pretty desperate, and the rest of the group had beaten him up pretty good. He had a gun and held it on me. I kicked it out of his hand. He took off and came back later with a gun. I'd only manage to walk a couple of blocks. He pointed the gun at me, then decided that he would shoot himself instead. He pulled the trigger and blew his brains out all over the back alley."

"Did you call it in?"

"I did," he said. "It would have traced back to me anyway."

"Yeah, it sure will," she said. "So, if you're at the ER, come straight down to the station, and we'll take your statement."

"As if," he said. "I need coffee, and I need food. I haven't slept, and my talk with the cheater was a little less than polite."

"How less than polite?" she asked.

"The worst," he said. "He shot at me first." And, with that, he hung up the phone.

She looked over at Colby, but he was already swearing. He turned to the others. "Find out from the street cops what the hell the deal was with the cheater's body last night. See where he was found, check out Simon's statement to see if that's correct, speak to the other poker players," he said. "This guy is in the middle of way the hell too much. I want him either cleared, or I want him charged. You guys got that?"

She glared at him, picked up her coffee, threw back the rest of it, sucking up the last drop. Then she snatched her half-eaten pretzel and said, "I'm gone." As she headed for the door, she heard a shout from behind her. She looked to see Rodney heading her way. "Colby wants me to go with you."

She shrugged. "Whatever," she said. "I'm calling Simon back to see where the hell he is."

"Don't you think he's still at the ER?"

"Knowing him? No. He's probably home."

"Where is home?"

"Penthouse in False Creek North," she said.

He whistled. "So this guy's got money, huh?"

"He's got money. What I don't know," she said, "is whether he got it legitimately or not."

"But we can't assume he did or he didn't," he said. "We have to look into this guy pretty closely."

"Yeah," she said, "he's all over the place. Particularly considering he's the one who found the dead little girl."

"And he's psychic?"

"*Psychic* is another word for *charlatan*, so maybe," she said.

Rodney looked at her. "My grandmother had the sight," he murmured in a calm, affable manner.

"Good for her, but she is still dead."

A hard snort came from him on that. "You know, believe it or not," he said, "death comes for all of us. You can do anything you want to avoid it, but death still has your name on its watch list."

"I got no problem with death," she said, "until it comes to people taking children's lives, and then there is no forgiveness."

"Got it," he said. "But back to the psychic."

"You mean charlatan. So what about him?"

"What if he is the real deal?" he said. "What if he actually can help us?"

"Oh. Well, he hasn't helped us yet," she said. "Why would he start now?"

"I don't know," he said, "but he called us on the little girl."

"And she would have been called in within the hour anyway," she said, the fatigue catching up with her. "I don't know if this guy is for us or against us, and, like Colby, I would like to place him securely on one side or the other."

"Not a problem," Rodney said. "I'm here to help."

And he gave her that big, affable overgrown-boy smile. She shrugged and not knowing what else to say, said, "Good. There's lots to do. And someone I need you go pick up for questioning."

SIMON KNEW HE would pay for his actions. "Everything had gone sideways," he muttered over a glass of scotch, sitting on his couch, trying to enjoy the view from his penthouse. He slowly swirled the drink in his hand, as he thought about the repercussions of calling in the little girl's location. Then the gambler's suicide. It had been a hell of a night.

He had connections on all levels, and murmurs in the underbelly had reached him.

An underground group of pedophiles—who passed children between themselves—had alerted the others in the group, when the cops got too close. So far, locations of those bastards eluded Simon. As soon as he had his hands on one, he could break the chain, could share some concise information with the detective then, but finding the weakest link was so much harder now. They closed ranks to keep their little hobby going. They were depraved excuses of humanity.

He took a sip of his scotch and leaned his head back to let the hot liquid burn its way down his throat. He was cold; he was tired, and his mind kept going over and over the fact that *she* had been there.

The detective shouldn't have been there, but he knew in his heart of hearts that, of course, she was there. She'd become his nemesis. At the same time, she'd also become that magnet he couldn't resist. Like a moth to the flame, he knew he would get burned the closer he got, but he just couldn't stop getting closer. In his mind, he could try to convince himself that it was all about the children, all about redemption for the past, but that wasn't even working for him anymore.

Something was magnetic about her. Yet she was abrasive and didn't suffer fools. More than didn't suffer fools, he highly suspected she didn't suffer very much at all in the way of human weakness. But everybody made mistakes, including her. His mind said that if he could find her mistakes, he could use it against her, but his heart told him not to. If it had been anyone else, he wouldn't care.

He stared down at the scotch, remembering the promise he'd made to his grandmother to not head down the same direction a friend of hers had, supposedly a no-good drunk. *Ne pas y aller.* Simon had no recollection of him whatsoever. For that matter, Simon had no recollection of his birth mother either. Yet he vividly remembered his grandmother, who was with him for such a short time, following the abuse with his foster father, only to be yanked into that system again upon the death of his grandmother.

Leaving a ten-year-old boy alone in the world. Vulnerable. Innocent. A victim to be preyed upon. Again. Just like those other kids the detective tried to save.

*Ne pas y aller.* Simon's promise to his grandmother had been easy to make at the age of eight, after suffering at the hands of his abusive foster father. Who knew that decades later, as Simon learned more and more, it was that much harder to separate right from wrong? And, for him, it was almost impossible anymore. The line had become such a knife-edge that he bled every day with the need to stand on that point. He did as much as he could on the right side to make up for every boy, like him, who had been wronged.

He leaned against the window and stared out at the bright morning. The city was stunning in its beauty, the sunrise scene absolutely glorious and rivaled any major city in the world, but, for him, this was home, the only place that felt right. He'd been home in the underbelly, and he was at home in the richness of the world above. The latter he'd worked long and hard to get to. And he had no intention of giving it up. Living behind bars was not for him either. Intriguing detective or not. One last flick of his wrist to toss back the last of the scotch in his glass, he prepared to get through the rest of his day.

HE STARED AT the TV image of his China Doll. How had they found her so soon? He'd thought about a dumpster, and he'd thought about the water. Then he'd decided the back alley was probably better. He studied the school photo on the TV. She looked so happy and so young and innocent. He smiled. "She'd been such fun. But she hadn't lasted. She'd been damaged," he murmured, as he studied the blond curls. He gave a hard laugh at that. But still, there was the missing Leonard, and that little boy was fresh and young, might be a really good replacement for Jason. He'd love that.

They flashed a picture of Leonard up on the TV.

And his heart gave a happy sigh. "Now, all I have to do is find you, Leonard. I'm working on it."

His group had made a pact a long time ago to share and to share alike, but they never actually had. It was like an open rule, where anyone would share, as long as you don't ask to share. But, in this case, he wanted that little boy, and he had no intention of sharing. But he had to find him first. As he stared out the curtained window, he wondered which one of his so-called cohorts in crime had Leonard. And what would it take to buy Leonard.

He wanted him badly. Especially after missing out on the toddler. Why was there no news coverage for him? Was somebody else holding out on him? Because he hadn't heard of Leonard being a guest with any of them.

And that made him angry. As he looked down at his fingers, clenched into balls, he was ready to punch a wall. He'd promised that he would keep the violence down, according to the landlord's dictate that he'd have to leave if he couldn't control himself. He should ask his sister for money again, so he could buy a small place, but she'd already told him no, that she had no money. Maybe that had been true before, but she was pulling in good money now.

At least he thought she was, just no way to tell. He didn't get to go to her place, and she never came to his. That was also one of those unspoken rules. *You're part of my world, only as long as you stay outside of my world.* That he was confined to his little apartment worked most of the time, and only now did he realize that he needed to reach out to grab what he wanted, and he didn't have another place to do that. This was the one place he had that was safe. Sometimes he wished he had a playroom somewhere else. But that took money. At least for something fancier.

He sat down with a pad of paper and wrote down a bunch more thoughts and tidbits to feed his sister. It was important that he keep up their relationship. The only way he could do what he was doing and survive was that tenuous connection to her. Sure, they were blood, and they were connected by his deeds, but, more than that, it was by her curiosity. And he knew to keep feeding it. He'd been doing this for years, for decades, so it was easy to keep going on and on in circles, as if trying to confuse her.

She usually saw through it, but the fact that he was even doing it, he knew that she was puzzled by it. And that was fine. He needed her. And Leonard. He didn't really care about his sister, as long as he could find another way to get a hold of that little boy. Then he was his. He didn't care what pedophile already had Leonard; he would make sure he took him. Now he had to find Leonard before the cops did.

So which of those assholes should he shake down first?

# CHAPTER 12

*Friday Midmorning*

"How is it that possible?" Kate sat here at her desk, in the early morning, sipping her coffee. The selfishness of people stunned her. "An Amber Alert goes out, and people pitch a fit because they were woken up by a text about a child gone missing," she said, shaking her head, staring out the window. It was a dreary Vancouver day, the coastline weather having hit and hit hard.

"Children go missing every day of the year," Lilliana said. "If they aren't personally affected, they don't care."

"Isn't that the truth."

"Don't you have something to work on for the meeting?"

"I do," Kate said. "But I have this nagging thought at the back of my head, and I don't like it."

"Since when is that new," Lilliana said. "You brought all these cases up to the front. Give your head a rest. We have that meeting now, so let's go."

Slowly Kate got to her feet, threw back the rest of her coffee, grabbed her notepad and pen, and walked through the bullpen, past the coffeepot. Lo and behold, there was a little bit left. She quickly drained it into her cup and carried on.

As she sat down in the meeting room, she mulled over

the fact that people from her supposed team were talking to her now, since Colby's lecture. Some still had the same ol' animosity. Back when she'd been a rookie—for a long time—as long as she did everything right, everybody who'd knocked her had eventually come to respect her. She thought she'd use the same tactic here, but, with her added experience, she no longer gave a shit about peer acceptance. And yet, if that were true, why the hell had these last few months been so hard on her?

When Colby walked in, he said, "You better have some news for me." And he looked directly at Kate.

She gave him a wan smile. "Outside of the fact that the little girl is dead, appears to have a broken neck, she was also sickly, so we're waiting on the autopsy report now," she said. "I spoke with the parents. Obviously they're devastated. They have no understanding, even at this point in time, that their little girl is gone," she said quietly.

He nodded. "What about your buddy?"

"I thought these two were picking him up." She turned to look at her other team members.

Colby turned his attention to Rodney and Owen. "Did you?"

"No," he said, "short of having a warrant to go into his place, he is not answering."

Colby shot his gaze back to her. "Will you have any better luck?"

Her eyebrows slowly rose. "I might," she acknowledged, with a nod.

"So, Rodney, you are her sidekick."

Rodney just nodded.

Colby turned his piercing gaze to Owen and Lilliana. "What about the other little boy?"

"He is in the hospital, sedated. He was sexually abused. A little bit of time will heal that physically—the mental, psychological, not likely. The parents are in the hospital with him."

"Good, do we have any DNA, any forensics, anything on the boy?"

"They're on it, but, so far, I haven't heard or seen any report of it."

He pivoted to Kate. "And you? Did you come up with anything regarding the other man who was approaching the child?"

She shook her head. "No, just an impression in my head. I haven't got it down on paper."

"Do you want to work with the sketch artist?"

"Nothing in my head for him to work with."

"I could comment on that," Rodney said from the front. Muttered titters came around room, and she just ignored them.

"People, at the end of the shift, I want something on my desk," snapped Colby. "I want something concrete. If you need to grab some street clothes cops to help with interviews, do so, but we need answers, and we need them today."

Everybody got up but her. Colby looked at her and asked, "What are you up to?"

"I'm going to set up my boards in the conference room. I brought them from home. Then I'm going to try and figure out why these cases were never solved."

He just stared at her.

She shrugged. "I get that we didn't have the links between them before. What I don't get," she said, "is that these dead children cases are still all unsolved."

"Some of them are from a long time ago," he reminded

her. "Don't criticize the teams who have gone before you. We didn't have DNA from any potential suspects. We didn't have countrywide digital connections to other PDs. You know that we have more pending cases to handle that do tend to overshadow the dead-end cold cases. We didn't have a lot of what you have today. The question really is, how long will it take you to solve this now?"

"No clue," she said, "but hopefully by next Monday."

He looked at her in surprise, his eyebrows slowly rising. "Why next Monday?"

She nodded. "I don't know if it's a coincidence or not," she said, "but those children were taken on different days of the week."

"And?"

"They go in cycles," she said. "We've got a Sunday, a Monday, a Tuesday, no Wednesday, and then there is a Thursday, no Friday, a Saturday, and now a Sunday. They are all different weeks, months, and years, but ..." She went through each of them for him, adding, "They are in order, but I can't be sure if I'm connecting them properly."

"Do you think we are missing other cases?"

"Yes, we are missing other cases. Reese is looking at all unsolved for the last thirty years for me," she confirmed. "What I don't know is if another child could go missing on this next Monday, which will be the next day of the cycle. I just don't know *which* Monday."

"Jesus," he said, frowning at that thought. He gave her a quick headshake. "Did you check out those two latest children? Do they fit the pattern? Have the same mark?"

"I checked the little boy that night," she said, with a nod, "but the evening light was really bad, and he was too traumatized. I've asked Forensics Division specifically to have photographs of his wrists."

"Maybe you should go check him yourself."

"I will," she said, but that's the last thing she wanted. That little boy had broken her heart and to see him now, today? If he even remembered her—yet it might be better if he *didn't* remember her—she would never forget him.

"What about the little girl?"

"I didn't see anything, but again," she said, "the same circumstances apply. It could take the autopsy to confirm."

"So you know what to do then, don't you?"

She nodded. "Do I have to take Rodney with me?"

"Is it a problem to have a partner?"

"Sure," she said, "it's like having a leech attached. I do better on my own."

"He doesn't have to go everywhere with you, but he should go when he can."

She gave a quick nod and got up.

As she walked out, he said, "Kate?"

She turned. "Yes?"

"Go easy on him," he said. "They are all good people."

"So am I." And she turned and walked out.

At her desk, she sat down long enough to check her email, realizing she didn't want to even look at the twenty-odd emails sitting there. Logging off her computer, she stood and grabbed her weapon. As she walked to the coatrack, she snatched her vest.

Rodney called out, "Where are we going?"

"To the hospital," she said. "To see the little boy who came in last night."

"The one you picked up?"

She nodded and walked to the door. She didn't care if he came or not, although she preferred to be alone. But, sure enough, the sounds of running feet had him coming up beside her.

"You could wait for me, you know?" he said good-naturedly.

"Or I could go alone," she said, hitting the button on the elevator.

They squeezed in, with the dozen other people in the elevator. When the door opened at the ground floor, it was just like a pressurized can popping, letting the contents spill out. At least she was at the forefront of the spill. Outside, she stopped, looked up at the weather, and smiled.

"You are the only one I know who smiles at the gloomy gray."

"Lots of reasons to smile at the Vancouver sky."

"Maybe, but it's usually not chilly weather that people smile about."

"Who said I'm smiling about that now either?"

He didn't have an answer for that.

At the hospital, she walked in and talked to the receptionist, got a room number, and headed to the stairs.

"We might see the parents here," he said.

"I highly doubt the parents left," she said. And, sure enough, as she shoved her hands into her pockets to walk down the last little bit of the hallway, she shut down on the inside as she prepared to see the little boy. The father stood outside, rubbing his exhausted face. At least she assumed that was his father.

When he looked up and saw them, he frowned immediately.

She reached out a hand and identified herself. "I'm the one who found your son last night."

Immediately the thundercloud in his face cleared, and he

threw his arms around her and hugged her tight. "Thank you, thank you," he whispered brokenly. "Oh my God, we are so grateful to have him back."

She gently disentangled herself. "How is he doing?"

He shook his head. "The doctors don't know. He keeps screaming, so they have him lightly sedated," he said. "He is a little bit awake, but he drifts off to sleep really fast. It's funny but not funny in a way. It's just, whenever he is fully awake, he screams again."

"I'm sorry," she said. "I do have some questions to ask of you."

His shoulders shrugged, and he nodded slowly. "Of course," he said, "the trouble is, I wish you could answer my questions. Like what was he doing on that street corner?" He raised his hands in disgust. "Anybody could have got him there."

She stopped, gave herself a headshake. *Maybe that was the point.* But that was another whole discussion she wanted to sort out in her head. Because this ugly impression was going on in her mind, she didn't quite understand it. "I need to ask you, did you recognize the clothing he was in?"

"Yes, of course. Although the big sweater wrapped around him wasn't his."

"And did the police come and take away all the clothing?"

He nodded. "They said they needed it to check over for forensic evidence."

"And I presume they checked him over too?"

He winced. "They went over his body, with a fine-tooth comb, magnifying glass, and tweezers. That was absolutely degrading."

She reached out a hand, gripped his with hers, and said,

"But remember. It's important. If we find just one hair, ... we might find the person who did this."

He closed his eyes and nodded. "But investigators do that to a dead body, not to my little son," he said, tearing up. He sat down on the bench outside the room, outside the window in the door, and motioned at Kate. "My wife is inside." He sobbed and just curled up and cried.

Leaving him alone, she rapped lightly, then she stepped inside. A woman stood, looked over at her. And Kate explained again who she was. The mother began to cry gently. "Thank you for finding him," she whispered. "We've been just so lost."

Kate walked closer and looked down at the little boy. He was sleeping lightly. She reached out a hand and gently stroked a curl off his temple.

"They didn't seem to have hurt him," his mother said anxiously, "but we haven't had a full report from the doctor."

Kate looked at her. "He was quite bloody when I brought him in," she said. "I don't know the extent or what damage was caused or even if it was his blood that he was covered in." She wished to God it wasn't, but she highly suspected that the sexual assault she already had confirmed had been a large part of it.

"And then there is, you know, that other part that they did to him," the mother said, motioning at her son's lower body, "but he could just forget about that."

Kate stared at her, wondering how that was even possible. She hoped, for the little boy's sake, that he could grow up and forget about what had been done to him. But she highly doubted he would walk away from it as quickly and as calmly as the mother thought.

Just then, the little boy's eyes opened; he looked at his mom and frowned a little bit. Started to whimper. She reached over to him immediately, calming him down—or trying to. "It's okay, baby. It's okay. Mum is here."

He shifted his gaze, saw Kate, and froze. And Kate feared he would start screaming now. She smiled at him and said softly, "Hey, buddy."

Maybe it was her voice, maybe it was just the way she reached down a hand, but tears came to his eyes, yet he didn't scream. Instead he did something that completely shocked her. He reached up his arms to her.

Everybody in the room stiffened. But unable to stop the request of the child, she reached down and hugged him gently. When she tried to stand back, he locked his arms around her neck, so that, as she straightened, he came up with her. He just cuddled in close, and she held him.

"Oh my God," his mother said, tears in her eyes. "He remembers you."

Kate looked over at Rodney, who stared at her in surprise. She felt awkward holding the child; she had zero experience with children. But just something was so needy about this one, and that broke her heart. She held him close for a long moment and then whispered, "I think your mother needs a hug too."

He looked up at Kate, looked over at his mother, who stood shaking, emotions racking her soul.

Kate walked around the bed, so he was closer to his mother, and he held out his arms, and his mother snatched him up, sat down in a chair with him in her arms, and just bawled. Kate looked at the empty bed, where the child had been, and looked at the mother and then back at Rodney, as if to say, *Now what?*

Rodney smiled at her—one of the truest smiles she'd ever seen on his face, at least directed at her—and he said, "That was a lovely thing to do." She looked up at him in surprise. And he motioned to the mother, who desperately hung on to her son.

Thankfully it looked like the little boy was also hanging on to his mother.

Kate sighed softly. "We'll come back another time," she said to the mother, but Kate was pretty-damn sure the mother hadn't even heard her. As Kate and Rodney stepped out of the doorway, realizing absolutely no answers were to be found here, she noted the father still sobbed at the bench. She reached down a hand, and he looked up startled.

She said, "You might want to go in and see your wife." He bolted to his feet and walked in. She turned in time to see the look on his face, when he saw his son holding on to his wife. And he jumped forward and snatched both of them into his arms.

Kate turned and walked away, once again shoving her hands in her pockets, as if that would lighten the blow of all those emotions running amok inside her. As she walked toward the elevators, Rodney said, "You dealt with her really well."

"Depending on what you mean by *dealt with*," she said. "It's not like we got any answers."

"What answers were you looking for?"

"Ones I've got actually, the little boy has the same mark," she said thoughtfully having seen the little boy's arms. She hit the button on the elevator panel that led to the morgue. Rodney stepped up beside her.

"Are we are going to see the coroner?"

She nodded. "Unless you've got something to do?"

"No, I'm totally okay to tag along."

"Well, if you get any leads," she said, "I'll be happy to tag along with you too."

He grinned at her. "This seems to be your show."

"Not my show," she said quietly. "I just feel I don't have any choice in the matter."

"That's how we all feel," he said. "You are not alone in this."

"Maybe," she said, "but sometimes it feels like it."

"And we get that," he said, "but that stage is over."

"Hope so." She didn't say anymore. At the basement, she checked in the coroner's office, but it was empty. As she walked past another office, she saw two people inside, talking. She stopped and asked, "Dr. Smidge?"

One of them just pointed her farther down the hall and turned back to their chattering. Following the direction given, she reached the autopsy room. As she pushed open the door, a buzzer went off inside the room, a warning for those working.

Smidge's voice rapped out, "No visitors."

She popped her face around the corner and said, "Unless you are working on my cases."

He looked up, frowned, and then nodded. "You can come in," he said, "but gown up."

She nodded, headed off to the side, pulled on a gown off a hook on the wall, scrubbed down, and snapped on gloves. As she joined the coroner, he had the little girl stretched out on the table, a sheet up to her collarbones. The doc worked on her head. Something was so devastating again about that tiny little body. So fragile and so broken. She felt Rodney's disquiet at her side. "She looks ethereal, like a fairy tale princess."

The coroner looked up and asked, "You have anything more for me?"

"No," she said. "The same early morning hours when we found this little girl," she said, "I found a little boy alive, about an hour earlier."

His eyebrows shot up. "I'm glad to hear that," he said. "I have more than enough work of my own, you know?"

"Oh, I know," she said. "I get it. Unfortunately there seems to be a never-ending supply of work for both of us."

"Isn't that a sad truth."

"Do you have a cause of death yet?"

"Broken neck," he said, "but she was a very sick little girl to begin with."

"In what way?"

"She has damage to her pancreas and undiagnosed diabetes."

"Interesting," she murmured, looking down at the pale white skin of the little girl. "Do you have a time of death?"

"I do," he said. "You're not gonna like it."

"Why is that?"

"Because it was several days ago. I would say anywhere from forty-eight to seventy-two hours."

She stared at him in shock. "What?"

"Yes," he said, "whoever had her, kept her for a couple days."

She stared down at the little girl. "Why?"

"I don't know why," he said, "but her body sat in one position, seated, until rigor left," he said. "We've still got a lot of lividity all around her lower buttocks and thighs, where she was sat up."

"Sat up?"

"My bet would be that she was propped up on a chair or

a couch."

Just a vision of a dead child sitting on a couch with her gave her the creeps. She shot a sidelong glance at Rodney to see the same disgust on his face. "Anything else you can give me?" she asked Smidge. "What about the same mark?"

"Yes, a single line. Other than that there's not a whole lot here to find," he said. He looked down at the little girl, then back at Kate and said, "You better find this asshole."

"I plan on it. I hope to not only find the perp but to add him to your work list," she snapped. With that, she turned and headed over to the door, removing her gown. She put it into the laundry bin and stormed off. She didn't care if Rodney followed or not. All she wanted was to be alone. Alone in a world where dead children didn't stare at her and where loved ones didn't cry out and reach for her.

As soon as she got outside to the fresh air, she stopped, took several deep breaths, Rodney calling out to her, behind her. She turned to face him. "What?"

He shook his head. "Why did you bolt like that?"

"Temper," she said easily. "I want to find this guy, so I can wring his neck, just like he wrung that little girl's neck. He doesn't deserve more."

SIMON SAT AT the breakfast table, the newspaper open in front of him. He had several monitors set up, facing him. He dealt in commodities, stocks, and real estate. After checking his regular reports, he went back to checking his emails. Always hundreds in a day. But then he had a lot of projects on the go, involving lots of people. He checked his watch, running late again. He tossed back his coffee.

Once dressed, he headed out again without breakfast. He'd tried to sleep, had woken up shortly thereafter, the same little boy screaming in his ears, followed by the little boy the detective had saved, as he'd seen on TV at the hospital this morning, then the little girl he'd found dead. All the time, he heard his ex-fiancée screaming about her nephew. He didn't know what the hell was going on, but his mind was focused on child to child to child.

Somewhere in there was the ghost child of the past; Simon just didn't understand why now. What was it about these children that kept him awake at night? He pushed open the stairwell door to the lobby of his apartment building and strode to the front door. The doorman called out a good morning. Simon lifted a hand in greeting and stepped out into the street.

He was a couple blocks from Starbucks and a block over from a favorite sandwich shop. Contemplating a breakfast sandwich, he decided to hit his first building project.

His foreman waited for him. He nodded, smiled in greeting. "Wasn't sure if you'd make it."

"I said I'd be here," Simon said. They studied the building and the blueprints.

"We're ninety percent complete on stage one. It's going well."

"Well enough. Let me know when you get the last of the framing done. Then we'll get on to the next stage." Content with the progress on this project, he headed down to the next. Passing the Starbucks, he popped in to grab himself a coffee. At the second project, he once again found problems. This one had been beset by problems since the beginning. Some projects just wouldn't finish on budget.

After seeing the crap of the existing plumbing in this old

building, Simon okayed a complete and full redo. The last thing he needed was ongoing plumbing problems on the many new apartments that would soon be here. Better to fix the issue now, before it caused further damage.

By the time he finished with the third building assessment, a refinish of an old apartment building, his stomach was growling. He looked around for a place to stop and to grab a bite. But not really seeing anything that caught his eye, he headed to the fourth project, and he wasn't alone. He blamed a lack of sleep and food for his dulled senses. He dealt with the problems at the fourth project and turned around to see somebody in plainclothes approaching him. From all outward appearances, he was a cop through and through.

Simon stopped and waited. "What can I do for you?"

"I've been following you all morning, trying to catch you," he said. "I wouldn't have to, but you've refused to return my calls."

Simon looked at him in surprise. "So you've resorted to following me?"

"We have some questions."

And, with that, his heart sank, and his jaw firmed. "I don't have anything to do with anything," he said, turning his back on the detective.

"You found the little girl on the street and called it in."

"You guys are a good reason to never do that again," he said.

"Maybe if you'd called her in earlier, she'd be still alive."

That was a low blow and wasn't helpful because that little girl was dead and had been for a while. But it wasn't for Simon to explain the guy's job to him. "Nothing more to tell you," Simon said. "I walked home from a poker game and saw something gleaming in the moonlight, found a little girl. I called it in. That's the end of it."

"Where was your poker game?"

He gave him the address. "Just a group of friends but feel free to check it out." He gave him a bunch of the names of the guys who had been there, carefully avoiding the cheater. So far, no one had said anything to him about that related incident.

"Fine," he said. "I'll check that out. What are you doing with all these buildings that you keep checking in on?"

Simon stopped, looked at him, and said, "They are my building projects. Is that against the law too?"

The detective just stared back at him, a blank look on his face.

"And how come Detective Morgan isn't on the case?" Simon asked in a derisive tone. "Or did she get pulled off for being too close to the cases?"

"She is dealing with the children right now," he said. "Like the little girl you found last night."

"And you're not?"

"No, I'm trying to figure out how you came upon the body."

"Well, I didn't know it was there ahead of time, if that's what you're asking," Simon said. "And, if you have any other questions for me, call my lawyer."

"Why do you need a lawyer?"

"Apparently I need a lawyer because of you," he said. And, with that, he strolled off again. He knew it was the wrong thing to get involved, but how could he not? Every decent human had to have a good side, and he had more than a few good qualities; he just preferred to keep them hidden. And cops had a habit of digging until they found shit that Simon didn't want them to find. Just another reason to avoid that lovely detective and everything she stood for.

Seeing a lunch spot ahead, Simon quickly dashed across the road and left the detective staring at him. He didn't care if he followed him all day or not.

From the looks of him, he could use the exercise.

———— ∽∽ ————

KEN, THAT'S WHO he'd check out first. He looked at the list of first names that he had written down. Ken lived the closest to him. They liked to talk on their private chat on the dark web. He knew Ken was in the downtown Vancouver area, while a couple guys were out in the valley, and one was even in Richmond. But Ken was close. That made him a really good place to start.

But he didn't have a photo or much else to track him down. Just a few tidbits gleaned from their conversations, where Ken often commented on walking to Stanley Park. It was one thing to have someone by the university, or maybe over by the Richmond International Airport, but close to downtown? That wasn't cool. That meant the two of them were hunting the same grounds; why hadn't he considered that before? He tapped his foot angrily on the floor. "Like hell I want competition that close by."

His notes said that Ken preferred boys. So another problem, as he himself liked boys. He liked girls too, but he didn't want Ken hunting the same boys.

As he sat here, he got angrier and angrier. If, for no other reason, he should go find Ken, kick him out of the city. Besides he'd be helping the cops now, wouldn't he? And, if he happened to find Leonard in the process, even better. He studied his list. It was incomplete. A bunch of people in the group didn't say anything at all. And, of course, it was a small group, which was a little disturbing too because what if other pedophiles were in the area that he didn't know about?

And, of course, there were. It seemed like pedophiles were on every corner. Now how could he find them? He knew in the US, they tracked pedophiles on a nation wide website, but Vancouver hadn't adopted that system yet. What the police didn't realize down south was that they were actually helping pedophiles to find other pedophiles, so they could join together in the hunt for more kids. Or pass around used goods. Although most pedophiles didn't want to share, and that fear and need for secrecy that surrounded what they were doing often caused them to maintain a very isolated lifestyle.

If he dug deep enough, he could always find court documents that would give more information. But it didn't always tell you where the defendants were living, after they had been released. And that would be helpful. At most the paperwork would give a town or a city but not street addresses.

Now to see Ken's neighborhood. He put on his boots and grabbed his jacket and his list and his wallet. He had a pretty good idea of Ken's favorite haunts. He talked about them all the time. Like a restaurant called Stevie's Place. He would check that out first. See if he could spot him.

Besides, he was hungry; he checked his wallet and still found twenty bucks cash. That would be enough for a meal. He didn't even remember the last time he ate more than bread and peanut butter. He frowned, picked up a can of Coke, opened it, and walked out of his tiny apartment, carrying his drink.

He used to live in much nicer places, was raised in a mansion. Getting back to that lifestyle would be impossible without help, like from his family. His sister had helped for a long time but not now. He wondered if she was still as broke as she said she was. Hardly. He should go to her place, just to make sure that she was still living at the same level as he was.

He doubted it, and it was okay if she were a little better off, but he wouldn't tolerate a ton better. That was just wrong. They were twins, siblings in mind and nature too. He should be doing as well as she was. Sure, he hadn't gone to school, and he hadn't gotten a medical degree, like she had. But that didn't mean he didn't have something good to offer.

He was just in between jobs now. It pissed him off when people said that he needed an education, that his experience wasn't anywhere near as good. He knew they were wrong. Experience was worth its weight in gold. And screw all these people who didn't believe him.

Stevie's Place was a hamburger joint that stayed open late every day of the week, in one of the worst areas in town. Known for large portions, good food, and cheap prices. He could do much worse than having dinner here tonight. A big chalkboard was outside, with a handwritten menu on it. The prices had jumped. His twenty bucks could still buy him a meal, but it would no longer buy him anything he wanted. And that pissed him off too.

"What can I get you?" asked the gum-chewing young woman with brassy hair, who looked like she'd seen way too much of the world already.

He gave her a half smile. "Just figuring out what appeals

tonight."

"Well, there is the steak burger," she said. "That's to-night's special. It comes with fries."

He looked at it and said, "That's pretty reasonable."

"It is," she said. "It's the biggest burger you ever saw. The fries are decent too."

"Can I get gravy on the fries and pickles on the burger?"

"Comes with the pickles," she said, writing it down. "Gravy is an extra buck."

With that decided, he ordered his dinner and grabbed the number that she gave him and headed off to find a table. Stevie's had tables on the sidewalk as well as inside. The rain had cleared, so he sat just under the overhang. It was warm with his jacket on, but it was a nice place to sit and to watch the world go by. He hadn't ordered a drink to go with his burger, so he just sat here, sipping his Coke. People came. People went. It was just that kind of an evening.

No children were out now, nothing to put a smile on his face. Everybody was eighteen and over, except for maybe a couple little chicks hanging around the corner. They looked like they were sixteen, maybe dolled up to look like they were twenty. But the look in their eyes said they were heading to forty.

Being a hooker at that age was hard. It sucked the life right out of you, turned your body into an ancient organic waste dump, and took your soul and spit it out in pieces. Good thing he hadn't had to resort to that kind of a life. Nothing over the age of eleven appealed to him at all. That was just gross.

When he heard his number called, he looked to see a big platter of food set off to the side on the front counter. He got up with his number, took it over, and exchanged his number for the plate, adding ketchup on the side, taking his plate with a fork outside to his table. He stared down at the food in amazement. It was a lot of food; he was lucky if he could eat it all. Maybe he could take it home for tomorrow. Leftovers were gold in his world. He didn't cook but had a microwave, so that was his lifeline.

He picked up half the burger and took a big bite, munching, as he watched the world go by. Down at the end of the block, he studied a man who approached. Just something about him set his jaw back a little bit. He chewed on his burger, slowly watching the man's progress. He looked at the girls with interest, talking to them in a cheeky, flirting manner, as if he were some friendly uncle.

Friendly uncles like that, he knew all too well.

They ended up being the kind who coerced little kids into their bed. He should know; he was that kind of friendly uncle. And he recognized another who was just the same.

It wasn't long before the same guy approached one of the other girls on the opposite corner, laughed, gave her a dollar, for whatever reason because it's not like it would buy her a coffee. It sure as hell wouldn't put more clothes on her body. Then the man stepped into Stevie's.

Watching him, he followed the stranger's progress, as he walked up to the counter and placed an order, without even looking at the menu. That's how often he came here.

He slowly worked his way through the first half of his burger, keeping an eye on the man.

The friendly uncle walked over, chose a table closer to the wall but still on the outside patio. Soon the uncle's order was ready. After he picked it up, he fixed his burger. He lifted the top bun, added ketchup and mustard, extras of both, took the pickle and tossed it off to the side.

Already he knew what kind of a guy this uncle was. Anybody who didn't eat pickles on his burger was wrong. He watched as the uncle squashed down the burger, picked it up, and gently took a bite. No big bite for him. No, it was all little tiny nibbles. And why was that? Burgers were meant to be chewed with gusto. Anything less was sacrilegious.

He sat here, eating his fries, as he watched the uncle. Realizing the fries needed salt, he grabbed the salt and gave a liberal shaking of it over his fries and then tasted them. Much better. By the time he finished his fries, the other guy had finally finished his burger.

He looked down at the other half of his burger still on his plate and decided he'd take it back with him. He got up and walked to the counter with it in his hand, and the same girl at the counter gave him a small container. He quickly transferred the last half of his burger to it, thanked her, and walked back outside.

As he passed the uncle, he studied his trench coat that had once been a high-end piece but was now older and had dragged the ground for too many years. He had big shoes that looked to be a little too big, and his pants, instead of fitting nicely at the top, scrunched over. So secondhand clothes all the way. He tried to look nice, but he was down on his luck and had been for a long time.

That's all right; he understood that too. As long as this uncle stayed out of his fucking way, it was all good.

As he walked past, he said, "Hey, Ken."

The man froze, then spun to see who'd called out to him. But he was too slow.

Standing at the corner of the restaurant, he watched as Ken nervously wolfed down the rest of his food. Then he sat back down outside with his Coke and waited until Ken finished his meal and got up and left. But he didn't go the way he'd come. He headed up the block.

He waited until Ken disappeared out of sight, before he rose and followed.

The city wasn't big enough for both of them. But he needed to know if Ken had Leonard first.

# CHAPTER 13

*Saturday, Wee Hours of the Morning*

"HEY, WE'VE GOT a new one," Rodney said into her phone.

Kate groaned and rubbed the sleep from her eyes. "What time is it?" She sat up in bed, realizing she was still half dressed.

"It's four-thirty."

"Great," she said. "When do we ever get a full night's sleep?"

"Not tonight, that's for sure," he said, "I'll meet you at Drake and Howe again."

"Shit, another one there in that same area?" She closed her eyes at the thought. "Please tell me that it's not a kid."

"It's not a kid." And he hung up on her.

She still didn't have time for a shower, so she hopped into the rest of her clothes, picked up her harness, buckled in her weapon, grabbed her jacket to cover it up, and wished she had time to even make coffee, but she didn't, which considering she had yet to get to a grocery store it wouldn't have made any difference. She walked out of her apartment, locking it behind her, hopped into her vehicle, and headed to the location. Parking was easy at this time of the night—early morning really—but she made sure that her vehicle could remain easily in her line of sight, as she inspected the crime scene. She stepped out to see street cops putting yellow tape around the area to keep the growing crowd back. Where had they all come from at this hour?

When she walked over, she noted Rodney standing by the body; he lifted a hand in greeting. At his side, she looked down. "Homeless man?"

"I don't think so," he said. "What would make you think that?"

"Clothes are too big. Boots are too long. Coat doesn't fit either." She added, "Looks like he hasn't shaved in a couple days."

"But the clothes are well-made," he said. "They are pretty high-end."

"Yeah, he used to afford them, but now he can't. So either these are somebody else's clothes or from a secondhand shop."

"Okay," he said. "I didn't even see that the pants were too big."

"And they hang down too long. The back of the pants scuffed along the sidewalk." She walked around the victim, looked at him, and asked, "Strangled?"

"Looks like it. No bullet wounds, no bleeding, and no blood splatter anywhere."

"Coroner?"

"On his way."

Just then the vehicle pulled up. She looked up to see Dr. Smidge.

He got out, glared at her, and said, "I told you to stop bringing me work."

"Well, I was trying to stop bringing you children," she said, "but I'm not able to stop the flow of work. That's beyond anybody."

He gave a sad smile and nodded. He looked down at the victim. "Interesting." And then he crouched beside him, pulled back his eyelids.

Kate asked, "Petechial hemorrhage?"

"Absolutely. Finger marks all around the neck too. Looks like two hands."

"That's not easy," she said. "Takes a bit of strength to manually strangle someone."

"No, it isn't easy. Using something—like a wire, a scarf, anything—would be easier."

"He is a big guy," she said. "What is he? Six-one, maybe six-two?"

"Possibly, I'll know more when I get him on the table." He stood, sighed. "Interesting time of night for it."

"Yeah, as in, what was he doing out here? Time of death?"

"Probably not more than a couple hours," he said looking around. "Which means, at first estimate, knowing you can't quote me on this, I'll say since two o'clock."

"Restaurants and pubs?" she asked, turning to Rodney. "This area, this day of the week, when do they close?"

"At one-thirty a.m.," he said, "but there are a couple coffee shops that stay open late around the place."

She nodded. "Good enough. We'll start knocking on doors and see if anybody saw this."

"Cameras? We need to check the street cams," Rodney said, as he stopped to look around.

"Yeah," she said. "This is an alleyway though, so I'm not sure there will be any coverage."

"Not far from here is a good restaurant," the coroner said. "It's open all night long."

"That's good to know. I'll check it out."

"It looks like he's still got particles of fries and hamburger in his mouth," he said, "and I can smell it on him."

"I'll head back to the street and take a look then," she said. "ID?"

"I'll check that for you." He pulled out the wallet from the back pocket of the dead body and handed it to Rodney.

"Ken Roscoe," Rodney said, and he gave her the driver's license. She quickly wrote down the number and handed the DL back. "Let me see the rest of that wallet."

Rodney laid the contents on the victim's belly, so she could photograph it.

"Cash totaling fifteen eighty-two, one credit card—but it's expired, at least in his real name—and that's about it." She looked up at Rodney. "Like I said, he was down on his luck."

"Okay, okay," he said. "Message received."

"Doc, does he have his own teeth?"

The doc checked, his finger inside the victim's mouth and nodded. "Appears to be."

"And they are in good shape, aren't they?"

"They are," he said. "What are you getting at?"

"Just makes me wonder how recent his fall from grace was," she said, as she straightened up. "Check the back of the coat collar for a brand name. Some places in town still customize and even tailor jackets," she said, "and that's very high quality, that one."

"It is," the coroner said, and he tugged the collar to the side. "It says, *Custom Made for James.*"

"Too bad his name isn't James."

"Anything in his pockets?"

They checked the coat pockets, pulled out a few more bits of change, and that was it.

She sighed. Nothing useful. She watched Smidge check the body over. She stopped and leaned closer. "What's on his wrist?" Holding her phone's flashlight over the dead guy's wrist, highlighting the shadows, she could barely see. "Please don't tell me that's the same mark."

He looked closer, then at her, back at the mark, and said, "Damn it. You know something? I think you're right."

"What mark?" Rodney asked, blustering forward.

She held the wrist in such a way that he saw. "This mark," she said. "It's been on every one of those child victims."

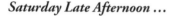

### Saturday Late Afternoon ...

SIMON WALKED INTO the casino, more unsettled than he wanted to acknowledge. Something was seriously wrong in his world, and he didn't know what had happened. He'd been a different person these last few days, and he didn't know who or what to blame. But he wanted a target, so he could beat it into little pieces.

His grandmother's voice slipped into his mind. *Once you start down this pathway ...*

"Screw that," he snapped. *Ne pas y aller.* He shrugged away that voice and the other messages, all pounding inside his skull, as he squeezed the yellow ball in his pocket, like some stress ball. He didn't even know why he felt compelled to phone in that first murder of the hopped-up husband killing his wife with a knife. Except that Simon knew for sure that it was a murder and that the asshole husband could get off scot-free if Simon *didn't* tell the cops. But he'd seen other assholes in the past do things that he knew needed to be turned in, so why hadn't he back then?

Everything was different now, and he didn't know why. Since when had he grown a conscience? And here he was, tonight, trying to shake it off and to lose himself in what he knew was comfortable and normal for him. As he walked through the carpeted craziness, with games going on around him, a friend of his called out.

"Simon, over here."

He looked over to find Reggie, sitting at the bar, having a drink. Feeling like that just might be the perfect answer, Simon walked over. "Hey, I haven't seen you in months. What? Six, seven, or more?"

"Maybe," Reggie said, with a tilt of his head. "It seems like you're here, and then you're gone. I don't know what the hell you've been up to lately, but you are never really here."

"I've been to a few private games," Simon said, with a shrug. "But, other than that, I've been busy."

"Busy doing what?" Reggie asked, with a smirk. "You don't work, just like I don't work."

"How the hell did we end up getting a lifestyle like that?" Simon asked, as he turned to the bartender and cocked his finger to get a whiskey.

"You hitting the hard stuff right off the bat, huh?" Reggie noted.

"It feels like a whiskey night," Simon said. In fact, that might be the fastest way to get drunk. And he was up for that. Anything to help him forget the changes in his world.

"Obviously something is wrong," Reggie said, snickering. "You only hit the whiskey when things are bad."

"Oh, well now, that's really nice," he said, mocking him. "Come on. It's the drink of choice in the evenings."

"Yeah, but you are not at home. You are not in your own bed, and you're sure as hell not tucked up and ready to go to sleep."

"No," he said recklessly. "I'm here to play and to play hard."

"Poker?"

He thought about it, and he didn't even want that anymore. Typically it was his game; it was how he won. He looked at the craps tables and said, "Maybe I'll try that tonight."

Reggie's eyebrows shot up. "Wow, it must be a really bad time in your life. You've always been very adamantly against the craps table."

"Maybe that's because I haven't tried it," he said. He didn't want to lose a ton of money tonight, but, at the same time, recklessness rode him hard. He walked over to the front table and watched the game go down. With Reggie at his side, they both placed bets, and, when Simon won, he snatched up the money, placed more bets indiscriminately. He won half, lost half, until he saw a sequence to the pattern, and he started playing more strategically. As he won more, the crowd behind him grew. Again and again and again.

Finally he placed it all on one number, staring at it because he knew it was the detective's badge number, the badge of the very cop who wouldn't leave him alone. The detective who was on his mind when he went to sleep and the same detective who was on his mind when he woke up. He'd memorized her badge number when she had flashed it for him: 9726. He placed everything on black 26 because he knew, as sure as hell, that one would be dark for his soul.

And when he threw the dice, the crowd erupted all around him. He stared in shock because he'd just quadrupled his earnings and had made more money tonight than he'd made in the last six months.

Reggie said quickly, "Damn. I don't know what the hell got into you tonight, but that was some serious craziness."

"It was," he murmured, just as unsettled now as he had been when he had arrived, only now he was disturbed for a completely different reason. He needed to get out of here and fast. He looked over at Reggie and said, "I was planning to stay and to close down the place, but I think I'll head home instead."

And again Reggie just studied him quietly. "Anytime you want to talk, you know you can, right?"

Simon gave a hard nod. "Thanks, I'm fine." He quickly handled the money aspect, getting a cashier's check in his name. Then left the place and, instead of walking, hailed a cab. He didn't want to take a chance with the check in his pocket. As he headed back to his place, he tipped the driver generously, got out, and walked into the front foyer. The doorman quickly opened the door, before he got there. "You weren't out long, were you?" Harry said. "I figured you wouldn't return until after my shift was over."

"I wasn't expecting to be back this early either."

"Well, that cop was here looking for you," Harry said.

"Which cop?" he asked cautiously, but he knew. Darn, he already knew.

"The one who was here before, Detective Morgan or something."

"Ah," he said, "did she say anything?"

He shook his head. "She said she would phone you later."

Simon nodded. Maybe that was partly what drove him, what had him so edgy. Maybe he knew that call was coming.

The problem with having a strong intuition, as he called it, was that it was just enough to get you in trouble, yet not enough to get you out. He would cheerfully never use his abilities again, if he could. But the fact of the matter was, something was going on, and his abilities had suddenly gotten stronger—and a little bit wilder. He had a connection to her that he hadn't seen and didn't know what to do with.

As soon as he got inside his penthouse apartment, he put away the cashier's check and reached for the open bottle of wine but stopped midway. Frowning, he walked over to the decanter on the side and poured himself a stiff whiskey. He headed to the couch, put down his glass, and threw himself atop the cushions.

"What the hell?" he said, reaching out both hands and rubbing his face. "It's like I'm not even the same person anymore. But, if I'm not the old Simon, who the hell am I?"

Because he'd spent his lifetime being multiple Simons: the one the public saw, the one his foster family saw, the one anybody with any psychic energy saw, and then the one the business people saw. He hid behind different personalities in order to make his world move. But the one personality he didn't let anybody see was the one deep inside. Even his girlfriends and ex-fiancée hadn't seen that one. And, speaking of which, he pulled out his phone and sent Caitlin a text, asking if her nephew had been found. The response came back brutally **No**.

"Shit," he said. He tossed his phone on the coffee table and stared blindly outside his windows at the lights of the night.

# CHAPTER 14

*Sunday Morning*

T HE NEXT DAY, Kate tore out of bed early, had a hot shower, and walked to work. Thankfully she only lived a couple blocks away. As soon as she got in, she realized how damn early it was. Not a soul was here. She perked up at that idea, headed over to put on a pot of coffee. She stood beside it to make sure nobody would come in and steal it from her. As soon as it dripped enough to fill her cup, she strolled back to her desk. She grabbed the new notebook she had been using and headed to the board, where she had posted all the names and related data from the other cases. This was a duplicate of the one she had at home.

With those details up, she added a couple new ones, including the one regarding Ken Roscoe, the subject of her recent conversation with the coroner. That one made absolutely no sense. And it really bothered her. There were ever-so-slight differences between the tattoos, but his was so faint that it was hard to see. It's almost as if there was a line differentiating some of them. She studied them for a long moment, hating the feeling that she was missing something obvious here.

Finally she stepped back and sat down at her desk. The autopsy reports weren't in on the little girl nor the adult male. She shook her head. But the new case bothered her.

And what was with that little girl? Until Kate got the autopsy report, she didn't have anything to move on. Street cops had canvassed the area, and nobody had seen anything. But then, nobody ever sees anything, she mused.

She sat back and checked on the night shift details. A peaceful night, thank God.

In a big city like Vancouver, fewer murders happened here than one often suspected, but still an awful lot of unexplained deaths occurred, so they had to check them all first, until the facts were ascertained, and the forensics were in. She also couldn't shake off the 9-1-1 call, reporting a man who had stabbed his wife to death. And that had been weeks ago.

According to all the neighbors, they had a decent relationship, and, every once in a while, they had some really bad fights. Nobody seemed to be surprised at the death, but some people seemed to think he had done it deliberately. Yet, until the forensics or coroner's reports came back, it was hard to say. She wondered how anybody ever managed to close their cases, since nobody ever saw anything.

Just then Rodney walked in. He stopped, took a look at her, and frowned. She frowned right back. He grinned. "You're getting pretty cheeky."

"I am?" she asked quizzically. "I didn't do jack shit."

"Nope," he said, "you're just being you."

"What else is new?" she said.

"Being you is a good thing," he said. He walked over, poured himself a cup of coffee, and said, "There is some advantage in you getting in early. At least there is coffee."

"Not necessarily," she said. "Depends on how much I drink before you drag your sorry ass in."

When he returned with his coffee and sat down at his

desk, she got up and refilled hers. As she hit her desk again, the others started to file in. She studied their faces; Andy and Owen looked like they had had very bad nights. Lilliana was bright and chipper, as always.

Kate sat back down, when Colby walked in and called a meeting. "Look, people. We need to get onto this missing child mess," he said. "We need answers before the press crucifies us." He stopped, looked down at Kate. "Do you have any update on the other cases?"

"Only in that Reese found two more," she said in a quiet voice. "The adult DB we picked up yesterday has a similar mark on the wrist."

At that, the rest of the room stilled. "The same mark?"

"Close enough," she confirmed. "It's more faded, so it's harder to see, but the coroner showed it to us. Rodney was there with me," she said, turning to look at her assigned sidekick.

Rodney nodded. "It appears to be so, yes."

"They are all exactly the same?"

She turned to Colby and shrugged. "No," she said. "Not exactly. They are at the base, and then some of them have an extra line or two on them."

"Have any idea what that means?"

"Not yet," she said. "But I will."

"He's actively connected to how many other children's cases?"

"We have found nine unsolved," she said. "Reese is still looking."

"Sounds like there might be a whole lot of cases we can close then," Owen said. "Providing we actually solve these."

She turned to him and frowned. "Not unless we have DNA that convicts him."

"But that's the connection," he protested, with his hand out. "What else are you looking for?"

"I'm not looking for anything," she said. "I'm open to seeing whatever the evidence shows us."

"Are you thinking someone else is involved?" Colby asked.

She hesitated, knowing all eyes were on her. "Yes," she finally said. "I don't know exactly how to explain it."

"Oh, here we go, the cop with the gut," Owen snapped.

Surprisingly Rodney defended her.

"Look," Rodney said. "We've all had opportunities when our guts overruled our brain," he said. "If she thinks something more is to it, then let her keep digging."

"Sure, but we have other cases too," Owen said. "This sounds like he's good for a lot of these."

"Like our victim from this morning. Finding out he's a registered pedophile opens the suspect list," she said. "Do we really not want to know about any other cases he might have been connected to?"

"Not to mention we can't close them, just assuming he's responsible to make it easy," Rodney continued. "Vancouver has hundreds of registered pedophiles. Any number of them could be involved."

"I was looking for somebody to help fill in the details," she said quietly. "The one I'm thinking of works in the Cold Case Division."

Colby stared at her for a moment and nodded slowly. "We need to know," he said. "Bring in whoever you think can help. Make it a priority."

She gave a clipped nod. "Will do, sir."

After the meeting, she headed to the Cold Case Division. She had a list of files she wanted to talk about with one of the detectives.

"Detective Morgan, nice to meet you." Detective Isaac St. Johns sat at the front desk, several folders to his side. His weary gaze matched the gray hair on his head, both speaking volumes about what he'd seen. "So, you are the one who contacted me about a couple of these cases, huh?"

She nodded and held out the case numbers. "We're considering a connection to a registered pedophile found dead early this morning."

He put down his pencil, steepled his fingers together, and stared at her for a moment. "Grab a seat, and tell me what you've got," he said, as she sat down beside him. She quickly went through the little bit of evidence they had. He shook his head. "So, one thing that ties them together is the mark?"

"Take a look," she urged.

He frowned at her and started pulling up information on the case files. "These photos are pretty indistinct."

"They are," she admitted. "Until you look at the left hand on the inside of the wrist." He clicked through several of the digital photos, until he found one that gave him a little bit of a mark. "That just looks like a scratch," he said, looking over at her.

"Bring up the next case file."

He brought up the old digital case files that he had access to. He saw exactly the same looking scratch. By the time he saw the third one, he turned and glared at her.

She shrugged. "I wouldn't have seen it, but I was looking at a bunch of others."

"This is insane," he said. "How many have you connected?"

"With these same scratches, about nine so far. But then,

we aren't done yet."

"And you are thinking they are all his?"

"I don't know," she admitted. "But these child abductions and subsequent deaths belong at the feet of someone."

SIMON HAD TRIED to reach out intuitively to Leonard again tonight, but it was no good. Somehow wanting to do something was completely different than actually doing it. He could only hope the boy was okay.

And that the detective would find Leonard in time.

The last thing Simon wanted to do was talk to this detective. She wasn't good for his peace of mind, and neither was she good for his work apparently. Although his performance tonight at the craps table had been spectacular, he was still a little disturbed by the push to play a game he'd never tried before. And, for the profit, he'd taken an incredible risk, something he didn't do lightly. Until now, since he was apparently somebody different these days. He poured himself another shot of whiskey, and, as he went to sit back down again, management called, saying the detective was downstairs.

"*Great*," he mumbled. "I will come down and talk to her."

"She wants to come up."

"Fine," he snapped. "She can come up." Slamming down the phone, he walked over to the door. At the door, he waited for it to open, leaning against the doorjamb, trying to settle his nerves. The last thing he would do was let her know how much she rattled him. At the same time, something was just so off at present that he had to guard himself as well.

With defenses firmly in place, he turned to face the elevator.

HE WOULDN'T BE living in these shitty digs if he had money. His sister had the money. That was a minor issue. That was just an irritant between siblings. Even if she did have a fancy Belleview mansion, what could he do about it? She should be making decent money with her education. She was the one who had gone to school; he, on the other hand, had been so used to his lifestyle that he wasn't at all interested in changing it. But now things were getting a little bit tighter, a little bit uglier, and that was changing everything.

He stared down at the names of pedophiles on his list, then drew a stroke through Ken's name. He remembered how much Ken had to say, before he'd taken the man's life. And there had been a certain satisfaction, almost justification, in purging the world of a seriously sad member of society. He didn't believe he was above Ken by any means. But, even within the hierarchy of the type of people they were, some pervs deserved respect, and some didn't. Ken was at the bottom of the list. He was no longer a problem, and that was a good thing. Good riddance. The police should be thanking him.

It had been odd killing him though. Harder than he had expected, until he climbed onto his chest, so Ken couldn't expand his chest either, couldn't inhale anymore.

He looked at the others on his list. There was a person he could ask next, but he was a whole lot harder to track down, being a whole lot farther away. Trust that guy to be somewhere close to a beach, where he could watch his prey, as they played in the sand. Lots of beaches were in Vancouver. The city was located at an incredible, beautiful ocean, with many opportunities to watch toddlers in all kinds of places.

He himself didn't want toddlers per se; he liked them a little bit older.

His tears caught unexpectedly in the back of his throat; he really missed Jason. He had had that little boy for so many months. Jason had been such a heartfelt part of his life that he just felt so empty right now. And that little girl had done absolutely nothing to fill the void.

His sister would probably say that he'd jumped back too quickly and would feed him all this replacement therapy bullshit. He didn't want to listen to that. He just didn't want to feel so empty inside, and that was a hard thing to fix. Instead he went online to their special dark web group and asked if any of his cohorts had any special friends lately. Several happy-face responses made him feel way worse.

**Damn it**, he snapped. **No way in hell you should have somebody, and I don't.** He'd be quite happy to forget about the fact he, of course, had been the one with the happy-face response for the last six months with Jason, but the tide had turned, and he was alone again. **Willing to share?**

And this time, he got a sad emoji and then a thumbs-down.

**Anybody have one to share?**

One name came back. **Nico.**

He stared at that name and smiled. So Nico had somebody too, did he? He quickly checked over his notes. Nico was in Richmond. And that sucked. While nothing in Vancouver was far away—Richmond only like ten miles south—but the drive was five times longer. Richmond was out by the airport, and that meant a forty-five-minute drive, dealing with traffic and anything else that might come up on the way over and the way back. The good thing about it was, by the time he got back home with his new friend, the police would still be looking for that missing child in Richmond and not in Vancouver, where he was. But, just in case, he asked, **Anyone else?**

Nothing.

"Damn," he said aloud. Okay, Nico it was. He quickly sent Nico a message, asking again if he had anything to share.

Nico came back. **Maybe.**

Wincing, he replied. **Maybe?**

**For a price.**

**What the hell is up with that? Since when do we charge?**

**Since I can't pay my rent.**

Shit. No fucking way he was paying if it wasn't something worth paying for though. Damn it. This girl's face popped up in the screen, and he stared. She had to be about four, maybe a little younger. He frowned because he hadn't heard of any missing little girls of her age and coloring. And he had to wonder how long this little girl had been Nico's.

He quickly typed in a question. **How old?**

**Five.**

Definitely doable. Although Nico normally lied about the age, just to make it hit his age-five-and-up preference range.

**How long?** He knew that Nico would be staring at that question, trying to figure it out, but they all had codes for answers.

Nico came back. **A year.**

A year in the system was a long time for a five-year-old. On the other hand, she'd be well adapted to it. **How much?**

Nico turned cagey. **What's your offer?**

He got up and paced his room. Grabbing a cigarette, he lit it. He stormed around and stared at the little girl's face. It might be easier if he just grabbed somebody himself, but the risk was pretty high, what with China Doll found and Leonard still not located.

He sighed. A girl that had been in the system this long would be used to the process, so much easier to travel with. Only he didn't have her dark hair or almond-shaped eyes. So, if anybody saw them together, it could get people asking questions. Nico, on the other hand, was a blend of many nationalities, and you couldn't really tell where he was from or what he was. It was convenient at times but caused him more trouble over white children in his possession.

He thought about her for a long moment.

Then Nico came back. **I have others interested too.**

He snorted. **Sure you do.**

The trouble was, he actually could have. At least twelve of them were in their small group, but they had access to much bigger groups too. And he hated that, damn it. He didn't want to have anything to do with everybody else. He thought about her for a long moment, and, just as he was about to type no, he feared the opportunity would be gone, and he'd still be alone. He frowned and then Nico came back.

**Two thousand.**

He swore again. He quickly typed an angry response and got an angry response back. They kept at it, badgering the price down, until he got as low as twelve hundred and that was it. Twelve hundred for a five-year-old Asian girl. Shit,

shit, shit. He could pick one up off the streets. That would be free. He quickly sent a last message, saying he would think about it, and immediately logged off.

Maybe Nico would get desperate and come back at half the price. Half, he could afford—more than that, not so much. He should have asked what the little girl's name was. But, with her image in his head, and one saved to his desktop, he put it up on the side while searching further. If the investigation into her disappearance was really hot, it would make his life so much more difficult. He came up with absolutely nothing to connect her to any missing child ring. So she'd been in the ring for a long time. A year was possible but more than that? Usually meant she had probably been sold into it much younger. Nico wouldn't have known very much of the girl's history.

Honestly none of them cared.

"Damn, damn, damn," he whispered. He got up, grabbed his jacket, and, with his lit cigarette, stormed out of the small apartment and headed to his favorite park. He sat on the swing in the children's playground and just let his mind go back and forth over his options.

On the far side he watched a mom with two kids trailing behind her. She was urging them to keep up, as her hands were full of groceries. One was a little girl, somewhere around the same age as the little sweetheart he had kept a picture of, only this one had red hair and pigtails. Beside her was a boy, a little bit older, kicking rocks down the street.

He was focused too. With fierce concentration on his face, he reached out with a sturdy foot and kicked the rock with all his might. Of course, it went forward about six feet, and that was it. But the little boy kept scampering after it and kicked it again.

He watched as they headed to a little row of condos up ahead. And surprise, surprise, she went inside and left the other two in the front yard. He stood and casually strolled in that direction. He took note of the street name and house number. As he got closer, the mother called the children in, and, as soon as they heard her voice—and something about her tone—they immediately swept inside, and she firmly closed and locked the door. He kept on walking past, but no way would he forget what was so carefully guarded inside that house.

Because, man, they were perfect. And he was so damn lonely.

# CHAPTER 15

THE ELEVATOR OPENED in front of Kate, and she stepped out to see Simon leaning against his living room doorjamb. She stared at him. "Thanks for seeing me," she said calmly. He just glared. She smiled a little bit. "You weren't busy, were you?"

He swirled some golden liquid in the glass he held. "I'm always busy."

"Interesting," she murmured. His gaze narrowed, until she spoke again. "So you don't happen to know anything about an earlier stabbing, do you?"

His eyebrows shot up, and his facial expression turned neutral. "No," he said. "Why would I?"

She shook her head and said, "Just something I heard on a 9-1-1 call." She studied his face, but absolutely no change was in his expression. "You must be good at poker. Especially as you didn't ask me, *What stabbing?*"

His gaze flattened. "Are you charging me with something, Detective?"

"No," she said. "Should I be?"

He gave a negligent shrug of those elegant shoulders. Something was just so damn appealing about him, and she had a hard personal line she'd never been tempted to cross, but he was damn hard to forget. But why was she here now, when she should have hauled him in for questioning? Anger over the attraction made her more brisk than normal. "Honestly I'm still not exactly sure what you are up to," she said. "I just wanted to keep track of you."

"You didn't have to personally come to my apartment to do that," he said.

"Maybe I'm looking for injuries," she said smoothly. She watched as he froze and then lifted his gaze, as he sipped his whiskey. Interesting reaction.

"*Injuries.* You already know I got into a fight with that dead guy you found beaten up downtown."

"I do," she said. "I also know what those bruises would look like if they were real."

He stared at her. "Did you have any other questions for me, Detective? If so, maybe I should call my lawyer."

"If you want to, feel free," she said, studying him. After a moment she confirmed, "Where were you two weeks ago, on that Monday, between four and six in the afternoon?"

He stared at her in surprise. "I'm always working. I have no clue for that time frame. Most likely I was moving through some of my building projects," he said. "You remember those. You followed me often enough."

She gave him a flat stare and asked, "Where were you?"

"Not sure," he said. "I'll have to think about it."

"You have five minutes," she stated.

He glared at her, turned, walked over to the side table, pulled out his little black journal, which he used to keep track of what he was doing, and said, "I was on a project on Denman Street."

"Any calls on your phone that will prove it?"

"Phone calls," he said, looking up at her. "You'll have to get a subpoena for my records, if that's the issue."

"I can do that easily enough if I have justification," she

said, with a nod.

"Which you don't," he said. "Which is why you are fishing. The question is, why, though?"

"Because I think you are the one who phoned in that stabbing," she said.

He stared at her, the corner of his lips twitching into a tiny smile. "Why the hell would I do that?"

"I'm not exactly sure," she said quietly. Her gaze was intent, as she studied him. "But I heard the 9-1-1 call. And there was something in that voice—your voice."

"And how would I have known about it?"

"That is what we all want to know. Most of my colleagues seem to think you are involved."

"Interesting," he said. "And does it matter what that involvement is, or are you just trying to ensure I'm guilty of something, so you can charge me?"

"No," she said, "but, if you did call that in, I want to know how you knew about it."

"Meaning, I must have been there. Is that what you're saying?"

Her gaze was steady. "You would think so, yes."

"Or was it *a psychic moment*?" he mocked. "Detective, you actually sound like you might believe in me."

"I wouldn't go that far," she said slowly. "But I have to admit there was something about that call."

When the phone in his hand rang, he said, "If you'll excuse me, I need to take this call."

She nodded. "I'll be in touch." And, with that, she turned, stepped into the elevator, and pushed the button to go down.

"JESUS CHRIST." SIMON glared down at the phone. "What's the matter, Caitlin?"

"Try to find him. Please!" his ex-fiancée whispered.

"I have tried," he said. "I don't have anything to tell you."

"How is that possible?" she said. "I know you have the skills."

"No," he said, "I don't. I don't have any of what you keep thinking I have."

"You have the sight," she whispered.

"Maybe, maybe sometimes. Every once in a while I get some inclination of something," he said, "but that's different than instinct or intuition."

"It's not," she cried out forcefully. "Do you know how much that little boy could be suffering right now?"

He closed his eyes and pinched the bridge of his nose. "I've tried," he said, and he hung up.

He tossed the phone onto his couch and stared out the window. He'd tried, but he hadn't tried everything. He bowed his head, fighting against the forces pushing against him. It's almost as if he heard his grandmother's voice in the background, repeating something she had said many times.

*You must do something, or it will crush you.*

Even growing up as a young boy, she had warned him, "The more you turn your back on your talent," she said, "the more it will rise up against you. Eventually it will crush you. There will come a time in your life when you must decide to go one way or the other."

And he heard that same voice in the background say, *That time is now. You must decide.*

# CHAPTER 16

*Fourth Monday in June, Morning*

T HE NEXT MORNING Kate stared at her board, her hands in her pockets, as she studied the various markings. The lines bothered her. She turned to look at Rodney. "What about the Integrated Child Exploitation Unit?" she asked.

"What about ICE?"

"I wonder if they'd seen anything like this."

He lifted his head and looked at her, looked at the photos. "The mark?"

She nodded.

"Ask. It's a good idea. Should have done that right off."

She nodded, walked to her desk, and sat down. Dennis, at ICE, answered the phone on the first ring. She quickly explained who she was and why she was calling.

"So, you have a dead pedophile you think might be connected somehow to a bunch of dead children with a strange mark on the wrist?"

"Yes. But most of these are cold cases," she said. "It occurred to me that maybe the marks have something to do with a sex ring. Or a sex trafficking site, club, or whatever these assholes call themselves these days."

"Can you send me a copy of the images?"

"We've got the same base image," she said, "with a couple minor differences. Some have additional lines on the side." She quickly got his email address and sent a few files over to him, while they talked.

"If you open the first one," she said, "that's from fifteen years ago. The second one is from eight years ago, and the third is from the dead convicted pedophile we found Saturday," she said.

He brought up the images on his end. "Interesting."

"Interesting why?" she asked.

"Because it's so faint," he said. "It's almost as if it's some secret marker. Deliberately made so it's hard to see."

"That's what I was thinking," she said in a dry tone. "Something they would know but nobody else. So faint it would get missed in the autopsy."

"I can take a look," he said. "We generally focus on facial recognition, scars, body deformities, things like that. If this was bold with heavy black markings, we'd have noted it. As it is, it's very faint."

"I know," she said, "but I just thought—"

"It's a good thought," he said, "a good find. I'll get back to you." And, with that, he was gone.

Rodney looked over at Kate. "And?"

"He'd never seen them before," she said. "He'll get back to me."

"There really could be a possible connection."

"Who else can access a ring like that?" she wondered out loud. "Is there some online chat room or somewhere these psychos go?"

"Lots of them," Rodney said. "The dark web is full of that shit."

"I want to go to Ken's place. Forensics should be through with it." She hopped to her feet, looked over at Rodney, and asked, "You up for it?"

He grabbed his jacket and said, "Always up for a road trip."

"It's not all that far away from here," she said, "maybe fifteen minutes."

"I'll drive," he said. Within minutes they were outside and in his car.

As they pulled up in front of the townhome, she whistled. "He wasn't terribly broke if he was living here."

"He was subleasing. The cops have been through the place already, as have we. You didn't get to go through it, did you?"

"No," she said. "Does forensics have the laptop?"

"They do."

She walked inside the townhome and stopped in the living room and stared. "It's so perfectly neat."

"He lived alone."

"Did he though?" Her gaze caught on some grime on the wall. She shifted closer, saw a bunch of smudge marks, but they were only like thirty inches high. She pointed them out down the hallway. "Look. It's almost like a child rubbed his hands all the way along the wall here."

Rodney squatted in front of her. "It's hardly a spot where an adult would touch, is it? But it lends credence to our theory."

"But," she said, taking a devil's advocate point of view, "he also could have dragged something or been carrying something. We'll have to keep looking for answers." Still, her mind was locked on the fact that something was off. But then again, it was the home of a pedophile, after all, so what the hell else should she expect? Some seriously ugly scenarios could have happened here. She wandered through the place slowly, checking and searching everything, until she got to the kitchen.

"What exactly are you looking for?"

"Nothing and everything," she said. She quickly went through the kitchen and found absolutely nothing suspicious. She sighed and said, "What about the basement?"

"Just a crawl space for utilities," he said.

"I want to go down there," she said instantly.

He shrugged and said, "Whatever. It's in the hallway here." They opened up a panel on the floor, and she dropped down with her cell on Flashlight mode. This space was only about three feet high. She asked, "Did Forensics come in here?"

"Yep, they did," Rodney said. He crouched again, so he saw where she was, had his flashlight shining down there too.

Kate saw all the utilities, pipes, and wires that kept the condo functional. As she searched around, she couldn't see much else. She didn't know what the hell she was looking for really, but at least maybe a scratch on the wall or something to show that a child had been here. There was nothing. She continued her search, tapping the walls for a hollow sound. "Nothing," she said, disgusted, as she made her way back up.

"We do know how to do our job, you know?"

"So do I," she snapped. She headed upstairs, where she went to the spare room, and found it completely clean and empty. Then she went into the master. And yet it too was nothing but plain and ordinary. She shot him a look. "What is it about this room that makes my skin crawl?"

He smiled and said, "I can see that it does. Maybe just the fact that he lived here. I don't know."

She quickly searched through the room, knowing that the Forensics Division had been here ahead of her, but she didn't care. She studied the worn wall, wallpapered in some strange purple and gray pattern. She slid her hand across the top of the wall, and, when she snagged her fingernail ever-so-slightly, she stopped and moved back. Then, using her nail, she followed the indention, outlining a space about two feet by two feet. She pressed inward ever-so-gently and out popped the secret door.

"Now this is interesting," she murmured.

Rodney was there instantly. "Well, I'm betting they didn't find this," he said in surprise. Behind it was a safe built into the wall. She looked at it, then turned to him. "You any good at this?"

"No," he said. "We could get somebody in here."

She nodded and frowned. "I could try anyway." She placed her ear against it and slowly turned the dial, but she couldn't make it open. "Damn it," she said. "How long will it take to get somebody in here to open it?"

"Unless you know somebody," he said, "we must bring in a locksmith."

She swore again. Just then her phone lit up, and a text came in from Simon. She sucked in her breath at the string of numbers in front of her. Was it possible? How could he know? Against her better judgment, but unable to ignore the impulse, she tried the numbers on the safe. When she heard the tumblers fall into place and then a *click*, she stepped back, snapped the lever down, and pulled it open. And stared. In front of her were DVDs, old VHS tapes, and what looked like a photo album.

"What have we here?" Rodney asked, beside her.

She groaned. "What we have is a motherfucking sick society. I really don't want to watch these videos."

They stared at it all, knowing these would be videos nobody wanted them to see.

"We need Forensics in here," he said. "A ton of finger-prints could be all over this stuff."

"And yet Ken is dead, so what I want to know is who else knew this shit was here?"

"How did you open it?" he asked curiously. "Surely that was more than a guess."

She lifted her phone in her hand and tapped the screen to open it up, so Rodney saw the text she had gotten from Simon.

Rodney stared at that, stared at her, and looked at the lock. "Holy shit. Call us Team Simon."

---

SIMON SHOULD HAVE just shot himself. He didn't know what the hell that was all about; he didn't know where the numbers came from, and he didn't know what the six numbers even meant. Too short to be a telephone number. But he knew that this had changed something forever. He stared at the phone in his hand and threw it down. It was fast becoming a habit with him.

He really wanted to throw it outside and forever shatter the window that linked him to this unknown world. But he also knew that this wouldn't go away. He had reached this point of doing something that was right *and* doing that something right every damn time.

It had been two hours since he'd sent that text, and now he waited. Waited for the phone call that said the detective was downstairs. Finally it came.

"Send her up," he said quietly. He didn't even meet her at the elevator this time. When the elevator opened, he listened to the footsteps, grateful to hear only one set.

She walked to the couch, where he sat. "How did you know?"

He looked up at her, exhausted and drained. "I don't even know what the numbers were for," he said. "I don't have the slightest idea what you did with them. I didn't get any interpretation."

"The numbers were the combination to open the safe of a pedophile," she said quietly. "The same man who's in the morgue."

He stared at her in shock. "A safe?"

She nodded and didn't say anything.

"I don't know what the hell is going on," he whispered, "but I got a message in my head that you needed these numbers, and I sent them to you. See? I get numbers in my head all the time. It's how I make money when gambling, buying stocks, investing in real estate. I've always called it *intuition* but this? ... I don't know what to call it."

"I was staring at the safe, figuring out how to get into it," she said, "and I was wondering what the numbers were, asking my team member to see if we could get a safecracker in, but wondering if we could get in faster before all that."

"And it worked?" he asked. Then he gave a broken laugh, lifted his whiskey glass, and threw back the rest of it, his eyes closed again.

"How much of that have you had to drink?"

"Not nearly enough," he said defiantly, and he opened his eyes and glared at her.

She smiled at him. "You know? I almost believe you."

"Almost?"

"Almost," she said. "Because that was a pretty smooth trick."

"How else would I have known?" he said.

"I presume no one knows about your parlor trick?"

"Would you tell anyone?" he challenged.

She frowned and stared at the carpet.

"No way in hell you would let anybody know," he snapped. "Your job would go out the window. The public would view you completely differently, and your privacy would be nonexistent. Do you have any idea how terrifying all this is?"

She raised her gaze and looked at him steadily.

He didn't feel so much the center of her gaze as much as her deep sense of goodness.

"If you have answers," she said, "you are honor bound to hand them over."

He cracked up with laughter. "Honor bound?" he snapped. "Like fucking hell."

"Do you think swearing makes a difference in my world?"

"I don't know," he said. "Why do you think your pretentious attitude makes any difference in mine?"

"I don't know," she said. "But I think you've been struggling against who you truly are for a lifetime."

He stopped and stared, her words echoing his grandmother's. "Like hell," he said, but he wasn't ready to concede anything. He just glared at her.

She nodded slowly. "See? I don't have any faith in what you do," she said. "I've seen too many charlatans. Somebody took my mother to the cleaners and burned her for over fifty thousand dollars," she said quietly, her gaze intent as she studied him. "At no point in time did that charlatan give her anything of value. What he gave my mother was the tiny glimmer of hope for what was an unreasonable expectation to begin with—the chance to contact my missing brother in the afterlife."

He just nodded. "There is a segment of society," he said, his voice just as quiet as hers, "who prey on the hopes, fears, and heartaches of others."

"She ended up marrying him, and, by the time he died, the inheritance and trust fund her father had left was completely gone. She is still alive and in a very sad state right now," she said. "So you should believe me when I tell you that I want you to be the charlatan, so I can throw your ass in the slammer."

"Got it," he said, his lips quirking but his gaze was steady.

"The fact of the matter is," she said, "that you keep squirreling around in my cases, which is suspicious as hell. Rest assured, if I find you've overstepped," she said, "I will do exactly as promised."

He believed her. "So, I might be squirreling around in your cases," he said, "but I don't have the slightest idea why the information I'm getting has anything to do with them," he said. "If I could find a way to get out of having this strange information, I would."

She looked at him for a long moment and then gave a quick nod. "I think I believe you, but the thing is, I don't have any way to justify these numbers." She held up her cell phone and the string of numbers he'd texted her. He stared at them for a long moment. "I can't really tell you how I got them either. I didn't even know where you were at the time."

"I know," she said. "I didn't tell anyone where my partner and I were going, and that's the part I really struggle with."

"Maybe it's more than either of us can imagine," he said.

"Maybe."

"And maybe it's something completely unrelated to your cases and just some weird connection we have."

"I don't know." She spun on her heels and headed to the elevator.

"Detective, you look tired," he said.

She froze, then turned to look at him. "It's hard to sleep when I know children are being abused, and I can't stop it."

"Is there something you can do about it?"

"I have to hope there is," she said sorrowfully. "Otherwise, what am I doing with my life?" Her gaze deepened, as she stared at him. "Maybe that's a question you should ask yourself," she said. "What are you doing with your life?"

And, with that, she was gone.

He leaned back against the couch again and stared out the window. *Trying to make amends.* Not so much for his actions but for all those who had suffered too. Giving to those who no longer believed that gifts, … hope, … happiness were possible any longer. That's what he was doing. He'd been hoping against hope that what he was doing was enough. But based on what was happening right now, he wasn't.

He still didn't understand his connection to her or her cases because that was the thing. They were *her cases*—not these people—that he was connecting to. It was all about his connection to her cases, which ultimately meant his connection to her. And that was something he didn't want at all. The last thing he needed was a cop in his life. Hell, the last thing he needed was anybody in his world, particularly somebody who would want something from him. But a cop, given his own lifestyle? Well, that was probably the worst-case scenario he could imagine yet.

Cursing, he poured another shot and threw back the

whiskey, feeling the burn all the way. His grandmother's voice came to him again. *You can run, but you can't hide.*

RICHMOND. EVERYTHING WAS done in secret on the dark web. Anonymously. But where in Richmond? That was the secret. His group didn't discuss addresses; they certainly didn't exchange phone numbers. Anonymously online. Ken had mentioned a couple spots he used to hang out in. Spots that he himself had recognized. What he was doing now was finding some similar details from Nico's past conversations. Anything, any message, any sign.

He went through everything that he ever had gotten from Nico. A couple photos of children. He kept trying to see locations, landmarks. One showed a McDonald's, so he quickly mapped out all the McDonald's locations in the Richmond area, trying to find one from that angle. He made one trip to Richmond and realized just how useless that would be, without more directions, more landmarks, more details.

If he could find that little girl, why should he pay money? Especially that kind of money? Nico shouldn't have been so damn greedy. It's not like he himself had any money. He used to have a lot of it but, well, not any longer. And that was pissing him off more and more every day. He had to get a little sneakier, a little more ingenious, on how to get through his month.

On his way back from Richmond, empty-handed, he pounded on the steering wheel. He parked at a coffee shop to use their Wi-Fi and quickly sent a message online, asking Nico if he'd reconsider. When there was no answer, he frowned. Then, getting a little trickier, he sent another message, saying he wanted proof of life, somewhere outside. **Send me a picture of her at a park or someplace I can identify and know you didn't Photoshop her in a scene.**

Then he tossed his phone on the passenger seat and, grinning, made his way back home.

The thought of having a little girl who had already been groomed and made ready for him had him salivating. He felt himself getting hard just walking to his apartment. He made a dash in half the time he normally did. And, once inside, instead of calming down, his bloodlust grew. Swearing, but still anticipating, he headed into the shower to take care of himself. As he ejaculated all over the shower wall, he groaned. If it wasn't that little girl, it had to be the little boy Leonard. Only he didn't know how to find that one, and that pissed him off too. He had to do something, and he had to do it soon.

# CHAPTER 17

*Tuesday Morning*

"FINDING THE SAFE in our DB's apartment is a huge break. The search for Leonard will never be called off," Colby said in the next morning's meeting, his tone quiet. "But now a week later, we are the hell a long way past the first forty-eight hours, and you all know what that means." The atmosphere was somber, silent, because everybody in that room knew exactly what it meant. "We are still looking obviously, and the Amber Alerts are out, but we have no vehicle, and we have no idea where or how. Somewhere from the school on the way home. If there is any connection from Leonard to that DB, let's find it—and fast."

"They checked the city street cams, right?" Kate asked.

Her sergeant nodded. "As is our standard procedure."

"I know," she said, "but sometimes the basics can get missed." Nobody laughed at her or made any comment because, in the case of a missing child, they'd rather double up on the work and request something twice, rather than assume and have a lead get missed.

"He's only seven," Colby said.

"Prime age," she murmured.

He shot her a hard look and then nodded in agreement. "We have a lot of city cops still looking," he said, "but we need to focus on *our* concurrent cases. You never know where the next tip will come from. Meanwhile an entire department is working on finding Leonard."

She winced at that. "And that just means he could end up as one of mine."

"What about that mark on the wrist? Did you track it down?" Colby asked her.

"I'm working on Ken's history now, every known associate, and whoever he was in jail with. A couple people he got close to in the prison system. I want to talk to them." She hesitated, then asked, "Can we bring in a profiler? Someone to help us build a profile on our future suspect in these related cases?"

He looked at her for a moment, frowned, then shrugged. "If you think it would further the Leonard case, but remember these others are cold cases and not yet linked to Leonard's disappearance."

"They are all connected," she said coolly. "One of the predators is now dead and is lying in the morgue, so it's hardly a cold case. Plus, our little girl bore the same mark."

Colby immediately nodded. "And that becomes our priority now. Contact Dr. Yolynda Brown. She's one of the PD's consultants on serial killers. She also specializes in child cases." He looked at the others. "What about the other cases?"

"We have the husband with his wife stabbed to the wall," he said. "And that odd 9-1-1 call."

Colby slid his gaze back to Kate.

She shrugged. "I asked Simon, and he said he didn't have anything to do with it."

"Do you believe him?"

She frowned, replaying the conversation in her mind. "You know what? He didn't come right out and say he didn't do it," she said, "so maybe not. He's definitely been a little cagey at times, as in all over the map."

"Did you tell the team about the safe?" Rodney asked her.

"The combination to the dead perv's safe did come from Simon, and I asked him about that. He said he had no idea where I was or what I was doing, but those numbers flashed in his mind associated with me, so he texted them to me."

Owen jumped up and said, "Seriously?"

She twisted in her seat, looked back at her team member. "Yes. I was standing in front of the safe with Rodney, talking about how to crack it and what we could do to get somebody in to look at it, when, out of the blue, I received a text. I looked down and saw the numbers. I tried them and opened the safe."

"And you hadn't told him where you were?"

She shook her head slowly. "I hadn't talked to him all day."

"Interesting," Owen said. "And kind of disturbing."

"In many ways," Kate said. "Like I said, I did ask him about it afterward, and all he said was that he felt compelled to provide me with those numbers, but he didn't know why."

"We do have a lot of videos to go through now," Rodney added.

"Forensics has them all at present," she said. "Although they sent the first group back already. Some of these go back fifteen to twenty years," she said quietly. "There'll be nothing on those videos that we want to see."

"But we have to," Owen said, his voice equally quiet. "Because we don't know what else we might find. Even if it's only to narrow down a location of where he may have held these children, because there's absolutely no indication that they were at Ken's home."

"No, he probably has a hidden location. I'm also wondering if he has a connection with other pedophiles," she said. "Then again there were those black marks on the walls at a child's height, so maybe Ken kept them there, then moved them."

"Possible. Online, definitely," Rodney said. "These guys tend to cluster."

"But, in person, I don't know," Owen said, shaking his head. "I don't think they share well."

"Space?" she asked him. "Or spoils?"

He winced. "I don't know. Either probably."

She nodded. "And yet it still seems like it's some sort of club."

"Because of the mark?"

"Yeah, some meaning must be behind it," she said. She pondered it for a moment, then nodded. "Like a tattoo or the stamp you get when you walk into a nightclub, isn't it?"

"Only this is a little bit deeper, and it's not something that rubs off," Rodney said.

"So then what is it?" Owen asked. "What makes the mark?"

"Likely a hot iron," Kate said. "At least that's what the coroner suggested. A brand."

"And it would be faster that way than a tattoo," Owen said. "These are children, after all."

"Branded, probably done while they're unconscious," she said. "And the marks aren't deep. A part of this club membership."

"So we focus on the DVDs first," Colby said. "Kate, you and Rodney handle that. See what you find. Then, Owen,

Lilliana, and Andy go through it again. Maybe Reese too depending ..."

"Reese is swamped, and, unless it's mandatory, no way she'll want to go through those tapes. If there's something to be identified, maybe, but likely forensics will hunt that down. She, on the other hand, is tracing Ken's history right now." Owen turned to look at Colby and nodded. "I'll set up the arrangements to speak to the two prisoners Ken did time with. I'll let everyone know if they have anything helpful."

"Yes, do that too."

Knowing she had a long ugly day ahead of her, she filled a coffee cup and headed into one of the boardrooms, where they had the VHS tapes and DVDs set up that had been released by that Forensics Division. She brought along a large notepad and said, "I really won't like today, will I?"

"None of us will," Rodney said. He sat down and popped the oldest one into the equipment.

She sighed. "These guys still use a VCR? Jesus."

"We still have machines that play them, so it's no biggie."

As it started, she saw it was an ugly home movie. A toddler sat quietly, clutching a teddy bear, rocking back and forth. His face—at least it looked like a little boy—seemed vacant. She sucked in her breath. "Ah, shit."

And that's how her day began. Unfortunately it didn't get any better, as Forensics Division dumped the rest of the VHS and DVD tapes with them about noon, having digital copies now for Forensics to work with.

Rodney and Kate made their way through seventeen different sets of home movies. By the time she was done, she had numbered them all and had written brief descriptions of what was in each. Some of them had interiors of houses but nothing to define where they were.

They'd gone back and forth on a couple, looking for street signs outside big windows, looking for something that identified the interiors of these houses. She'd written down descriptions of the wallpaper patterns, though everything was black-and-white, so it may not be that helpful.

"I think that's all I can handle for the day," she whispered.

"Yeah, me too," Rodney said, looking more than a little tired and sick.

And, so far, they hadn't seen anything of much value.

"Not only that," he said, "I don't think most of these victims have been located."

She looked at him and said, "Ken's record said he was charged with four?"

"Yes, but at one point in time he supposedly confessed to three times that many."

"So twelve." Kate shook her head. "Just by him."

Still rattled by the videos, Rodney said, "We haven't seen any duplicates yet caught on tape, so just these initial tapes that we've been through account for at least four times if not more than that. Forty-eight kids and counting. Some of the kids in the other tapes that we haven't seen yet could be more recent too."

It was almost 10:00 p.m. when they called it a night.

---

### Wednesday

KATE AND RODNEY resumed their second day of going through Ken's pervert videos. It made for a soul-crushing day. Meanwhile, Andy, Lilliana, and Owen were set up in another boardroom, going through the first batch of tapes that Kate and Rodney had scoured yesterday. Maybe the other team members would find something they had missed.

Hours later, Kate frowned, looked at Rodney, and said, "Well, we have the DVDs yet too, and those would likely be newer." Shaking her head, she swore. "Fuck! I'll stay here and go through them. I don't want to get up and have to see this shit tomorrow. If we can use anything here, we need to find it now. Leonard, if he's part of this same vicious group, is out of time."

"Hell, you're right," Rodney said. "Come on then. Let's get through them."

### Thursday, Wee Hours of the Morning

IT WAS AFTER midnight by the time Kate and Rodney got to the third-to-last DVD; she had shut down inside, almost numb to the abuse going on in front of her.

From the crying children of every age, barely crawling to about ten years old. And she wouldn't count on that age being correct either. Some of the children appeared to be fairly stunted. Also mostly a blend of Asian and Caucasian children. What she wasn't seeing was too many other ethnic groups, but the old black-and-white videos didn't help.

"Stop!" Rodney said. "Look at that."

She hit the Stop button, turned to him. "What is it?"

"Back up," he said, "About thirty seconds."

While she'd been too numb to notice, he'd caught sight of something. She leaned forward, as she replayed the last thirty seconds. "What is it?"

"That," he said, "is a different room, in a different house."

"Sure, and what does that mean?"

"I'm thinking that either he moved, or this is his and that child's home."

They quickly went through the video again and then once more. On the third time through, she stopped and said, "That's a living room." She got up, walked over to the large screen and tapped at the corner. "Can we get a close-up on this? A street sign is there, which means the house is on a corner."

"We'll send this to Forensics and see if they can get it blown up a little more."

Kate said, "Just use the controls on that and see if we can get anything now."

They managed to get it blown up enough to see the RD for *road* on the sign.

"Can you make out anything else beside it?" she murmured.

"It ends in an *E*, and I see either a *T* or an *L* right before it," Rodney said.

"Well, that's something," she said. "Let's get somebody from Forensics on this, and we'll work this angle."

Feeling better after having found something, they quickly went through the last two videos. When they finally got to the last one, she gasped. "Oh my God!"

"What?"

"It's our little princess, Candice Ferguson," she said. "That bastard Ken had her."

"Are you sure?" Rodney leaned forward and shook his head slowly. "I think you're wrong. I think it's a different one."

She turned and stared at him. "Seriously?"

"I hope so," he said. "This DVD file is dated more than four months ago."

"How long ago did she go missing?"

"About four months." He nodded slowly and then frowned. "You're thinking that he had her all that time?" he asked, clearly disturbed by the thought.

"I don't know what to think," she said flatly, "but at least now we've got the two of them together."

"We don't actually," he said softly. "What we have is him taking a photo of her, but she is even a little bit farther away. She is walking on a street here. Almost as if he were casing her as his next victim."

"But there aren't any images of her as a victim, are there?" She quickly got up and checked to make sure they had been through all the DVDs. "Maybe he didn't have time to make one?"

"Or he wasn't the one who actually had her," Rodney said, staring at her. "Which kind of supports your theory that more than one perv could be involved, a ring of deviants."

Her stomach churned. "We have to do a wider circle, do a complete canvass of the neighborhood, all the streets around, to see if Ken was ever seen with a child, if he was ever seen taking photos, movies, things like that."

"I'll get someone on that," Rodney said. "And we'd better get back to Forensics, to see if they can find anything more on that address in that screen."

"And I think fresh eyes need to go through some of these," she said, rubbing at her eyes. "We're exhausted."

"And we could be going through this again and again," he said. "It's a horrible stash of child porn from a pedophile.

We don't know what all else could be there."

"What about his little black book that we found in the safe?"

"Forensics kept it," he said. "But I've asked for photocopies. Let me check." He pulled out his phone, nodded, and said, "Yeah, we've got them here."

"Send them to the printer," she said. "I'll take a copy home with me." The idea of going home, even as exhausted as she was, seemed wrong. Maybe with a shower and a couple hours sleep she'd be refreshed. She said, "I don't know what else is going on here, but we've got enough that we should crack something. And to think that Ken's already dead? Well, that just pisses me off even more."

"But who murdered him? Who would do that? That is the question."

"The little girl's father," she said instantly. "Think about it. If that was your daughter, and you knew who'd taken and abused her ..." She said to him, "Spin it around. Wouldn't you?"

He looked at her and winced and said, "Yeah. Damn right, I would. If it was my son or daughter that he'd done all that to, hell yeah. You know that most of the people on the planet would say the world is better off without the sick son of a bitch. But, of all those people, who is the one who had the balls to do it? And why now? Why not when he had the little girl—if he had her—and rescue the child?"

"I don't know, but I'm damned determined to find out."

### Friday Afternoon

SIMON WALKED ONTO the cruise boat, heading out for the

weekend. If nothing else, he needed to get away, to just refresh his mind and to go back to something he knew. It wasn't about making some money by gambling, not that he ever said no to money. Still, after getting that cashier's check from the local land-based casino, he was fine. But one never had enough money, not in this world. As he walked into his cabin, he shrugged off his jacket and hung it up. He brought three suits with him for the evenings. They had another hour until they set sail. He was restless and headed out onto the deck.

He was in jeans and a T-shirt at the moment, and the Vancouver air was warm and a perfect temperature for this cruise. By the time he got to the front side, he stopped, picked up a gin and tonic from the bar, took a sip. He knew instinctively that the detective would return to his place to look for him, and maybe it was cowardly, but he didn't want to see her.

Every time he saw her, the connection between them deepened, and so did his abilities. It only occurred to him this morning that somehow *she* was strengthening his abilities—a scary thought. But all the more reason to stay away. His phone rang just then, and he glared at it but didn't answer it. It wouldn't stop ringing. He swore, downed the rest of his drink, and answered it.

"Detective, I'm on a cruise, and I'll be heading into international waters soon," he said. "So I won't be answering your calls."

"When are you back?" she asked, all businesslike.

"Early Monday. I plan to have a late breakfast and debark midmorning on Monday. Why?"

"We've had some breaks in the case."

"Interesting," he said. And, in spite of himself, he asked,

"Something that's useable?"

"The safe had a lot of videos," she said. "I'm sure you can imagine of what."

"From those numbers I gave you?" Pleased, he leaned over the railings and stared at the deep dark ocean beneath him. "I know it's just a drop in the hat," he said, "but I'm glad that I contributed in some way."

"A lot of the things you've done have contributed," she said. "I just haven't figured out if it's in a good way or a bad way just yet."

"Neither have I," he said, with a crack of laughter. "But we can count on the fact that this time, at least, it was worthwhile."

"Maybe so," she said. Then she hesitated.

He waited. "What's up, Detective?"

"God help me, but I was just wondering if you'd seen anything else," she said.

He stopped, and then he laughed. "What's this?" he asked. "Aren't you the one who can't stand charlatans?"

"You're absolutely right. I can't," she said. "And, if I ever find out that you're making up all this shit, you can bet I'll fuck with you every bit as much as you've been fucking with me. But, in the meantime, as long as any of the visions you have are helpful," she said, "I still have a seven-year-old boy missing and a dead six-year-old girl in the morgue."

"I'm sorry about the little girl," he said softly. "She was so young, so beautiful. So perfect."

"Maybe that's what got her killed," she said. "A lot of parents don't realize how much a pedophile can lock on to a look and can't think of anything else until they get what they want."

"Then a lot of these parents dress up their children like

models and take them for dancing classes, thinking how cute they are."

"There's no justifying taste," she said. "But it doesn't matter what these parents did. No child deserves what these pedophiles have done to them."

"Agreed. So, no locations or anything identifiable in the videos?"

"No," she said, "at least nothing yet."

"I don't envy you going through all that." That would ruin his faith in humanity if he had to do that. Not that he had any left.

"No," she said. "So, if you find anything or something else comes up, please let me know."

"Like I said, I won't be answering the phone."

"So then what? You're off to fleece a bunch of people to get more money to build your rehab projects?"

Simon was stunned; her words were very close to the truth. Close enough that he stopped and stared out at the city lights, playing on the ocean waters. "What's this? Trying to be psychic on your own?"

"Not at all, but you have no visible means of support, and yet your building projects aren't cheap."

"Gambling is like that," he said. "I had a really good run here the other day."

"Believe it or not, I found out about that," she said, "and you're right, especially considering it wasn't even your game." And, with that, she hung up.

He swore, as he stared down at the phone. "Are you following me, Detective Morgan?"

Of course she was. Not only was she following him, she was keeping track of every step he made. Which meant, in theory, that she should know exactly where he was right now. He pocketed his phone and, feeling that same disquiet, turned and headed back to his room. He'd spend some time on the paperwork that had piled up, while he waited for dinner and the night's activities.

This was his chance to lose himself in something that he knew very well, something that he was comfortable in. He wondered who else would be here. He knew a large group of guys came and went on these short weekend gambling cruises. He could only hope that he knew somebody who would make the trip a little bit easier. As he walked toward his room, he thought he saw someone he recognized. He called out.

His buddy turned, raised a hand. "See you tonight," he said. "First drinks on me."

Simon laughed, his spirits picking up. This is what he needed—friends in a world that he was used to.

"THE OLD BASTARD," he said aloud about Nico, as he stared at the photo of the little girl, but it was definitely doctored. **That's a manipulated image.**

**Don't dare take her outside.**

**Don't you have any photos of where she was originally?**

**That's hardly a proof of life.**

He swore because, of course, that's quite true. **Then give me proof of life in your house**, he wrote. **Unless you live in a tent or something?**

**I have a house**, he replied. **It's a decent one too.**

**Are you sure you are not renting some squalid little basement?**

**Nope, it's my house, been living in it a good thirty**

**years**, Nico typed. **Bought it a long time ago, when I was still a prof at the university.**

"Interesting," he murmured. He immediately wrote down notes because, if Nico owned a property, he should find out which one it was. How the hell to do this? Pull a few connections. But Nico was not being any more open than that. And was still not being very agreeable on the photos. **No money without proof of life**, he wrote, then quickly logged off. He called his sister. "Can you get a record of property ownership?"

Her voice was distracted, as she said, "I don't know, probably. Maybe. I'd have to pull a favor to get it. Why?"

"I'm just trying to find where somebody lives, and he owns a house in Richmond."

"Why?"

But at least he heard just curiosity in her voice. "Sorry, I guess you are at work," he said, wishing he'd thought first before he'd called.

"I'm always at work these days," she said. "You know me."

"Well, that's good," he said. "At least you should be bringing in lots of money."

"I am," she said quietly. "But it's lots of stress, lots of bills."

He winced. "Bills suck."

"They suck the life out of you and take your income down to far less than half. Listen. I don't know about this address thing. Why don't you just call the cops? You had a couple friends on the force."

"I did, but I don't know if I still do," he said.

"Well, check online first then," she said. With those words, she hung up on him.

He frowned. He still wanted to drive past her house. Maybe when he was out driving one of these times. He quickly did an internet search about checking property ownership sites, then headed to the county assessor site, looking to see if he found any help there. But his first attempt only allowed him to look up by address.

What he needed was a way to look up by name. It didn't take too long, and, after a couple phone calls to government entities, he found how to track down what property a person owned. The trouble was, he only had Nico's first name, and he needed the last name. Where to start? Then he remembered what Nico had said about being a professor.

It took the rest of the day for him to figure out where Nico had been a professor, based on the little scraps of information he knew about him. Over time the little snippets of information added up, and, once he applied himself, he found he knew quite a lot about Nico.

Before long he'd determined where Professor Nico had worked for close to fifteen years. He didn't know if Nico's hobby was the reason he got sidelined from that very profitable venture or if he'd actually retired. Nonetheless, now armed with a name, he backtracked and found the property ownership records, including the physical address. A further search led him to discover that it hadn't been sold in the last several years, and the value on it had his eyebrows shooting straight up.

Three million dollars? Goddammit! What the hell was Nico doing fleecing him for twelve hundred for that little girl, if he had that kind of a house? Furious, he grabbed his wallet and keys, then headed to his truck. With the GPS programmed for Nico's address, he drove over the bridge to Richmond. It really pissed him off that somebody living in a multimillion-dollar house wanted to be paid for this little girl, when *he* needed her and was broke.

It didn't take too long, and, after an extra ten minutes or so, he neared the side of the bridge, and the GPS gave him quick instructions, turning left or turning right. Before he knew it, he was going down a tree-lined street, with decent-size houses. This was a much older part of town. All of these were likely to have been built before the airport became such an international hot spot. Richmond itself was reclaimed land, and this area looked to be part of the original settlements.

It was a beautiful area, with huge brick mansions. Very similar to the house where he'd grown up, in the Point Grey area of Vancouver. But this was more regal.

The GPS announced his arrival at the destination address. Stopping, he looked around and found it on the right. He stared at this huge old house, with a big brick fence across the front and a wide iron gate. An alleyway must be at the back for parking because no driveway was in the front. He drove forward a bit more and came around the rear, where, sure enough, he found an alleyway.

He drove around the block a couple times and finally parked one block away, got out, and walked back. No way for Nico to know who he was, what he looked like, or what vehicle he was driving, but that sense, that awareness, that he could get caught, rode him hard. He walked down one way and across up the four sides, then he walked down the alleyway, slowing his steps, as he studied the massive building.

"Christ, he could have a half-dozen kids in there," he murmured. "How the hell is that fair?"

The more he stared at what this guy had for wealth, the

angrier he became. It was all too possible that he might have been the most broke, the most in debt, and the most borderline destitute person in the whole damn group. For somebody who came from such high beginnings, this was bullshit. It was dark outside, and the lights were on inside the house, but there didn't appear to be movement inside.

The dark alleyway had a garage and a side gate. He tried to open it, but it was latched from the inside. He could probably jump the gate in the front of the house because it was much lower. The one at the back was very inaccessible. He suspected it was also locked, which meant the garage was probably where the vehicle was parked. And he didn't see any side door, outside of the massive front door and the one rear entryway, to get in either. The fence came right up to the side of the gate and went all the way around the property.

Muttering to himself and getting more pissed by the minute, he headed to the front. In the darkness, he stepped onto the neighbor's side and studied the fence between the two homes. It wasn't as high on this side, about the same as the front. However, it was a bit out of the view from the front windows and the house on the sides. No lights were on in the neighbor's house, and the For Sale sign in the front yard seemed to say that nobody would be home and probably hadn't been for a while.

Damn, a cop car pulled slowly through the area. Damn. He froze up against the fence. The cop made the block and came by slowly once more. Damn, damn, damn. *If he runs my plates* ... Running back to the alleyway, he watched for the black-and-white. Taking a chance, he jumped in his vehicle and left as fast as he could.

He hit the steering wheel over and over, still cussing. *I'll have to come back. Damn it.* Meanwhile he searched for a coffee shop, pulled in, using their Wi-Fi to connect with Nico. **Give me until Monday 5:00 p.m. to get some cash.**

.

# CHAPTER 18

*Friday Late Afternoon*

I T WAS STILL Friday, another busy day, but, so far, Kate hadn't accomplished anything. She got the canvassing back from the entire neighborhood and everybody except for one person said the same thing—that they hadn't seen Ken. But one person reported seeing him walking in his property, using a cell phone. With the name of the person and the address, she quickly bolted to her feet and told Rodney, "I'll go talk to the one person who saw our pedophile."

"Okay," he said. "I'm working with Forensics on that street."

"I'll be back," she said. She raced outside, picked up a pretzel from the vendor on the corner of the block, grabbed a coffee, and headed to her car, taking off to Ken's place. She knocked on the neighbor's door and waited, in her hand. A little old lady opened the door and stared up at her in worry.

Kate smiled. "Hello, I'm Detective Morgan," she said. "I understand that you saw one of your neighbors, Ken, out walking in his yard."

The little old lady nodded and tilted her head, sending bubbled lavender-colored hair in all directions. "I did talk to that one young gentleman about Ken," she said, with a smile. "A nice young cop."

"How often did you see Ken?" Kate asked, in a conversational tone. The problem with witnesses is that you never knew what they knew, and they didn't know themselves, until they were given the right questions in order to pry out the information.

"I used to see him a fair bit," she said, "but less and less as time went by."

"Do you know how long he's lived here?"

"Quite a while," she said. "Maybe ten years."

"And he doesn't work?"

"Well, I imagine you know more about him than I do," she said, with a trilling laugh.

"Yes," Kate said, with a half laugh. "He doesn't appear to have been working constructively for the last five years."

"No. I'm sure he told me at one point in time that he was looking after his sister's kids."

"Did you ever see him with children?"

"At the odd times," she said, "but not for quite a few years now."

"You know that he hasn't been out of prison for all that long?"

The little old lady's eyebrows shot up. "I didn't know that," she said. "I guess maybe that's why I haven't seen him all that often recently."

"He served four years," she said.

"But he's been home for several weeks now at least, if not several months," the lady protested.

"Exactly," she said. "He's been home at least six months, I think."

The old lady looked relieved. "For a moment there, I thought I was losing it."

"No. He was away but has been back for some time."

"And did you say what was he in for?"

Kate looked around, as if checking to see if anybody was close by. "He was a pedophile," she said quietly.

The little old lady's face blanched. "Oh no, please don't tell me that he hurt those little children."

"I'm not sure which little children you mean," she said, "but I'm afraid it's all too possible. He didn't have a sister."

The little old lady immediately brought her hands to her chest and started patting herself, as if trying to recover from a shock.

"Ma'am, can I help you sit down somewhere? I know this is a bit much."

"Come in. Come in," she said, and she let herself be led to the couch, where she sank into a corner.

Kate walked back over and closed the door. "I'm sorry. It's been such a shock."

"You just never know, do you?" she said. "My name is Alice. And I've been alone for a long time, so I love to take an interest in my neighbors, though I find most people don't really like to have an interest taken in them."

"I think most people prefer privacy these days," Kate said, with a smile.

"It's very sad. Nobody does anything for each other anymore."

"Well, in this case, it's quite possible that your neighbor had something to hide."

"I won't sleep now, thinking about the children I saw him with."

"Maybe you could describe those children to me," she said.

The old lady looked at her for a moment, concentrating on something. "You know what? I think I might have a picture of them too."

Kate sat back, her heart slamming against her chest. "If you could show us any pictures you have, that would be a huge help."

"Let me take a look," she said. "I have a bunch that are unsorted." She got up and disappeared. While she was away, Kate got up and walked around the living room, checking out the photos on the wall. They were obviously of an era gone by. There was her husband and what looked like two children of her own.

When Alice walked back in, she pointed at the picture Kate was looking at and said, "That's my husband and two sons. They are all gone now."

"Even your sons?"

Alice nodded sadly. "Yes. I didn't realize it, but I had passed down a rare disorder to them," she said. "They both had it and were gone before thirty."

Such sadness and grief were in her voice that Kate couldn't speak for a moment. "I'm so sorry," she said. "That's got to be difficult."

"It's even worse when you find out you're responsible," she said, "but there was no testing back then, no way to know."

"That must have been emotional," Kate said gently. "But what if you had known? Surely that wouldn't have been easier."

Alice looked at her, understanding. "Isn't that the truth? Maybe I'm blessed as it is."

"You at least had them for a time," she said. "It looks like you were all very happy then."

"Indeed," Alice said, with a smile. "My husband died about ten, eleven years ago now," she said. "God rest his soul. He found the loss of the boys even more difficult to bear than I did."

"I think every man wants a son," Kate said.

Alice sat down, placing a thin six-inch-long plastic bin on the coffee table.

"Where are these photos from?"

"I had a camera for a while," Alice said. "I was trying to fill my time after my husband's death, and I thought maybe I could pick up a hobby. So I started taking pictures, but I found that, once we moved into the digital photos, it was so much cheaper, yet I had nobody to show the photos to anyway," she said. "So it didn't seem to make any sense to even take them, you know? I'd look at them once and never look at them again."

She pointed at the ones in the bin. "Originally I started printing off some of the digital pictures," she said. "I had a photo printer, though you can see that they aren't very good. But here's what I have." There were some full-size sheets of photos in the bin and a bunch of smaller ones too. Some were film paper, as if she had had them done at a store, and others were, indeed, just on plain printer paper.

Kate looked at Alice and asked, "Do you mind if I look through them?"

"I'll give you half, and I'll take half," she said, "to see if I can find the ones I was thinking of."

And that's what they did.

Kate went through them, noticing that the pictures were everything from flowers to vehicles to storms and the odd person. When Kate got down to the bottom of her pile, there were more photos of people, and she studied them, as she tried to figure out which ones might be Ken and which ones might be other people. She stopped at one and tapped her finger on it. "That's Ken, isn't it?"

Alice looked over at the picture and nodded. "That's him."

"Who is he talking to? Do you know?"

"No," she said, "no idea."

Kate put that picture off to the side and went through several more photos. Another one of Ken, standing alone. She put it off to the side as well.

Alice was going through her pile much more slowly. Then she picked up one and said, "Here. This is one of them." In the photo, Ken was walking on the street, holding the hand of a little boy.

Kate stared at the picture and shook her head. "I don't recognize the little boy."

"Maybe that's a good thing," Alice said. "I keep hoping that maybe it's a neighbor's child he was looking after for a little bit."

"Maybe," she said. "Do you mind if I take this photo?"

"Please take all of them," she said. "I don't want any of him left around." She found one more, and, in that one, he was pushing a little buggy.

"Was a baby in there?"

"It was a toddler, but I don't know how old."

Kate took that photo too. "Also I'd like any photos showing people coming and going at Ken's house," she said. "Not that you would have been watching or anything."

"Oh, I watch," Alice said somewhat derisively. "I was looking for anything to keep myself busy." She grabbed a few of the remaining photos and went through them. "That one, that one, and that one," she said. "They were all of Ken's place, and, indeed, people are standing there, talking to him."

Armed with a new collection of photographs, Kate stood

and thanked Alice for her time and for the photos. "Should you come across any more, Alice, just give me a shout." Kate placed her card on the coffee table. "If you remember anything about times that you've met him or things he might have said, I'll like to hear from you."

"What is it you're trying to find?" Alice asked.

"Friends and associates and, of course, any children he may have come into contact with," Kate said bluntly. "We are looking for other victims and potentially other people like him."

"Now that just doesn't bear thinking about," Alice said.

"I know, which is exactly why we have to do this," she said, and, with that, she took her leave.

Back in the office, she showed Rodney. "This is what we came up with." He stared at the photos in surprise.

"Wow," he said, "that's one nosy neighbor."

"Maybe so, but what I want to know is who this guy is," she said, pointing to one of the pictures.

"What about the other ones?" he asked, tapping the three at the end.

"They look more like they were just passing by," she said. "Looks like they walked down the sidewalk, and he was there, talking to them. Could have been friends, but might only have been strangers stopping to talk for a few moments."

"So get on that one," Rodney said.

"How though? These photos aren't even that good," she murmured, frowning at the photo in her hand.

"Some of the tech guys are really good with that stuff," he said. "Show it to them."

She turned to head back to her corner. She was not a computer whiz, but she was decent at some of it. She scanned a photo in and sent it to the tech guys.

When Kaplan contacted her, he asked, "Where did you get that photo from?"

"From one of the neighbors," she said. "Why?"

"I was hoping for the original, like a digital file. And poor quality."

"I'm not sure it's available," she said and quickly explained. "Any chance of facial recognition on that guy talking to our dead pedophile Ken?"

"I can do my best," he said, "but the face is twisted, so it's not an easy one. So first impression—not a hope."

"It's connected to the pedophile cases that we have ongoing," she said. "The same for these other two I just sent you. Two little children."

"*Great*," he said sarcastically. "I always love looking for images of children."

"I'll send copies of them to the Missing Persons Division and to the International Sex Crimes Division too," she said.

"Let's hope you don't get any hits."

"I know." When she hung up, she realized just how much everybody hated working cases involving children.

### Saturday Noon

THE NEXT DAY, Saturday, at about noon, just as Kate was trying to get some healthy food into her body for a change, she got a call from Detective Martins in the International Sex Crimes Division.

"Dennis Fragipano of ICE sent on your images. The female child in the photo," he said, "she's shown up in over ten thousand different images."

"How long ago?"

"As far as we can tell, about twelve years ago," he said. "It's one of the earliest as far as we can tell."

"So it probably started with our dead pedophile Ken?"

"Or he was one of the earlier ones to get her."

"*Get* her?"

"Yes," he ended up saying. "Chances are she was taken early and kept within the ring."

Kate sank back in the chair. "See? That's what I was wondering," she said. "Are these children being handed around?"

"In some cases, yes. Sometimes these are big rings, and it's all about the images, the photos, and the videos. In other cases, small groups pass the children around."

"That's sick."

"It's all sick," he said. "I have something else I want to send you. I tried to get to you at your office late yesterday and missed you."

"What is it?"

"That mark on the wrist," he said.

She straightened. "Did you find somebody with it?"

"Two photos," he said. "Images of just the hands, but both showing what appears to be, or what could be, that same mark."

"Send them to me."

"Already done," he said cheerfully.

She got up and walked over to her laptop, just as the images came in. And, sure enough, it was the same mark. She called him back and said, "This one in particular has three lines. Are these both from the same guy?"

"Same hand, different angles."

"Okay, that's why I can't see the same lines in the other

ones. You have no idea who this man is, right?"

"Not yet, but it's one of our priorities," he said. "We have quite a few images with him in it. But it could take years," he cautioned.

"Great," she said. "Lots of different children?"

"Different children, but it's like he is keeping them for a while, maybe a month. It depends on how many photos we have of each one, and we can't really give a time frame. If we don't get an outside image, then we don't know what day, what time of the year, that sort of thing," he said. "We don't know if these pedophiles have had them for one week or for six months."

*Six months* rang a bell to her. "We have a deceased little boy who was found," she said. "He was in pretty rough shape. We're still waiting on the autopsy, but he'd been missing six months."

"And in that case," he said, "he could have been with one pedophile, or he could have been passed around to a dozen."

"God, that doesn't bear thinking about," she cried out.

"Which is why most of us can't do this job for too long," he said. "We see terrible things and can't imagine anything like that happening to our loved ones, but, the fact of the matter is, it does happen. And it happens more than we would like to think."

"Scumbags," she said.

"So you do your job," he said. "Just think that, for every time we find something, we're getting another piece of the puzzle."

"I want the noose," she said harshly. "I want the noose, and I want to tighten it on this asshole's neck."

"In your case, this perv is already dead and gone, isn't

he?"

"Yes," she said, "Ken is, but I'm starting to suspect we have a ring here in Vancouver."

"Unfortunately I think you're right."

### Saturday, Late Afternoon, through Sunday Dawn

SIMON WOKE UP from his nap late Saturday afternoon and sat up, swinging his legs over the bed. He got up and walked onto the balcony. He never went on a cruise unless he could get a balconied room. Last night had been fun, getting back into the swing of things, as it always had been. Normal routine, he won a few, lost a few, won a little more, and then finally called it quits. He had several drinks with a friend and several other acquaintances here.

But he'd yet to even figure out who else was here because he hadn't cared. He'd just been so busy losing himself in his hobby. Tonight would be a whole different deal though. He had a quick shower and headed off to get his first meal of the day, and, with that under his belt, he headed in to prepare for a heavy evening again. Back in his room, he quickly got changed and headed out again. They were on international waters, but he found himself wondering what the detective was up to. He had checked the news, but he found nothing new, and that was good with him.

As he headed toward the casino a couple hours later, he looked up to find Yale sitting there, with Ben and Jerry, two other guys Simon knew well. He sat down and had a drink with them.

"Are we keeping up this lifestyle forever?" Ben asked.

"My wife has given me an ultimatum," Jerry said. "This

is the last weekend, or she is gone."

"Ouch," Yale said, "maybe it's time you got rid of her."

Jerry nodded. "But I love her," he said, "so this is my last hurrah."

"Then we need to make it a good one," Simon said in a joking manner. With the others in agreement, that started them onto heavy drinking, heavy gambling, and Simon didn't even worry about winning. By the time it was dawn, Jerry stood ten grand to the good, and he'd had a blast. They walked him to his stateroom.

As he closed the door behind him, he called out, "You guys are the best."

They split up at that point, and Simon headed back to his room. He dropped on his bed. He was only a couple rooms away from where the others were, but he wanted time alone. He'd made a good fourteen, fifteen thousand tonight, and, considering he hadn't even worked at it, it was just an easy win. He closed his eyes, and almost immediately his phone rang. He groaned, lifted it, and knew that everything else he did would cost him, but it was the detective. He swore. "What the fuck do you want on a Sunday morning? I haven't slept yet. You know where I am?"

"I know where you are," she said calmly. "I want you to come in and see me Monday when you get home."

"Why?" he said.

"I have some guys I want to see if you know," she said. "I think that one pedophile was working with a local ring."

His stomach twisted, churning at the thought. "What's that got to do with me?"

"I don't know," she said. "But, just like you sent me those numbers because it had to do with me, I'm calling you because I think it has to do with you." And, on that note, she hung up.

He dropped back onto the bed and groaned. He needed sleep. He had to be rested up for whatever the hell she had planned for him. As he slowly drifted off to sleep, he was once again assailed by the same nightmares that had driven him to the police station the first time.

# CHAPTER 19

*First Monday in July, Morning*

KATE WASN'T AT all surprised when she got a text message this morning on her phone, saying that Simon had docked but wasn't coming in for several hours, as he needed a shower and a change of clothes.

**One o'clock**, she sent back and didn't get a response. It was Monday, after all, but then she didn't seem to know the difference. She worked most of the time and didn't have a partner or a family. By the time one o'clock rolled around, she stepped out of the station to wait for him, just in time to catch him arriving.

He glared at her. "Why the hell did I have to come in right now?"

"Because," she said and led the way back to her desk. She motioned at the chair and then handed him a bunch of photos.

He stared at the old pictures, some just printed on regular paper. "What are these?"

"That's the dead pedophile in the morgue," she said. "The one with the safe that you helped to open."

He shrugged and handed them back. "I don't know who he is," he said. She handed him a more recent photo.

He winced. "Is this a mug shot?"

"It is. This is one"—she splayed out another one on

top—"from a couple months ago."

He handed it back and then stopped, snatched it back from her hand again. He frowned. "I've seen him down at a restaurant," he said. "At Stevie's. A burger joint downtown."

"A favorite hangout of his apparently," she said. "And we were wondering—because we found out he'd been there that evening before his death—if you'd been around at the same time."

He looked up at her and said, "That was the night of that local poker game with the cheater."

"Right," she said. "But did you go to Stevie's?"

"No," he said, "I didn't."

"Nobody there has cameras," she said sadly. "It would be nice if we had video cameras of the patrons, so we saw if he talked to anybody."

"Guys like that don't have to talk to anybody," he said, his voice still harsh. "They live in their own world."

"Look here," she said, handing him the third photo, with the two men talking.

Simon turned the photo ever-so-slightly and frowned.

"Do you know him?"

"Not sure," he said. He held it out at arm's length and then shrugged. "It's a really shitty photo."

"We're working on that," she said. "I was just wondering if you knew him. They appear to be quite friendly."

"Doesn't matter," he said. "They don't generally have anything to do with anybody in their own field."

"That's true, … unless they are part of the ring," she said. "And that's the theory I'm operating on."

"There's probably what? One hundred and fifty, two hundred released pedophiles in the city? Or maybe a couple thousand."

"I know," she said. "We've been keeping an eye on a bunch of them."

"No way to really check unless you get into their group chat."

"We're doing that too," she said. "But, so far, nothing." Just then, her phone rang. She glanced down and answered it. "You got into his laptop? Ah, now that's exactly what I want to hear," she said. "I'll be there in a few minutes." She stood up, looked at Simon, and said, "You can go now."

He sat back and glared at her. "What if I don't want to?"

"Too damn bad," she said cheerfully. "Our forensic techs got into Ken's laptop. Apparently they've found some interesting chats."

He nodded, stood, and said, "Good. The question is whether they are local or not."

"Well, hopefully," she said, "we just found something that will crack this wide open."

"Good," he said. "Then you don't have to hassle me anymore."

"Am I hassling you?" she asked curiously.

He just glared at her.

She shrugged and said, "Thanks for coming in." She watched as he turned and walked away. As soon as he was out of sight, she headed for the Forensic Department. As she walked in, she said, "What have you got for me?"

"All kinds of goodies," the tech said. "Looks like this case is starting to pop."

———❦❦———

SIMON HAD TO admit that he was a little miffed. He wanted to see what forensics had found. Curiosity was one thing, but this was something else. He knew the cops needed a break in the case, but he did too. He wished he could do something to help. He brought himself up short, shocked and surprised. After a lifetime of trying to stay uninvolved, he was doing a hell of a lot worse on that whole plan than he'd ever had before.

Was it the detective? Or was it the series of unending nightmares about kids? He didn't want any more of that. As long as he kept fooling himself, he could keep believing that it was all about the nightmares. But he knew the detective was affecting him in some way, and it didn't appear to be in a good way.

As he stepped outside the police station, he walked a few blocks to get his bearings, seeing an outdoor café up ahead. Still unsettled, he walked in, ordered a coffee, and then sat outside on the little patio deck, watching the world go by. It had been a successful gambling weekend, but something was seriously unsettling about coming off the docks and heading straight to the police station.

He pulled up his phone and downloaded all the messages that he couldn't receive while out in international waters. He went often enough, but he also took it as a break from so many problems that always seemed to assail him on a daily basis. It was a pain in the ass in most cases, but, right now, as he sat here drinking his coffee, he quickly sorted through his emails. He had no intention of calling anybody back at this point. He would have to, soon enough, but not right now.

With nothing else popping up as being major, he finished his coffee and got up, then started slowly back toward where he wanted to be. It was a good walk, and he might just catch an Uber on the way.

As he headed out, he caught sight of Yale. He looked at

him in surprise, as the two met in the middle of the block. "Hey, what are you doing here?" Simon asked.

Yale smirked. "That's what I would ask you."

"Not doing a whole lot," Simon said. "Just heading home."

"You were in a hell of a hurry to get off the boat this morning."

"I had an appointment. Otherwise I would have stayed on until the end, as I normally do."

Yale shrugged. "Stayed on as long as I could for the crowd, and then I had to go." He lifted a hand and walked past. "Have a good day. See you in a couple weeks." With that, he strolled down the street in the opposite direction.

Simon turned to watch his old friend go by; Yale was really aging. He'd always been what Simon thought was maybe a decade older, but he wasn't sure. Now it was obvious that the lifestyle was starting to get to Yale. Something Simon himself needed to consider. Shrugging, he headed home, choosing to take the long walk instead of grabbing a ride.

He couldn't help but still be irritated that he wasn't allowed in on the investigation. The detective had no reason to trust him, but then she also had no reason to consider him a suspect, especially not since he sent her those numbers for the safe. And it was a damn good thing he had done that.

As he thought about her and considered what they were doing, another series of numbers popped into his head. He frowned and shook his head.

"Ha, no way." No way he would send that to her. But, with every step he took, it was like a nail being driven into his skull. Finally he pulled out his phone and sent the numbers to her, then put away his cell. Realizing that she would likely call, he pulled it back out, shut it off. When he finally got home, he was cold and tired. When he stood in the front lobby and headed toward the stairs to his apartment, the doorman at the front smiled at him.

"Good morning, sir."

He nodded. And then he stopped and asked, "Was it a quiet weekend, Harry?"

The doorman walked over and checked the log. "Looks like it."

"Good, that's the way I like it."

"In that case, he said, "that was the weekend you should have stayed home."

"So damn true," he said, with a groan and a chuckle. He headed toward his apartment, then put on a small pot of coffee. It seemed like all he was doing was drinking alcohol and coffee. He brought out his laptop and checked his accounts and his projects. So far, everything was reasonably on target. That always made him suspicious as hell. He turned his phone back on and had missed several phone calls. They were all from the same number. He snorted.

"Tough shit, not everybody is on your time frame," he snapped. Just then, the phone rang again. He figured it was her. "What?"

"Did you try?" his ex said, in a trembling and tearful voice.

Shit, this was the last thing he needed. "I've tried, and I've tried," he said. "I'm sorry, but I haven't had any luck."

"You know you could if you wanted to," she said.

"If it was that damn easy," he said, "I wouldn't have been dealing with all this shit, now would I? It would already be solved."

"Would it?" she asked. "Or would you still be trying to

avoid it all?"

"That's not what I'm trying to do," he said. "I'm sorry this is happening, but I don't know anything."

He hung up on her, so frustrated because, if he did know something at this point, he would say so, even if just to get rid of Caitlin. No, that wasn't true at all; he would do it to help Leonard. That was the right thing to do, and, when he could, he would always help children. Hell, some of his real estate projects were geared toward helping single women and children who had no money. But it was all just such a crapshoot. He sat outside on the small deck and called out to his grandmother.

"You could have warned me," he said. Of course there would be no answer; his grandmother had no cares at this point. In a situation like this, he would do a lot to help. Anybody who thought otherwise didn't know who he was at all. And that was the problem because he'd practiced that whole isolation thing for a lifetime. When his phone rang again, he looked down at it, and this time it was the detective. "What?" he snapped irritably.

"Did you know?"

"Know what?" he said. "I'm sitting in my damn apartment, looking out at the city and wishing to hell all of you people would just leave me alone."

"Listen. The numbers you sent me were the password to the online chat for these ugly little pedophile pukes. So why would I ever leave you alone?"

"It was?" He bolted to his feet. "Jesus, did you get something decent?"

"Well, I got something sick," she said, and her tone revealed the depression and the disgust at whatever she'd found.

"Yes, but did it help?"

"We're hoping so, but, of course, we didn't get real names or anything. But we're trying to track them down and find locations."

"And what about children?"

She hesitated, and then her voice broke into the softest of whispers and said, "Yes, an online transaction is happening right now with one little girl."

"Oh, shit," he said. "How old?"

"Five, and she's been in the system for a couple years."

"Oh God," he said. "Can you find her?"

"We're working on it," she said. "If you get anything else, let me know."

### Monday, Late Afternoon

STILL PISSED FROM Friday's excursion to Nico's house in Richmond being interrupted by the cops, he returned to Nico's the following Monday, late in the day, wanting cover of darkness, cussing the whole trip, but watching for cop cars. At least he had scoped out the exterior the first time here. So, deciding to jump the neighbor's fence, he quickly hopped the shared side fence, wincing as his bones rattled all the way down to the jarring landing on the other side. He wasn't anywhere as agile as he used to be. Life hadn't been all that easy on him either. He'd also aged a lot faster than many of his peers had. Prison would do that to a person.

He snuck up to the side of Nico's house and just stood here, waiting for something, … for anything really. When he couldn't hear anything inside or out, he crept down the house, closer to where he thought the kitchen might be, so he could peer inside. No light was on except for one over the stove, sending out a warm glow across the kitchen. He snorted at that. It was such a high-end kitchen that it made him sick. He used to live in a house like this. Had grown up in a house like this.

He swept around the corner to the back-porch door and, with a gentle hand, reached out and twisted it. It opened easily enough. No alarm went off, at least not an audible alarm. He studied the back side of the house, looking for video cameras, sensors or the like, but found nothing. With the door cracked open ever-so-slightly, he pushed it open another few inches, and, when still no alarm was raised from inside or out, he slipped into the kitchen and let the door close silently behind him.

"Now," he whispered to himself, "where is she?"

He went through the whole main floor and hadn't found anyone yet. He didn't know if Nico was even here. He had found some mail in the kitchen that had Nico's name on it. He quickly took photographs of several places around the house. He didn't dare stay too long, in case Nico came back. So far, he hadn't found what he was looking for. He may have to come back for a third trip this way, but it would be faster now because he knew the layout.

He did a quick circle of the upstairs and then raced downstairs, knowing that time was of the essence. And then he saw the basement door. Of course the house had a basement, though it was pretty damn stupid, considering Richmond sat on reclaimed land. But, hey, if they wanted to play the water-in-the-basement game, that was fine with him.

He slipped downstairs, staying in the dark, until he got to the bottom, where he searched for a light switch. He quickly turned it on, only to find that it was just a basement, storage and all. He quickly swept around to inspect the side walls, and finally, behind a bunch of boxes, he found another door. He brought his hand up in anticipation and slowly reached for the doorknob.

# CHAPTER 20

"SO NOW THAT we are in on the chat, what have we got?" Kate asked the forensic tech. "And is this something we should be involving ICE, Sex Crimes Unit, and the International Crime Division?" It was enough to make her head spin. But if there was any chance that these men and their sick games went farther than Vancouver, which the images at least had, she wanted everyone on board.

"I'll update them when I'm done," Doran said.

"The talk was about the sale of a little girl, with a price war between these two online handles," said one the techs. She didn't know his name. "But currently we have no idea who they are. Nor do we have a location for the little girl. Correct, David?" he asked his coworker.

"Not yet," he said. "We've seen a couple similar versions of these handles in other chats though."

"So, it's likely the same guys?" Kate asked.

"I would think so. They are fairly distinctive. And usually so on a child porn site," David said, having both downloaded and uploaded images.

"So, what do we have to do to catch these guys?" Kate asked David.

"We are trying to track back the IP addresses, and we'll see if we can get the data from that in order to find out where they are coming from."

"Another one of those laws we can't break, right? We don't have access to them?" Kate sighed with frustration.

"No, the communications companies have the information."

"So, what else are we supposed to do?" she whined.

Just then, one of the men at the side leaned over and said, "We've got a chat here that's making me a little suspicious."

"Bring it up on the screen, Aaron," David said, now standing beside her. They brought it up and quickly went through the conversation. "So, he got the price down to twelve hundred, and then what?"

"He wants until Monday night—tonight—to get the money together, But I think he's fishing," Aaron said. "He is asking for proof of life, but he also wants something outside. Like a photo from outside."

"Meaning?" Kate asked.

Aaron hesitated and said, "Honestly, I'm wondering if he is looking for a landmark to pinpoint the child's location, possibly to kidnap the child himself instead of paying that price."

"Wow. That takes a lot of nerve. Do you think they are local?" Kate asked him.

"I'm not sure," he said. "They are obviously still being very cagey with each other, and, although they are friendly, they aren't giving up personal information."

"Which would be the stupidest thing anybody here in this chat could do," she muttered.

"But we do see it happen, and these guys have been online for a while. We've gone back at least four or five years with these two, plus Ken."

"But part of the time Ken had been in prison. How does

that work?"

"Yeah, he sure was, and sometimes he managed to get onto the chat anyway."

She shook her head at that. "What? Isn't that restricted?"

"These guys make a life of finding ways to get around the rules."

"What about that image that I sent you earlier with the street number?"

"I've got it right here," Aaron said. He switched to a second monitor, with a different window up, and brought up a street.

She looked at it and frowned. "Do you think that's it?"

"Not only do I think that's it," he said, "but I think it's taken from inside this house here." He brought up a Google map and quickly pointed, placing himself right on the street.

She nodded. "Give me that address, and I'll go check it out."

"It's in Richmond," Aaron said.

"Even better. I can get there in twenty minutes and check this out." And, with that, she grabbed the address and walked away. She called back as she left, "Let me know if you get anything on that chat room."

"Will do," he said, and she headed out.

She didn't bother telling Rodney or Owen because there wasn't anything specific to tell them. They were working on the other murder.

For Jason, they were still waiting on the drug tests.

The traffic was heavy at this time of day—rush-hour traffic on a Monday evening no less—and, by the time she made it to the address, she was swearing at the forty-five-minute trip. She quickly drove around the block and back and then checked out who else was living on this street.

None of the names rang a bell, and none of them had popped up in her criminal database.

Until she got to the search of the house at the far end. Some names of owners for houses in the middle of the block didn't appear yet either. She quickly brought up the corner house on her tablet and then phoned Rodney from her car.

"I'm in the middle of the block on the road that we saw on that video," she said. "The picture we found inside Ken's living room? Well, Aaron thinks the photo was taken from inside the house on the corner—just like we thought with the road signs we found. A porch goes around the front side of the house. So that road sign is just barely visible through the front window. The online record states Ken Roscoe is the owner—a pedophile, convicted, served his time, released to a halfway house, now lives here. No issues since his release. So that's Ken's property. It's all dark right now, which we would expect with a dead guy as the owner."

"Well, he should have popped immediately with that address. I'll get Forensics out there pronto."

"Good. Now I've run across another registered perv. This Nico guy, also living in this same block, he did show up in my search, but we hadn't had any problems with him either, and it's his family residence, so it's not like he's just out of the halfway house."

"So, as long as he stayed low and out of trouble, he just was a name."

"Exactly. The database tells us he lives here, but it doesn't tell us anything else. So ... I'm wondering if that house on the corner was another playhouse for Nico to share with Ken? Or is it possible for two pervs to live on this same street and operate out of the same child porn ring, sharing children?"

"Anything's possible. Any sign of life around Nico's place?"

"Lights are on," she said. "It's early evening on a Monday. A vehicle is parked in the back alley, but it just appears to be one of the neighbors."

"Well, go on up and ask. See if anybody is there," Rodney said. "You should have called me though. I would have come with you. And we need to call Richmond RCMP. You're in their turf," he warned.

"I would have if the tech guys had found anything constructive on the two players trying to buy slash sell the little girl online," she said, "but they didn't—not yet anyway—except that these two guys had been in this child ring online for at least four to five years."

"They got access while they were in prison?"

"Aaron in IT doesn't seem to think that's out of reason."

"That's even sicker than normal," Rodney said. "We send them to prison as a punishment, not to create support groups to help each other hurt kids."

"Exactly. Call Richmond RCMP for me, will you? I'll take a walk and see what I see." She pocketed her phone, hopped out of her vehicle, and walked through the gate and up to the front door. She rang the doorbell and waited. There was a big long echo, a hollow emptiness on the inside. Yet it made no sense if he were living here. It was obvious that he could have gone somewhere for the afternoon, but it didn't have that kind of feeling. It had an unlived-in feeling.

She walked the porch and peered in through the big windows on the ground to catch a glimpse. But it was all full of furniture, old-money kind of furniture. She frowned again, walked back to the front door, and rang the doorbell again, then quickly sent Rodney a text, saying she'd gotten no answer.

"Not surprising," Rodney said, when he called her instead of texting. "According to the record, there's been no calls to that address. At least not in the last couple years."

"I wonder if this guy went to jail," she asked.

"Seven years ago," Rodney said. "He'd been quiet before then. *Nico Dunfer.* He's a professor, a botany professor. Richmond RCMP are on their way to your location."

"Interesting. Okay, I'll keep it up." She popped her phone back into her pocket, and, just as she was about to come down the front steps, she heard a sound. She moved around the side of the house, and, sure enough, somebody was sneaking out a window. Annoyed, she held up her badge and called out, "Police. Stop!"

Instead he shot her a terrified look and bolted. He jumped over the fence, even though she came racing behind and jumped over after him. But she was just that split second behind. He had dumped the garbage can, so she landed on it and rolled to the ground. She was on her feet in seconds, racing down the same direction, but he hopped into the vehicle that she'd seen parked up ahead and took off.

Good thing she had taken a photo of the license plate. She swore and called Rodney back. "Somebody escaped out the rear window," she said. She quickly gave him the license plate number.

"I'm on it," he said. "Hold up." And then he swore. "Well, damn, that's registered to another convicted pedophile."

"What are you talking about?"

"A different one entirely," he said.

"Do you have an address for him?"

"Yeah, but its back down in this corner."

"So, what the hell is he doing in his buddy Nico's house in Richmond?" She stopped, turned, and looked back at the house. "I need a warrant to get in. No Richmond RCMP here yet either. I can't get rid of the feeling something is going on here."

"Hang on," he said. "Let me make some calls."

She stepped back to the open window, knowing that she needed an official warrant, unless she had justifiable cause. As far as she was concerned, having one pedophile in another pedophile's house, while several kids were missing, was a good enough reason for her.

She pulled on a pair of latex gloves from her pocket. She always carried them. Then climbed through the window and stepped into the kitchen. The basement door was open; she made her way downstairs with the lights on and found just storage. It didn't look to be anything other than that, until she came around the corner and saw another door. She walked over, and it was locked.

Kate swore and pushed her ear against the door. She couldn't hear anything, but that wasn't good enough for her. She'd learned a long time ago how to pick locks; she just wasn't allowed to use that method. But, right now, she didn't have a whole lot of choice. She pulled her tools out of her back pocket and quickly popped the lock. She pushed open the door and turned on the light. There in front of her, curled up in the bed, was a child. She raced over and checked, and the child was alive. It was a little girl. She called Rodney. "I'm inside. I found a child in the basement. Behind a locked door. She's alive but comatose."

"Jesus!" he said.

"Get me an ambulance and get your ass out here. I think this is the girl from the chat room."

"Watch your back," he said. "You only ran off one of the pedophiles. So where's the second one?"

"Good point," she said. "Get your ass here and fast." She didn't want to leave the child, so she got up and walked over to the door and locked it again. She took several photographs of the little girl's face and sent it to Aaron and the IT Division, and then to the guys following up on sex trafficking rings. Something had to be here that she could use to get this little girl out of here.

As she turned, she stared at the closet; the small solemn room was all dolled up as a little child's room, with a child's bed, all kinds of toys, and a bookshelf off to the side. But in a corner of the room were cameras. She quickly grabbed pieces of clothing and put them over the cameras, in case somebody was watching her right now. Then she heard footsteps.

Swearing under her breath, she raced behind the door and waited. She didn't know who the hell it was, but no way she would let anybody take this little girl again. Not on her watch.

## Monday Evening

SIMON COULDN'T RELAX; he couldn't seem to settle into doing anything. It was Monday evening, and all he could do was think about those kids. It was pissing him off. He hopped up, grabbed his wallet, and walked down the stairs this time, forgoing the elevators, hoping to burn through some of that ugly energy. He strolled out to the street. He needed to pick up something for dinner, simply too damn tired to do much. And he was frustrated, angry. A fish-and-chips shop was not too far from here, so he walked that way and ordered some, along with a beer, and sat down with it.

As long as he was within the boundary of the shop, he could have his beer, but he longed to get a walk around the block. As he sat here, he knew something was going on. He saw it—just vague disjointed visions. He felt it. And, damn it, he tasted it, and that made the fish and chips taste like shit. He looked down at it in disgust, knowing he needed it for sustenance, but he sure as hell didn't want to eat the rest of this.

His fingers itched to contact the detective, just knowing that she'd found something. He could only hope that what she found was the right something. Finally he couldn't help himself. He quickly sent her a text. **Progress?**

When there was no answer, he got pissed again. Of course he got no answer because she wasn't allowed to tell him anything. But there had to be some progress. He sent her a second text. **Follow up when you can.**

Then he got up, tossed back the rest of his beer, dumped the last of the fish and chips he couldn't eat, and headed home again. Instead of walking the normal route, he went via some old buildings he was rehabbing; then he walked back to where he had found the little girl's body. Children were in every corner of this damn world, and it was distressing, bringing back so many ugly memories. Memories he had no intention of dealing with.

As he went to cross the street, a pickup truck bolted in front of him; it didn't even have its lights on. He stepped back quickly to avoid getting run over and swore at him. The guy had a fist out the window, with a finger straight up to the sky. Simon just glared at the small little truck as it tore off. Then he saw the license plate numbers, yet he shouldn't have been able to read them. The truck was going by too fast, but the numbers were emblazoned in his head.

He frowned and didn't know what to make of it. But he had no instinctive urge to send those to her, so he carried on. Soon his footsteps took him in the same direction as the truck had gone. That didn't seem logical either, since no way he would catch up with a speeding vehicle; the asshole would be miles away by now. Except, as he came around the corner, he saw the same truck, parked off to the side.

He frowned at that, but he approached slowly, not sure what he was looking for. He walked past, and the driver was sitting in the truck with his head back, deep breathing, as if trying to calm down. Simon pounded on the window and heard a shriek from the inside, as the guy woke from whatever meditative nap he was trying to take. He rolled his window down and screamed, "Asshole, you fucking asshole!"

But a tremble was in his voice, as if he were terrified. He had had a rough life too, proven by the little bit of his aging face Simon could see. He looked to be in his fifties easily. Whatever his age, he was scared. Catching that note, Simon looked at him and snapped, "You are the one who flipped me off, after nearly killing me on the road."

But the other guy just started up the truck, shaking his head. Wordlessly he pulled away at a much more sedate pace.

"What was that all about?" Simon wondered aloud. Was the jerk just out here, trying to recover from some shock of his own? And recover from what? But, in this location, it could be anything. It was a pretty ugly side of town. As Simon watched the blue truck head up the street, it took a right, heading toward the area where Simon had found the little dead girl. Suspicious, Simon quickly took several shortcuts through the back alleyways and came out on the same corner, about a block or two down from where the little girl had been.

As he stood here and watched, the same blue truck came around the corner, slowed, and then picked up speed again. Simon pulled out his phone and texted the license plate to the detective. She didn't answer, but then what did he expect? He pocketed his phone and, this time, headed home for good.

# CHAPTER 21

*Monday, Later that Evening*

THE FOOTSTEPS STOPPED. Kate held her breath and waited because that last stair had a bit of a creak to it. It was almost as if he understood that somebody was down here. A man called out, "Hello, anybody here?"

She tilted her head, not sure who was there.

"I'm the neighbor. I saw the door open. Is everybody okay?"

She groaned silently and rolled her eyes. But she didn't dare say anything. Because what if it was him, the Nico perv? And the neighbor bit was just a ruse? She waited and finally heard the footsteps turn back around and go upstairs. He called out several more times on the main floor; then she heard him go out the kitchen door and close it. She was grateful for that. She raced to the window to see if she saw where he went. And, indeed, he headed to the house on her side of the basement and went back inside.

She checked her phone. It hadn't been twenty minutes since her original text about the little girl. The little thing was still curled up, her skin waxy cold. But she was alive, and that's how Kate was trying to keep her—alive. This little girl had been through way too much already.

With great relief Kate heard sirens approaching. She didn't want to leave the little girl even then, but her phone buzzed, and she saw it was Rodney. She gave him instructions about coming down to the basement. He arrived within minutes, paramedics at his side. Richmond RCMP officers following behind. As soon as she opened the door, he saw the little girl and, shaking his head, whispered, "Dear God in heaven."

"I know," Kate said, her tone low.

The paramedic went straight to the little girl's side, checked her out, and frowned. "We need to get her to the hospital immediately," he said. "Her vitals are really low. I suspect she's been drugged."

"It's probably to keep her calm and quiet, while she's alone," Rodney said.

"Yeah, I agree," Kate said. She watched, that same burning fury building inside her as the little girl was quickly bundled up, loaded onto a gurney, and, sirens blazing, taken away. Kate stood here for a long moment and said, "Forensics needs to go over this room with a fine-tooth comb."

"Richmond RCMP will handle it," Rodney said quietly. "What are you expecting them to find?"

"You mean, outside of evidence of the pedophile?" She saw him acknowledge her words with a nod and looked at him directly, angst in her eyes. "DNA from other children." With that, she turned abruptly and headed upstairs. Outside, on the back porch, off the kitchen, she took several deep, calming breaths. Forensics would be here soon, but it would take them a little bit.

Rodney joined her. "Do we need to check the rest of the house?"

"Yeah, we do," she said, "plus that neighbor." She pointed to the right. "He came over and was all over up here and even came downstairs, calling out to see if anybody was there because the door had been left open. We also need to track down the driver of that truck who got away."

"Sounds like the neighbor is somebody we can talk to then," he said. "Did you let him know you were here?"

She shook her head. "I couldn't take the chance, in case it was actually this Nico guy who lives here."

"Good point," he said. "I guess other children could be here somewhere?"

Her shoulders hunched in. "Oh, God, I haven't looked," she said, turning to stare at him in horror. "I didn't want to leave the little girl alone."

"The police are searching right now, but we can join in. Let's go together," he said. "We'll search the downstairs and tear it apart, make sure nobody else is here."

"We must search every corner," she said. "He had one child hidden and God only knows for how long."

"That girl was the one for sale in the chat room, wasn't it?"

She nodded slowly. "And what I'm wondering is," she said, "if that rat's ass I'd missed escaping the kitchen was trying to steal her out from under the other one, instead of buying her."

"Well, we have an address for him too," he said. "Let's finish this job, hand the scene off to Forensics, and then we can go find him."

"I already sent out a request to have him picked up," she said. "And I want to talk to him no matter what."

"Did you get a good look at him?"

She shook her head. "No, not the facial details. Just the general frame. Sure glad I took that photo of the license plate when I got here."

"Have you heard if they've got him yet?"

"Nope," she said, "but, as long as they are doing that, we can do this." And, with that, they headed back downstairs to the basement, systematically measuring off the space, and checked that no other hiding spots were in that basement. Then they moved upstairs and searched the main floor. By the time they had done that, a Forensics Division team was on the scene, and Kate and Rodney turned over the basement to them. Then she and Rodney headed back up to search the rest of the house. In the master bedroom, now that they were fully allowed to do a thorough search, she said, "I think we should also look for a safe."

"Good point," he said. "A house like this would have one."

"Where the hell is the owner?"

"I'm not sure," he said. "He hasn't left the country, at least not by any means that requires his passport."

"Of course, now that we've found the child, even if he planned on coming home, chances are he's not anymore."

"Well, it's not like you or I would anyway," he said. "And I hardly doubt that he can pass this off as being anything other than his house."

"I wouldn't think so," she said, "but we've seen guys act like they had absolutely nothing to do with anything before. It always amazes me."

"I know," he said. "Come on. Let's finish up."

They went room by room on the second story and ended up back in the master bedroom once again. They checked under the bed and the night tables, also for hidden pockets in the walls, inspecting everything they could think of. And found nothing.

She shook her head. "You know a safe is here somewhere." She walked over to the huge closet again and moved all the clothes back, pulling them out this time. "Here it is." And she pointed to the safe. She stared at the combination lock and said, "This one looks even older than the last one."

"Maybe your friend will send you the combination."

She pulled out her phone, checked it, and said, "He's been asking for updates."

"Well, tell him you need the number." She looked at him, startled, as he shrugged. "Hey, he sent it to you last time. Maybe he would send you another one."

"Oh my God, he already did send some numbers," she said, scrolling through her messages. She held it up and said, "Look at the license plate."

"That's the same one as the guy who escaped from the kitchen?"

"Yes," she said. On a whim, she sent him a message.

**Need a number.**

Instead of texting her back, her phone rang.

"What kind of a number?" he said briskly.

"It's a safe again," she said. "I have no clue."

"Did you get anywhere tonight?"

She turned to Rodney and smiled. "Yes. We found a little girl. Alive."

"Well, thank God for that," he said. "Twelve, nine, for-ty-two." Then he hung up.

She stared down at her phone, then looked at Rodney and shrugged. "He said, twelve, nine, and forty-two." She quickly ran the tumblers back and forth, dialing to the numbers he gave her, and, when it clicked, she just stared. She turned to look back at Rodney and said, "This guy is dangerous."

"Or a huge asset," he said.

"I don't think I like the asset part." She pulled open the

safe and stared. "Holy shit." It was full of albums and binders. Still gloved up, she pulled out the top binder, and it was full of children. Grim-faced, she handed it off to Rodney and pulled out more. "Jesus Christ," she said. "These are all photos of children."

"But that doesn't mean they are photos he had anything to do with," he said. "It could be just a picture album."

"I guess our online forensic techs could tell us that. They can do a facial recognition on these kids. We'll need to send those to ICE at bare minimum." With all the albums collected, she found an envelope in the back of the safe. She pulled it forward, a paper clip holding it shut. She popped that open, took a look, and whistled.

"What is it?" Rodney asked.

"Dates and codes," she said, "maybe for names?"

"Meaning?"

"I'm not sure, but maybe children," she said. She turned to Rodney. "Crap. I didn't check the little girl's wrist," she said. "I should have."

"We still can," he said. "She's at the hospital."

Kate nodded. "That's where I'm going first," she said, "and we need to take this in, see if we can get confirmation of what the hell is going on here."

"I don't think these albums are trophies," he said. "I suspect they are more like wish books. I hate to say it but think *ordering catalogs*."

Just the suggestion made her stomach churn. "Please don't use that term," she said hoarsely.

"I'm not sure we have a choice. It's almost like this is an online catalogue," he said. "Each one of these photos has a number."

She stared down at the photo album, looked up at him,

back at the photo album. "So what is this then?" she asked, holding up the envelope. "Some of the numbers are here."

"I'm thinking it's a sales record on these *products.*"

They stared at each other in horror because that was a truth nobody wanted to believe.

### Tuesday, 1:00 a.m.

SIMON DIDN'T KNOW why he assumed Kate would come to him because there was absolutely no reason for it. Except that she'd come at other times. When he still had no sign of her at one o'clock in the morning, he threw in the towel, got dressed in jeans, grabbed a leather jacket, and walked out. He hopped into his car and drove in the direction of her address. She probably didn't even know that he knew where she lived. But it was something he had learned almost immediately.

He stared from the sidewalk up at the old apartment building. She lived at the top right corner, and her light was on. Did she leave the light on, or was she there? Maybe she slept with it on. More than likely she was still working. Speaking of which, he turned, looked around, and saw a Chinese restaurant still open at the corner. He walked in and found the place was empty. He asked if they were still taking orders, and the old man told him they were closed.

"I just want to get enough for tonight, right now. Do you have anything left over?" They haggled back and forth, and Simon finally convinced the man to sell him the leftovers. Equipped with two large bags, he walked over to her apartment, let himself in the main door, and entered the elevator. When he got to her hallway, he headed toward her number and knocked. He almost felt her jump at the sound.

When he heard her call out, he answered quietly, "It's Simon."

She opened the door, and he stared at her calmly. She was shocked, dumbfounded even. "What are you doing here?" she asked.

He held out the Chinese food, the aroma wafting through the place. "I figured you probably hadn't eaten."

She frowned instantly, stared at the food, then looked back at him and said, "No, I haven't. But what has that got to do with you?"

He didn't give her a chance to argue, just pushed his way inside, and placed the bags on the table. "I figured you were still working, when I saw the lights on."

"Again, what does that have to do with you?"

He smiled and said, "You can't fight all these guys on your own."

"I can do whatever the hell I need to do," she snapped.

"Maybe," he said, "but, at this point in time, it's not an issue."

"You can't do this. It's bad news."

"Why?" he asked, turning and looking at her. Already hating the sense of rejection coming.

"You're a suspect."

He gave a bitter laugh. "Like hell," he said. "I've already proven that I had nothing to do with this. You're just looking for excuses."

She shook her head and said, "It's not allowed."

And he could sense the desperation in her voice. "You don't like to fraternize with suspects?"

"No," she said. "I can't."

"So, it's a good thing I'm not a suspect anymore then, isn't it?" He started taking the food out of the bags. "Come eat," he said. "There's lots. And you ruin my sense of peace and quiet as it is."

"Why?" she asked, as she came to stare down at the food in front of them. "What did you do? You ordered enough for ten people."

"No, they were shutting down, and this is all the leftovers."

"Hardly," she said, "unless they had orders that didn't get picked up, or they just make it all way ahead. Wait—is this the place at the corner?"

He nodded.

"Then they are leftovers," she said grudgingly. "They have a buffet open until one o'clock."

"So there," he said. "Eat." She looked at him, her mouth open, until he reached across and gently pushed her jaw closed. "Now," he said, "eat." And he walked into the kitchen and searched for plates. He pulled out two and handed her one. He saw she was getting angry, but, at the same time, she wanted the food. He grabbed a large spoon and served up two plates. "There's so much food here that we can't even try it all. You'll have enough for leftovers."

And they settled down at the table and ate. He sat across from her and started working on his. Now that he was here, and she was beside him, he felt more settled again. He shook his head. "This is a really bad idea."

"Pretty sure I just said that," she muttered around her food.

"Maybe," he said, "but I couldn't *not* come." He looked up to see her staring at him in shock. He shrugged. "Now I feel like I'm constantly waiting for you to contact me."

"I shouldn't have been contacting you at all," she said.

"Maybe so," he said, "but it doesn't change the fact that

I'm here, and now I'm not leaving until I've eaten."

"OH MY GOD, oh my God." He couldn't stop the litany going through his head. What if the cop had seen his face? His truck? What if she knew who he was now? He had to disappear. He had to do something. Somehow he had to get out of this. He hadn't been this close to getting caught since forever—well, since he did get caught.

And no way he could afford to go to jail again. His sister would disown him. She'd already told him once, if he ever got caught again, that was it, and he would be dead to her. That wasn't fair; it wasn't fair at all. He could drive home but he didn't dare. He bolted toward his sister's house, even though it was across the river and clear on the other side of town.

He drove carefully, making sure he didn't attract any undue attention. The last thing he needed was to be pulled over right now. His hands were still shaking, but he didn't know how to determine if the cop had gotten a good look at his truck. If she got his license plate, what was he supposed to do now? *Should I call it in as stolen?*

Without giving himself a chance to think, he pulled off to the side of the road and quickly called in the fact that his truck was stolen. That he hadn't seen it since the previous day. With that done and promising to come in and to fill out a statement, he continued on toward his sister's place. He double-checked the GPS, swearing, as he drove through one massive mansion after another. Surely he was in the wrong area, right?

He kept driving until he got to the address, then stopped

and stared. *It couldn't be*, his mind screamed at him. He knew his sister was doing okay, but he hadn't realized she was still living like they used to live. He was barely scraping by in a run-down little flat, but this? This was like a twelve-bedroom mansion. Brick and ivy, a gated driveway, and a grand front entrance.

He pulled his phone toward him, and, with a shaky hand, he dialed his sister. When she answered, he asked, "Are you really living in that goddamned mansion?"

After a pause on the other end, she said in a curious tone, "Well, I haven't moved, so I don't know what you're talking about."

He tried to regroup his brain cells into some coherence, so he could actually talk to her, but this was just too flabbergasting. "I'm outside," he said abruptly.

"What?" she said, her tone coming alive, with a fury that he recognized. He winced. "We had an agreement," she snapped.

"I know. I know. I know," he said, sounding whiny, even though it's the opposite of what he wanted. "It's just been a really bad day," he said. And, as much as he tried, he couldn't hide the trembling in his voice.

"What happened?" she snapped.

"Nothing," he said. "Nothing really. It's okay. I'm fine."

"Are you though?" she asked. "Then why are you scared? You sound terrified, as a matter of fact."

He gave a laugh. "But you aren't worried about me though, are you? You're just worried in case it comes back on you."

"It won't come back on me," she said. "And what the hell are you doing outside my house?"

He looked to see if she was looking out a window, but

even that was too much effort for her, so of course she wasn't. "I needed to reach out," he said.

"Well, reaching out is making a phone call, not sitting outside my house. That is stalking."

"You're my sister," he said, with outrage.

"Go home then," she said, her tone filled with a banked rage.

He'd used his rage and had let it boil over, while she kept hers contained. He knew that meant she was just a time bomb waiting to blow because she had done nothing to dispel the fury inside her.

"I will," he said, in an effort to calm her down, yet, at the same time, he stared at the house, taking in the lifestyle she was living versus what he had. "How come you've left me in that tiny little hovel, while you're living in this great big mansion?" he asked. "You know what I've been through."

"I also know that you got caught," she said. "Getting caught a second time will be the end of even that little hovel, so remember that," she said and hung up on him.

He'd been visibly shaking when he managed to escape the house in Richmond, but now he was deeply shaken inside. Because he had no doubt that she meant what she said. If he got caught again, he would be dead to her. She was the only person in this life that he'd ever been able to count on. But she'd always made it clear, after he got caught the first time, that, if he ever did it again, that was it.

And now today, he'd actually pushed the line to the point that may have set things into motion that could result in him getting caught. He shook his head, started the engine, took a photo of her house, and, with that done, he drove toward his own home.

Having already called in the theft of his vehicle, he decided to park it a few blocks away, then took a rag and quickly wiped it down. Nothing incriminating was inside; he'd always made sure of that. But he left it unlocked, just parked off to the side, so somebody could find it and hopefully return it to him. Then he got out and walked back home again. Inside, he was quaking. He had a sense of something crumbling, his world breaking apart around him.

Once inside, he locked the door, warmed up a slice of cold pizza, and sat down in front of the TV. Even his China Doll would have been a welcome comfort right now, but he didn't have even that. He turned on the news and watched, hoping nothing would be reported.

And then, just when he felt like he was safe, a breaking news story came on, saying a missing five-year-old girl had been found.

With that, his throat closed. And tears came to his eyes. He'd been so close. She'd been right there, where he could have just grabbed her. He shouldn't have run. He should have waited until that cop had left. He could have just taken that little girl, and she would be here with him right now. He closed in on himself and started to bawl, the sense of hopeless loneliness overtaking him once again.

# CHAPTER 22

*Tuesday, Wee Hours of the Morning*

KATE DIDN'T KNOW what had gotten into Simon's head to think that this was a good idea. The fact that he'd brought her Chinese food, when she was desperately hungry, just added to it. The fact that he was so comfortable here, even though her place was such a dump compared to his incredible penthouse, only added to her sense of unease. "You're crazy."

"So are you," he said.

And they both continued to eat in silence. When she finally had the first level of her massive hunger appeased, she settled back and said, "I just would have had some toast."

"And white bread presumably, which has no nutrition, no protein, no good fats," he said. "You can't function on that."

"I've been functioning on that for a lot of years," she said.

"But, if you ate better," he said, "you'd function better."

"Maybe," she said, "or maybe I just won't get used to this kind of food because I can't afford it."

He stopped, looked up at her, and asked, "Do they pay you that badly?"

She just smiled.

"Of course you won't tell me anyway, will you?"

"No, I won't," she said. "Why the hell would I?"

He shrugged and said, "Well, it's a good thing I brought this tonight then, isn't it? There should be enough leftovers for you for a few days. So can you tell me what you found?"

"No," she said briskly. She got up, marched over to the sink, and filled a glass of water. "That I cannot do."

"You already told me that you found a little girl," he said.

She turned to lean back against the counter, looked at him, and smiled. "Yes, but she's not the only one who has been on our radar today."

"Ouch," he said, staring at her in shock. "Does that mean this is going on all around us?"

Her grim face turned to him with a nod. "Unfortunately, yes. But if you came here to get information from me," she said, "I can't tell you anything."

"Fine," he said. Then he picked up one of the other dishes in front of him and served more food. "Still hungry?"

"I am stuffed," she said, "and so are you."

He motioned at her plate and said, "You want to try some of this?"

She stared, then realized she did, in fact, have room for some more. "I'll never sleep after this."

"I doubt you were planning on sleeping anyway," he said. "Let's get real. You're all about this case."

She sat back down and glared at him. "You don't know me," she said. "You don't know anything about me."

"I know you are incredibly driven. You look after the children first. You can't stand injustice, and you hate criminals," he said. "What more is there to understand?"

"A hell of a lot more," she said. "That describes most of the cops in the city."

"No, it doesn't," he said. "It doesn't describe a lot of them." He shook his head. "And you've clawed your way up to where you are now, and something about you says you have to prove yourself."

"I've only been there for three months," she admitted.

"Ah," he said. "So you still feel like you have to prove you belong."

"I do feel that way," she said. She looked down at her phone and said, "Crap. I was supposed to go to the hospital, and I forgot." She pinched the bridge of her nose.

"It could wait," he said.

"No," she said, "I need to know."

"Then call them," he said. "Just use the phone."

"I don't know about that," she said.

"Doesn't matter," he said. "You're making too much of this."

"Not true," she said, but she continued to stare at her phone, as she munched her way through one of the vegetable dishes that he'd dumped on her plate. "It's a sad world out there," she said. Shaking her head, she tried to take her gaze off her phone.

He pushed it toward her. "Being obsessive is one thing, but not allowing yourself to make a simple decision is another."

"You shouldn't be hearing my conversations," she said.

He snorted at that. "In case you haven't figured it out by now, I'm hearing way more than I would like to about you, whether you're right in front of me or not," he said.

"Oh." With that, she snatched her phone off the table and called the hospital. When she got one of the nurses, she asked about the status of the little girl. The nurse quickly came back on the line.

"Detective Morgan? The child is still in a drugged state, but, healthwise, she appears to be okay. We are monitoring her, as we try to sort out the drugs. I don't think the doctors have analyzed what she's been given yet."

"Are you in her room right now, or can you go there?" she asked. "I need a picture of the inside of her wrist."

"Her wrist?"

Kate heard the footsteps as the nurse headed down the hallway. "Have you heard any news on locating family for her?"

"No," the nurse said. "And that's breaking all our hearts."

"Yeah, ours too, but hopefully somebody will pop up soon," she said.

"Maybe. But how long has this little girl been in the system?" the nurse asked with bitterness.

"I don't know. It could be quite a while to sort it all out. We'll run her DNA, of course, but that, in itself, takes time."

"Seems like everything takes longer than it should. I know," the nurse said. "Okay, I'm in her room right now. She's not showing any signs of change."

"That won't necessarily hurt her right now."

"You think she's been living like this for a long time?"

"It's quite possible. It stops her from being difficult, right?"

"Bastards," the nurse said. "Okay, I'm here, looking at her wrist. What is it you need?"

"Her left wrist," Kate said. "Can you take a photo of the inside of it and text it to me, please, at this number?"

"Will do," she said. "A couple scratches are here, but I don't see anything else."

"I need to see those scratches," she said.

"It's coming your way then. Give it a minute."

"Thank you." Kate hung up the phone and laid it on the table beside her. She took another bite of food but kept her gaze on the phone.

"What's all this about scratches on the wrist?"

She held up her hand like a stop sign. "Remember that part about you not being allowed to hear my phone conversations?"

He fell silent, and, when her phone buzzed, she snatched it up, swiped to open the screen, and accessed the photo. She sank back and nodded, exhaling.

"As much as I didn't want it to be," she said, "it confirms what I was really hoping to confirm. Or rather hoping I couldn't confirm."

"I still don't understand. What's on her wrist?"

"A series of scratches, that's all," she said. "And in this case, pretty faint ones."

"So, old ones?"

She nodded slowly. "Yeah. Old ones."

"And what is it? What do they mean?" he asked.

"It's like a club stamp," she said sadly. She looked up at him. "And this little girl has been part of the club for a long time."

He winced. "Are you talking about a pedophile ring? Is that what you mean? Are these pedophiles buying and selling children?"

She nodded slowly. "A lot of pedophiles won't share, but there are others, in groups sometimes, who actually pass around their victims. And it looks like this little girl has been with this one guy for a while."

"I hope you find him," he said, "and put a bullet between his eyes."

She snorted. "Yeah, not likely," she said. "I have to work within the law."

"I can do it, if need be," he said, his tone harsh.

She glared at him. "No vigilante justice," she snapped. But, inside, she understood his anger and his rage. "I get it," she said. "We all do. But we still have to make sure we take them all down, not just this one."

"If I can do something to help," he said, "you just have to tell me."

She looked up at him intensely. "Why? Why do you care?"

He said, "Show me that photo first."

She knew she shouldn't. But she couldn't *not* do it either, so she brought it up and showed it to him.

"I need to be in on this," he said, his gaze rising to stare at her.

"Hell no," she said. "You don't need to be in on anything."

He turned his left wrist up and reached across the table, so she could take a look.

Gasping, she stared down at very faded lines on his wrist. So faint they were mostly scar tissue. Still shocked, she looked from the photo to his wrist and then back up to him.

"You were one of them?" She narrowed her gaze. "But were you a pedophile or a victim?"

He glared at her. "I was a victim," he said. "But I already know who put these marks on my wrist," he snapped.

She stared at him in shock. "Who?" she demanded. "Who was it, Simon?"

# CHAPTER 23

*Tuesday, 8:00 a.m.*

KATE BOLTED INTO the station later that morning at eight. She was still rubbing the sleep from her eyes, having only collapsed in her bed at four. After dropping his bombshell the previous night, Simon had disappeared almost immediately. She'd done everything she could to hold him there, but he walked, and she saw how terribly difficult it all was for him. Just as he left, she made a plea. "The station, eight a.m., this morning. Please."

He'd frozen in the hallway, turned to look at her, and then stepped inside the elevator, disappearing. She hoped not forever, but a part of her wondered.

As she raced into the office, the rest of the crew looked up and frowned. She said, "Ground zero."

Eyebrows shot up, and people bolted to their feet. "Another body?"

She took a slow deep breath. "Not quite," she said. "I need to write down some stuff that we should go over, and I must do some research."

Colby walked in and said, "No. First you tell us what's going on." She glared at him, but he didn't waver.

"Well, I can't really tell you right now. I found somebody with that same mark on their wrist. Someone who is alive today, but was a victim of a pedophile decades ago."

"Who?" Colby asked.

She shoved her hands in her pockets, hating to even bring it up. "Simon."

He just stared at her, and his eyebrows went up. "Are you serious?"

She nodded slowly. "I saw it last night," she said. "He said that his foster father gave it to him, and that he'd been a victim for many years when he was just a child." Several gasps came from those around her. She turned her gaze on each, trying to decide if they believed her or if they thought she was making it up. Or worse, that Simon was making it up. It was Lilliana though, who offered another theory that Kate hadn't considered.

"You do realize," Lilliana said, "that he probably wasn't the victim of a pedophile but was part of the adult pedophile ring, correct?"

Colby's frown deepened, and he looked at Lilliana and said, "Go pick him up."

"Wait," Kate said. "I guess that, to you guys, that probably is the next logical step. But he gave me combos, license numbers, and names."

At that, they all turned and stared at her. She nodded. "He didn't want to share anything personal, but he told me to look it up, if I didn't believe him. I think he realized, once that symbol came up, and he showed me his wrist, that he would be assumed to be part of the ring," she said quietly. "At least let's give him the respect of checking out the case number."

"What's the number?" Owen said from his computer. She pulled out her phone, checked the note she'd made for herself, and read the number out loud. He typed it in and brought it up. "Jesus, well, this is pretty ugly. It's definitely a pedophile case involving a six-year-old boy named Simon."

His gaze shot up over the top of the monitor to look at her.

Behind him, Lilliana said, "That doesn't mean it's the same Simon."

"What year?" Kate asked.

"Thirty-one years ago," he said. "We've got just a bit of a digital file here."

"Who was the abuser?"

He continued to read, handing out bits and pieces of information. "The child had been abused for years by the suspect, his own foster father. Wow," he said. "This is a pretty shitty deal."

"It is," Kate said. "And it follows everything he said."

"But nothing is in there about the marks on his wrist, is there?"

"Not that I've read yet," he said. "Not to mention, no photograph of it either."

"What about his foster father?" Lilliana asked, from behind him, coming up to read the monitor. "Where is that bastard?"

"I haven't got that far yet," Owen said. "His name is Josh, Josh Cameron. I'm still checking the case file to see if he was taken down and if he served his time."

"A hell of a lot of pedophiles are in our world right now," Kate muttered, staring at Owen, willing him to come up with the information. She hated to think that Simon might be classified as guilty of crimes he didn't commit, having that ring connected to him in ways that she hadn't expected. But, if his words were true, it would exonerate him.

"You also can't walk away from the concept that victims of pedophiles often turn around and become abusers themselves," her sergeant said. "I know that's not a theory you are looking to explore," he said, "but we've seen it time and time again."

She nodded, hating the truth of the words. "That's true," she said. "But we haven't linked him to any of these children, have we?"

"Not sure we tried that hard," Owen said.

Immediately Colby jumped up. "And that's your job today," he said. "Go through all these current cases and see if there's anything you can lay at Simon's feet. Any kind of connection, no matter how small, and we bring him in and talk to him here," he said. "Because, no matter what, we need to know just what the hell happened to him since then."

She turned to look at him. "What we need to know is whether he was involved with anybody else. Pedophiles often had other children," she said. "And maybe some of those are still around too."

"Good. Keep thinking. This is breaking wide open," Colby said. "Everybody at it."

People got up and headed toward various corners of the office, all energized at this new link in their case. She walked over to stand beside Owen. "Anything else in there?"

"I'm sending them to the printer," he said. "Back then there wasn't a whole lot in the report. He couldn't be interviewed because of his age, and he didn't have much to say. It was his own foster father, after all. So a lot of intimidation tactics at play here."

"Also, at that age," she said, "he wouldn't have known that this was anything but normal. But where the hell was the damn foster mother?"

"I'm not seeing anything in here about the mother,"

Owen said.

"Did you send it all to the printer yet?" she asked.

"Yeah, the whole file," he said. "Two copies."

Lilliana from behind him said, "Print me one too."

"I'll do one for everybody," Owen said. "So we'll all be on the same page."

Kate walked over to the printer and sorted out the copies as they came out. She delivered one to everybody and then sat down with a cup of coffee and read hers. In black-and-white, it was easier at a distance, but the minute she saw the picture of the little boy, his wrist in a cast and bruises all over his face and his arms, she knew that this wasn't just an ordinary sexual abuse case.

"More than just sex abuse going on in this one," Kate said. "This kid had been beaten to a pulp."

"According to the interview, that was after Simon told the police what his foster father had done to him," Owen said.

"So the beating was punishment. Interesting," Rodney said. "Makes sense though. Pedophiles will do anything to keep themselves safe."

"So they left Simon with his abusive foster father, even after he told on him?" Lilliana asked, incredulous.

Owen nodded, his lips pressed in a firm line. "You know as well as we do that they probably couldn't prove the abuse. Hell, they might not even have tried."

"Until his foster father beat him up." Lilliana shook her head.

Just then, the phone on Kate's desk rang. She picked it up, her thoughts still on the picture of the little boy in front of her. Audrey from the front desk was on the line.

"A man here to see you," she said, "Simon St. Laurant."

She hopped to her feet and said, "I'll come out and get him." She stopped, hung up the phone, turned, and addressed the group. "Simon came in on his own. I asked him to show up at eight this morning, and he did."

"Good," Owen said.

"I don't want you interviewing him at all though," Colby said, stalking out of his office, obviously having heard her.

"Why not?" she asked.

"Because you're too attached," he said bluntly.

Her eyebrows shot up. "Attached to the case, yes," she said. "To him, no."

"Maybe not," he said, "but let's get other people on this too."

She nodded agreeably. "I was planning on taking him to interview room A, unless you have a problem with that, sir."

He shook his head. "No, Owen and Rodney, you're on this."

"Good," they said. "We'll want to do some more research before we go in and talk to him."

Steaming on the inside at Colby's suggestion, yet understanding his position, and even wondering if there was something to his words, Kate headed out to the front. When she saw Simon standing there in a black power suit, she knew this was extremely difficult for him.

"Simon," she called out. He turned and looked at her. "Come this way, please." He didn't even acknowledge her words with a nod or show that he knew what this was all about in any way. His face was blank, his gaze hard. As she walked him to interview room A, she said, "Two other detectives are to interview you."

"Why is that?"

She hesitated. "Colby said I'm too involved."

"Makes sense," he said in a noncommittal voice. She led him into the interview area, one of the larger rooms they had for this purpose. He looked in, sat down on one of the chairs, and asked, "Any chance of a coffee?"

"Sure, I'll go get you one," she said, and she walked out, leaving the door open. He hadn't been called in for questioning. He'd come in on his own, and she afforded him the respect he deserved for that. With a cup of coffee in hand, she headed back in. He looked up at her, smiled, and said, "I presume I have to wait for a bit."

"Sorry," she said. "They'll be along as soon as they can."

He nodded and then ignored her.

She appreciated that. This would be hard enough on everybody as it was, but, damn it, she wanted to be in that room. And she doubted she would be allowed in the observation room either. As she walked back to her desk, Owen and Rodney stood. Lilliana looked at her and said, "I'll go in and observe. What about you?"

"If I'm not crossing some line, that's what I want to do too. I believe Colby is joining us," she said. She grabbed a notepad and headed in to the adjoining observation room. She watched as both Owen and Rodney walked in, introduced themselves, closed the door, and sat down.

Simon just sat there and waited, seemingly calm, but then he played poker, and, in some ways, she realized just how unequal this interview was. Rodney and Owen had their hands full, and they weren't likely to be any match for Simon. She pulled up a chair and sat down, interested to see how this played out.

Owen started off fairly easily. "It's come to our attention from one of our coworkers that you have a mark that involves you somehow with our cases."

In response, Simon pulled up his shirt cuff and suit jacket and popped his wrist out. They leaned forward, took a look, and frowned. "It's likely much fainter in my case," Simon said easily. "The marks were administered when I was a child."

That was one for him right there, by showing how old the scars were. It was obvious that these weren't done recently. She admired the smooth openness that he expressed. He wouldn't lash out, which she knew, but she was willing to sit here and listen, as much as she could.

"Can you tell us how you got it?" Owen went on.

"My foster father gave it to me," he said.

"Why?"

"I was supposed to be a founding member of a club I didn't want to belong to," Simon said.

"A club for what?" Owen asked.

"Pedophiles," he said. "Assuming your coworker gave you the case number, you've probably already looked it up."

Owen nodded and tapped a folder in front of him. "We have the notes, but it was many years ago, and unfortunately it's not as extensive as we would like it to be."

"Well, if it was more extensive," Simon said, "surely they would have done something about the case then?"

"What is it you want done?"

"Find my foster father," he said easily. "And put him in jail where he belongs."

"There's been no sign of him since?" Rodney asked.

Simon shook his head.

"Has he ever contacted you?"

"No," Simon whispered in a clipped tone.

"Where is your foster mother?"

"I have no idea," he said. "And I have no recollection of

a foster mother."

Kate's heart slammed against her chest. It helped her understand why he was so elusive and so much of a loner. Self-made in whatever direction he'd gone in, and not because of someone behind him giving him a helping hand.

"Your foster father didn't mention her?"

"Not that I remember at this time."

"Was he ever married?"

"That's for you to find out."

She watched as Owen started taking notes. They didn't have data, and a lot of research needed to be done. In a way, this was to Simon's benefit. It was good that he'd shown up this morning because, in another few hours, they would have been armed with a lot more information and likely would have a lot more questions. This went on and on, and the more questions that they came around to and repeated, the less cooperative his response. By the end of an hour, he was down to yes or no answers.

Lilliana looked over at her. "What do you think?"

"His patience is thin. His tolerance is less than thin," she said. "But I'm not hearing or seeing any signs of deception."

"I hate to say it, but I agree with you. It's not giving us anything to go on."

She looked over at her coworker. "What did you think he would have to give?" Kate asked curiously. "He was picked up as a sexual abuse victim at the age of six. Luckily his blood grandmother found him somehow, and he was with her until age ten, when she died. Simon went back into the system and, as should surprise no one, was a handful and was moved through a series of foster homes before he walked away at eighteen. And that was after running away many times and being hauled back. What could he give us that we shouldn't have on file already?"

Lilliana nodded. "It's hard when the children have been through the system like that."

"I just wonder what the system did for him—or to him," she said. "That hard edge to him isn't showing any sign of relaxing."

"No, he probably built up the barriers as a little child and kept them in place the whole time," Lilliana said. "If he has no idea where his foster father is, doesn't know anything about his foster mother—or his biological parents—never met any other family members, then it's up to us to start doing the genealogy."

Just then Owen made a request that caused everyone to freeze. "We'd like a sample of your DNA," he said calmly. "Do you have any objection to that?"

SIMON STARED AT him, knowing that this question would come. He looked at the smoked mirror behind him, knowing perfectly well that people were back there, that Kate would be among them. He looked back at the detective and said, "No objection, that's fine. But you shouldn't even have to ask me, it's already in the system."

Owen looked down at his notes and said, "They collected a lot of forensic evidence back then, didn't they?"

"They did."

When asked whether he was ever tested with modern and up-to-date DNA testing, he replied, "I have no idea."

"Maybe that's something we need to put some money back into," Rodney said, frowning. "We have a lot of cold cases that were never solved."

"In this case, you're looking for my foster father, who is who-knows-where," he said. "For all I know, he's living a happy life on an island somewhere."

"But somebody else in your life might have some idea of what's going on or who was involved back then," he said. "Do you have any memories of that time in your life?"

He took a slow deep breath and let it out. "A child between the ages of four to six doesn't remember much, except for the really bad stuff he went through." His patience was already clawing away at him to get out of here, to run, but he didn't dare show any outward sign of it. Any sign of weakness was something they'd jump on. No way he could let these men know how hard this conversation was for him. "And none of that I care to remember," he said coolly. "To be honest, most of it is a complete blank at this point."

He watched as a grimace whispered across one man's face, revealing that at least one of these two had enough empathy to understand what he, as a child, had gone through. "There were other men," Simon said suddenly.

Both of the men raised their gazes from the folders in front of them to stare at him. "But I don't suppose you have any names. Or do you?"

Simon gave him the briefest of smiles. "Even if I did," he said, "I doubt if they were the names that the members used at any other time." He stood suddenly. "Gentlemen, if there's nothing else," he said, shooting his left wrist out of his suit jacket and checking the time, "I am due for a meeting."

The two detectives looked at each other and slowly stood. "Please make yourself available for more questions."

"When you have some questions," he said, "you can ask them. Until then, let's not waste either of our time." He tilted his head in a regal incline and strolled to the doorway. He lifted a hand to the smoke mirror and knew that she'd seen him wave. Nobody tried to stop him as he exited the police station.

He stood outside and took some really deep breaths of air. That was one of the dirtiest little tasks he'd had to do in a very long time. And it wasn't something he wanted to repeat. He'd had no intention of ever dredging up any of that in his life. But to think that his foster father was still out there, laughing at him, was just something Simon couldn't bear right now. He wanted to go home, have a shower, and a stiff drink. Make that a half-dozen stiff drinks. Instead he strolled to the harbor and let the splash of the waves, the sound of the tugs, the sight of the sailboats and everything else that happened on the water soothe his soul.

He had a sailboat himself that he hadn't taken out in a few weeks, and that was something he needed to change. He needed less work, more downtime. He needed to remember why he was where he was, how he got here, and how stupid it would be to not ever enjoy it because of a heart attack or some stupid thing down the road.

He wished he knew where his foster father was right now but had no clue.

"Hope you're rotting in hell," he muttered. He had tried as a young boy and again as an angry young man to track him down, but Josh hadn't been easy to track. Hopefully somebody in his own ring had killed him. But Simon knew that the man was a slippery slimeball and had likely just set up at a new location somewhere else in the world, where he was likely abusing another dozen little boys. And, even as his heart went out to them, finding his foster father was just something that he couldn't do, even though he'd tried so hard before. He wondered if it was time to try again.

He'd successfully forgotten all about his abusive foster father for decades. Would he even be alive now? Simon thought his foster father very old at his tender age of six. Adjusting for that, maybe his foster father was only in his late sixties, seventies? Regardless, still able to cause havoc for any number of children.

At that age, many of the older generation lost their filters and didn't give a shit anymore, doing whatever they wanted, regardless of who they hurt. His foster father already didn't have much of a filter, so Simon highly doubted that anything was left now but evil in the old man. If Simon could, he'd stop him from hurting others. Maybe he'd let the cops do the work for him and then wait.

If they tracked down his foster father, that was something else again. Simon thought about the vague ghostly faces that he'd seen as a child. Other men, the occasional woman's laughter. That had always taunted him because any woman who knew what was going on couldn't have been much of a mother figure. How could anybody allow something like that to happen to a child?

But then some women had no maternal qualities, allowing their children to be abused, or even putting their own children up for sale for sexual purposes for others. Just a sad part of the world out there. Then there were ghostly children's faces. But none clear enough to identity or to even understand what role they played in his history.

Weighed down heavily with a sense of disturbance and trauma, he walked slowly back to his place. As soon as he got inside his penthouse, even though it was only about ten or ten-thirty in the morning, he stripped off and walked into the shower. He might be clean on the outside but cleansing the stain in his soul? That would take a lifetime. Maybe even longer.

### *Tuesday Midmorning*

HE KEPT LOOKING at the front door, expecting the police to come barging in. Yet, so far, they hadn't even knocked. He knew that his quick call about the stolen vehicle had been a brilliant idea, and he knew they would still come to his door and check up on him. That he was more or less prepared for. He was stressed and had spent some time cleaning up as much as he could.

When the knock came on his door, he froze and swore inside his head. He knew exactly who it was. With a smile plastered on his face, he walked over and opened the door. He smiled at the officers in front of him. "What can I help you with, Officers?"

"You reported your vehicle stolen?"

He nodded. Then gave a gasp of surprise. "Don't tell me. Did you find it?"

The cop nodded. "It was parked a couple blocks away," he said.

"Oh my," he said. "Can I get it back then?"

"Well, we need you to sign some paperwork on it and to check to see if there's any damage."

He stepped out on the front stoop, as if to look up and down the block. "Where is it?"

"It's literally around the corner," he said.

"Where? I wonder if they planned to return it and forgot where they got it."

"Anything is possible," the cop said, as if he didn't really care. "We've seen all kinds of things happen for a lot less reason."

"Well, I have my keys," he said. "Give me a moment, and I'll just grab my shoes and a jacket." While they waited, he quickly tied his shoes, grabbed his jacket and his truck keys, and followed them down to where he'd left it parked. He looked at it, walked clear around, and said, "This is great. I'm so happy to have this back," he said. "What do you want me to do?"

"I can send you the forms," the officer said. "Then just sign and send them back. As long as you're sure there's no damage, we won't have to involve insurance at all."

"No, it looks fine. As long as it runs," he said, with laughter. He waved at the officers, hopped into his truck, started it up, slowly pulled out and drove it back home again, where he parked it. That was one of the most brilliant ideas he'd had in a long time, and, so far, it looked like it worked. He knew the cops were still watching, as he pulled up into his parking spot. He hopped out, gave them a wave, and walked back inside, an obvious leap in his steps.

The fact that they were leaving was something to be joyous about. The fact that he had his wheels back was awesome. The fact that they didn't know where he'd been and what he'd done was another huge plus. He'd been researching information on the little girl that they found. It just drove him crazy to think that he'd been so close but had failed.

Yet to think the cops had been that close to finding him trying to steal her, then he figured that it was all good and for the best. Now he would track down his friend Nico, who was still not responding to his messages. With the cops now safely out of his way, he sat back, his front door locked, and was back on his laptop and signed in to the chat. He talked to a couple of the other guys, just general conversation to see if anything was there from Nico, and there wasn't. **Hey, anybody seen Nico lately?**

**Not since your conversation with him**, one of the other guys wrote.

A couple new guys were in the group, which always made him go quiet for a while, as they figured out just who they were. He sent Nico a couple messages and got no response. Finally realizing that it was fruitless, he logged off. He sat back in his mostly clean apartment and smiled.

"Looks like I'm the man," he said, and he rubbed his hands together. "Just means I need to find another friend." He got up, found his list, and drew a line through Nico because there was absolutely no point in returning to his place, if the child had already been collected.

He did want to find out where Nico was though. He had a vague recollection of seeing him somewhere else but couldn't place where it was. When he heard a *ding* from his computer, he walked over to see a message from Nico.

**On the run.**

**Why?**

**Cops onto me. Was coming home, saw them at my place.**

**Shit.**

**Got a couch to sleep on?**

He thought about it for a quick second and typed, **You can't come here. I've had the cops here because my truck was stolen.**

**I'm going underground.**

**I can meet you somewhere.**

**What good will that do?** Nico typed.

**I've got a bit of money I can give you. I could pull**

**out some traveling money.**

**Money would be good. I really appreciate that.**

**Have they frozen your accounts?**

**Jesus, I hope not,** Nico typed. **I've got several.**

**Maybe pack and I'll meet you on your way out of the city or something.**

**How about a coffee shop?** Nico suggested.

**Okay, so I'll meet you at the Starbucks on the way out of town.**

And, now that he had his truck back, he could do this. He waited until he heard back from Nico that it was a go. He got up, slipped on his shoes, and grabbed his keys again, his mind buzzing to identify his options. One of the things that he really wanted to know was whether Nico had accessed his bank accounts and how much he'd taken out.

He wondered what it would take to get that same information, so somebody else could take money out of that account on another day. Maybe he should suggest that Nico make it look like he was still in town. As Nico's good buddy, he could wander all around town and take out a little bit here and a bit there. It could be a hell of a pot. Something he desperately needed for himself.

He hopped into his truck and slowly started down the street that led out of the city. His mind churned with possibilities.

# CHAPTER 24

A S KATE STEPPED out of the observation room, Owen looked at her and said, with a shrug, "I don't know what to say about him."

"The question is whether there was anything to find or not," she said briskly. "Personally I believe him."

"That's a turnaround for you, isn't it?" Lilliana asked. "Though I have to agree that nothing here suggests he was part of the ring."

"But we've been wrong before," Rodney said. "So let's make sure we do our due diligence and see if any connection exists between him and any of these cases."

"And he is right about the DNA," Lilliana said. "His DNA should have been collected when he was rescued."

"I'm looking into that too," Rodney said.

When he walked out of the office, Kate sat down and asked Owen, "Would they have actually collected the forensics evidence from that?"

"Well, they should have," Owen said. "Was standard procedure even back then. Although there might not have been any to find. Interesting that his foster father just disappeared."

"I wonder what happened to him," she mused out loud. Rodney walked in just then, headed for the coffee then returned to go to his desk, listening to the conversation going on around him.

"I wouldn't be surprised if your Simon didn't take him out and deep-six him in the ocean, when he got old enough," Owen said. She looked at him in surprise, but he just shrugged. "Hey, it's what I'd do."

"Maybe, but I think the formative years would have shaped him, yet the years that came afterward would have done an awful lot too because of who he was and who he is now today. I'm thinking the years with his grandmother should have helped," Kate said, not sure that same destroyed little boy had the same anger as a young man and even now. "Besides, to kill his foster father, he had to find his foster father, and that might not have been quite so easy."

Lilliana said, "I'm still not sure I believe him about the foster mother. Surely to be approved to foster kids you needed a married couple, right?"

"Who aren't pedophiles preferably," Owen quipped.

"Do we have anything on her?" Kate asked Lilliana, ignoring Owen.

Lilliana clicked away on the keys of her computer. "Josh Cameron was married. Seems she's in an old folks home with mental decline. So that's a dead end." She typed again. "He was born to a woman named Meggie Smith—if that's really her last name," she said. "The father isn't listed on the birth certificate."

"So how did Simon end up in foster care? Did he go from Meggie to live with his biological father or what?" Rodney asked.

"Or Simon was given away," Owen said, looking at Kate. "It could be that he was kidnapped as a child, or this Meggie person sold him into the pedophile ring."

"And is this Meggie person alive or deceased?" Kate

asked.

"I'm not finding a death certificate on file for her," Lilliana said. "So she could possibly be alive. We have no surname though."

"Interesting. Is there anything on her in a missing persons file?" Kate asked.

Lilliana looked at Kate over her monitor. "Why would you think she's a missing person?"

"It just occurs to me that the birth father or the foster father probably didn't want any baggage," Kate said, thinking about it. "It's one thing to take a child who you want to abuse, but to have the blood mother there, who could whine and try to defend the child, would get tedious very quickly. Maybe Josh Cameron took Meggie out for a walk and left her in a ditch someplace."

"It's possible," Rodney said.

"I'll have to hunt through the missing persons data," Kate said, frowning.

"We can't just contact that department?" Owen asked. "Or better yet, get Reese to check it. That's why we have an analyst in the first place."

With a smile, Lilliana said, "You know what? That's exactly what I'll do." And she reached for her phone.

Kate added, "Plus, what about any possible Jane Doe IDs in the Vancouver morgue? Just keep our search here locally in Vancouver for the moment."

Owen nodded. "I'll take a stab at that."

Kate got up, grabbed her purse, and said, "I'll check out the address for the truck I saw last night, fleeing Nico's place. Apparently the vehicle was reported as stolen. I need to talk to the owner," she said.

"Do you want somebody to go along?" Rodney asked.

She thought about it and shook her head. "No, we're spread too thin as it is," she said. "I'll just be an hour, as I'll head over there and come right back."

"Maybe," Rodney said, "but we've seen things turn sideways very quickly."

"In that case," she said, "I have you on speed dial." She turned and walked out. The last thing she ever expected was to get support. Chances were the offers to help were something other than the goodwill she thought they were—probably more about confirming Simon was an active pedophile, involved in these current cases of dead abused children—but, hey, she appreciated the assistance. The problem was, she had been working alone all her life, and she wasn't too keen to have a partner now.

Her good intentions to talk to the truck owner went out the window when she stood in front of the small apartment and realized nobody was home. And neither was the truck. She'd gotten a follow-up that the truck had been found and returned to the owner earlier. Apparently he had subsequently left. She frowned and wished she'd had a chance to see him and the truck. It would help revive her memory of the man she'd seen Monday evening escaping out a window at Nico's place.

She should go to the hospital now and check on the little drugged girl found in Nico's basement. After the initial check at Richmond General, she'd been transferred to Vancouver General. That little girl and also the little toddler she had scooped up just in time in that alleyway. She hated to face these children again, but she had to. So she got into her vehicle and headed to the hospital. When she walked in, she flashed her ID and asked for the location of the little girl. She was given the room number, and, as she approached, she saw some family members, kept outside of the girl's room by a burly unhappy orderly. At least Kate hoped they were family members. Only when she approached, everybody went silent. She frowned.

"Who are you all, and what's your relationship to this little girl?" she asked, her tone especially authoritative. She found that, when she used that tone, most people jumped up and answered her.

But one man, larger than the others and on the belligerent side, spoke up. "Why should we tell you?"

She pulled out her badge and said, "Because I'm the one who found this little girl," she said, "and I want to know who you all are and what your roles are in this little girl's life." With that, she pulled out a notebook and her phone. What she really wanted was photos of each and every one of them. One person in the background was inching away. She immediately put her phone on Camera mode and snapped a picture of him. "You," she said, pointing at him. "Let's start with you, since you're trying to sneak off."

He glared at her. "I just came because I'm with him," he said, pointing at the belligerent guy.

"Good," she said. "Name, address, phone number. Let's have it."

"Like hell," he said. "You don't have anything on me."

"I didn't," she said, "but I will in about two minutes, if I don't get some cooperation," she said, her tone flat and hard.

The belligerent guy said, "Come on, Jackson. Shut the fuck up with the whining and give her what she wants."

He gave her the name of Buddy Malone—she figured Buddy was a nickname for Jackson—and said he lived downtown on Houston Street. He gave her a cell phone number that she knew would be completely bogus.

"What do you do for a living, ... Buddy?"

"I don't work," he said. "I don't have to." She looked at him, studied his clothing, made a mental note that he definitely had a trust fund look, and wrote down *unemployed*.

Then she turned to the belligerent man. "Name, address, cell phone number, and occupation." He gave her the information. His name was Benjy. She mentally cracked up at that. Some of the names that people gave their kids, jeez. Would they still do it when they realized how they turned out as adults? "And what do you do for a living?"

"Construction," he said briefly.

That stopped her pen on the paper because this guy couldn't bend over and swing a hammer. He was too big, too fat, and too out of shape. "You own your own company?"

"I manage a bunch of contractors," he said, with a nod.

She wrote that down. "What is your relationship to this little girl?"

"That's what we're trying to figure out," he said, with a sour tone. "We all lost a niece a couple years back, and we're trying to figure out if this is her."

"Do you show up in every hospital when a little girl is found?" Kate asked, studying the faces of those around her. A couple looked guilty.

One, a woman, her arms across her very ample bosom, nodded. "That's right," she said. "That's exactly what I do."

"Name, address, and cell phone number," she asked. And she quickly took down that woman's information. "So, Susan, what makes you think this could be your niece?"

"I don't know," she said. "But I saw the picture on the TV, and she just looked like my sister's little girl."

"Where is your sister?"

"She died of a drug overdose a few years back," she said.

"She gave her daughter to a friend of hers, but, by the time we went and contacted the friend, there was no way to find her, and the little girl had disappeared."

"What was the friend's name?"

"Trish Bell," she said. "But she was another druggie on the street, so I don't know why the hell my sister would have thought her daughter would be safe with her."

"And how many of you opened your arms to accept this little girl and raise her as your own, so your sister would be sure her child would be safe?"

"Not one of us," said another woman, young, leaning against the wall off to the side. "Not one of us gives a shit."

"Then why are you here?"

"Because I live and stay with Mom, and she says I have to come." She pointed at Susan, the big-breasted angry woman, as the young woman chewed bubble gum, blew a big bubble in front of her, popped it, and said, "But don't kid yourself, nobody here cares."

"You're all here," Kate said, "so something matters."

"An inheritance," the young woman said.

Susan turned and said, "Shut the fuck up!"

"Ah, so the inheritance falls to this little girl, is that it?" Kate asked. "So whoever gets to look after the child in that hospital bed gets a hold of the money?"

"So much more for us to figure out now," Susan said, with a groan, acting like it was all too much.

"Nothing to figure out at all," said one of the other men. "I don't know anything about an inheritance, but that little girl, she was family."

"*Was?*" Kate raised her head, her gaze pinning the other man in place. "Why do you say *was?*"

He tried to backtrack, but it wasn't working.

Shaking her head, Kate said, "All right. Every one of you stretch out your left hand, please. I want to see your wrist." They all looked at her in confusion. She popped her own out and held her wrist so that they saw. "Like this." Frowning, they all did it. She was pretty sure the women wouldn't be involved, but she'd seen the lesser dregs of society and didn't want to make an assumption here. Then she went through each of the men. Not one of them had the mark. She nodded. "Good."

By the time she had everybody's names and address, she asked Susan, "Who is the lawyer handling the inheritance?"

"Terry something or the other," Susan said, with an angry shrug, just getting angrier.

Kate faced Susan, her feet planted apart. "What's his name?" she repeated. "Now."

Susan just glared at her.

Then Kate said, "Fine. Let me do a full rundown on your history and see what else we'll come up with."

"It's Terry Masters," Susan said, "but I don't know anything about an inheritance. It's just my daughter making up shit. She's always doing that stuff. She's pissed off at me right now because I wouldn't let her boyfriend sleep over last night."

Kate wasn't too worried about their reasons because it was usually deception like that which brought out the truth. "I'll be checking it out regardless," she said.

"You don't have to," she said. "It's all bullshit."

"Maybe. And one other thing," she said, "we need DNA from everyone here."

*Silence.*

Kate gave a brief smile. "I know how absolutely thrilled you all are," she said, "but not one of you could claim to be family in this case without a DNA match. Particularly if an inheritance is involved. The lawyer should have mentioned that to you in the first place."

"It's my sister's daughter," Susan said, her tone consistently angry and frustrated, but no fear was there.

"Understood," Kate said. "That's why we do DNA testing to ensure she is. A lot of children go missing. The fact that we have found one with no family we can hand her off to means that we must be very careful that she goes home with the right people," she said quietly. "Anybody here have a problem with that?"

"You don't need to test all of us," the big belligerent guy said. "The only one you need to test is Susan."

The others nodded in agreement and stepped back a little.

Kate smiled. If anything set corrupt people's back on edge, it was DNA testing. It had a way of revealing all kinds of shit about people. She looked at Susan. "Is that a problem?"

She shook her head. "No, it's not a problem at all."

"So, you'll be here when I get back in five minutes with the DNA kit from the doctor, correct?"

Susan gave her a solemn nod. "As long as you're fast," she said.

"Five minutes isn't fast enough for you, huh?" With that, Kate turned and strolled to the front reception area. She got a kit and headed back to the little girl's room. Thankfully they were still out in the hallway, not inside the girl's room, because not one of them seemed like family at this point in time. At least not as far as Kate was concerned. She would talk with the doctor to see what he'd said to them too.

As soon as she collected the DNA from Susan, she put it

back into the tube and labeled it. "Thank you," she said. "I will get this tested, along with that of the little girl."

"How long?"

"I can't say," she said. "But, given the circumstances, we would put a rush on it." And then she deliberately stepped past them all and went into the little girl's room, closing the door in their faces. She walked over, not surprised to see a doctor standing there, over his patient. "How is she doing?"

He turned to look at her, just as she flashed her badge at him. He asked, "Are you the one who found her last night?"

She nodded. "I am."

"She's coming off the drugs in her system," he said. "She was given a heavy sedative, and, from the amount in her system, I think it's been a regular occurrence."

"Of course, by keeping her sedated, he could do whatever he wanted." She studied the sleeping cherub. "How's her general health?"

"Relatively okay. Some of her deficiencies are nutritional, as if she's lived on mostly carbs, without vitamins, healthy foods, or vegetables."

Kate said, "That's consistent with what we've seen on a lot of these types of cases. Have any family members showed up yet?"

He nodded at the hallway.

"I mean, besides those who just *say* they are," she said. "I've pulled DNA from the so-called aunt, but I'm not so sure that any of them are family."

He looked at her, dumbfounded, so she continued. "One of them mentioned an inheritance for a child missing in their family, so they are all jumping on the bandwagon."

He made a sound of disgust. "Of course they are," he said. "People are just—" And then he stopped, as if words completely failed him.

She looked down at the little girl and reached over to turn her left wrist upward, so she saw the mark for herself.

"I saw that mark," he said. "Are you the one who called to have the nurse look at it?"

"Yes," she said. "We've got children in the morgue, both sporting the same mark, plus others from older cases," she said. "We also have a murdered pedophile with the same mark."

"Jesus," he said. "I can't believe this little girl is even alive then."

"I don't think she was supposed to be for too much longer, or, if she was, she's very lucky to be here right now," she said sadly. "We need to find some real family for her."

"We don't even have a name," he said suddenly.

"No, we don't." Then she quickly explained what they knew about her being offered for sale.

"Such sickos in this world," he said. He turned and studied the doorway, leading out to the group. "Do you think they are a danger to her?"

"I don't know," she said, "but I want to make sure they don't get in here. Nobody but verified family is allowed in here, and, until they are proven by blood to be family, even then, I need to make sure they didn't have anything to do with her ending up where she did."

"That is just sad," he said.

"If they did this," she said, shooting him a hard gaze, "I'll nail their asses to the back wall of a jail cell."

"Do that." He turned and looked back at the little girl. "No matter where she ends up, she'll need a lot of therapy."

"How much damage physically?"

"Long-term sexual abuse," he said, his voice low. "Most

of that would eventually heal," he said, "but the rest?" He shook his head. "I'm not so sure. Sometimes they just don't recover."

She couldn't help but think about Simon. "That doesn't sound too good," she said. "You'd like to think that, if we save them, they can have a decent life again."

"It's possible," he said, "even though I wouldn't think it's very realistic. But we must keep trying. She's young and, with any luck, she'll forget a lot of this and move on to something that's much better."

"I hope so," she said. "It's pretty traumatizing for everybody involved." With a final look at the little girl, Kate turned and walked out.

### *Tuesday Evening*

SIMON WORKED HIS ass off for the rest of the day, bluntly trying to forget what he'd been through and the childhood memories dredged up. As he went from project to project, to the bank, and then back to another project, swearing and cursing at problems, most of the men around him ducked and avoided him. He knew it wasn't fair, but it's what he needed to do, as he straightened out things that had gone wrong. By the time he made it home, it was after seven.

He was more than pissed off and fed up. He opened the front door to the building himself and saw no sign of a doorman around. He headed to the stairs, too tired to go up them, yet knowing he still had more of the same frustrating anger driving him. He strolled up the stairs, flight after flight after flight, and, by the time he got to the top and headed into his penthouse, he was beyond exhausted.

He stripped off right from the front door for his second shower of the day. And he knew the demons wouldn't let up anytime soon. When he came out, he dressed again in jeans and a T-shirt, poured himself a stiff drink. Nursing it, he headed to the front window, where he sat down and stared at the incredible view before him. But he didn't see the view. It was his history; it was his past; it was everything bad. All he saw was the mocking darkness hidden underneath all those bright lights. And something was so wrong about it all. When his phone rang, he grabbed it, check the Caller ID on his screen. It was Kate. "What do you want?" he barked.

"You have a right to snap," she said, "but I'm bringing dinner, so let me up."

"I'm not hungry."

"Too damn bad," she said. "Let me up." Her tone was as inflexible as his.

He gave a snort. "Your funeral," he said, and he buzzed her in. He could just imagine her walking across the front foyer, and he wondered again for a moment where the hell the doorman was. But didn't waste any more time on that issue. He got up and walked to his doorway, then leaned against the doorjamb and waited for the elevator to open. When it did, she strolled out, and he looked down at the bag in her hand. "There should have been leftover Chinese still."

"I left that at my place," she said. "I haven't been home yet. I stopped on the way from the hospital."

"That sounds like a lovely visit."

"It should have been," she said. "Two children were saved. But somehow it just leaves me with that terrible feeling inside."

He nodded in understanding, realizing her mood equaled his. He watched as she walked into the kitchen and took out containers. He didn't recognize the brown paper bag or the smell coming from the containers. Some sort of Middle Eastern dish. "Smells interesting," he said cautiously.

"It's good, but don't eat it if you don't want to. I don't give a shit," she grumped. He gave a bark of laughter and brought plates over. She quickly served two platefuls, pulled up a stool, and sat down right where she was. He repeated the move on his side, and the two of them munched through some food.

"What is it about food," he said, studying the folded wrapped thing in his hand, "that soothes the soul?"

"And add not being alone," she said quietly. "I'm sorry that I couldn't be in the interview room with you today."

"Whatever," he said. "They didn't do anything that crossed the line."

She nodded. "No, not yet," she said. "If they find anything that connects you to any of the cases, they will though."

He stared at her and then shrugged. "They can waste all their time if they want," he said. "I don't give a shit."

"Good. No sign of your foster father or your biological mother so far," she said. "We found your birth certificate, but no death certificate for either of them."

"Check the Jane Does," he said. "My foster father said she was nothing but a junkie."

"Maybe," she said. "A family was at the hospital today, who said the little girl who I found in Richmond was their niece. Missing for a couple years." She filled him in on the story, and he just stared.

"And they want her now? Even though, when her mother was in trouble and needed a safe place for her daughter, they weren't there?"

"Family, right?" she said, with a snort. "Something about an inheritance. I've started a few searches on my laptop, but I haven't gotten any further."

"An inheritance would do it," he said. "But why so many people?"

"I think they don't trust each other," she said. "And they want to make sure they are all in there to grab some money."

"They want to help spend the inheritance."

"I've got calls in to the lawyer," she said. "So far, nobody is talking. So we don't have a connection yet."

"Sorry," he said, "that sucks too."

"It does, but I'm looking for a solution, not more shit."

"And you are the one who found this little girl?"

She nodded. "And I also saw somebody coming out of a window in the house, but I didn't get him," she said, with another snort of disgust. "That same blue truck was stolen that night, and, when I went to talk to the witness, he was gone. I did get a license plate, and so did you apparently."

"All a little too convenient."

She stared down at the wrap in her hand, looked over at him, gave a small smile, and said, "That's what I thought."

"So why are you here?" he asked.

She studied him, her gaze blank, and then she smiled. "I'm not sure," she said. "But, when I came out of the hospital, it was instinctive to grab a meal for two. And, when I did, I realized who it was I was supposed to share it with."

"What is that, like being psychic?"

"Like hell," she said forcibly. "I don't know anything about that part of your life, and I don't really want to know," she said. "But something is here, and *that* may be something I need to reconsider."

"An awful lot of somethings you just mentioned," he

said.

She smiled and nodded. "There is, indeed. Don't know if that's good or bad though."

"Don't think it matters much," he said, "because you're still talking in circles."

She cleaned her plate, stood, and walked to the sink. There she washed her hands, took his empty whiskey glass from the counter, rinsed it out, then filled it with water and took a long drink, while she studied his face. "Maybe so," she said. "But I didn't think you were the kind to beat around the bush."

He got up, repeated her actions exactly, placing his lips where hers had been, and, by the time he'd swallowed a glass of water, with just the counter between them, she walked around and packed up the garbage.

"I can leave though, if you prefer."

Grabbing her by the shoulders, he spun her around, cupped her face, and kissed her. Almost immediately her arms swept around his neck and held him in a grip that was harder and stronger than he'd ever felt before. Lips locked, it was as if something had been unleashed between them. Their hands were busy, as they pulled out shirttails, unbuttoned buttons, dragged down zippers, and sent clothes flying.

He dragged her backward, down a couple steps to his bedroom, and, by the time they collapsed onto the bed itself, not a stitch of clothes stood between them. The sex was hard, fast, riveting, and nothing short of wild.

Then she collapsed back down again and groaned. "I know we shouldn't be doing this," she whispered. He rolled over on top of her and slammed his mouth down over hers. She got the message and pivoted, spinning him over onto his back, where she immediately climbed on top of his already growing erection and rode him, taking them both to the edge of collapse again.

Finally he lay on the sheet beside her. Reaching down, he gripped her fingers with his, lacing their fingers together. "I'm glad you came," he whispered.

She snuggled close, and, with the lights of Vancouver shining in an odd ethereal array in front of them, she whispered, "So am I."

# CHAPTER 25

*Wednesday Morning*

K ATE STOOD ON the side of the commercial street, studying the vehicle near Starbucks. It wasn't the one she had seen at the pedophile's house on Monday night. But it was registered to the pedophile named Nico, the owner of the house where they'd found the little girl. Somebody had decided to make sure the pedophile drew his last breath, before he'd face justice for that little girl in his basement. Appeared to be another strangulation of a pedophile. A part of her was furious about that. She wanted to see this guy locked up and treated the same way he had treated those poor kids.

In this case it was a saving grace on the taxpayer's money and the legal system to have Nico put out of his misery permanently. At least this way, he couldn't get off on a technicality or do his time and be released again to hurt more kids. He'd already done that. Still, did they have a vigilante trying to take down pedophiles on his own? 'Cause that would never go down well.

At her side, Rodney pulled his coat jacket edges closer together against the Vancouver rain.

"The world is crying today," she murmured.

"Not for this asshole," he snapped.

She looked at him and shook her head. "No, but let's

hope he has answers for us."

"I doubt it," he said. "We haven't been lucky yet."

"We haven't been lucky," she said, "because we didn't know the big picture. But the pieces are coming together."

"How the hell can you have so much faith in that Simon guy?" he asked abruptly.

She looked at him, shrugged, and said, "I don't know. All I can tell you is that I do."

"Well, nobody came up with anything to tie him to the cases," he said grudgingly. "So Colby's backed off on Simon being our number one suspect." Then Rodney gave a snort and said, "Depends on if we can lock down his alibi for last night though."

Kate froze, struggling to not show her shock. She was about to face one of the hardest times of her career. She didn't say anything at the time, as she stared at the dead pedophile, sitting in the driver's seat of his registered vehicle, the Forensics team working around the body even now. "Do we have a time of death?" she asked the coroner.

He shook his head. "He's been dead at least six to eight hours. So, somewhere between midnight and four a.m. would be close."

She nodded slowly. "That's a small window. We need to find out how long the vehicle was parked here." With that, she headed into the coffee shop and asked the staff. Most of them had come back on at six this morning, and the vehicle had already been there. One of the new staffers coming on for his shift had called in the scene.

With the names of those who had closed the night before, Kate stood outside and started phoning them. A couple she woke up, and some were angry, although their tone changed once she explained what the problem was.

One had seen the vehicle there, but he wasn't sure that anybody had been inside it. He'd left at 1:30 a.m., and the only reason he had noticed it was because he'd parked out back too. He couldn't give any specific identification on the vehicle, just that a small truck was in the parking lot when he left, and it was a dark color. Which matched the description of this one perfectly. "Did you see anybody around it? Anybody coming to or from it?"

"No," he said. "Should be camera footage though."

"We're getting that," she said. After she hung up, she sought out the manager and asked, "Do you have security cameras?"

He nodded and handed her a phone number. "I already requested that it be prepared for you. This number is for the security company. They should have the video feeds ready."

"Do you have any access?"

"No," he said. "If there's anything suspicious, we contact them."

"Good enough," she said. She headed back outside to call them. When she heard somebody at the end of the line, she identified herself, the business name involved, and the property address. "I'm looking for any activity around the parking lot in the back," she said.

"We can scan through it here, or do you want the feeds sent to you?"

"I need the feeds," she said instantly. "And I need them now. I'll be in my office in about twenty minutes."

"Sure. Give me your email address, and we'll send it to you immediately," he said.

When she hung up the phone, she walked to where Rodney was, glad to see the coroner here too. "I have the security feeds coming to my email, so I'm heading to the office to go over them."

Rodney nodded. "Let's hope we have some forensics evidence on this one."

She stopped, turned to look back at the deceased male, and asked the nearby cops, "Anybody check his wallet yet?"

"I have it here, if you want to take a look," the coroner said.

Kate and Rodney walked around to the side. "Anything missing?"

"No cash—which makes it look like a robbery—and, even more so, no cards."

"So maybe it's completely unrelated," she murmured. "Or made to look like a robbery." As she glanced into the back seat of the vehicle, she noted, "He's got several suitcases here. I presume he was running."

"He probably had a decent amount of cash on him too," Rodney pointed out. "So a robbery is then quite likely."

She thought about it and said, "That would make sense. We can check his bank records to see if he'd pulled out any money."

They spent another ten minutes studying the scene, before they returned to the office. By the time they made it back, she was chilled and damp. That was the thing about living in a coastal town like Vancouver; sometimes it was absolutely stunning, but, when the rains started, you felt like you would never get dry or warm again.

At her desk, she searched through the video feeds. Lots of vehicles in the hours just before Starbucks closed, an amazing amount. She hadn't realized just how many people were out at that hour. But then the nightlife in the city was always active.

As she watched, vehicles came and went; then their victim's truck pulled in slowly. She watched as Nico got out, looked around nervously, then walked rapidly into Starbucks. He came out a good ten or fifteen minutes later, a cup in his hand. He was joined by another man, whose back was to the video cameras. She studied the frame, straightening slowly. "I think it's him," she said in amazement.

Rodney came to stand behind her. "You think who is him?"

She reached out and tapped the man talking to the victim on her frozen screen. "I think this is the guy I saw outside Nico's house."

"It would make sense," he said.

But then the one guy disappeared, and Nico got back into his vehicle. He sat there for a long moment. The other guy came back again with a cup of coffee and slipped into the passenger seat. They stayed like that, talking for at least another ten or fifteen minutes, while she waited impatiently. She didn't want to speed up the video camera, even though she was dying to see what else happened. She didn't want to miss anything.

Then the second man got out, wearing a hat pulled low over his face. With the cup of coffee in his hands, he walked to his vehicle, which was just out of the shot.

She swore and said, "Damn. I need to know what vehicle he drove."

"We can pick it up on the city cameras," Rodney said, going over to his computer. "What time frame are you looking at?"

"It's one-fifteen a.m.," she said, reading the time off the security footage. And, from that point on, she saw no action in that vehicle. The man who had been sitting in the passenger seat was the last person to see Nico alive. She watched clear through the recording, until the new shift of staff arrived, and somebody noticed he was in there. Then she shut it down and went back to the beginning and watched it again. "Blue pickup," Rodney announced. "Same license plate as in your photo."

She turned in her seat. "The same one?"

"Yep," he said.

She gave him a fat smile. Same one as Simon gave her too. "Now check," she said, "to see if there was a second phone call, saying that his truck was stolen?"

He looked over at her in surprise.

"It was stolen the other night," she said, "but I checked with the cops, and it was returned to him the next day."

He nodded in understanding. "So now the question is whether it was stolen again—which is highly unlikely—or whether he was driving that vehicle himself."

"From what I see on this video camera," she said, "it's him, the guy crawling out Nico's window. Same stature, same framework, but I can't get a picture of his face."

"Well, that won't have been accidental," he said. "He knew the cameras were there."

Owen spoke up from the other side of the room. "I've also run Nico's bank account," he said, "and five hundred was removed very early that morning—before his death at about one-fifteen a.m.—from a branch downtown."

"Get those ATM camera feeds."

"Already ordered," Owen said.

"So, looks like our guy took Nico's cash and his cards as well," she said, with a nod. "No honor among thieves."

"Considering they were selling that little girl and bickering over the price, no honor at all," Rodney said.

"I need to talk to that little runt," she muttered. She

stood and pulled her wallet from inside her drawer and shoved it deep into her jacket pocket and zipped it up. With her keys in her hands, she looked at the two of them. "Anybody coming?"

Rodney gave her a big smile and said, "Oh, thank you for the invitation."

She rolled her eyes at him. "I don't know if our killer's armed and dangerous," she said, "or just dangerous to little kids."

"Are we gonna kick some butt?" he asked, with interest.

Her smile widened and deepened. "I hope so," she said fervently. "I really hope so." Just as she was about to head out, Colby called out to her.

"Kate, come back here, please."

She held up a finger to Rodney, saying, "Just a minute." As she walked into Colby's office, he motioned at the door.

"Close that, will you?"

She closed it and said, "Sure. What's up?"

"I understand we have a new victim, and it's connected to the existing cases. I want you to double-check Simon's alibi for last night to make sure he's not involved."

She knew this was it. Her D-day had come. She took slow deep breaths and said, "Sergeant, I can tell you right now that his alibi is good."

Colby looked at her, and a thunderous cloud crossed his face. "Please tell me that you didn't—"

Shoving her hands in her pockets, she rocked back on her heels and then gave a nod. "Actually I did."

"Fucking hell," he roared.

She took two steps and collapsed in the nearby chair.

"He is a suspect," he snapped.

She shook her head. "No, he wasn't. You guys were trying to make it *look* like he was a suspect, but he had no connection, outside of being a rescued child from thirty-one years ago," she said boldly. "I get that everybody wanted him to look good for it, but he didn't."

"He wasn't cleared," Colby snapped.

She stiffened. "He was," she said. "I listened to everything yesterday. Rodney did a full workup, trying to match him to everything, and couldn't find anything. And, for the record, I didn't plan it," she said. He just glared at her. She shrugged and straightened. "Can I leave now?"

"You know I should pull you off the case," he snapped.

"You don't need to do that, Sergeant," she said wearily.

"Where are you heading?"

"Out to the home of the same pedophile I saw leaving Nico's place, where we found the child," she said. "He was on the camera as the last person who approached Nico in his vehicle."

"And it's definitely not Simon?" His gaze probed hers.

"Definitely not," she said, with emphasis. Inside she was trembling. The last thing she wanted to do was get sidelined for having done something improper. In her own mind, she knew Simon had nothing to do with it, but that didn't mean everybody else was as sure.

He gave a brief nod and added, "This isn't over."

She gulped. "Thank you, Sergeant," she whispered and quickly disappeared. She met Rodney at the elevator. He looked at her and said, "Problem?"

"No," she said, calmer than she felt. "Nothing more than usual." As they approached the apartment she'd been to earlier—but both owner and truck were gone that first time—she walked over and knocked on the front door. There was no answer. Rodney went around to the parking lot to check for a vehicle.

She knocked again and then picked up the phone and called Owen.

As soon as he answered, he said, "We have a warrant."

"Good. I'm going in," she said. She brought out her tools, popped the knob, and opened the door ever-so-slightly. Rodney came up beside her, one of them on either side the door. As he went high, and she went low, they pushed the door open and entered, calling out, "Police coming in. We have a warrant!"

Only silence greeted them.

She frowned as she stepped inside and looked around, doing a quick sweep around the small apartment first. Bedroom off to the left, living room straight ahead, kitchen on the right. Small bathroom between the living room and the bedroom. And the place was a hovel. It smelled as if no fresh air had been through here in weeks. It was nasty. But what was that odor from? She lifted her nose and sniffed the air again, frowning.

Rodney looked at her and nodded. "Something dead was in here."

"But what?" she said quietly. They did a general search first and then got into the nitty-gritty details. She focused on the living room. Just something about it really drove her crazy. As she worked her way through it, moving pizza boxes, take-out containers, rolled-up bags of garbage, she realized they could have moved any number of things in here, and the resident never would have noticed.

But the couch, where he sat in front of the TV, was clear, both sides. She removed the cushions, finding a number of things she didn't want to question too closely, and one was a piece of pink ribbon. She stared at it quietly for a long moment, then picked it up with her gloved hand and placed it in a small evidence bag. "A pink ribbon here," she said.

"And that means what?"

"Maybe nothing," she said, "but our little princess had pink ribbons on her clothes."

He popped his head around the corner, looked at her, frowned, and said, "She was here?"

She shrugged. "I don't know. I'm just telling you." She kept going. When she came to a small notebook, listing a series of names, she frowned and put it into an evidence bag as well. But not before she took a couple photos of the list. She knew that the Forensic teams would come, but she wanted this moment to see for herself just exactly what was here and what was not.

"I wish we had his phone," she murmured. She quickly sent Reese a text, asking her to apply for a list of the phone calls from this perv's phone. If they could get his phone records, that would help too. The kitchen itself was the cleanest part of the house, but clearly that was because he didn't use it. She opened the fridge to find milk, cookies, a couple half-eaten sandwiches, a random jar of pickled jalapenos, and not a whole lot else.

Obviously this was the fridge of a man who didn't cook and had no intention of learning. He'd lived this way for a very long time. She was doing the run of his history, even as she searched the place. He was forty-nine years old and a twin. She froze at that and researched who his sibling was. When she got the name, she froze again.

"Oh my God," she said.

Rodney poked his head out of the bedroom. "Now what?"

"He's a twin, and his sister is one of the most preeminent psychologists in town. Dr. Yolynda Brown. We use her a lot for our cases and often call her in on our criminal trials. I was supposed to contact her about these cases but never got a chance to do so."

He looked over and frowned. "Well, I guess even pedophiles have family," he said.

She nodded, but something about it just felt terribly off. "I've notified Colby." She kept reading the summary and realized that this perv had been picked up once and had served a couple years. He was on the record as an abuser but had kept a very low profile ever since.

She pocketed her phone and kept going through the apartment. As long as they were here, she knew the perv wouldn't come back, but she didn't know if he understood that he'd lost his home base. Surely he had another base too. Yet, considering his current lifestyle, she was uncertain of that. She walked through to the bedroom and asked Rodney, "You find anything?"

"Nothing incriminating, just nasty-assty shit," he said. "All kinds of condoms in the drawers, but all the packages are unopened."

"So he's ready but not here maybe?"

"Maybe, or he stopped using them."

"That's possible too," she said. "I hope so. Surely his DNA is bound to show up somewhere." She glanced around, walked over to the window, drew back the curtains, and opened it wide. "Ground floor, minimal light, kept the curtains closed," she murmured. "He was hiding."

"Pedophiles are always hiding," Rodney said, "but hiding in plain sight. So we never know who the hell they are."

"Well, this one is about to be exposed," she said, "because we're about to get him." She knew it was false confidence, but she was determined to solve this.

"It would sure be good timing to have any fancy numbers your boyfriend could provide for you."

She froze at his use of the term. "Simon is hardly my boyfriend," she said carefully.

"Whatever," he said.

"Could a safe be here?" She viewed the walls with interest, and he immediately stopped his search and started helping her.

"It doesn't look like the kind of place that would have a safe, does it?"

"No, and I'm not too sure if this is actually a place he'd bring victims to or not," she said. "It's pretty *un*lived-in."

"You mean overly lived-in, don't you?" he asked.

"Yeah, I mean, it looks lived-in for him but not for a child."

"Depends on how long he had them for," he said. "That little girl Simon called in had been drugged all to hell before her neck was broken. Then the lost little girl you found at Nico's place had also been heavily drugged for a long time too, so she's not been consciously aware of what she went through for the last while. Which is a blessing in a way. I wonder how long Nico actually held her at his place."

"Good point," she murmured. She studied the apartment with a new eye. "So this is where this perv lived," she said, "but there's no hiding place for kids in this dive."

"Storage lockers," Rodney suggested. "Usually in the basement."

She looked at him, frowned. Then, as she walked out, she said, "I'll go talk to the manager." She roused the manager from his apartment and had a quick conversation.

"How long has he been here?"

"Since he got out of prison."

"So you know about his prison record?"

He nodded. "It was part of the reason I gave it to him."

She stared at him in surprise. "He came with good references?"

"Ready to turn over a new leaf."

"And yet children are in this building, and, as a registered pedophile, he has to stay a certain distance away from children."

"I don't know anything about that," he said, backing up. "Besides, I don't think we have any kids right now."

"It's an apartment building, and you don't have any children living here?"

He frowned, studied the hallway, as if mentally clicking through his renters, and said, "I'm not so sure there is right now. In the past we certainly have, but it's an older building, and there aren't any amenities for kids."

"That just means the lower-income families could live here," she said.

"He came with references, and I was asked to take him in, so I did," he said. "This isn't on me."

"Who asked you to take him in?"

He hesitated.

"A preeminent psychologist, by any chance?" she asked.

"Yes," he said, answering with relief. "I figured, if he came with that kind of reference, he was good to go."

"Except in this case, it was a family member," she said.

He looked at her in shock. "What?"

"His twin sister," she said. "Have you ever seen him around any children?"

"No, I haven't. Look. To be honest, he's been quiet,

stays out of trouble, and hasn't been an issue."

"Does he have a storage locker?"

"Everybody does. Downstairs," he said. "They're allowed to do pretty much whatever they want with that space."

"What number is his?"

"Just a minute." When he came back, he said, "Eighty-four."

"How do I get into it?"

"I can lead you there," he said. Then he took her down a set of stairs, followed along the main hallway here, a series of plywood-looking cages on each side. "His is at the far end," he said.

She followed him to the locker in question to see it was mostly sealed up. She noted the lock on it, looked at him, and asked, "Do you have a key?"

"No," he said. "This is their private property."

She nodded, pulled the pick from her back pocket, and popped it open in seconds.

"You do have a warrant, right?" he asked nervously. "I can't let you do this if you don't."

"Yes, of course I do," she said. She jerked up on one of the metal gates and pulled open the door. Then she stopped. Turning, she faced him and said, "Please go back to your apartment, and stay there for further questioning."

He looked at her, then tried to peek into the storage locker, but she stepped into his view.

"Now!" she snapped.

He looked at her resentfully, shrugged, and said, "Fine. But I've done everything you've asked. None of this is on me."

She watched him leave, then turned to look at the storage locker. They might not have anything on the apartment manager, but this sure as hell put some things on the pedophile's shoulders. The space contained children's toys, clothes, beds, and all kinds of paraphernalia that went along with having children. Only this guy had no children. So what in the hell had he used all this stuff for? And where?

### *Thursday, Almost Noon*

AS DAYS WENT, Simon felt pretty damn good about this one. He didn't dare contact her, but he felt too good about the night they'd spent together to not be thinking about her. He went about his business from jobsite to jobsite, happy that, for once, things were moving along and functioning well. For a little while he could put all the nastiness behind him. When his phone rang, he looked at it, realized it was almost noon. "Yale, what's up?"

"Private game Friday, if you're up for it," he said.

"I might be," he replied, "but I might have plans too."

"You?" he said, with a sneer.

Something about Yale had been pissing him off a little more every time. "I do have relationships," he said. "Don't you?"

"Not in a while," Yale said grudgingly. "But I might need a place to crash for a couple nights."

"Why is that?"

"Some odd smell in my bloody apartment building," he said. "Management is asking us to vacate for a few days."

"What will they do, fumigate?" And what happened to the mansion? But Simon didn't want to ask. Yale had poor money management skills. Always had. And he should never gamble. That combination was deadly.

"Maybe," he said. "I don't know."

"Time to go on a cruise then," Simon said, not interested in offering his friend a room. Not when it was possible that Kate would be back.

"Fine," he said. "I wasn't asking for a place to stay, you know."

"I hear you, and that's a good thing because I'm full up at the moment."

"I doubt it," he said. "You've got all that money."

"What does money have to do with it?" Simon asked curiously.

"Just that you can go anywhere you want to," Yale said.

"I could," he said. "The bottom line is that I don't need to."

"But you made enough money on the last weekend cruise to take you to a hotel for quite a while too."

"Maybe so," he said. "I don't think I made as much as you seem to think."

"Maybe not," he said. "Doesn't matter. I'll work it out, whatever."

"Where's the game at?"

"Same as last time," he said abruptly.

"Ah," he said mentally, certain it was one he wouldn't attend.

"What? You not giving anybody a chance to earn their money back again?" he asked. "I'm sorry I missed that game, although I've lost plenty over the last year."

"I hardly got anything off you," Simon said in a mild tone.

"Sure didn't feel that way at the time."

Simon noted an edge to Yale's voice. "Look. If you've got a problem, just come on out and say it."

"You cheated."

"*You* cheated," Simon snapped, biting back his true response.

There was a sigh on the other end. "How did you know?"

"The signs and tells were all there," he said. "Besides, you've always been cheating. Whether it's at the casino, on the cruises, or in a club," he said. "But you're losing your grip on it."

"Hardly," he said. "I just haven't made enough money to handle what I needed to handle."

"Why is that?"

"I have to go away for a bit," he said.

"So, go away," he said. "Casinos are everywhere. Maybe nobody will figure out what you're doing in a new one."

"I had hoped, on Friday, I'd make a big score and then maybe move on from Vancouver. Find a place where I can start fresh."

"Well," he said, "whatever you need to do, I've got to get back to business." And he hung up. He was more than a little disturbed about Yale's phone call. It didn't make a whole lot of sense. Simon finished his work and slowly headed toward his apartment. He wondered how Kate's day was going. He'd heard on the news that a man had been found dead at the Starbucks on the way out of town.

Simon figured it was the one she had tracked down, but it also could be the one in the blue truck that Simon had seen. On the way home he stopped, picked up fish and chips. Just as he walked inside and headed to his elevator, a series of numbers flashed before his eyes. He frowned, grabbed his notepad, and wrote them down. He often had no clue what the numbers were until later.

These were right in his face, as if to say something was deadly important about them. He looked down at his notes, but it made no sense. It was just 4441 4441 4441. He didn't know, but, with her on his mind, he quickly texted her, sending **4441 4441 4441**. Hoped that maybe it made sense to her. When she phoned him almost immediately, just as he was walking into the kitchen, he answered the call.

"What's that number for?"

"I don't know," he said. "I really don't know."

"Well, that's no help," she snapped.

"No, it isn't," he said, "and I've just gotten home with dinner, so I'll talk to you later."

And, with that, he put down his cell. He smiled because it's not what she would have expected, but, hell, it wasn't what he expected either. But it's what he needed to do. He took off his jacket, hung it up, and then turned his attention to his fish. He sat down and ate it, having missed lunch. He still didn't understand why his friend Yale suddenly needed to leave.

Then he remembered the in-town poker game with the cheater and how some strange looks had been directed at Simon. Maybe they suspected Simon of cheating. Knowing Simon and Yale were friends, maybe the other poker players were looking at Yale as well. If that were the case, they would be coming after him sooner or later. He phoned his friend back. "You should probably leave sooner," he said. "I'm remembering the looks on their faces at that last game. I think they're going to be hard-asses from here on in."

"Of course they will, but I had nothing to do with it. You on the other hand ..."

"I only cheated the one guy," Simon said, "and that's because he was cheating everyone else."

There was silence, and Yale said, "Seriously?"

"Yes. You should know that about me by now," he said. "I don't cheat friends, and I don't cheat at all, unless I need to deal with somebody like that."

"How the hell can you always win at cards then, if you don't cheat all the time?"

"I happen to be good with numbers," he said. "But it's another thing to have somebody take everybody for a ride, even ones who couldn't afford it."

Yale sucked in his breath. "Are you saying they might know I cheated?"

"Oh, I know it's you, so, yeah, maybe so."

"Great, so I guess no game on Friday."

"Probably not," Simon agreed. "Me neither."

"Don't suppose you have any spare cash you can lend me, do you?" Yale said humorously.

"No, can't say I keep any at home."

"You could always go to the bank," Yale said, this time with a bit more of an edge to his voice.

"Stop off and get into a local game at the casino," Simon said. "Pick yourself up a grand and don't do anything to attract any attention."

"Too risky," he said. "I just want enough money to fill up a gas tank and get going."

"You should have that," he said.

"It's been a tough few months," he said. "More than a tough few months, I guess."

"You walked away with a couple grand on that last game."

He said, "Yeah, but I had bills to pay. So not a whole lot of that left."

Not knowing why he was even doing it, except they'd

been friends for so long, … Simon said, "Fine. I can spot you a grand, but that's it."

"I'll take it," Yale said immediately.

"What the hell happened to your trust fund?"

"It dried up," Yale said in a dry tone. "I haven't managed to find another way to replenish it, besides games."

"Games are dangerous," Simon said. "And, when you cheat, you get noticed."

"So I don't understand how the hell you get off scot-free."

"Because I'm not cheating when I gamble," he said. "Again, I did cheat that one asshole, but that's because of what he did to the other guy, Baine."

"He really lost his wife, didn't he?"

"Lost his wife and his home and everything important to him. Hopefully he'll wake up and find something else to do with his life."

"I don't know," Yale said. "We get stuck on a pathway, and it's hard to deviate."

"It's not that hard to deviate," Simon said. "The trouble is, nobody wants to. You're on that pathway yourself because it gives you something," he said. "So stop fooling anybody else and make the hard choices." And, with that, he hung up. Just as he put down his phone, he realized he hadn't told Yale where to meet up for the money. He thought about it and texted him to meet at a coffee shop downtown in twenty minutes.

He got a thumbs-up in return.

Simon hoped he could make it in twenty minutes. He checked his wallet and, of course, he didn't have that kind of cash. Going to his safe, he opened it and pulled out $1,000. One of the few things he did keep at home was cash. If anybody ever got into his safe, he'd also know about it. He'd spent a lifetime building up what he had, so no way in hell he would let anybody take it without a fight.

He had a lot of security, and most of it he'd designed himself. He picked up the rest of his fish and chips, tossed it in the garbage, and figured he'd grab a coffee at the shop. Then he headed out. As he exited the front door, he stopped, noting the rain had started again. But still, the coffee shop was only about five blocks away. He took a shortcut through the alleyways and arrived within a short time. He ordered a coffee and sat down outside at one of the little patio tables under the awning. Yale should be here soon. Sure enough, Simon turned around, and there he was, walking toward him, a grim look on his face. His truck was parked around the corner.

Simon looked at the blue truck and frowned. "Is that your truck?"

Yale looked back at it, shrugged, and said, "Belongs to a friend of mine. We exchanged wheels for me to leave."

"Interesting," Simon said, studying Yale's features, wondering what the hell was going on. "A good friend?"

"Maybe," he said. "Why?"

"Because that truck has been in some trouble."

"He said it was stolen a little bit ago, but he got it back."

"Right." Simon didn't say anything more, but his friend went inside, grabbed himself a coffee, came back, sat down, and he asked Yale, "You're sure about this?"

"I'm sure."

Simon handed him the envelope and said, "Good luck with that, but seriously you may want to ditch that vehicle."

He looked at the truck and said, "I need it."

"Not that bad. How good of a friend?"

"Really good," he said. "Why?"

Simon shrugged and didn't say anything.

They finished their coffee, and Yale stood and shook Simon's hand. "Thanks, I appreciate this." He pocketed the money and headed off to the truck. As soon as he got inside, he left.

Simon called Kate and explained what had just happened.

"Which direction?" she asked.

He told her, along with the little bit he knew.

"I'll put out notice to pick him up."

He put away his phone and sat here, wondering just what his friend was doing mixed up with that blue truck. Then he considered how long he'd actually known Yale. As he tossed his mind back, it was hard to actually pinpoint the time they had first met. They'd both been in a private college for a short time, what with Simon's gifted mind, skipping several grades, graduating from high school much earlier than most. A scholarship had gotten Simon there. He'd filled out the forms and had gotten the funding and the acceptance on his own.

But, after a year, he realized just how useless a stuck-up education was, and he'd walked away. But a lot of kids attended there, and Yale had been one of them. Because Simon had been there, everybody assumed he had a trust fund. That's because they all did. He knew for sure that Yale did. He quickly typed Yale's name into Google and did a search on him, found an address for him, but it was years old. It didn't tell Simon anything new or current. He picked up his phone and texted Yale. **Where are you heading, by the way?**

**Not sure. I haven't decided if I'm going south or**

**north.**

Simon left it at that, frowning. As he got up and headed toward home, he started across the street. Too late, he heard a vehicle racing toward him. He bolted out of the way, but it caught the corner of his hip and flung him onto the sidewalk. He rolled and jumped to his feet, furious, turning to face whoever it was.

It was a damn blue truck, and Yale stood there, gun in his hand.

He pointed it at Simon. "Why the fuck do you want to know where I'm going?"

Simon stared at him in surprise. "I thought we were friends," he said. "Are you saying you don't want to keep in touch?"

Suspicion battled on Yale's face.

Simon stared at him. "It's your truck, isn't it?"

"This?" he said, with a disgusted look at the ugly truck.

"Yeah, that," he said.

Yale shook his head. "No, it's not mine."

"Really?" Simon said, walking slowly toward him. "I saw it the other night, going through town."

"Well, it wasn't me driving," Yale said.

"No, you are right about that," he said. "It was some other geezer. I didn't know who it was at the time, but he shot me a look, but the area was too shadowed to see him clearly."

"It's got nothing to do with me though."

"Maybe it does," Simon said slowly.

Yale glared at him.

"Does your family know?" Simon asked.

"Know what?" he said, with exasperation.

"That you're hanging around with pedophiles?"

Yale froze. "Fuck off," he said. "You don't know anything about me."

"I know that you were abused as a young boy," he said. "I remember that from school."

"That was just a rumor," he said. "It doesn't mean anything."

"And I know that you are part of a family who all have trust funds," Simon said slowly, trying to read his way through his memories and to sort through the little bit of information popping up.

"So what? Everybody who went through that damn school had trust funds."

"And," he said, "you have siblings. A brother and a sister."

Yale glared at him. "And?"

"And," he said, slowly reaching for the information seemingly buried in the recesses of his brain, "your brother is a mess. Didn't he get into a spot of trouble a while back?"

"So? He's the black sheep in the family. My sister is also a highly regarded doctor," he said. "She's the good side of the family. I didn't go either way, just stayed there in the same place and did nothing."

"Maybe. Or maybe not," Simon said quietly. "It sounds to me like you've made a lot of decisions on the dark side that you're trying to avoid getting caught up in."

"I didn't do anything," he said.

"That remains to be seen."

Just then, Yale's phone rang. Swearing, but the gun never wavering, he pulled out his phone, looked down at it, and held it up to his ear, shaking his head. "Yes, we're leaving," Yale said into the phone. "Yes, I know. The cops were at your place. I'll get to you in a few minutes." With that, he hung up.

"And that just confirms it," Simon said. "Because I already know the police were after the owner of that blue truck," he said.

"So what? It's got nothing to do with me," he said.

"Were you the one who conveniently stole the vehicle the other night?"

His eyebrows shot up, and he chuckled. "You don't know anything. You're just fishing now."

"All right, put away that damn gun," Simon said, "and get the fuck out of here."

"I'd get lost if I thought I could," he said. "But the fact that you recognized the truck, that's a problem."

"Hardly," Simon said, growing irritated. "I figured your good buddy, the owner of that blue truck, he was out looking for children."

"That's an awful lot of figuring you're doing," he said.

"It is," he said. But, instead of taking a step back, he took a step forward.

"Stop right there," Yale said. His phone rang again, so he looked down, then swore. "I told you that I'm on the way. ... Right, I know. I know." He put away his phone and said to Simon, "I need you to disappear."

"I can do that," Simon said readily.

"No," he said, "like forever."

Simon's eyebrows shot up. "Why is that?"

"You really don't know, do you?"

"I don't know anything," he said. "I think that's pretty obvious by now."

"That's how you got into school, you know?"

"I got into that school on a scholarship," he said.

"And because of your foster father," he snapped.

341

At the words *foster father*, Simon stared at him. "I don't remember anything about my foster father."

"That's too bad," he said, "because he was a wealthy man. I suspect your trust fund should have been equal to mine. But mine is dried up, after a series of bad business decisions. Wish I could pay the lawyers to handle them."

"Go back to the part about my foster father for a moment," Simon said, taking a step closer. "What the fuck are you talking about?"

"Everybody knew who he was and that you were born on the wrong side of the blanket. To a barmaid. He said the stories made it around town without too much trouble, especially for everybody in the school. Everybody was supposed to keep it a secret, and, as such, everybody soon knew everything."

"I was only in the damn school for one year."

"But we all knew who you were. Your foster father was Josh Cameron," he said. "A businessman. A banker and a married man too."

"What's this got to do with anything?" Simon said, completely confused.

"That's the thing. You don't get it. Because your mother dumped you in with my family. Your foster father was *my* father. He *bought* you off your mother. Your foster father—my father—was a pedophile," he said, with a broken laugh. "And you were one of his victims."

"*One* of his victims?"

Yale nodded slowly. "He abused the rest of us," he said. "I don't really know how the hell you were rescued, but nobody else was."

"Is he dead?"

"Yes," Yale said. "Thus the trust funds, remember? For

us—not you of course. He disappeared a long time ago and was declared legally dead after seven years. Sometime after he put you in the hospital. Of course we might have had a hand in his disappearance."

That statement made Simon pause. "But your last name is different."

Yale gave him a one-arm shrug. "We didn't want the old man's curse on us too. When that came out, and he promptly disappeared, looking guilty as hell, we all changed our last names."

"I didn't know anything about this," Simon said, staring at Yale in shock. "After all this time ..."

"I was of two minds, whether I should say anything or not, but you didn't seem to know or to care."

"Oh, I care," Simon said in a harsh voice. "I just can't believe that nobody said anything to me in all this time."

"You were so young. I was really surprised when you showed up at that school."

"And you're what? Eight years older than I am?"

"When you were rescued, you were only six and I was fourteen," he said. "I was just coming out of it because, as long as you were there, I wasn't abused."

"And your brother and sister?"

"Same thing. As long as our dad had a pet, we were safe."

Simon's stomach churned at the term. "So you never told anyone, and you never helped me?"

Yale winced. "I stayed friends with you," he said. "I always wanted to tell you how and why, but I never could."

"What about your brother? And your sister?"

"My sister is okay," he said. "She helps my brother."

"Your pedophile brother? Who owns that blue truck you

are driving?"

"Yes," he said. "But he's been clean for a long time."

Simon glanced at the blue truck, then at Yale, and said, "So you and him are abusing the kids?"

"Neither of us," he said in outrage.

But Simon no longer believed him. "I don't think that's quite true," he said. "I'm pretty damn sure he's either supplying the kids to you, or you're paying him for the kids."

"Oh, well, since you can't tell anyone after I kill you ..." He shrugged. "After you've been abused, it's hard to relate to the world around you," he said. "I can relate to the little kids. So he supplies them for me."

"Where?"

"My place," Yale said. "That's another reason why I have to leave. They are searching my brother's place right now, and they'll find my place next." Abruptly he raised the gun and fired.

Simon swore as the bullet tore through the top of his shoulder, slamming him against a brick wall. He heard footsteps as Yale walked closer, and Simon knew it would be a killing shot. He gasped in pain and waited for just the right moment. When Yale came close enough, Simon hooked the back of Yale's knee with his foot, then bolted upright and swung around, landing a hard right fist. The gun fired again and once more, but Yale was already on the way down. Simon kicked the gun free and stomped on his wrist, hard. With his left foot holding Yale's wrist, Simon slammed his right knee hard into Yale's gut and held him down.

Incongruously the yellow ball always in Simon's pocket rolled free to land on the sidewalk beside Yale.

Yale laughed uncontrollably. "Oh my God, how appropriate. It was yours, you know? I kept it all this time."

Simon responded by jamming his knee deeper in Yale's gut, as he stared at the man he no longer knew. To even think the ball had been a memento of his nightmare at Yale's father's hand and that Yale had even wanted to keep it ...

Looking up at him, Yale gasped. "Just shoot me," he said. "I don't dare get caught."

"Seems like you should have been caught a long time ago," Simon said bitterly. "It wouldn't have taken anything to get the help you needed. Your sister was right there."

"She's always been there, but she knows more about what we do than any of us. She's been trying to help us through it, trying to get us to understand what we're doing."

"Is she really though? If two of you are pedophiles, are you sure she isn't one too?"

Yale laughed. "It's our only connection to her. It's the only connection we have to our past and our history. We do whatever we can to keep her. She's tried to walk away from us many times, but we know how to keep her."

"What do you mean?" Simon asked.

"Curiosity. Professional curiosity," he said, with a chilling voice. "As long as we can keep her engaged, we're part of her life. And that's what we need. What we desperately need. She is the only family we have. The only family we've ever had."

"So she knows what you do?" Simon asked him, his stomach wrenching in disgust.

"She knows it and questions us constantly on it."

"How many?"

Yale shook his head. "No clue," he said.

"Hazard a guess," Simon said.

"Too many," he said sadly. "I've known this day would come, but I didn't know when."

"So why didn't you get out early?" he asked.

"Because you're right. I'm a terrible cheater, and I need money," he said. "I don't have a job, and it's getting harder and harder to keep the house. And anything I do that separates me from my brother takes me away from what I really love."

"Children," he said.

Yale nodded. "I never abused them, you know?" he said. "I loved them. I just wanted to keep them. My brother couldn't do anything but abuse them. But he wouldn't call it abuse either. He would say he loved them."

"And that little dead girl I found?"

"*You* found her? She was my China Doll after I got her from the pedo that kidnapped her, but I think it was my brother's idea to snatch her after he became obsessed with her," he said, "but she was sick right from the beginning. I knew that she didn't belong to this world. There was just something very ethereal about her. Still, I held her for a long time, and then my brother took her. He wanted her bad to replace Jason. His beloved pet of so long. He kept that boy for six months, and, after he lost him, he was so depressed that I got worried. He had my little girl only a short time before somehow he broke her neck, but I don't think he meant to. Still she wasn't meant for this world. I miss her terribly."

"You're sick," Simon said, staring at Yale, a banked rage inside him. He wanted to blow him apart, but he still had to get information.

"I am sick," he said. "I'm so very sick. I'm just so tired of it all."

"Tired of what?"

"The lies, the deceit, the struggle," he said. He looked up

at Simon. "Kill me, please. Just kill me."

But Simon shook his head. He got up off him, slowly twisted, then rolled him over and pulled his hands behind his back, biting back a groan at his own pain. "You're not getting out of this that easy." And he bent down, looking for something to tie Yale's hands with, when his phone rang. He swore when he realized who it was. "I'm at Hemlock and Broadway area," he said, "and I have one of your two pedophiles."

"What?" she roared.

"I don't have time to talk, please come," he snapped.

"Be there in five," she snapped back.

Simon told Yale, "The cops are on the way."

Yale started to cry. Deep sobs.

"What the hell?" Simon said, sitting atop Yale's back to keep him here. "What did you know about my biological father?"

"Not a whole lot other than your mother said he was a useless drunk," he said. "I do know that you were born to a tavern girl, and she was a nightmare. She ended up selling you to my father for barely any money. You were a toddler at the time."

Simon just stared at him.

"You better take your money back, or the cops will wonder where I got it from."

Simon looked down at his ex-friend and lifted the money from his pocket, realizing that part was true. He shoved it inside his own jacket pocket, glaring. "Goddammit, Yale."

"What do you want me to say, Simon? I stayed friends with you because I was part of that whole mess," he said, "caught between guilt and hatred. I don't know which was worse."

"You could have asked for help to get away anytime," he snapped.

"Maybe I didn't want to get away," he said. "Maybe I just want to die."

"And how the hell will you manage that?" he said. "It's not that easy to commit suicide while you're in prison."

"I figured that, if I told you the truth," he said, "you'd kill me."

"Well, I'm not," he said. "And the cops aren't either."

"It would be easier if you did."

"Not happening."

"Damn it," Yale said, starting to get angry.

"Whatever," Simon said. "You have to pay the penalty, just like everybody else." It wasn't long before he heard sirens, and, as he turned, Kate raced toward him. At least one other and possibly a second vehicle were coming in too. He couldn't see them yet. He nodded at the gun by his side. "The gun is his. He was trying to figure out what to do with me, when I took him out."

"And you're bleeding," she snapped.

"It's just a scratch," he lied, refusing to give in to the pain. "If you take this asshole from me, I can clean it up."

"Well, what the hell?" she said, looking down at the man on the ground. "We've got cops out looking to pick up your brother, by the way."

Stunned, Yale looked up at her. "What?"

"We've got you. We'll have your brother soon. Now the question is, what we can do about your sister. We're picking her up right now too."

At that, Yale started to laugh, but there was a bitterness to it. "You can't do anything," he said. "She's a doctor. It's client confidentiality. She's known what we've done and what we are all along," he said. "She's the same, just that she lives it through us and not through deeds of her own."

"Which makes a lot of difference but not enough," Kate said, staring at him in disgust.

"Maybe," he said, "but you won't pin anything on her. She's too smart."

"That's not my problem right now." Kate stood him up, putting handcuffs on him. "What I want to be sure of is that we've got you too."

"It won't matter," Yale said. "He's dead already."

She stopped, staring at him in shock. "Who's dead?"

He just shrugged, but Simon knew. He walked round to face Yale, reached out, and clenched Yale's neck. "He's talking about Leonard. Tell me where he is. You know that that little boy is Caitlin's nephew."

Yale looked at him in surprise and then nodded. "I figured you wouldn't care. I mean you hate the whole family."

"That little boy didn't do anything to anybody. Things would go a lot easier on you if you help the police find that little boy."

"If you're here, and my brother has been picked up, it's already too late."

"Has he done all the killing for you?"

Yale looked at him, pleading with tears in his eyes. "I didn't want them to die," he said. "I just wanted to love them."

"Address," Kate barked. As she led him over to the police car, she asked again. "What's the address?"

Yale shrugged.

Simon said, "Don't do this, Yale. Tell us."

He gave the address and said, "In the basement."

She nodded, and two cops grabbed him. "Get him

downtown. We're heading over to the address he gave us." Simon raced to her side. She looked at him and said, "I can't let you come."

"No way in hell I'm not coming," he said, and he got in the back seat of her cruiser, wincing at the pull on his shoulder. But, if he said anything, it would just be more ammunition to stop him from coming. Whoever the other cop was got into the passenger side, and she tore off.

The cop just looked at her. "This isn't a good idea."

"Fine," she said. "You push him out of the car."

He gave a snort and settled back.

Simon knew he didn't belong here, but he wanted an end to it. All of it.

"I didn't know, Kate," Simon said. "I didn't know."

"Know what?" she asked him, looking at him through the rearview mirror.

"That Yale was a pedophile and right in the middle of this," he said, his voice soft. "I didn't know."

# CHAPTER 26

K ATE BELIEVED SIMON, but she didn't know about her partner. But anybody who'd been abused as a child would understand how absolutely unacceptable it was to be around anybody who thought it was okay to do the same. She turned onto the street where the address was. "Whose house is this anyway?"

"It's Yale's," Rodney said. "The siblings all got one from the trust fund."

Simon snorted. Yale had never been short of money.

"How come the sister lives in a big fancy house like this," Kate asked, "and the brother Yale does too. But that one called York doesn't?"

"They had to sell his to pay for his legal defense, when he got caught as a pedophile," Rodney said, reading the note off his phone. "That makes sense. The other two never got caught, so they still hold their own assets."

She pulled up front and shut off the headlights. It was dark out. "You stay in the vehicle," she said to Simon, behind her. He just nodded. She glared. "I mean it. We're here with guns, and, with a child in danger, we're not checking too closely who it is we're firing on."

He just gave her the same blank look back.

Frustrated, she hopped out and closed the door quietly. She looked over at Rodney. "Did you call for backup?"

"Already did," he said.

She approached the gate and studied it for a long moment. It was locked, and a wrought iron fence went all the way around. She checked to see if it was electrified, but it wasn't. Rodney went to a big brick corner post and quickly climbed it and jumped into the main part of the front yard. She followed suit. Rodney raced around to the back, and she went up to the front. No sign of life inside. It was a big brick mansion, similar in age to Nico's they had found in Richmond. But a very different layout, and it was completely black inside.

She moved around the front of the house, looking for any windows she could reach. Working her way around, she tried to look through the basement windows. Curtains were on every one of them.

Around the back at the kitchen, Rodney was there, searching through the windows. He looked at her when she joined him. "No sign of anyone."

"A garage is at the back in the alley," she said. "The asshole could be anywhere."

"And maybe a vehicle's there, maybe not," he said, "but I want to go in and see if that child is here. Just because the perv says 'basement' doesn't mean I'll believe him." With just cause, he quickly popped the door and pushed it open. They entered, calling out that they were the police and had a search warrant.

She didn't know that they actually had one yet, but that was a moot point, since they were looking for a missing child and already had a confession with a confirmation that the child was in imminent danger. They raced through the main floor and headed toward the basement. With the door opened, they slipped down the stairs quietly. At the bottom was all dark shadows. With little alternatives, they waited for their eyes to adjust for a moment and quickly swept through.

There was a large locker room, with massive storage rooms off to one side. Several other smaller rooms were on the opposite side, all with doors. She checked one, placing her ear against it, but she heard nothing inside. She opened it quietly and found nothing. They went to the next one, and it was already open. The last one had a lock on it. She stared at it, pulled out her pick, and quickly popped the lock.

The presence of the lock meant that no adult should be inside, but they didn't dare take a chance. She dropped low with her gun out, and Rodney went in high. There on the floor, in the corner, was a little boy. Maybe five or six. She picked up her phone, turned on the flashlight, and saw that he slept. The same drugged sleep that she'd seen before. But she didn't recognize this child. *Not Leonard.* She turned to Rodney and nodded. He had his phone out in seconds, sending out a call for expedited backup and an ambulance.

SIMON SAT IN the vehicle, as he'd been ordered to. His shoulder burned, and the bloody wound was making a mess of his clothing. He'd pulled off his jacket and used it to staunch the bleeding. Something in his pocket kept getting in his way.

He pulled it out. And snorted. It was the yellow ball Yale had tossed him. He'd automatically picked it up and pocketed it. The damn thing wasn't leaving him alone. He vaguely remembered the ball from his childhood, but he'd blocked so many memories; this was just one more.

As he studied it, something, ... someone, spoke to him.

"Mommy ..." a young boy whimpered.

Simon studied the interior of the vehicle before dropping his gaze to the ball on the seat beside him.

He picked it up carefully, closed his eyes, and whispered, "Leonard?"

Instead of a *yes*, he felt the boy jolt.

"It's Simon, a friend of your aunt's."

"Aunty Caitlin?"

Simon gave a silent *whoop*. "Yes, her. Are you alone?"

"I'm in a room all alone." He started to cry. "I want to go home."

"I know. That's what we're trying to do. I need you to hide though. The bad man is in there looking for you."

"I know. I hid under the bedcovers. But he will find me again. He got angry with me. And gave me some more medicine. But this one tasted different." His voice was fading, getting woozy.

"Can you find a better hiding place?"

"I'm too scared," Leonard whimpered. "No place to hide."

"Can you get out of the room?"

"Only to go to the bathroom."

Simon exited the detective's vehicle and stared up at the massive house. "Can you see a window anywhere?"

"No, no windows. Huge boxes are everywhere."

Simon smiled, as an idea came to him. "Leonard, listen to me. I need you to find a box that you can climb into. It will slow him down. The police are at the house, but we don't want the bad man to find you first." Sensing movement, Simon whispered, "Look for a box just big enough for you. Best if other boxes are stacked around it."

"I can't move them," he announced, his voice panicky.

"Calm down. Can you hide behind them? Can you see a ripped one that you could crawl into? Are they small enough you could stack them around you?" He knew a seven-year-old didn't have much strength, but there was no counting how much could be summoned when needed.

*He's coming*, Leonard said into Simon's head. And he went quiet.

# CHAPTER 27

$\mathbf{K}$ATE AND RODNEY moved from room to room. Most were empty; several contained boxes, as if packing were underway.

Suddenly a voice from the doorway said, "Hold it right there."

She also heard the unmistakable sound of a gun being readied to fire. She turned slowly, her hands in the air, to face the other brother, standing in front of the doorway to the poor drugged little boy. "So, you're York, the pedophile who likes to hurt the children. The cops are looking for you," she said. "And your brother Yale is the one who just likes to cuddle them."

"He likes to do it all too, no matter what he says." he said, slowly leaning against the doorway. "And our sister just likes to hear all about it."

"We've been to your place," she said. "It's quite a mess."

"What do you expect? It's not like I get the money they get."

"No," she said, "but you had it once. Just that yours had to go toward your defense."

"Well, Yale could lose his too," he said. "I'm not going down alone this time. He was supposed to look after me when I came out, and he didn't."

"He's paying your rent, isn't he? And your sister? Or is

357

she covering everything else?"

"They both pay a couple thousand a month, just barely enough to keep me in what I need. My sister should be paying more, but she figures she's paid enough. I'll see about that."

"I'm hearing a little anger there," she said.

"More than a little," he snapped. "But mostly because you could take me away from this again."

"Don't you think you should give up?"

"I don't give a fuck," he said. "I want to live the life that I want. I don't want all these rules and restrictions."

"I don't think that's an option anymore," she said quietly.

"Well, it should be," he said, with a sneer. "And who's to stop me? You? Either of you? I don't think so." As he spoke he waved the gun at their faces.

"Have you killed anybody here?" Rodney asked. "In this house?"

"A couple," he said. "I mean, they're just children—and very fragile. It's just like a chicken. You snap their necks, and they die within seconds."

Her stomach hit the bottom of her toes and bounced back up to the top of her head before exploding outward. "*Chicken*? Goddammit," she said. "These are children you killed. They had lives ahead of them."

"What kind of life?" he said, with another sneer. "They are all just so fucked up."

"Because of you," she said.

"Doesn't matter if it's because of me or somebody else. They are all useless. I did miss a couple of them though afterward. My brother let me take one, I called her my China Doll, back to my place for a few days. I was supposed to get rid of her, so he didn't technically know what I did, but I took her to my little place and kept her for a couple days, just so I could enjoy her company, but it wasn't the same."

"Dear God," she said. "That was her pink ribbon I found in your couch."

"Really?" he said, looking at her in surprise. "I was pretty damn sure I cleaned all that up."

"I don't think so," she said. "I also found your notebook."

"Yeah, well, that notebook—I'd only gotten a little way into my lists," he said, "when I decided I needed to get out and elevate my tactics a little more."

"Why did you kill the other pedophiles?" she asked, curious.

He just gave her a blank look. "Why not? They were losers."

"No. There was a reason," she said. "What was it?"

"They wouldn't share," he said simply. "They had what I wanted, and they wouldn't let me have it."

"Besides the little Asian girl, who you were trying to buy?"

He frowned and straightened up. "Did you get into Nico's laptop?"

"Oh, yeah, we got into his and your laptops," Rodney said. "Interesting read. We got into the chat and saw that you didn't like the price."

"Then you came after me and rescued the little girl anyway," he said. "What a waste."

"Well, I don't think so," she said. "I'm pretty damn sure there is more to that than meets the eye."

"Whatever," he said. "That stupid Nico. He was a mess, and he should have just given me the damn girl. Then none of this would have happened."

"Instead you killed him."

"And took all the money he had with him," he said. "There was a lot, and I was grateful to have it."

"You speak so casually," she said, "as if you don't really care."

"Well, I don't," he said in surprise. "What's to care about after you've been through jail? Life is not the same anymore."

"That doesn't mean you have to go around making it worse," she said.

"It's just a fact of life," he said. "It's all about surviving, making something out of life for yourself to enjoy."

"Says you."

"Yep, says me," he said. "Besides, that's not what my life could be like now. I've got my brother's cards now too. I could take the money, whatever I can get, and run. He will lose this house, just like I lost mine."

"What makes you think you'll just walk away so easily?" she asked.

He smiled and said, "Remember the gun?" He looked down at the little boy in the bed, drugged, and lined up his gun to the child's head.

"And you would kill a child for that?"

"Well, I have to clean up loose ends," he said.

"If you fire at that child, I will take you out."

He looked at her, smiled, and said, "Women are so simple." Just then, he moved and pointed the gun her way. But she was already running toward him. He immediately fired once and then turned it on Rodney and fired a second time. She felt the hit slamming into her shoulder, as she went down from the blast. But she refused to listen and had already bounced onto her feet, heading toward him again.

"Fuck you," he snapped, lined up for a shot again.

But an arm snaked around his neck from behind, pulling York backward, his gun arm flying upward, as another arm came around, grabbed his trigger finger, and fired into the ceiling, until all the bullets were spent. She watched in shock as Simon slammed York into the ground and dropped on top of him, pinning him there. Simon grabbed York's hands, pulled them behind his back, then looked at her. "Are you okay?"

She nodded, wavering a little bit on her feet. "I'm fine."

Simon pointed at her partner. "What about him?" She raced to Rodney's side and saw that he was out cold. "He'll be okay," she said. "The bullet wound is just a graze. He must have hit his head when he fell or something. He'll be pissed off when he wakes up."

"But at least he will wake up," Simon said. He looked down at Yale's brother, York, and said, "So, asshole, Yale finally told me all about my childhood and my connection to your family."

"Yale told you, did he? That's funny," York said. "Did he also tell you that he used to curl up in bed beside you at nighttime and that you were the child who made him want to cuddle and to save everybody? The one who made him want to collect all these poor souls," he said. "I bet he didn't. He's just that much older than you that, of course, you don't remember."

"No, I don't," he said. His voice hard, bland. "I don't plan on remembering him anymore either. Now that we've got the two of you down, it's over, as far as I'm concerned."

"I don't think so," the older brother said. "Yale could bring it all out and make sure everybody in the whole world knows."

"Knows what?" Simon asked.

"That you are a victim yourself," he said. "He might even detail how he abused you and all the others. The world will look at you differently. Our father marked you. Some kids go through several rings and every new one gets a new line. But it always made me smile to know that my brother insisted you get the same mark. The one that says who owns you."

"I'm not an unprotected vulnerable six-year-old anymore," Simon said. "So fuck off, asshole." And, with that, he hit him hard in the head, knocking him out cold.

Looking around, he saw her standing there, leaning against the doorjamb, placing pressure on her wound. He checked her out and said, "It's not too bad. I've got one to match."

"I said it was okay," she snapped. "So they were involved in your victimization?"

"Apparently my foster father was their biological father," he said, with a hard sigh. "According to Yale, *my* biological father was a no good drunk while his was a prominent local businessman. My birth mother was some bar-hopping floozy he got pregnant, and Yale didn't give me her name. When my father refused to acknowledge me, she ended up selling me to Yale's father for a pittance. I wouldn't doubt that that they deep-sixed her somewhere. I don't know that for sure however. Yale did say they killed Josh, his own father, so that's another cold case file covered in dust somewhere that needs to be closed."

"Sounds like she didn't know what to do as a single mother with her lifestyle," she said. "Maybe she deluded herself into thinking a better life was there for her baby."

"I'm not sure what kind of rosy scenario you're dreaming up in that head of yours, Detective," he said calmly, "but that's not reality." He tossed the ball up in the air, as he waited for her to answer. Her gaze locked on the ball. Had she not seen him in the park that day tossing that same ball?

"Maybe not," she said, "but it makes it easier to sleep at night. And, when you do this shit all day long, you realize a hell of a lot of monsters are in the world who are worse than you ever thought."

"But this time," he said, "you won the day, and now you get to go on and fight some more." And that's why he was keeping the ball. He'd beaten that memory, that nightmare. He figured touching the ball had triggered his slide into the darkness, but now he was back in the light. And that's where he would stay.

"Maybe," she said, straightening up and groaning. "But not today. No way in hell today. The focus is finding Leonard, the little boy."

"Look for packing boxes," he said, suddenly staring around at the mess. "He's hiding here somewhere." And he called out, "Leonard, it's Simon. Let me know where you are."

"What the hell?" she snapped, staring at him.

"Don't ask," he said, with a head shake. "But we need to find him. His voice sounded funny. And he said York gave him medicine, a different one this time."

"JESUS." SHE ASSESSED their space. "Let's split up and look for him. We've got cops coming. We'll tear this place apart to find him." She bolted out of the room and, ignoring her shoulder, moved as fast as she could through the basement area filled with boxes. When she came to a roomful of boxes, she groaned. "Leonard, are you in here?"

No answer.

She walked through the stacks, looking for the little boy. Nothing. Not behind the boxes or anywhere close. She found a bathroom and a small bedroom, but no sign of the boy. She turned to study the boxes. A packing slip crossed her gaze. She walked closer. The box was large, slumped to one side. The numbers running along the sticker were 4441 4441 4441.

She jumped into action, shuffling boxes, until she could get to the one she wanted. As she reached for the side and tried to shift it, Simon suddenly appeared beside her. He ripped open the top of the carton.

Out tumbled a little boy to lie at their feet. Simon dropped down beside him.

"Is he alive?" she asked, struggling against the dizziness attacking her. Using his back for support she crumpled to the floor beside them.

Simon put his finger on the boy's neck, then looked at her. A huge grin broke across his face.

"Yes, he's alive."

# CHAPTER 28

*Friday*

"YOU WILL STAND and will accept the commendations," Colby said in exasperation, "with a smile on your face."

Kate glared at him. "I don't want to go."

"Doesn't matter if you want to go or not," he said. "You helped crack a very major child abuse ring," he said, shaking his head. "I still can't believe this has been going on so long right under our noses."

"I think it's more about them keeping track of each other, sliding victims back and forth, depending on who was in jail and who wasn't. They covered each other's asses and stayed in their own dark little shadows, only coming out enough to touch base with each other, only as much as they needed to."

"And Simon?"

"Simon is fine," she said, her tone brittle.

He gave her a half smirk. "So, one-night stands don't work for you, do they?"

"I guess not, sir. I haven't seen him since."

His eyebrows shot up. "Well, he was pretty-damned worried about you when he came in to the hospital yesterday."

"I think he was afraid that I might die on his watch."

He shrugged and said, "Get yourself suited up, and we'll see you at the media show."

"Three-ring circus, you mean. That's all it is," she said.

"Its politics," he said, his voice hardening. "And you will be there. Both you and Rodney."

She shrugged and then winced because the last thing she should do is move that shoulder.

He laughed at her. "See there? If you weren't so stubborn," he said, "you'd be home in bed."

"Fuck that," she said. "An awful lot needs to be settled up in this case yet. So much paper to fill out, reports to write …"

"There is," he said. "Not the least of which is that we've pulled in seven others from that chat room."

"Do the names match up with the notebook?"

"They do, indeed," he said with a fat grin, "and make sure that you're there."

She glared at him. "But, sir—"

He returned the glare. "No," he said. "Dismissed."

She turned and walked out. She didn't bother going to her desk, just headed outside to the front of the police station. She stood here for a long moment, watching the hustle and bustle of the street and the traffic, something inside her calming down. This was her city. Her streets. And these were her people. She would do her damnedest to look after them. Even when they didn't want her to. But the children in the hospital really broke her heart.

With that thought, she turned and her feet headed in the direction of the hospital all on their own. As she walked in, she found the family of the latest boy they'd found, Leonard. Was Simon here too? She saw him, happy at first, then remembered it was his ex-fiancée's nephew. She stiffened and glared at him. He glared right back.

But the aunt had absolutely no problem showing her emotions. She raced over and tried to hug Kate, but, when Caitlin saw the shoulder sling, she stopped and smiled. "I really just want to say, *Thank you for finding him.*"

Kate smiled and nodded. "Hopefully he'll get some help and recover from this without too much trauma." She didn't even go into what he might have gone through. Nobody wanted to go into that. She quickly escaped and headed up to the little girl's room. As she arrived, grateful to see no greedy group of people gathered around, a young woman sat off to the side of the hospital bed. Kate looked at her and asked, "And who are you?"

"I'm her mother," she said, tears in her eyes.

At that, Kate stopped and stared. "Verified by DNA?"

She nodded and whispered, "Yes. She's my child. I was only seventeen when I got pregnant. At the hospital my parents told me that she'd died, but apparently they gave her to my sister for some damn reason, who then passed her on to someone else," she said. "But I'm here now, and I'm much older. I'm stable and have nothing to do with my parents. I've grown up a lot, and nothing is more important than my little girl."

Kate looked at the little girl and said, "Let's hope that the rest of the years of her life are a whole lot easier than the first few she's had so far."

The mother had her jaw locked down, a small tic playing on her face. She nodded and said, "I am committed to making sure of that," she said. "My family will have nothing more to do with her."

"Good," she said. "Because, somewhere in the middle of all that, she ended up on the street and then got sold into this nasty life."

"That wasn't my fault," the mother said, standing up

determinedly.

"I know that," Kate said, noticing the shining wedding ring on her hand. "Your husband?"

"He's talking to the doctors right now," she said. "We want to know how long before we can take her home."

"And is he on board with this little girl?"

"Very much so," she said, with a loving smile. "I'm not sure I can even have any more children," she said. "Giving birth to Samantha here was really hard."

"Well, let's hope you realize what a gift you have."

"Like I said, Detective, I don't have anything to do with my parents anymore," she said. "This is my life, and I will protect my child."

With those words, feeling much better, Kate stepped out of that room. Four children alive, several dead, and God only knows how many more to be found in this case. She stepped into the little boy's room to see him sitting up and eating some Jell-O. She laughed at him because his face was covered in green goo. More food was going into his face than his mouth. But his mother sat beside him, laughing. They both looked up when Kate came in, and the mother immediately bounced up, took one look at her injured shoulder, and cried out.

Kate hushed her. "It's fine," she said. "I'm fine." She walked to the opposite side of the bed. "I had to stop in and see my favorite patient." The little boy reached up his arms, and she winced, knowing this would hurt her arm for sure.

"Really?" But she came closer and, wrapping her good arm behind him, tucked him up close, grabbing both of his dirty hands in hers. She kissed him on the cheek and rocked him gently, subtly checking the inside of his left wrist. The mark was there.

The mother had tears in her eyes. "He's acting so normal," she whispered to Kate.

"A child's mind is a wonderful thing," Kate said. "Just love him, take care of him."

"I will," she said, "and thank you."

With tears pooling in her eyes and uncharacteristic emotions flooding her heart, Kate quickly made her escape back outside. When she walked outside the front entrance to the hospital, a Porsche pulled up in front. As she stopped and stared, Simon hopped out, complete with his own sling, leaned over the hood, and asked, "Can I buy you lunch?"

She frowned at him.

He frowned right back. "I know. It's not a good idea."

"It's a terrible idea," she said.

He nodded. "So, lunch it is. Come on. Let's go."

She hesitated and then shook off her doubts. As she got in, she said, "I have to be at the police station at three."

"Wow, try not to sound so eager," he said.

"I'm not," she said. "I'm supposed to get some award." She said it in such a grudgingly harsh tone of voice that he laughed really hard, which made her smile. They were still grinning as they headed out of the parking lot. A whole lot of worse things she could be doing with her day. She looked over at Simon and said, "You know that it's still a bad idea."

"I know," he said, "but I figured that we've made it this far, so we might as well see what comes next."

She had to admit there was something to his logic. She had no idea what came next, but she knew what had come so far—and what was coming next—looked to be a damn good deal.

This concludes Book 1 of Kate Morgan: Simon Says... Hide.

Read about Simon Says... Jump: Kate Morgan, Book 2

# Simon Says... Jump: Kate Morgan (Book #2)

Introducing a new thriller series that keeps you guessing and on your toes through every twist and unexpected turn....

*USA Today Best-Selling* Author Dale Mayer does it again in this mind-blowing thriller series.

The unlikely team of Detective Kate Morgan and Simon St. Laurant, an unwilling psychic, marries all the unpredictable and passionate elements of Mayer's work that readers have come to love and crave.

Detective Kate Morgan has settled into her position and, although straining under her new caseload, is working hard. Simon is still a big question mark in her world—and his "gift" even more so. Dealing with a frustrating series of drive-by shootings has brought a three-year-old drive-by case to the forefront ...

Simon had hoped that his visions would have stopped, especially now that the police had solved the pedophile murders. No such luck. But these new visions are confusing, chaotic, and nonsensical. Unwilling to share yet more disjointed and meaningless information with Kate, he keeps it to himself. Until he sees a pattern and connects to a woman, … one who is suicidal.

While Kate understands his physical and mental torment, she's underwhelmed by the lack of detail in his latest visions—until she looks into another issue and finds out that the number of suicides are higher than normal, as in way higher …

### *Vancouver, BC; Third Monday in July*

DETECTIVE KATE MORGAN, a homicide detective for just over four months of her thirty-two years of life, walked slowly across the Lions Gate Bridge—officially known as First Narrows Bridge. Parked off to the side were several cruisers, their lights flashing in the gloomy light. It was not quite morning, and vestiges of the night still clouded the air around her. But the pair of ladies' white three-inch-heeled pumps, placed carefully at the side of the railing of the bridge, shone with an eerie glow.

It was a well-known fact that suicide victims who jumped off bridges often took off their shoes, placing them to the side, as if shoes couldn't get wet. But nobody thought about their coats or anything else. Sometimes they left purses, keys, or wallets, anything to identify that they'd gone over the bridge, in an effort to help find closure for families and friends, if the body never surfaced.

As Kate walked toward the group of police officers, standing and talking in a huddle, one turned to look at her and nodded. "Good morning, Detective."

"Morning, Slater," she murmured, recognizing the officer from her earlier department, her gaze still on the woman's pumps. "Did we find the body?"

He nodded. "The divers are bringing her out now."

Kate stepped closer to the railing and looked over. "If she'd been any closer to the park, she would have hit the rocks first."

"Right," he said. "Most of them jump from the middle of the bridge."

Kate looked out and saw that they were not much farther than the lions mounted on either side of the bridge, heading toward West Vancouver. "Depending on the force of her fall, she might easily have hit the rocks, just under the surface," she murmured.

"We'll find out soon enough," he said.

"Any identification left with the shoes?"

"Not that we know of."

Kate nodded. "Sure seems to be an awful lot of jumpers already." She had done a quick search a few days ago, and the stats had stuck with her.

"This year has been pretty tough on everybody."

"I know, but we've had what? A fifty percent increase in jumpers from last year?"

Two men nodded. "A lot of businesses went under, and people are suffering financially, not to mention the mental health aspect."

She sighed. "And there's never enough we can do for them either."

"Were you called in on this?"

"No, I heard it on the news. I was already close by."

"Ah, that explains it. I'm surprised to see you here so fast."

She waited until everything was dealt with as much as

they could on scene, while they waited on the coroner. At that point, she walked back to where she had parked up the hill. Not very many places to get out of the way of the normal heavy traffic, but she'd parked on a service road. She would have to go across the bridge in order to get back where she needed to go. But that was all right; it wasn't a very long turnaround.

She quickly drove across the bridge and turned around to head back into Vancouver. Instead of going to the office, she headed to False Creek area, to a small harbor café that should be open by now. She parked, got out, and walked, the brisk air hitting her senses, the saltwater breeze lifting her hair. She watched as the sun rose, its light shining on the city she loved so much.

Picking up a coffee, she found a bench and sat. She had a morose feeling inside, once again confronted with the realization of just how many people willingly took their own lives because they felt that was better than any other option, unable to see a way out of whatever hell they were in. It made her sad, but it also made her angry.

She'd never gotten to that point herself, but she'd gotten close, and she certainly could understand it. As she sat here, she recognized a man's voice behind her, ordering coffee at the counter. She waited, knowing that he would come in her direction.

Finally he stepped up beside her. "May I sit?"

She nodded with a half smile. "Why not?"

"I haven't seen you in a few days."

"It's been busy," she said, with a wave of her hand.

"Why are you here so early now?" Simon St. Laurant asked.

"Why are you?" she replied, her eyes going wide.

He smiled. "Deflecting a question with a question, huh?"

"Are you a lawyer now?"

"No, God help me," he said. "That would not be what I would choose to do. Not in this lifetime."

"Neither would I," she said. "In some ways it was simpler in the olden days. Guilty was guilty, and they were swiftly handled," she said, shaking her head. "Now the lawyers get in on it, delaying justice, and criminals carry on with their lives, without ever being punished, filing one appeal after another."

"It doesn't sound like you have much faith in the judiciary system."

"Oh, I have a lot of faith in it," she said. "It's the process that I struggle with sometimes."

He nodded slowly. "It's got to be frustrating when you keep taking bad guys off the streets, only to see them there again, free to commit more crimes. Then it's up to you to go back out and hunt them down once more."

She looked over at this man, someone she was struggling to keep at arm's length. But the more she tried to do that, the less it worked. After all, she'd found her way to his corner of the world, hadn't she? As if her body had a mind of its own. She sipped her coffee and studied him over the rim of her cup. "Why are you up so early?"

"Couldn't sleep," he said. He spread his arms along the back of the bench, studying her. "Why are you?"

She shrugged. "I was awake already and heard news on the scanner about a jumper."

He winced. "That's always tough, isn't it?" Then his gaze sharpened. "But you're a homicide detective," he said. "So surely suicides don't come under your domain."

"All unattended deaths are investigated."

"So you just follow police scanners for fun? Don't have enough cases now, so you have to go find new ones?"

She laughed.

"You're just not ready to tell me."

She shrugged. "It's probably nothing. I guess I'm wondering if there's anything to be done for the mental health problems we have in town," she murmured, giving him a partial answer.

He looked over at her, then reached a hand across to cover one of hers. "You know that you can't help everyone, right?"

"Wasn't planning on it. Yet I care about a lot of things," she said, "and kids are number one."

"Missing kids, you mean."

She glared at him. She still couldn't believe she had opened up enough to tell him about Timmy. Then, given Simon's history, it had seemed like a good idea at the time.

"That's better," he said, with a nod. "I was wondering what was going on that made you look so maudlin."

"I wasn't," she protested.

"Were too."

"Was not," she snapped back. He left it at that. After a moment, her shoulders eased. He was right. "I guess just seeing another jumper ..." she said. "I mean, it's like there's one every day right now."

He looked startled at that. "Is it really that high?"

"Not quite. If I were to count all the bridges on the Lower Mainland, it's especially bad," she said. "It seems much higher than normal."

"Well, last year was bad overall, and this year has been a pretty ugly one so far too."

"I know," she said, "and I get that people are losing their loved ones, their businesses, their homes, plus their families are breaking up. We didn't even need the pandemic for all that to happen, yet just so much else is going on all the time. The pressures of today's world are immense, and handling it all seems to be a special skill set that a lot of people don't have. And, all too often, I think drugs and other enabling issues help bring it all down too."

He shrugged. "And again, there's only so much you can do."

"I know," she said. "A whim sent me down there. I hadn't been there at that wee hour of the morning in a long time."

"Why would you ever be in that area at that hour?" he asked in surprise.

"When I was a teenager," she said, "sometimes I would go sit on the bridge."

He sat back and stared at her in shock. It wasn't hard to understand what he was thinking...

Find Book 2 here!

To find out more visit Dale Mayer's website.

smarturl.it/DMSSSJump

# Author's Note

Thank you for reading Simon Says… Hide: Kate Morgan, Book 1! If you enjoyed the book, please take a moment and leave a short review.

Dear reader,

I love to hear from readers, and you can contact me at my website: www.dalemayer.com or at my Facebook author page. To be informed of new releases and special offers, sign up for my newsletter or follow me on BookBub. And if you are interested in joining Dale Mayer's Reader Group, here is the Facebook sign up page.
https://smarturl.it/DaleMayerFBGroup

Cheers,
Dale Mayer

# Get THREE Free Books Now!

Have you tried the Psychic Vision series?

Read Tuesday's Child, Hide'n Go Seek, Maddy's Floor right now for FREE.

Go here to get them!

https://dalemayer.com/tuesdayschildfree

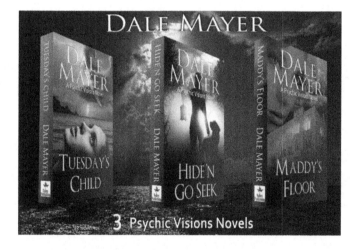

# About the Author

Dale Mayer is a *USA Today* best-selling author, best known for her SEALs military romances, her Psychic Visions series, and her Lovely Lethal Garden cozy series. Her contemporary romances are raw and full of passion and emotion (Broken But … Mending series). Her thrillers will keep you guessing (By Death series), and her romantic comedies will keep you giggling (*It's a Dog's Life*, a stand-alone novella; and the Broken Protocols series, starring Charming Marvin, the cat).

Dale honors the stories that come to her—and some of them are crazy and break all the rules and cross multiple genres!

To go with her fiction, she also writes nonfiction in many different fields, with books available on résumé writing, companion gardening, and the US mortgage system. She has recently published her Career Essentials series. All her books are available in print and ebook format.

## Connect with Dale Mayer Online

*Dale's Website – www.dalemayer.com*
*Twitter – @DaleMayer*
*Facebook – facebook.com/DaleMayer.author*
*BookBub – bookbub.com/authors/dale-mayer*

# Also by Dale Mayer

## Published Adult Books:

### Bullard's Battle

Ryland's Reach, Book 1

Cain's Cross, Book 2

Eton's Escape, Book 3

Garret's Gambit, Book 4

Kano's Keep, Book 5

Fallon's Flaw, Book 6

Quinn's Quest, Book 7

Bullard's Beauty, Book 8

Bullard's Best, Book 9

### Terkel's Team

Damon's Deal, Book 1

### Kate Morgan

Simon Says… Hide, Book 1

Simon Says… Jump, Book 2

### Hathaway House

Aaron, Book 1

Brock, Book 2

Cole, Book 3

## The K9 Files

## Lovely Lethal Gardens

Lovely Lethal Gardens, Books 5–6
Lovely Lethal Gardens, Books 7–8
Lovely Lethal Gardens, Books 9–10

## Psychic Vision Series
Tuesday's Child
Hide 'n Go Seek
Maddy's Floor
Garden of Sorrow
Knock Knock...
Rare Find
Eyes to the Soul
Now You See Her
Shattered
Into the Abyss
Seeds of Malice
Eye of the Falcon
Itsy-Bitsy Spider
Unmasked
Deep Beneath
From the Ashes
Stroke of Death
Ice Maiden
Snap, Crackle...
What If...
Psychic Visions Books 1–3
Psychic Visions Books 4–6
Psychic Visions Books 7–9

## By Death Series

Touched by Death

Haunted by Death

Chilled by Death

By Death Books 1–3

## Broken Protocols – Romantic Comedy Series

Cat's Meow

Cat's Pajamas

Cat's Cradle

Cat's Claus

Broken Protocols 1-4

## Broken and... Mending

Skin

Scars

Scales (of Justice)

Broken but... Mending 1-3

## Glory

Genesis

Tori

Celeste

Glory Trilogy

## Biker Blues

Morgan: Biker Blues, Volume 1

Cash: Biker Blues, Volume 2

## SEALs of Honor

## Heroes for Hire

## SEALs of Steel

## The Mavericks

Kerrick, Book 1

Griffin, Book 2

Jax, Book 3

Beau, Book 4

Asher, Book 5

Ryker, Book 6

Miles, Book 7

Nico, Book 8

Keane, Book 9

Lennox, Book 10

Gavin, Book 11

Shane, Book 12

Diesel, Book 13

Jerricho, Book 14

Killian, Book 15

Hatch, Book 16

The Mavericks, Books 1–2

The Mavericks, Books 3–4

The Mavericks, Books 5–6

The Mavericks, Books 7–8

The Mavericks, Books 9–10

The Mavericks, Books 11–12

## Collections

Dare to Be You…

Dare to Love…

Dare to be Strong…

RomanceX3

## Standalone Novellas

It's a Dog's Life

Riana's Revenge

Second Chances

# Published Young Adult Books:

## Family Blood Ties Series

Vampire in Denial

Vampire in Distress

Vampire in Design

Vampire in Deceit

Vampire in Defiance

Vampire in Conflict

Vampire in Chaos

Vampire in Crisis

Vampire in Control

Vampire in Charge

Family Blood Ties Set 1–3

Family Blood Ties Set 1–5

Family Blood Ties Set 4–6

Family Blood Ties Set 7–9

Sian's Solution, A Family Blood Ties Series Prequel
Novelette

## Design series

Dangerous Designs

Deadly Designs

Darkest Designs

Design Series Trilogy

## Standalone

In Cassie's Corner

Gem Stone (a Gemma Stone Mystery)

Time Thieves

# Published Non-Fiction Books:

## Career Essentials

Career Essentials: The Résumé

Career Essentials: The Cover Letter

Career Essentials: The Interview

Career Essentials: 3 in 1

Made in the USA
Monee, IL
03 January 2022

87785041R00223